NIGHT
OF THE
WOLF

BY ALICE BORCHARDT

NIGHT
OF THE
WOLF

ALICE
BORCHARDT

DEL REY

THE BALLANTINE PUBLISHING GROUP
NEW YORK

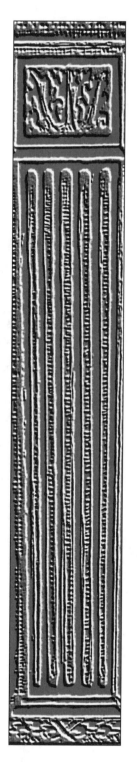

A Del Rey® Book
Published by The Ballantine Publishing Group

Copyright © 1999 by Alice Borchardt

www.randomhouse.com/delrey/

LIBRARY OF CONGRESS CATALOGING-IN-PUBLICATION DATA
Borchardt, Alice.
Night of the wolf / Alice Borchardt.
p.   cm.
ISBN 0-345-42362-3 (hc.: alk. paper)
1. Rome—History—Empire, 30 B.C.–476 A.D. Fiction.   I. Title.
PS3552.0687N54   1999
813'.54—dc21   99-31102
                                                          CIP

Book design by Holly Johnson

Manufactured in the United States of America

First Edition: August 1999

10   9   8   7   6   5   4   3   2   1

TO MY BELOVED SISTER,
KNOWN TO THE WORLD AS ANNE RICE.

Out of darkness smile on me faces I may never see.
Out of sleep are reaching still arms
that I may never fill.

At every important junction in my career,
you have always been there for me.

Ad memoriam.

In the deepest place of sorrow, there is no time.

T**HE WOLF AWOKE. HE LIFTED HIS HEAD FROM**
his paws. Above, the moon was full, but only a drifting ghost
through the mixed pine and cedar on the mountainside.
The rest of the pack slept.

He alone felt the touch of . . . he knew not what. Wolves don't
grieve. Not even for themselves.

He rose and went through the rite of fur straightening, then drifted
down silently to a stream formed by overflow from a lake above. It was
just wide enough to mirror the sky in its water.

Since she died . . . no, since she was killed, he had awakened every
night at this hour, an hour when all else sleeps . . . remembering.

The night has rhythms of its own. Rhythms that resonate in the
flesh, blood, and bones of all earth's creatures. Man, alone, has forgotten them, forgotten they ever mattered.

But to the wolf, they came as memories, memories not his own,
fragments of a dream. He touched an immortal consciousness as old
as life, the experience of a creature not yet self-aware and so immortal. The first of our kind, swimming in the water column of the
Cambrian sea. At this time in the night, it ceased the flexions of its
muscular body and drowsed in a shimmer of moonlight.

He, the wolf, understood that a catastrophic disruption of his consciousness had taken place, depriving him of the birthright handed
down to him by that first dreamer of the ocean sea.

His muzzle shattered the image of the moon in the water in the
way sorrow shattered his sleep.

1

Above, the drifting clouds drowned the moon. Near their kill, the wolves of his pack slept soundlessly and without dreams.

The air around him was cold. It was late autumn, nearly winter again, but he felt a fire within himself—a fire that the wind from the glaciers towering over the mountain passes couldn't quench. A fire that heated his skin under his heavy winter coat.

Fire! They were creatures of fire. And fire followed them everywhere. The smell of burning always tainted the air around their dwellings. Earth, air, fire, and water. All living beings on earth partook of those elements, but of them all, only man was the master of fire.

Why? How did they seize such power? Nothing in his memories could tell him.

When his kind first met them in the darkness and struggle of the world's winter, they controlled flames, extinguishing and kindling them at will, their only advantage in a ruthless battle for simple survival against the omnipresent night and cold. Otherwise, they were pitiable, naked things.

Pitiable, naked things like he himself was, at this moment, because as the last rays of moonlight were caught by the drifting clouds, he became a man.

He remembered that she said—she told him—fire was a gift of the gods.

He had laughed at the word *gift*. He had already seen enough of the humans to know they stole and despoiled without conscience or compunction and read in the minds of the gods the things they most wanted for themselves. Worship and submission to the feckless, arbitrary commands of those who maneuvered themselves into a position to rule their own kind.

"A gift," he had asked, "stolen perhaps?"

"Perhaps," she answered with a shrug. "The thieves were mocked by their theft, because, as always, power is a two-edged sword."

But power, the man by the stream thought, *whatever it costs, power is life.* Without the theft, they and all their kind could never have survived that long-ago endless winter and they would have been winnowed out, as were so many others.

The man stretched his arms upward as if to embrace the moon, just as the cloud in its passage was silvered at the edges by the returning glow.

Then the silver light shone full in his face. He wondered what the gods really did want.

She, whose touch gave him the power to change from wolf to man and back again, seemed careless of worship and had never asked for thanks.

And, indeed, he didn't even know if he should thank her because, like fire, this gift brought suffering and sorrow in its wake. A gift garnished with cruel knowledge and an awareness of absolute loss.

Then he was wolf again, satisfied to extinguish a comprehension of life that he didn't, at the moment, want.

He remembered fire, and only fire—that spirit, that everlasting ambiguity that could protect, create, and destroy.

And the wolf set out, the only wakeful creature in a sleeping world.

Being aware and knowing awareness was a gnawing curse . . . a curse to be extinguished in blood, fire, and vengeance.

How did he know who the man was? He had seen. Why was he sure of his guilt? To the wolf this would have seemed a ridiculous question. He had smelled it, with a certainty that could not be denied— the scent of guilt that is beyond resolve, or anger, or fear.

Even his most ancient ancestor swimming in that first sea had seen, had known. And somewhere its rudimentary consciousness had been able to store the information presented by its deployed senses.

Humans, in their blindness, think intelligence has one path— theirs! But his brain—older and wiser, though not as acute—knew knowledge has many facets and routes.

None of us is any one thing. No more than a bush, a tree, or even an unloved weed is. We are all a combination of many factors, shapes, sizes, odors, movements, habits. Each impinging on the consciousness of others—others we never notice.

So the wolf knew this man. He had marked him, along with those others, in the hour between day and night, in the place that was neither water nor land, never guessing the man's fell purpose until it was too late. Too late to stop him and the others from the completion of their task. A task his mind, as a wolf or human, could never comprehend, understand, or, for that matter, forgive—not in the year since, not ever.

Now the man in question had seen his tracks near the watercourse that ran past his farm and so was on guard.

This one was not the only man whose guilt the wolf had felt, had seen and smelled. But the first had had no suspicion he was hunted and so had fallen easily into his trap. This one gratified the wolf by suffering more than the first.

So he had deliberately prolonged the stalk for several months. Now it was time to see who would emerge the winner in the contest of wills.

The wolf moved silently onto a deer trail, through a dark second-growth forest toward more settled lands below. As he traveled, the night wore on. The earth gave up its heat. Air movement ceased. Dew began settling on the grass and bushes. The hunters of midnight and dawn slept, with either full bellies or empty, as did their prey.

Nothing stirred at this hour. The wolf looked down at the farm-stead. The house was round with a conical thatch roof. A bare, tramped, corduroy yard led to a round barn very similar to the house, differing only in being smaller and open at the sides. Near the barn stood the wolf's target—a wicker sheepfold.

The house and barn were set at the edge of a wheat field that led to a graveled stream, its channel forming another tiny tributary to the river in the gorge. The farmer had begun taking the sheep in for the night.

The wolf moved from his perch to the wheat field. It didn't offer much concealment. The stalks were only tall enough to brush his shoulders and belly. Curlicues of ground mist hung over the laden heads of grain and they wet the wolf's fur as he pushed his way through. The bare earth between the rows was cold under his feet.

As he neared the farm buildings, he dropped lower, slinking along the ground, looking for all the world like a bit of dust driven by a breeze moving across the furrows. However, an alert observer would have noted, in this darkest hour before dawn, there was no wind.

A mastiff the size of a calf was sleeping chained to a post in front of the sheepfold.

So confident, the wolf thought, *you are asleep. How silly. I would not sleep if I were nearby. Well . . . you will not awaken.* The dog didn't.

The wolf dropped into the sheepfold.

The sheep, awakened from sleep by a roaring predator among them, tried to flee in all directions at once. Two went into, not over, the sides. The sheepfold disintegrated. The terrified animals bolted into the yard and then the ripe wheat. One old ram tried to make a stand. The wolf flanked the lowered horns and slammed into his shoulder, sending him rolling. Nerve broken, the ram fled with the rest.

The wolf paused. He stood in the yard, panting. One of the sheep impaled on the broken wickerwork of the ruined fold was making the night hideous with hoarse cries of anguish. The other hung dead beside it.

There was a light in the circular farmhouse. Inside, a woman screamed curses and imprecations. The wolf sat down, tongue lolling. It should take them a little time to get up their courage.

A few seconds later, a man charged out of the house, spear in one hand, torch in the other. Two others, armed only with cudgels, followed more cautiously. The first gave a horrified glance at the dead mastiff, then at the ruined sheepfold and the two—by now the one who'd been crying out was dead also—dead ewes. And the wolf sitting, taking his ease before them all.

He charged the wolf, spear high.

The wolf turned, then vanished into the darkness, the way a puff of dust does when taken by the wind.

The farmer, incensed almost beyond reason, chased him into the wheat field—followed, very much more slowly, by the two others.

The wolf heard one of them whisper, "Let's go back to the rath. It's gone, fled. We can search in the morning."

The wolf flattened himself expertly against the ground amidst the thick growth of wheat and slunk forward.

The farmer shivered. He raised the torch higher and shifted his grip on the spear shaft. His perspiration made the rough wood slippery. He could feel sweat on his brow and more running from his armpits. He couldn't see his two companions, only a circle of darkness beyond the torchlight.

He waded through a sea of ripe, red wheat. It stirred, softly rustling in the dawn wind. Dear God! Dear God! No! There was no wind. The air was utterly still.

The wolf hit him high between the shoulder blades. A pair of unbelievably powerful jaws crushed his shoulder and left arm as he fell—the arm that held the torch.

He saw it flip out of his hand, fly free, and land about ten feet away. He had a few seconds to realize the ripe wheat was tinder dry . . .

The wolf paused on the mountainside and glanced back at the dreadful tableau behind him. The man he'd felled no longer struggled. He was a blackened shape lying in a sea of flame. Another one of the cowardly followers was on fire, running madly through the fields, spreading the flames even faster. The third escaped. He and the other women from the rath were holding the farmer's wife back, keeping her from dashing frantically and uselessly to her death.

Closer to the tree line, the wolf looked back again. The wheat fields were a lake of flame. The house was now involved, wood and thatch throwing a column of fire at the sky. Even the apple and quince orchards burned, as wheat had been planted in rows between the trees. The surviving humans fled down the watercourse toward the river and safety.

THE MAN WHO GREETED BLAZE WAS FEEBLE, WHITE haired, and nearly blind. *Oh, ye gods,* Blaze thought. *How many years has it been?* He remembered a healthy, vigorous man in his sixties. This man was eighty if he was a day.

He tottered ahead of Blaze into a one-room house, really a ramshackle thatched hut. The fields, once intended to feed the old Druid, were neglected and empty of livestock, filled with tall weeds. Someone had been tending the small kitchen garden and fishpond. Onions, leeks, and turnips flourished near the door.

With a sigh, Blaze followed the old man into the house. Mir should have been replaced years ago, allowed to live out his life in peace. Sent home to Ireland where he could be cared for by his family. But in these troubled times, not one of his fellows had cared enough to bother. Or had been able to take the time.

The interior of the house was dark, the only light a small hearth fire. A woman bent over an earthenware pot sunk in charcoal near the flames.

Mir pointed to her. "My wife," he said. "I can't remember her name." The girl lifted her head and Blaze saw she was very young, no more than sixteen. He looked more closely and realized she was horribly scarred. Her face was crosshatched with swollen stripes. She looked as if someone had taken a very sharp blade, then slashed and slashed.

When she saw Blaze, she tried to smile. A twisted grimace was all she could manage.

"Go away," Mir said. "We men need to talk."

She nodded and pulled the pot out of the coals.

"The stew is done?" Mir asked.

She nodded again and slipped out.

Blaze and Mir sat down at a table. Blaze looked out at the green and gold sunlight beyond the door. He shivered. Being in this house was like sitting in a cave and staring out on the bright world beyond. He watched the girl cross the overgrown meadow and vanish into the pines.

A very strange odor hung in the room. It was rising from the bubbling pot.

"What sort of stew is that?" Blaze asked.

"I can't say," Mir replied. "I never eat it. I make do with a little bread and cheese. My people give me leftovers from their own tables. And my garden fills in from time to time."

"She's a bad cook?" Blaze asked.

"I don't know. I just don't care to eat the things she cooks. I once saw her put a snake, a handful of grasshoppers, and a dove into the kettle. The snake was alive. It got away. So were the grasshoppers; some of them got away. The dove was dead, its neck wrung, but it was not cleaned and still had all its feathers. Then she tossed in three live mice. I was able to rescue the cat before she added it to the brew. It ran away, though, anyway."

Blaze shook his head as though trying to clear it. "The cat . . . ran away?"

"Yes," Mir said. "She picked it up by the tail. The cat didn't like it."

"Why does she do such things? Have you asked her?" Blaze queried him.

"She doesn't talk," Mir answered.

"Oh," Blaze said.

Mir shrugged. "She belongs here with us. She needs protection. She isn't dangerous and she's warm at night. I could do worse. I will designate someone to take her when I am gone. But I didn't call you here to talk about the half-wit, but the wolf."

"Ah, yes," Blaze said. "The wolf. This wolf that behaves like a man."

THE NEXT NIGHT THE BIG GRAY LEFT WELL AHEAD of his pack. It was his duty to do so. He had attacked humans, thereby risking the lives of his companions. Humans did not discriminate. They saw all wolves as ravening killers and would destroy, sometimes after torture, any wolf they could catch.

A retreating glacier had carved the pool eons ago. It was part of a small stream fed by snowmelt in the summer and by native artesian springs in winter. Somehow the water never froze. The wolf had long wondered about this and had been puzzled by his own bent toward curiosity. His kind seldom bothered about such things.

The first people to come to the valley called it the Lady's Mirror. The Lady in question was already ancient by then, clouded by a host of other deities, but still remembered, especially during her hours, dawn and dusk. At those times, the inhabitants of the valley avoided the place, fearing they might see her walking there and be accosted, to who knows what end. The Lady was revered, respected, loved, and feared. Meetings with her could be very unlucky, and besides, who knows what a goddess is thinking? Perhaps they also avoided the place at such times because they knew it was the haunt of wolves moving down from the mountains at dusk to hunt in the valleys below. At dawn they gathered again, returning to their dens beyond the tree line.

The sun was sending up long rays from beyond the western peaks when the wolves came to drink. The sunset forest sighed in the wind's passage.

The water, true to its name, mirrored the dark forest of spruce and fir, the sun-flushed evening sky. The pool ended in a falls flowing in shining smoothness over a flight of black basalt steps into another smaller lake. From there it became a torrent cascading down a steep slope into the roaring flood racing through the valley below.

He approached the pool cautiously, searching through all the nearby coverts where bowmen could hide. He feared an ambush. He found nothing. Oh, someone had been there all right. An old someone with a light step. He sensed this and saw no cause for alarm.

When he reached the pool he found it deserted by all but swallows skimming for insects over the glasslike surface. The women who bathed below the falls had been there and were gone.

Women reminded him of those tender parts of prey animals, and reduced him to something as close to guilt as a wolf could ever feel. Yet he found them irresistible. A female wolf at midwinter, all fangs, her belly swollen with whelps, eyes blazing yellow with fear for her unborn young, was often her mate's best argument for celibacy.

But human women were a walking seduction. They covered their naked pink and brown skin with cloth almost as soft as fur was. Hairless, they felt like flower petals, velvet, silken, and fragrant. The hot places of their bodies misted the air at their groins with a variety of odors, some enticing, intoxicating, and, finally, as they approached orgasm . . . maddening. But most succulent of all was their surrender. At the finality of desire, they yielded bonelessly, melting around his body, into his arms, and into their own boundless pleasures as though they yielded to death. Indeed, when the first he embraced reached the culmination of her desire, for a moment he feared she had perished in his arms. Only the loud, persistent drumming of her heart reassured him that he had not, in his own urgency, destroyed her.

They are slaves, he thought at first, shaped by the torrent of their own males' desires the way the water-smooth stones in the riverbed were sculpted by the unending flow. Drawn by Eros himself from the earth's womb and shaped only for the delight of the savage killer mates who surrounded them and sought madly to possess them as often as possible. They were created head to toe to madden. There was nothing about them that could not inspire pleasure.

Small, high-arched feet, narrow ankles, curving smooth legs, silken thighs, velvety buttocks, a spine one could follow to the nape of the neck with lips and tongue while they squeaked with delight, writhing and purring with ecstasy like wild cats. And the breasts. Ah, God, those things. Wolves are born blind, struggling against each other for their mother's teats in the dark. Those breasts as he cupped them with his hands and sucked with his lips brought back the memory of that first triumphant spurt of milk into his mouth. The soft globes, shaped almost like cups, were a reminder of a giving world where a man might drink and fulfillment pour into his loins, heating his whole body the way that first warm taste of life had told him he would live. Haunted by the first fear of independent life that he would not reach warmth, food, and love—the abject terror that he would not survive. That first taste told him that he would—it tracked its way into his stomach and the warmth filled his whole body.

The dark wolf huntresses concealed their endowments except when they needed to feed their pups. The women didn't. They pushed their soft beauties into plain sight, reminding men of woman power, making them sit up and beg. Yes, at first he thought women slaves, playthings of their savage mates. Why not? Didn't these women know even the fiercest of beasts go in terror of man? Surely they were slaves to this endless unstoppable male lechery. Or did they first create it, then encourage it until the obsessed and goaded male became a creature of his desires rather than the possessor of them? A creature of the woman who gratified him.

He had encountered her in a dark wood, she who changed his mind about men. To his nose, the aromatic signals their bodies were giving off would have attracted him in preference to food.

The men were clustered at the edge of the wood, and raw sexuality and violence hung about them like a thick mist. At the other end of the wood, the sacrificial victims were gathered. The dozen young girls, standing with the dark-robed priestesses, were grouped near a pile of smoldering logs. They were naked and their skins gleamed with oil. Some green herb had been thrown onto the fire and the women were dancing slowly, uncoordinatedly, in the thick fumes, half steam and half smoke, rising from the sputtering fire.

The wolf knew the rite. He had seen it before. He also knew men fought among themselves for the privilege of joining the chase.

The procedure was a simple one. When the rising moon's tip touched the top of the standing stone, the girls would be driven into the grove. The men would follow. The girls were sixteen, at most, and all virgins. They would not be virgin when they emerged in the morning. Some would be weeping. All would be bleeding because if they didn't bleed when entered, they would be flogged by the men until the blood came. And some, not a few, would be crowned with flowers and have strange smiles on their faces.

The gray wolf found himself drawn into human shape by the powerful magic hanging over the grove. Every hair on his body had stood up like a cat's. Then, as though drenched with icy water, he was a man, the spring night air cold against his skin. He gasped, shivered all over as the canine in him tried to shake off what felt to it like a waterfall of ice. He stood shivering violently, his eyes fixed on the women.

The priestess who had been watching the moonrise shouted something to the group guarding the girls.

He heard the slap of a switch on flesh. The girls milled near the fire like frightened mares; one screamed. They tossed their heads, long hair flying. The priestesses held long, flexible willow canes. The women twisted and turned, screaming, trying to escape the blows. But still they fought, refusing to enter the wood, less afraid of what, after all, amounted only to a switching rather than face what awaited in the darkness under the trees. It wasn't until they saw the men coming full tilt across the meadow—charging silently, fists clenched, eyes wild—that they broke and ran.

The one he'd chosen, a lithe, black-haired girl, flew through last year's autumn leaves like a wounded deer. Fast as she was, he could have had her in seconds, but with the deliberate skill of a predator, he held back until they were deep in the grove, enmeshed in thick, black, velvet night. The only light from the stars, dense, brilliant, glowing dust everywhere the sky could be seen through the branches above.

He caught her.

She screamed.

His wolf senses told him about a bed of ferns. He threw her down, knocking the wind out of her for a second.

Not for a wolf was the savage penetration. She was already screeching and kicking, clawing at where she hoped his face was in the darkness. He wanted to smell, to touch, to taste, and, finally, to drink her substance. He buried his head at the most exciting spot his wolf's brain could find. A place whose emanations outstripped all the rest. Her groin. He lapped vigorously. Her screams and struggles changed to something else. She lay still. He found structures not existing on wolves. Delve . . . the place was soft with a rich taste.

She was kicking violently, but not at him. Something else here to suck. She gasped, moaned, laughed wildly, then howled, giving rent to such noises as he felt might shame a bitch in heat. Arching her body back with her buttocks pounding the ground. He tried to pull away. She caught his head between her thighs, his hair in her hands. He found himself wanting to drink her dry. He tried.

She was swollen, normal; wolves also did this. Other things were not so normal. She heated like a branch charring in a fire until she seemed one burning with fever. Her heart thundered. It went on and on until she reared up and shouted, "Quench me! Do it now!"

"Pain," he said. The unpracticed word was almost a snarl.

"By all the gods!" Her body shuddered; her nails dug into his back, scoring his skin. "Do you think I give a damn about pain?"

But she did. He found out when he forced admission to her intimate domain.

She fell back, biting the side of her open hand so as not to scream, her body suddenly drenched with perspiration.

"Wait," she whispered, placing her other hand palm open against his chest. She was breathing rapidly, deeply, not quite panting. "The sacrifice is a good one. I feel the blood. He takes his tribute, the male spirit, the bull of the woods. A woman's pain, her terror, her blood belong to him. I have given him mine, as I was chosen by lot to do."

Maeniel, now more man than he had ever been, tried to draw away. His mind chased the words through the blind pathways of his brain and couldn't find them. He wanted to say, "No more, you're hurt, bleeding. Your god should be content." But he couldn't fashion the thought into speech. "No," was the only reply he could manage. He tried to free his member from her body.

She embraced him, pressing his lips to hers. Her teeth met through his bottom lip.

Red rage wiped out all wolf and all humanity. For a second he was, as she wanted him to be, a conscienceless primal being. He completed the act of penetration brutally, vengefully, finally.

Her skin went cold, her heartbeat faltered. For a moment he thought he'd killed her, but then she stirred. She wept, but her skin was warming faster and faster. Seemingly almost against her will, a deep throbbing began. "Oh, no," she sobbed. "It will hurt. I can't stand it again."

"Not now!" he said.

For a moment she was balanced perfectly between pleasure and pain, then pleasure tripped the scales and they were both caught up in a firestorm of mutual desire that burned away caution and hesitation.

They explored each other's bodies passionately, constantly, with unceasing energy, as the night wore on. The moon set and then the Pleiades. All that remained were the cold, lonely stars when the dawn wind began to blow.

She was melting with exhaustion when she surrendered to him for the last time, the final pulsations of her body drawing him into flame. She lay in the ferns, a rag of flesh, breathing the deep, strong inhalations of sleep.

He found another, a man, also sleeping, clutching a half-full wineskin and wearing a woolen mantle. He woke when Maeniel took both. A blow of the gray wolf's fist returned him to the arms of Morpheus.

She swallowed the wine without waking, snuggled under the mantle. He found a bay tree nearby and crowned her with the victor's laurels. The mist was a silver glow among the trees as he left her for the sun to find.

Memory faded. Over the mountains the sun was sinking into the clouds. The wolf circled the lake, then trotted down the falls themselves, breasted the water in the lower pond. Helpless, his head clearly outlined against the perfectly still water, he invited attack if any huntsmen were concealed in the trees. None came.

The wolf reached the shore, puzzled. Men were vengeful creatures. The wolf was sure they would greet him here. But no. He reached the soft, beige sand beach at the edge of the lake, loped out of the water, and shook himself dry.

He owned them his superiors in cunning and, for that matter, in cruelty. He couldn't imagine what they might be planning. Some incomprehensible madness like the one that had taken her?

Guilt. A feeling known by dogs and wolves as well as men. None enjoys the emotion. The gray wolf didn't either. He didn't like remembering her. The memory of the fleshy passion they'd shared was tainted by the image of her ending.

For a moment, the wolf felt terror that he sometimes walked on two legs. They were cruel with an inventiveness and a delight he couldn't comprehend. Yet he partook of their nature. In fact, he was being tempted away from his wild innocence more and more often. This frightened him, but she and others of her kind drew him onward.

It would take him a hundred years to find out she really hadn't been beautiful. She hadn't been young, either. She had borne three children; one died in infancy. She brought up the other two; they were grown when he had met their mother. After the gray wolf found out about this, he was grateful. Grateful they hadn't met earlier and she had led a good long life before they had their chance encounter.

The sun dipped below the mountain. The evening breeze ruffled the lake's mirrored surface and the wolf's fur.

He saw the man.

My, the wolf thought, *he is a clever one.* The wolf froze. The observer stood in the woods near the top of the hill. He had chosen his position carefully. The breeze blew his scent away from the wolf, and he waited in the long shadow of one of the pines. Only the dark outline of one shoulder and the unmistakable silhouette of a human neck and face gave him away. As the wolf watched, the day faded, his eyes gathered in the last light, and he saw a gleam—the white of a human eye.

He turned his head deliberately and studied the observer, letting him know he'd been seen. The man made no move, threatening or otherwise, so the wolf slipped into the water, swam the pond, and was gone.

WHAT IS IT? BLAZE WONDERED AS HE MADE HIS way back to Mir's house. All he'd seen was a wolf. True, the thing was a very large wolf, bigger than most men. The thick gray pelt suggested a mountain hunter, one who made his home in the high passes, moving with his fellows across glaciers. Blaze had seen him clearly in the shadows near the lake. But that thick gray and white pelt would be invisible against snow.

Blaze shivered and not entirely at the rapidly deepening chill of evening. Yes, one struggling along through the drifts might look directly at this gray creature and not see him until he realized he was staring into a pair of large, yellow-brown eyes only a few feet away . . . and ahead of him. By then, there would be time for only a few seconds of prayer.

He'd heard of men taken by these aristocratic wild killers, even men traveling with large armed parties. When he was told the stories, he'd always felt some impatience with these fools and with their escorts, who had sometimes been brought before him, asking for mercy. Telling their tale of having lost a companion or an important individual, and pleading it was not their fault, saying they either heard no cry or only a very brief one. Then, when they quickly retraced their steps, of finding only a few drops of blood soaking into the snow. After seeing this one, even at a distance, he suddenly felt a great deal more sympathy for their plight.

As he was pushing his way through an exceptionally thick patch of undergrowth, he heard a whisper of sound behind him. Blaze's mouth went suddenly dry and he found his knees weren't steady. Mir claimed this wolf was sometimes a man, and seemed always able to think like a man.

The creature had seen him and there was nothing to prevent the giant predator from misleading him by going off in one direction, then—as soon as he was out of sight—turning and following him through the dark wood.

Blaze punched at his clothing and found the lantern Mir had given him under his mantle, hanging by a strap from his shoulder. He kindled a flame quickly by striking flint against an iron ring on his finger. As the wick caught, he realized his hands were shaking. He lifted the lantern high and saw he was in a small clearing. The boughs of a huge oak stretched out over him. The ground under him was covered with a mosaic of brown oak leaves.

He almost turned to look back, but realized at the last moment he really didn't want to. "Father of the gods, protect me," he whispered as he passed the big oak. At just that moment, he saw the fire Mir had kindled in the clearing in front of his house.

He heaved a sigh of relief and hurried onward. When he reached the edge of the wood, he stopped for a second, intending to blow out the lantern.

Something tugged at his mantle. Thinking it was caught on a twig, he turned and reached down to free it.

The eyes were only inches away.

He knew he screamed. Screamed like a woman. He hadn't believed he could scream like that, but he did.

He tore free of the mantle—the wolf had it—then flung the lantern at the wolf's back. Somehow, without seeming to move, the wolf dodged the flaming missile.

Blaze ran, ran as he didn't think he could still run . . . like a terrified twenty-year-old.

Mir was awaiting for him at the door.

Gasping, Blaze looked back across the empty clearing. The bonfire continued to crackle, flames whipping with small tearing sounds, points reaching for the heavens above. At the edge of the forest he saw his mantle, lying like a dark splotch near the flickering lantern slowly being extinguished by the damp leaves.

"Tell me," Blaze gasped hoarsely. "Tell me I didn't dream that."

"No," Mir answered in a weary voice. "you didn't. Try not to worry about it too much. Go inside. The people hereabouts have honored you with the best of mead and there are covered dishes, roast meats, and fish on the table. I'll go fetch the lantern and your mantle."

"No," Blaze cried hoarsely, clutching at Mir's arm. "He might still be nearby."

Mir gazed at him sadly. "I'm sure he is. He but played with you. Had he wanted you, he would have taken you before you ever reached my home. I have known for a long time he could take me any time he wanted.

"The night, the night after . . . she . . . died, I awakened. I believe it to have been the ninth hour, the longest, darkest of the night. The forest was silent; at that time even fish ghosting in deep pools at the river bottom sleep. But he sat awake, upright on his haunches, tail around his body, near my hearth. His eyes glowed green in the firelight. Such a look he gave me, and I knew whatever our intentions— my intentions, her intentions, even—he didn't . . ." The old man's voice trailed off. "Well, no matter. I'll fetch the mantle and lantern. You go inside and eat."

Blaze entered the house. The hearth fire blazed high. As promised, there were a number of dishes on the table. Savory aromas rose from them. The girl he'd seen earlier lay on the bed sleeping, her thumb in her mouth.

He poured himself a cup of wine. The beaker rattled against the neck of the cup. He gulped the dark fluid.

Mir returned, carrying the mantle and the lamp. "I know you didn't believe me before. I know what you thought. 'Doddering old fool living in a tumbledown shack at the edge of the waste. He has kept company with the birds and deer, the deep forest loneliness and his mad little wife far, far too long. His brain is turned.' That was what you thought, wasn't it? Eh?"

"I suppose I might have," Blaze sighed. "Well, I don't now. I most emphatically don't now."

Mir nodded. "He is a curse. We must be freed from that curse. You are the greatest of our order still remaining in Gaul. Help us."

Blaze sat down at the table. Absently, he poured himself another cup of wine. His eyes narrowed as his fear faded and he began to think.

F AR AWAY, THE WOLF MET HIS PACK IN A GROVE where a wooden female image held sway. Sometimes, at certain feasts, women cursed with barrenness came here to dance in the moonlight. They asked the Lady—she had no other name—for a child. Supposedly it was death for men to come here, but many braved the gesa and sneaked in, concealing themselves in the trees surrounding the image. They did so because the women danced naked, danced themselves into hot desire, and they would often couple in supple abandonment with those whose voices charmed them into the darkness and whose hot spill of seed might quicken the empty womb. After all, bees in the drunken springtime plunder the dreaming orchards by both sun and moonlight. What couldn't be earned in the marriage bed might be stolen by starlight. But all this came about in the springtime.

Now it was autumn with the mountain winter hurrying in on its heels. Now only the wolves danced and played here in the chill moonlight. They rolled in the short, brown grass, rubbed their heads and jaws against her pillared image, and, at last, sang to the rising moon before the hunt.

N O, SHE HADN'T BEEN BEAUTIFUL, BUT THEN HE'D never understood the canons of human beauty. How quick they were to try to hammer something so effervescent, so changeable into a narrow mold. Catch the wind on a net or freeze the play of sunlight on moving water, then you will know what beauty is, but you still will not have been able to lay hold of desire, the fire in the belly that brings us to triumph, heartbreak, or despair.

He had been determined to make the human she in the grove his last. Her pain had scared him. No bitch wolf knew such suffering and perhaps none found it the gateway to the almost transcendent pleasure she displayed so freely at the last. So he stayed away from the lake and devoted himself to his duty—leading the pack, keeping them fed, ensuring the weaker members were protected, and maintaining proper order. Perhaps if he hadn't lost his leader counterpart, the she who complemented his powers among the females, he might have escaped the trap awaiting him. But the pack's great female died under the claws of a bear and, for a season, he had no proper mate.

The winter had been harsh. No individual but he could remember a harsher one. The Romans haunted the valley—though he didn't know them as Romans, only as heavily armed, mounted men who carried powerful compound bows and wanted wolf skins for some purpose of their own. A pack living in the valley was decimated.

He led his to the heights. The men encamped in the valley slaughtered game with both hands. And, as winter wore on and the snows deepened, prey became more and more difficult to find. So when his pack pursued a lean elk into a snow bank and pulled him down, they weren't about to yield their prey to a snarling bear who appeared and tried to take it from them.

He and she were the leaders. They knew their duty. As the stronger, he led the attack, circling the bear, snapping at her, distracting her while the wolves fed on the steaming meat and blood of the fallen elk. The ravenous bear, her reserves of fat exhausted by the long winter and drained by her cub, wasn't intimidated or drawn off by their tactics. She turned back toward the feeding wolves and was nearly able to maul one of the yearling males. The wolves drew away, snarling, from the carcass.

They had to have the food, and the gray knew it. A few of the older members of the pack were already weak. He could tell by the smell of the air that a blizzard was sweeping across the pass. If they didn't feed now, the wind and freezing temperatures would end some of their lives tonight.

He faced the bear, backing her away from the kill with an open-mouthed roar of fury. She reared on her hind legs and swiped at him. He wasn't quite quick enough and she left a strip of fine marks all along one side of his body. He circled, trying to get behind her, but she followed him. The she-wolf leaped, diving for a haunch. The bear whipped around, dropped to all fours, and in a movement too rapid for the eye to follow, sent the she-wolf rolling, yipping, spraying blood into the snow. But the pack mother had given the gray his chance. He went for the giant thighbone. The bone crumbled in his jaws. He was able to leap away just in time to avoid a last vicious swipe of the bear's claws. The broken bone leaped out through the skin like a javelin. The bear gave a cry of anguish, spinning 'round and 'round, snow packing under her paws as her blood pulsed, fountained from the shattered leg and drenched the snow. 'Round and 'round she went, snapping desperately at the wound that was killing her until, at last, her struggles ended and she sank down in the scarlet pool and died.

Ignoring the bear's stiffening body, the wolves returned to the kill. The she-wolf stood, shook off the snow, limped over, stood next to him, and took her share. The blizzard's first clouds reached them. Snow flurries spattered their fur even as they cleaned the elk's bones. The bear was only a mound of white near the bloody scraps of the kill when they finished. The she-wolf limped away from the elk and the rest.

He knew where she was going—to the den where she had borne her pups for many seasons. Her head was down, her ears back. She was limping badly now, and looked as if she were in great pain. The rest had another shelter and they would seek it.

He followed her.

The den was beyond the tree line. Up and up she went. The snow flurries had settled into a steady downfall that seemed to grow thicker by the minute. The sky was a uniform deep gray that imperceptibly darkened, washing color out of the world, then slowly strangling light. He moved behind the she over the high windswept waste.

The light was blue-gray when they came to the den. The entrance was choked with snow. She wiggled in and found a corner piled with dried moss. She lay still.

He followed, resting next to her, lending her the only support and help he could. His big, warm body stretched out next to her. He heard her sigh, the same sound she made after sex. The previous springtime's loving hadn't taken. She was having a barren year.

Her eyes were closed and her muzzle rested on his back, just below the neck. He curled his body around hers as well as he could. Outside, blue evening became black. The wind howled louder and louder as the blizzard ripped through the mountains, tearing at the naked stony peaks and the glacial heights with frigid fingers, wrapping any unsheltered, warm living thing in a cocoon of icy death. Wailing, sobbing, moaning, and, at last, screaming out the triumph of cold and dark over light and warmth. Of an eternal frozen death over the fleeting loves of a transient springtime.

He didn't know when she died. All he knew was that sometime in those blackest, wildest, cruelest hours before dawn, he woke to find he could no longer feel her heartbeat and that in spite of his warmth, her body was cooling. When he moved, her head slipped from his back and landed with a soft thud on the moss. She lay on her side, jaws slightly open, the tongue protruding a bit between them, eyes staring unseeingly out into the last darkness. He rested his head on his front paws and awaited the dawn.

When it came, he slipped out of the den. The storm had passed. Sun shone on the snow. The sky was blue.

He returned to the den. She lay where she'd been before. He pushed her with his nose and found her already stiffening.

He turned and went outside. He became human. God, it was cold, but this wouldn't take long. He pulled at the snow above the entrance to the den. A miniavalanche ensued, sealing the entrance not just with snow, but with rock and pebbles that had been piled on the granite slab that formed its roof.

When he was finished, he turned wolf again and marked the den. He marked in a way humans don't understand, the way wolves mark traps.

This is a place of death. Stay away!

Wolves don't grieve. What he had done showed respect for what she had done and been. No more.

Then he left to join the rest under an overhang where they'd found shelter from the storm.

S HE IS YOUNG, BLAZE THOUGHT DISAPPROVINGLY as she rode up to Mir's hut. *Too young to be what she purports to be.* "You are?" he asked.

"Dryas," she answered. She was mounted on a beautiful blood bay mare. She wore a leather overblouse and a dark, divided skirt that hung almost to her ankles. It was thickly embroidered with gold at the hem. The long brown mantle that covered her shoulders was clasped at her breast by a broach formed of poppy flowers and leaves.

"Did you come through the Roman lines?" Blaze asked. "They patrol the countryside of Gaul everywhere."

"I wasn't far away," she answered. "Most of the ruling men seem to be gone, but a few of their women remain. Some retain power. They wanted my advice on how to survive now that the Roman conquest is complete." She dismounted, keeping the reins in her hands.

"The answer is, we can't," Blaze snapped. "Our only hope is to continue—"

"Oh my, yes," she said irritably, "and tempt these demons to slaughter and mutilate the remainder of our menfolk and sell more of our women into slavery, a slavery that is only a slower kind of death. Don't be fools, I told them. Preserve what you can, make any accommodation you must, but live. Teach our traditions to your sons and daughters. The old world is finished. A new has begun, and who knows where it will lead?"

Blaze fixed her with an icy stare. "That is what I would expect of a woman's counsel. No more. No less. But I didn't invite you here for a lesson in politics."

She pulled off her leather cap. A coil of long black hair fell from under it and spread fan-wise down her back, crackling a little with electricity. "I wouldn't expect you to ask. You *men* have done so wonderfully well up to now. At least half the people in this wretched realm are dead or carried away as slaves. The rest, their lives shattered, scramble for survival among the ruins of all they once held dear. And you, Arch Druid of Gaul, send letters to me asking that I dispatch one of my women—and you dare to specify an attractive one—to play the whore with a . . . a . . . wolf. What nonsense have you connived at?"

Blaze's face went scarlet with fury. He stepped toward her. To do what he had no idea; he'd never struck a woman in his life. But her words scalded the deepest part of his being, the place in his soul where his people's agony was his own.

She dropped the cap and the horse's reins and shrugged the mantle aside. She wore a sword. In less than a second, it flashed in the sun. "Back off," she whispered between bared teeth. "One more step, I take your hand. Another and it will be your head."

Mir, who had been standing by quietly, just as quietly stepped between them. "For shame," he said. "For shame," he repeated, looking at Dryas. "He is unarmed, and I so old a child could overpower me. And it is cruel to berate a brave man over things perhaps no one could change. My girl, outstanding member of your order that you may be, there is a truth that age teaches. We do all we can, but sometimes fate takes us by the throat and we are helpless."

Dryas stepped back and sheathed her sword. "Forgive me, my father," she said respectfully to Mir. "I have been long in the saddle. What I have seen here sickens me."

At this moment, the girl Mir called his wife stepped through the door and looked at Dryas.

"Oh," Dryas whispered, taking in the vacant stare and the hideously scarred face. "In the name of all good spirits, you didn't tell me you had this kind of problem."

Mir stepped aside. "Do what you can," he said. "I know that those of your order can often ease the despair of those driven beyond reason by private grief, and sometimes even reclaim the lost. Help her if you can."

The girl drifted toward Dryas, who took her by the hand and led her into the forest.

B LAZE WAS SITTING AT THE TABLE, HAVING SOME wine, when Mir entered. "How did you find Dryas?" he asked.

"Very like the men," Mir answered, taking the seat across from him. "It's disappointing. Somehow one expects more from women. I can't think why. But we turn to them when we have exhausted our strength and our solutions, as if they don't share the same weakness and faults we do. As if they might bring a new eye and finally loose the leashings of our Gordian knots without a sword. But I do believe she will help my 'wife.' It is the first time I've ever seen the child show trust to anyone."

Dryas entered just then. She carried her mantle and was freshly washed. She, too, took a seat at the table. "I suppose I should be flattered to be compared to a man, but I can't say that I am, and I have no solutions for your problems. And you, Mir, as for your wife, there's little enough I can do for her, trust or no. The damage is already done. I left her a few medicines that will ease her pain and even one that will permanently end it, if she so chooses; and I listened to her tale."

Mir's head jerked up in surprise. "She spoke!"

"To me, yes," Dryas said. "We are known to each other. I met her family; they were a great one. She may be the last remaining living member. The Romans killed or enslaved the rest."

"Then she's not mad?" Mir asked.

"Oh, yes, she is," Dryas said. "But she is lucid about certain things sometimes. She can grow most of the simples I left her in the garden. She tends it, does she not?"

"Yes." Mir nodded.

"By the way," Dryas asked, "what is her name?"

"I don't remember." Mir avoided her gaze.

"Good," Dryas said. "Continue not to remember. It's just as well. Now, if you please, give me some of that wine and tell me about the wolf, in that order."

Mir and Blaze stared at each other. They both looked uncomfortable. Dryas sighed and reached for a cup and the jug herself.

"I believe you are the senior," Mir said guilelessly to Blaze.

"And I believe you are the best acquainted with the problem," Blaze returned smoothly.

Dryas poured herself some wine. "While you are each trying to get the other to precede you through the door, I believe I'll have a drink."

AFTER THE MOTHER OF THE PACK DIED, THE WINter did not go well. The oldest female, she who knows always where to go to find prey, failed. She died in the grayness, the stony hardness of midwinter. She lay down to sleep in the snow with the rest and did not awaken in the morning. He was deprived of her counsel as well.

The virgin females fought with escalating fury for the position of pack mother. The most promising two inflicted such dreadful injuries on each other that both died, leaving a third the winner by default. This greatly cut the pack's hunting ability since they had been the swiftest and most dangerous killers. Their loss taxed all his cunning and ability.

In the spring he was, of course, at the disposal of the winning female. She was a rangy, nervous bitch, very jealous of her prerogatives as pack mother. She constantly harassed the remaining females. This led to endless squabbling and ill temper among the younger pack members.

Despite his feeling of coldness toward her, he would have accommodated her desires. She had, after all, earned the mother right. This was what pack law demanded of him—that he meet her graciously as a mate and then assist in rearing her offspring.

But to his mild surprise, she showed no interest in him at all and took up with two males who were all that remained of the pack destroyed by the Romans. This was also her right, that she choose her own partners if she wished. He might have asserted himself more strongly. Other leaders would have, but he was more relieved than otherwise at her decision and left her alone.

She returned from her forays, finally satisfied, pregnant, and much calmer than when she left, and he found himself pleased not to be bothered about her needs. And besides, he had already met the strawberry-blond woman at the pool.

The woman came from the small village of herdsmen and farmers, down the slope and to the pond to refresh herself in the cool water, bathe, and dress her thick, reddish blond hair. She was wide hipped; her breasts were large, upright with only a slight droop. The nipples jutted invitingly. Her skin was very fair, and he noticed she kept to the shade. That skin didn't tan; it probably burned. She was covered head to toe with freckles.

He grew accustomed to seeing her each day as he dozed on the flat rock overlooking the waterfall. He thought she looked delectable, but not in the manner of food. Usually she left when the sun was high in the sky. The pool, even at midsummer, could become very cool in the afternoon when the sun's rays no longer shone on it and the forest shadow crept in.

He found the change difficult and sometimes impossible by day. By the time he felt the long evening shadows pull at his flesh and he could sense a bridge forming between his world and the human's, she was gone.

Just as well, he thought. A few times he was tempted to slink after her when she returned to the rath where she lived. Once or twice he even entertained the fantasy of entering the circular, thatched dwelling by night. He wasn't blind in even the deepest darkness. He knew her scents. They were in certain ways more real to him than the way she looked.

Often, after bathing, she took her ease in one of the few sunny spots not choked by undergrowth or shadowed by ancient trees. The big granite rock was buried, but enough of it thrust into the water to create a platform a few feet above the lake. The top was too bare to sustain growth, but it was thickly carpeted with pine and fir needles. It got sun three or four hours a day. The radiant light would peer down, deep down, into the lake's clear water, flashing on pike, trout, and the occasional small sturgeon that would come and go like ghosts in the gloom.

All year, except during the darkest months, wild flowers surrounded the pine-needle carpet. Mother of thyme would rise from beneath the snow and twine with blue-flowered bergamot mint. Violets bloomed in the springtime, white, deepest purple, yellow. Later in summer wild carrots, the yellow composite daisies, sunflowers, and dandelions lit up the thickening grass. Harebells peered from the shelter of tall pines, hiding their drooping beauty in the shade of tile-barked trunks and thick, clustered needles.

All unknowing she left her mark on the fallen brown needles. For instance, he knew that desire rose in her, answering the moon queen's magnetism at least three times a week. He didn't know where she expressed that desire since she came to the lake alone. Her skin had a flowerlike scent. It took him a while to understand the smell wasn't just satiny flesh, but the oil of roses she anointed herself with after her bath. The smell at her armpits in the heat was mildly oniony—sweet, wild onions wrapped in clay and caramelized by a fire. When she was gone, he drifted down to drink in her complex perfume and sometimes roll on the pine carpet near the trees.

Of course, one day, perhaps accidentally, perhaps inevitably, she remained too long. She came rather late in the afternoon. The water was in shadow, but the trees on the slopes and the little clearing were suffused with golden light. She took a quick swim. The water was icy, and she retreated quickly to shore to rest in her usual spot, and let the late-afternoon sun warm her chilled body.

She stretched out on her perch. The wolf could also feel her languor, the relaxation as the deep heat flowed through her and the fiery light shone orange through her eyelids. He was a bit surprised when the fingers of her right hand sought her groin. It took him a few seconds to comprehend what she was doing. Then he understood and watched avidly.

She had some swelling and moisture that brightened the red-gold hairs on her vulva. They shone gilt blond in the sun. Her lips parted slightly. He could see the tip of her tongue between them. Finally, her back arched. The expression of deep concentration became a quiet smile. She heaved a deep breath as the first wave broke over her, then a second gasp and a soft "Oh" as the one following caught her up in its greater intensity. Her hips began to pound as if she entertained an invisible lover. Her belly muscles tightened as her hips closed on the dream penis. Then she sighed deeply, reminding him strangely of the mother of the pack. She relaxed bonelessly, sighed again with pleasure and satisfaction, then slept.

The wolf rose to his feet. His decision was made. He was cursed, and yet delight coursed like pure fire in his veins. He remembered the glade. He and the wolves knew more of the Lady who dwelt there than humans did, because they had sometimes seen her shadow walking there. No one had ever seen her face and lived. A few caught sight of her in the pool when they stooped to drink. No one, brute or human, ever turned to stare directly at what gazed down into the water over their shoulder. But he knew he had just seen one of her images mirrored in a human face.

She awakened, a bit alarmed to see that it was late, the sun long behind the mountain and lighting only the rocky slopes above the tree line. She rose quickly, wrapped herself in her mantle, ready to hurry up the well-beaten path between the trees. When she lifted her head, her breath caught in her throat.

He was standing only a few feet away. Naked, but clothed in profound beauty. She had married, she had taken lovers, and she was something of a maven where looks were concerned; he was the most magnificent specimen she'd ever seen. Frank, open desire burned in his eyes: a question, a plea, a promise, an urgency, and last but not least, a command.

"WELL, WELL, WELL," DRYAS CHUCKLED, "HE CERtainly wasted no time taking you down a peg."

"Thank you for reminding me," Blaze said sourly.

"What do you want me to do about him?" she asked.

"Kill him," Mir said.

Dryas burst out laughing. She leaped to her feet, then kicked the chair across the room. It clattered across the ramshackle hut and crashed into the wall.

"Oh, you're a pair of beauties, you are." She drank from the cup of wine she held in her hand, then walked over and picked up the chair and tossed it back at the table. It landed accurately on its legs where it had been before. She slammed her heel into the wall. Mud rained down from the wickerwork structure. "Wattle and daub," she said.

She walked over to the fireplace, picked up a pan and a flesh fork, and made a circuit of the room, pounding the pan loudly with the fork. She exited the hut and walked around it, pounding loudly, then returned, closing the door behind her.

Both men looked completely stunned and bewildered.

"Listen!" she ordered. "You tell me this creature can walk on two legs like a man. And there is a good chance he can understand what we're saying to each other. So you sit in this dilapidated dwelling and talk of our plans in loud voices. How do you know the creature is not, in fact, lying in the weeds not far from here? Listening to *every* . . . *word . . . you . . . say.*"

Dryas was tired. She'd come a long way and all she'd seen on the journey were death, destruction, and pain. The Romans had broken the people's will to resist, and worse, the chieftains who should have been the backbone of that resistance were all too often murdered, enslaved, or bought by Roman power, helpless to change the fate of their people.

Enclaves like this were all that remained of a once-proud and brilliant nation. The scarred, broken, despairing girl eked out existence where once a family, intelligent, valiant, and handsome, ruled. No, not ruled: led a society that tried to live together in justice and peace.

In her journey across Gaul, Dryas had seen something she had not even known existed . . . die. The sorrow that ruled her heart was so deep it seemed to blot out the sun, even on a bright day. Something was perishing here. Something more important than any mere human who shared it. A thing greater than the sum of its human parts.

She was frightened not only by its destruction, but also by her inability to comprehend what her deepest instincts told her was happening. She was not an intellectual, but a warrior, a person of action. So the feelings of grief threatening to drown her soul in a tidal wave of pain caused her to lash out in fury at these two old fools—the few surviving remnants of a class of thinkers and teachers who had shaped the only world she knew since the beginning of time.

She drew a deep, shuddering breath and covered her eyes with her hand. Then she felt on her other hand the dry touch of Mir's fingers. He patted it softly, gently, as he might comfort a child.

Tears leaked out from her eyelids and, when she opened her eyes to look at his face, she saw an understanding, a weary comprehension deeper than any she thought possible.

Her fury and sorrow faded together, leaving her drained and feeling slightly foolish for having taken so much wine on an empty stomach.

"Are you then refusing to help us?" Blaze's question carried the full freight of outraged authority.

Dryas turned toward him, anger beginning to flush her face again.

Mir clasped her hand. "Wait! Wait! I pray you both. Consider, Blaze: you have little of your former power. We are more than ever dependent on each other's goodwill. And you, girl, think. With most of the strongest warriors gone, I must, as the shepherd of an almost defenseless flock, preserve them from a scourge that can destroy them as surely as the Romans."

Dryas subsided. She snatched up the cup and swallowed more of the vintage there.

"All right," Blaze snarled. "You've made your point. I should say you've both made your respective points."

Dryas leaned forward and spoke in a very low voice and in another language, the tongue of her own people. "Yes, I'll help you." But her gaze shot to the door and walls. "*He* doesn't need to know that. Do you understand me?"

Mir simply nodded, but Blaze replied in the same language. "God! It's been years. My command of the language is . . . flawed and I'm cursed slow, but yes, I do understand simple sentences."

She nodded. "Tomorrow. In the sun . . . in the open."

Both men nodded, and she finished the wine in one pull. Then she kicked back her chair, walked over to the corner, shouldered her pack, and turned toward the door.

"Wait!" Blaze cried, "he—"

Dryas stepped toward him and spoke again in Caledonian. "Don't help me. Shut up! I know what I'm doing." Then she turned and vanished into the night.

S HE WAS A LUSH, FORBIDDEN FRUIT TO THE WOLF. A mature woman, redolent of an almost incenselike confusion of fragrances. Soft, yet tight openings and velvet surfaces.

As he took her, she communicated an exquisite and unknown sensation to his mind and body as he invaded hers. He could tell, as she fell first to her knees before him and then as he pushed her backward to sprawl on the pine needles, that she both feared and desired him. And that she felt both sensations deeply.

"Don't hurt me," she pleaded.

He didn't.

It was growing dark when he released her, allowing her to scramble to where her clothing lay. He slipped into the shadows and realized she was trembling as she donned her few simple garments and began her run to the village.

Wolflike, he was puzzled by her reaction to him. He knew he'd given her pleasure, ecstatic pleasure. And more than one time. He understood that her fear lent a sharper edge to both of their desires. But what he couldn't understand was the reason for that fear. Did she think he would attack, harm her during an act that brought so much mutual delight, an act of joy?

When he was sure she could no longer see him, he shifted to his wolf shape and shadowed her up through the pines, back to the rath, the rude Celtic farmstead where she lived.

He stood at the edge of the forest when she pushed aside the skin curtain that covered the opening to her dwelling.

"Imona!" someone cried. "We were about to go down to the lake. Look, our torches are kindled. What happened? Where have you been?"

"I'm sorry." Her voice was low, almost a stammer. "I drifted off to sleep after my bath. I had no idea I'd sleep so long. The sun was already behind the mountains when I awakened . . . I came back as quickly—"

The other she's voice broke in on her. "You should be more careful. I swear I believe you do these things to bring misery on your unhappy kin."

"Kat, I'm so sorry. I never meant to worry you."

Kat, eh, and Imona, the wolf thought. *Screech Kat.* Maeniel had met a few small, furred, clawed beasts. Loud voices, they had. They hung about and scavenged near human dwellings. They were quick and could run straight up trees. Imona's voice was low and lovely. This Kat sounded like a shrew.

The night wind was rising as the mountains let go their heat and the roar of the forest drowned out further conversation in the ringfort.

Imona, the wolf thought. *They have names. She has a name. Wolves don't. Only me—the name She gave me when She made me more—or less—than wolf. Maeniel.* High above, small clouds scudded past the glowing half moon. *The gray ones are like those clouds. Each one different, but somehow all the same. We come, we pass through life, we drift over the mountains as those clouds drift past the moon, then descend into darkness and are forgotten. They give each other names that they can remember. Remember at least for a time when they once loved. Do they try to reach beyond death?* The wolf was baffled. He thought of the mother of the pack, now surely only bones cradled in the overhang's moist earth.

And suddenly, he knew his difference from the rest of the pack. To them, if they thought of her at all, she was but a dim memory. He voiced a soft whine and shook himself.

Far away, a wolf howled. Then, smoothly and swiftly as water tumbles over a streambed in the teeming rain, others joined the chorus. The new pack mother gave the first cry, then the young males, and last of all the fleet virgin shes. Each voice was known to him, each conjured up an image and an emotional association in his mind. He raised his head, but then, with very unwolflike calculation, realized how close he was to human dwellings. It was unwise to provoke them or their powerful mastiff watchdogs.

He knew his pack would gather at the pool before the hunt, so he turned and entered the forest.

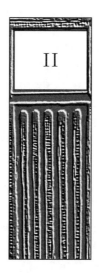

II

OUTSIDE OF MIR'S HUT, DRYAS WRAPPED HER-self tightly in a woolen mantle. The first chill of winter gripped the mountain meadow. She paused a moment to allow her eyes to grow used to the darkness. *I didn't have to wait when I was younger,* she thought ruefully. Then, the transition had been in-stantaneous. She was still young, but age was beginning its slow work, blunting the warrior skills of her youth.

As for the wolf, if Mir could be believed, this creature had an-other use for women than it did for men. In fact, if it partook of any-thing of the dog's nature, it might be harmless to her. The woman scent couldn't always be relied upon, but she'd often seen vicious mastiffs reduced to fawning submission at a brush of a woman's skirts.

Gradually, her eyes began to pick out the tree trunks and other structures surrounding Mir's hut. She moved slowly within the shadows.

Mir's little wife had described a well-worn path that led to a clearing and a standing stone that overlooked the whole valley. So she moved slowly over the treacherous rocky ground until her boots found the well-tramped footway. It was deeply cut. *Old,* Dryas thought, *very ancient and sacred.* Around her the giant firs and pines blotted out even the stars above. There was no moon.

Just as well the path was so deeply beaten; she could see nothing under the trees.

At first the slope was gentle, but it swiftly grew steeper, climbing with a minimum of switchbacks toward the tree line. She wasn't sure when the forest began to thin out, but gradually, as she climbed higher and higher, the sensation of walking in a cavern diminished as the trees became increasingly sparse and short, giving way, at last, to brush and then scattered wind-twisted dwarves. As she drew closer to the open, the wind began to bite alarmingly.

Frost, she thought. *There will be frost on the grass before dawn.* All at once she became aware she was walking across level ground. She stood in a tiny mountain meadow overlooking a deep gorge where the river ran. The grass was long and silken, gleaming like raw flax in the starlight.

She remembered the girl's words. No tame beast grazes there, only the deer, the mountain goat, and the chamois. Everyone has forgotten why. All they will say when they speak of it is "It's bad luck" or "There's not enough grass there to be worth the trouble and the trail is too steep. A fine cow or sheep might break a leg."

On one end of the meadow, a lump of dark granite crouched like a giant fist. Water bubbled from a brush-covered cleft in the stone near the top, fell from one ledge to another until it created a basin at the foot, then overflowed into the little creek that bubbled past Mir's door.

She paused to get her bearings and then walked forward carefully. The meadow ended on her right in a steep slope, rocky at first, then clothed in thick spruce and fir, and, finally, virgin pine forest near the river in the valley below. On her left stood a sheer cliff. Up and up it rose—steep, unclimbable—until it gave way to a series of rocky terraces leading to a snow-capped peak.

Go to the spring, the girl had instructed her. Near the spring you will find the stair.

As she approached the granite lump, she saw the hand- and footholds chipped out of the rock. Had the girl not called it a stairway, Dryas would have believed the small notches were simply natural features hollowed out over uncounted centuries by wind and rain.

Dropping her pack on the ground, Dryas reached out and slid her hand into the first. She found it much deeper than it had appeared. She began to climb and became aware, to her chagrin, that there was something the child had not told her. The rude ladder led her around the giant granite boulder and out over the valley below.

When the first handhold became a foothold, she found herself hanging over a sheer drop to the river at the bottom of the gorge. She pressed her breasts and stomach against the fissured stone. Her belly muscles quivered.

Pride awakened. She was Dryas of the royal line. Guardian to queens and queen herself. *Yes, Dryas,* her common sense informed her, *but the girl is mad as a bull in rut and these hollows may not lead anywhere.* Yet, even as she thought that, she found herself impatiently fumbling for another handhold. When she placed her foot where her hand had been only a few moments before, she realized her left hand was sliding over a rock ledge. A moment later, she was over the top and resting on the flat of a tiny dell looking eastward.

The dell was only thirty feet wide and qualified more as a large ledge, but it also supported the same thick growth of grass as the meadow below. Up so high, the wind seemed to blow without end. Sometimes a roaring blast, at others, a gentle breeze, but it never quite ceased, and in a few moments, her cheeks and fingers began to grow numb. The warmth of her exertion drained away and the cold crept in. Well, the girl said they were here. Where were they?

The moon began to rise over a distant peak. By its light, as the builders intended, she saw the ellipse of white stones among the grass and the pale, flat slab in the middle, glowing in the icy moonlight. Dryas nodded. She could even read this one. Part of her training had been learning what such structures meant. This one spoke as clearly as the wedge of a sundial. *There are,* she thought, *much easier ways now, but the creatures of this moon calendar probably invented them. Yes, it is important for us to know.*

The shadow appeared near the stone in the center of the circle, something darker than the rising moonglow and the misty, distant starblaze. It didn't coalesce out of the night. One moment it was not there; the next it was.

Dryas shivered. Yes, the girl had been right. She stood, backed up to the edge, then began to make her way down the same ways he'd come up. Only this time her entire concentration was on the openings that served as the ladder. She didn't look up. She wanted to, but she found she couldn't. She had encountered a phenomenon more frightening than a journey down a sheer cliff, hand over hand. She was afraid if she looked up she would see something, only God knows what . . . looking over the edge . . . down at her.

———————

FLOWERS, ANY FLOWERS, MADE HIM REMEMBER HER. While he loved her, the world had basked in summer, and the high alpine valley and lowland meadows were ablaze with their fire.

Beyond the mountains, other fires burned. They were not so beautiful, left only ashes and created dark smudges across a fair blue sky. Caesar was on the march. He would climb to the top of a pile of corpses and, at last, achieve primacy in the world.

But the wolf knew nothing of this and would not have cared if he did. What were the doings of men to him? He and his kind had settled their affairs with the universe millennia ago. They lived according to a fixed code, one that evolved with his species out of the darkness of mammalian beginnings. He and his kind were guided by it, though they never tried to understand it. He gave it no thought at all while he stalked Imona and her companions as they hurried downhill through the dawn mist to bathe in the lake.

She hung back a bit from the others, trailing along last, as if she sensed his presence and was waiting for him.

His arms closed around her from behind. He swung her off the path and behind a tree.

She gasped, but didn't cry out.

He gave her every opportunity to scream, but she didn't. In fact, when she turned and saw who he was, she threw her arms around his neck and kissed him.

He'd never been kissed before, but he was a quick study. He decided he liked this form of human contact and wanted to learn more about it. Time enough for that. He swept her up, carrying her uphill to a secluded spot only a wolf would know.

One bitter winter long ago an avalanche had cut a swath of violence through the tree line. When, at length, the summer came and melted the remaining ice and snow, it left a jumble of boulders, broken trees, and thick brush piles that extended down into the pine forest.

It wasn't a popular spot with humans, though the wolves and wild cats liked it well enough. The area around the vast piles of broken stone was haunted by vipers and pitfalls. You might think you were climbing along solid ground when the rotten timber and broken branches gave way, sending a foot or leg into a hole, twisting muscles or shattering bones. Whitened trees killed in the mountain's convulsive rock falls were always ready to slip, drop, and drive splintered limbs into a careless explorer. All in all, not a salubrious place to wander.

She kissed him on the neck as he carried her along. "Sweet merciful mother," she whispered. "I didn't think I'd ever see you again."

He laughed.

"Aren't you afraid . . . The men of my tribe would kill you if they caught you."

"I don't think I'd be that easy to kill."

Just at that moment, he reached the spot he had been seeking, a tiny clearing shaded by the heavy boughs of a broken pine and surrounded by boulders of granite and huge fragments of shale driven into the ground in enormous shards by the landslip. He placed her on the ground in a circle of broken stone knives.

She paused for a moment, but only to pull off her dress. She was naked under it. She cupped her breasts and offered them to him. He licked at first and then sucked. She writhed and moaned.

"I shouldn't be doing this," she sobbed.

He paused for a second, profoundly puzzled.

"No," she groaned, "don't stop."

Her back arched. He could feel her hot, wet sex pressing against his stomach. The perfume of her desire hung in the morning air as thickly as the soft, damp dew that bathed the grass around them.

"You want me?" he asked.

"I could devour you!" Her whisper was frantic. She clawed his shoulder, her nails ripping into his skin.

He felt her orgasmic spasms begin when he entered her. In the brief relaxation between her first and second she gasped, "I have a husband."

Maeniel withheld comment until she reached her third climax. Then, as she settled back into tranquility, he asked, "What's a husband?"

HE WAS NOT SATISFIED WITH HER REPLY. AMONG wolves, none possessed such rights over another. Wolves did not mate for life. Properly speaking, in human sense, they did not mate at all.

The strongest male in a pack achieved the privilege of breeding, as did the strongest female. But they didn't necessarily choose one another.

Desire depended entirely on the receptivity of the female. If she was not receptive, better not to try. In fact, it could become quite dangerous to try.

Imona lay in his arms. Around them the mist burned away. The sun began to warm the rocks. She dozed. He cradled her. He was used to sleeping with his pack mates piled up in company, safe against the cold. It seemed natural to him that in his human form, they would sleep in each other's arms. She roused once. "The food! I made a lunch. It's in a leather bag. I must have dropped it near the trail to the pond."

Maeniel stood and walked into the sun-struck clearing. Naked, the heat from above dazzled his eyes and warmed his skin almost painfully. He wanted to change, but sensed it wasn't possible. Then he fled into the cool darkness under the trees.

But the forest here, thinned by the avalanche, didn't offer much protection, and it wasn't until he found a sort of grotto created by thick vines growing over the top of a boulder that he was able to drop shuddering into the change and resume his wolf form.

He found the leather sack near where he'd intercepted her. Suddenly voices rang out. He recognized Kat's voice.

"She's gone, I tell you! And I saw wolf tracks near her carry bag."

Maeniel snatched up the bag as a second voice replied, "Wolf, my old fat ass! What are you . . . a fool, girl? That man of hers hasn't been any good since he marched off to war. The Romans took his hand and his manhood went with it. He doesn't even make a pretense of lying with her or wanting to anymore. Depend on it, she's meeting some man."

"Clarissa!" Kat's voice held the high whine of an angry wasp. "Leon is my brother and your age doesn't give you any right—"

The gray wolf melted into the forest just as they reached the spot where the bag had been lying.

Kat broke off. "What!" She looked at the ground where the bag had been a moment before. "It's gone!"

Screened by a thick stand of fruiting elder and—to humans—an almost impenetrable thicket of blackberry vines, the wolf was invisible to them.

Kat, a scrawny, dark-haired woman, began to search. "It was here," she insisted frantically. "I know it was! Just a few minutes ago. I saw it."

Clarissa, a thick-bodied woman with a long mane of graying auburn hair, broke into shrill, cackling laughter. "That's because they've finished having their first tumble and it made them hungry. They came back and got it." Her remarks sounded a bit incoherent because they were choked out between gales of salacious merriment.

Kat didn't look amused. "Curse her! Curse the day we let her into the family. A curse on the eyes in her head, the tongue in her mouth, the ears she hears with, the throat she swallows—"

The gray wolf's whole body jerked as Clarissa brought the tirade to an end. She slapped Kat's face hard. Crack! The sound of her palm meeting flesh echoed among the trees.

Kat took two steps backward, tripped, and landed on her backside a few steps away from the elder thicket that concealed the gray wolf. She lifted her hand to her cheek, an expression of pure shock on her face.

"Bitch!" Clarissa said. "Do you fancy yourself a witch? Shut your foul mouth and keep your evil ill wishes to yourself. Heaven knows it's little enough Imona asks of your family. She's a hard worker, ready to turn her hand to any task, an unpaid servant to you, your man, and that lazy old crone mother of yours. She's reached her climacteric. She can't have any more children, so she can't disgrace your family. And the two girls she bore Leon were an obvious disappointment to the whole bunch of you. Have a little compassion, woman. Life hasn't been kind to Imona."

"She's the daughter of a chieftain," Kat screeched as she scrambled to her feet.

"Yes, and that always stuck in your craw, didn't it?" Clarissa shot back. "Well, now it doesn't matter. Only the gods know what happened to her people when the Romans came."

Both women were silent, glaring at each other. The gray wolf thought, *It was the very mention of the word* Roman *that sent a thrill of fear through the air.*

Kat made a sign against the evil eye. "Don't mention them," she whispered. "They burned a town in the valley last summer. This year everyone is afraid they may come here again."

Clarissa shivered. A small cloud covered the sun and the thick pine woods grew darker around them. "Kat, don't be a fool. Try not to see whatever it is Imona is doing. Your farmstead needs every pair of hands you have right now. Your mother and Leon are useless. You, Imona, and Des are the ones carrying the main burden. Without her, you might all starve. We have too many enemies to begin clawing at each other."

Even though Clarissa's tone was conciliatory, Kat didn't seem mollified. "You vicious old carrion crow. Lay hands on me again and I'll claw your eyes out." Then she turned and stalked off toward the lake below. Clarissa followed, shaking her head.

The cloud passed. Sun warmed the forest and lark songs began. The gray wolf carried the leather sack until he reached the same grotto. He sniffed the air. Dampness. Rain must be falling on the pass through the mountains.

Drop the sack, something in his mind told him. *Leave it here . . . Go. Find the pack. The hunting will be good in the high passes. Lead them away from here. Away, far away . . . to the glaciers where the snow never melts. The high timberlands will be filled with game clustering around lakes frozen for all but three months of the year. In forests so thick the sun on the brightest day never breaks through to the ground, you can remain hidden from man forever. Go!*

The wolf felt again the pull of desire. He could imagine her, a graceful sprawl of sleeping woman lying in the cool shade among the delicate fronds of spring ferns. The wolf shape seemed a thick, uncomfortable garment, the heavy fur overheating him as the sun rose high in the sky. He cast it off as one will a thick woolen mantle on the first warm spring day, and rose to his feet . . . a man.

When he returned, she extended her arms to embrace him. "I was afraid you'd gone and left me," she whispered, stroking his hair.

He studied her face as they lay together side by side. He wanted to tell her about her sister-in-law's bitter envy and Clarissa's defense, but he found he hadn't the words. A wolf would remember these things, but not necessarily communicate them to another wolf.

For a few moments he puzzled over what and how much to tell her, but by then her nearness began to rouse him and he forgot what he considered to be the spiteful bickering of jealous whelps. The lower-ranking females and males were very protective of what little status they had and spent a lot of their free time snapping and snarling at one another. These adolescent spats rarely caused injury, as the participants almost never came to blows. He was sure it was something like this that he'd heard. The strong among the pack would ignore them unless the young ones made too much of a nuisance of themselves. Then he usually settled matters with a loud snarl and a few nips on the backside.

The surging tides of desire wiped the memory from his mind. In his arms he had a woman naked, helpless, and compliant, more than willing . . . starved for the attentions of a man. He could explore this body, an unending engine of mad delight, a heap of flowers yielding new colors, fragrances, textures, and vivid emotion with every experiment suggested by an imagination, driving hands, lips, and sex.

By the time the sun slipped behind the western peaks, they were both exhausted. For the first time, he tasted human food, sharing bread, cheese, and a little wine with her.

She drank most of the wine and ended up weeping on his shoulder, her arms clinging around his neck.

"What's wrong?" he asked between kisses. "Did I do anything to you . . . you didn't want done?"

She hiccuped and pulled herself to her feet, then slid the dress on over her head. "No . . . no . . . no . . . no. You're wonderful. I love you." She wiped the tears from her cheeks with her fingers.

He reached out and picked her up. She felt featherlight to him. He carried her into the growing shadows under the trees. The sky above was suffused with sunglow. Golden light poured down through the broken pines. The shadows of rock, brush, and trees were inky. The gold of sky and forest seemed to burn like molten metal splashed on charcoal.

He scented the reptile before he saw it. A viper lay sunning itself high on a rock in the day's last radiance, its skin mottled to match the brown pine needles and dusky dead leaves where it rested.

He saw it as it raised its head to strike and he interposed one massive shoulder between the woman in his arms and the snake. She gasped. A low deep snarl rumbled in his chest. If the sound had been speech, it would warn, "No, not if you're smart, you won't."

The reptile pulled back its head, dropped, and vanished into the shadows and leaf litter on the forest floor.

She sighed, a long breath of relief. Above, the light was fading, the shadows around them deepening. "You're not a man, are you?" she asked.

"No." He set her on her feet at the path.

They could both hear the women chattering as they returned to the village above.

"Whatever you are, don't let them catch you. And come back, come back . . . please."

He felt the wolf pulling him away into the darkening wood, but he carried her hand to his lips in brief, tender farewell before he slid into the night.

S TILL SHAKING AFTER HER CLIMB, DRYAS CROSSED the mountain meadow, looking for a sheltered spot to sleep.

Deadfalls from the few dwarfed, twisted trees surviving on the slopes nearby littered the clearing, weathered bone-white by the unending wind and cold.

She found a spot near where the spring appeared from the rock. Such places were always sacred. Anyone found polluting the purity of the water could be punished with death. She made an offering of bread and wine, only a few crumbs of one and a sprinkle of the other, then set up her camp with her back to the cliff. She built a fire with dried wood from the meadow.

The broken limbs had rested so long in the thin grass they contained no more moisture than driftwood baked by sun on a shore. They flared into a fire, burning white-hot; one moment a fierce conflagration, the next dark red coals winking like demons' eyes in the darkness.

Dryas piled on the fuel. The fire warmed the rock and the resulting radiant heat would keep her warm through the night. When only coals glimmered where the fire had been, she rolled herself into a bearskin and slept.

As usual, she dreamed.

Once, and not long ago, dreams had been so much of a torment that she drank herself into a stupor rather than allow a natural rest to fall upon her.

But that bad, very bad time had ended, and though she sometimes woke with tears on her cheeks, the nightmare and her ninefold could no longer wrench her heart by presenting the dead as still living and the eternally lost as hers. Even in the deepest sleep, she knew her grief and accepted the pain and emptiness.

She was Dryas, the warrior, the teacher of sword, shield, and spear. Expert in methods by which an unarmed man could overcome even a well-armed one. Mistress of the hero's salmon leap with all its lethal permutations. One who could read the trajectory of an enemy's sword swing and leap over it to decapitate him. Mistress of the battle spell and the battle madness. Keeper of knowledge, forgotten by even these Gauls. Reader of stone circles and chamber tomb patterns whose origin was lost in the mist of time.

She had accepted the task Blaze set her. She must stop this man-wolf who so savagely harassed Mir's people, trap him. While Mir and Blaze were speaking, she had roughed out a plan for dealing with this menace. Tonight she'd taken the first steps to carry out her plan, but she certainly didn't want this supernatural wolf to guess her aims and ends.

No, that wouldn't do at all.

She woke once as she drifted off to sleep. All that remained of the fire were coals, glowing and blinking in the shadows. Above, the stars in absolute splendor arched over her head. Their cold fire mapped the past, present, and future to an eye able to read them, tracing mystery of time's beginning and end for all eternity.

Her stomach knotted. She was sure someone was watching her. The wolf or simply one of the dark denizens who guarded the eagle's temple above.

She didn't know, couldn't guess which, but then it didn't matter, not really. Either could kill her if they chose to do so. She was the bait in her own trap. All she could do was trust in her judgment and press on. This wolf wouldn't be conquered by sword and javelin, but by stealth and trickery. And while she was uncertain of her skills in this direction . . . she must discipline herself to show no fear. So she simply yawned, turned to one side, and drifted off to sleep.

THE ROMANS CAME . . .
The women covered the steep slopes surrounding the more level meadows with flax. Resistant to both drought and cold, it grew rampantly, each year reseeding itself. In autumn, the weavers harvested as much of it as they cared to. Imona was one of those weavers. She would move her warp-weighed loom to the dooryard of the rather humble dwelling, feed the chickens, ducks, and geese clustered in the farmyard, then begin work on her latest project.

Summer brought plenty of game with it. The reason, though the wolf didn't know it, was a bit sinister. The Roman garrison in the valley had felled trees to build its walls and palisades, then burned other forest cover to prevent revolts and ambushes.

Elk, deer, and even hare and wild fowl found these particular clearings filled with an abundance of forage.

So the wolves prospered, taking prey easily and quickly among the old and young in the herds moving up toward the high pastures. Even the most desultory hunt yielded enough food to allow the pack to feast to repletion and then doze and play through the beautiful early summer nights.

At dawn he drifted away and took shelter among the rocky overhangs above her farmstead. He slept off his night meal and, even before the pinkish glow began to burn in the eastern sky, he would watch her movements through the wicker walls as she built up the fire and began to cook the flat breads and porridge that constituted the morning meal.

Later, after sunrise, he would watch over her as she stood before her loom under the ancient linden tree, shuttle flying to and fro as she created one or another strip of brilliant-colored cloth.

By noon, the breeze dropped. The sun beat down mercilessly. The rest of her family retreated to the round house or other shady spots to sleep through the afternoon's heat.

This was his hour. She wandered up the mountainside, "to tend the flax," as she told Kat, and they met. She didn't know how or why he was always able to find her. She only knew he did, and that seemed sufficient for her.

By now he'd managed to acquire some minimal clothing—a worn tunic he'd stolen from a Roman soldier who'd spent an afternoon bathing in the river. It was doubtful if the man regretted his loss long or deeply. The wretched thing was old, faded to a dull gray and ragged beyond belief. The wolf noticed none of these things. One garment was the same as another to him. This one was long and thick enough to protect his epidermis. He'd found, after an unhappy encounter with a tangle of blackberry vines, that human skin is tender.

In any case, he wore it only long enough to reach her, pull it off, and enter her embraces. Because that was what they did—make love, eat, and sleep away the long afternoons. Sometimes they talked. In fact, they talked often. Or rather, she talked and he listened. After the first and only question she'd asked him about his humanity, she never asked another. He didn't expect her to, realizing instinctively that she feared to disturb the delicate balance that preserved the happiness between them, an almost unearthly happiness.

When their daily lovemaking ended, she unpacked the food she always brought. She was an excellent cook. At first, he didn't understand this. Wolflike, he simply made it disappear. But human teeth and jaws, shaped by thousands of years of savoring and sharing, don't lend themselves easily to a wolf's method of tearing and swallowing whole.

After he nearly strangled himself for the third time, he learned to savor his food as humans did. He became aware of her skill. She made flat bread with flour, enlivening its flavor with honey, hazelnuts, and even hard cheese. He learned to love the taste of ham and bacon she'd smoked through the long winters. The innumerable sausages she made from pork, venison, and beef were an unending gustatory delight. And then there was wine and sometimes mead. Ahhhh . . .

He found a cave near the top of the ridge overlooking her house. It was small with a sandy floor, but deep enough to be cool on the hottest days.

They went there during the dog days, when even the overhangs sweltered in the summer sun. There, in the dim quiet place, she taught him the joys of becoming a bit fuddled by strong drink and the languorous relaxation of a summer siesta taken together before and after lovemaking.

When the tree shadows grew long, Kat began calling her. Imona quickly knelt and pulled on her dress.

"Odd," he said one day. "She never comes looking for you."

"She doesn't want to find me."

"No?" he asked.

"No," she replied, coming to her feet and peering through the gooseberry bushes that choked the entrance. "She knows what's going on, but she needs me. The cheeses I make and my weavings bring in what little money we have."

The wolf remembered Clarissa's words.

"Besides," she added as she kissed him good-bye, "I believe she's a little afraid of the unknown. You know: Who could he be, this man? By now, she's probably certain you aren't anyone from the families in this little enclave. Yes, I'm sure she's satisfied about that. She's not sure she wants to meet you."

"I don't think she'd care for me," he said.

Imona shook her head. "She wouldn't." Then she pushed her way through the cave's cover and took her zigzag path down the hillside.

Sometimes she did tend the flax. Its patches of blue flowers lay the way a fine dyestuff would if spilled by a careless hand, soaking into the deeper pine green covering the steep sides of the ridge, creating a patchwork effect up to the hilltop.

During the worst and driest part of the summer, drought resistant as flax is, it needed watering. She carried water from a stream flowing down the ridge from garden to garden, a difficult task even with his help.

Flax wasn't the only thing she tended. On the driest, hottest, most exposed outer parts of the hillside, she cultivated the herbs she used to dye her thread. Tiny aromatic chamomile, yarrow, elecampane, and a multitude of others he couldn't put a name to. Some grew wild. All she needed to do with these was to protect and encourage them. Others, like the elder, needed no encouragement, but grew rampantly and required only harvesting at the right season.

Her knowledge of weaving and dyeing was handed down to her by the women in her family—noble women who didn't do most of the work themselves, but were trained to supervise the multitude of workers attached to their households in the manufacture of large amounts of cloth. These fine weavings were sold or traded as far as Greece on the one hand, and some even crossed the channel to the British Isles on the other.

Here on this farm she was alone, so she was forced to do all the work herself. Yet still her manufactures were always in demand during the quarterly fairs accompanying the great feasts at each season of the year.

Over time, he came to know the whole family—not difficult since they were now very few. All of Kat's brothers but one had died in the wars that raged over Gaul after Caesar's invasion. As Clarissa had said, the work was done by Imona, Kat, and Kat's husband, Des.

Des was a big, quiet man who feared his wife's tongue and temper. The wolf was puzzled by his industry, sustained labor being as foreign to the gray wolf's nature as Imona's weaving skills, until Imona told him that Des' work in the fields allowed him to escape Kat's continual hectoring.

Maeniel knew the odors of each. Imona was a collection of seductive fragrances. Kat was sour, as if her frustration with life communicated itself to her clothing in a succession of harsh statements. Des smelled of the work he did, brassy sunlight and perspiration.

Imona's husband, Leon, was the strangest of all. To the wolf, he smelled dead. Not the raw scent of the newly slain or even the heavy carrion smell of a carcass rotting in the sun, but the dry, moldy smell of a pile of bones lying in the shadows, covered with dark splotches of lichen and gray patches of moss.

When it grew dark, the wolf crept down. He peered through chinks in the walls of the hut. They were eating, gathered near the fire. A rushlight illuminated the round house. Leon ate without seeming to be aware of anything around him. Des appeared to enjoy his food and the company of his sister-in-law.

Kat's elderly mother, toothless and exiled from the table because of her sloppy habits, sat in a corner, slobbering over a bowl of porridge.

"I like the one you have on the loom now," Des said to Imona.

She laughed and replied in a low voice. "Red is hard to get. Finding a red dye that will set and not run when it's washed is the very devil."

The wolf surmised they were speaking about Imona's newest weaving. He'd watched Imona struggle long and hard warping the loom. It had taken up most of the last three mornings. And even when she'd been with him, Imona had seemed preoccupied. But when he saw her intentions turned into cloth, he reveled as much as she did in its loveliness.

She'd used the softest flax she had, and dyed it with just enough blue to make it glow with a pearl's sheen, then added a sprinkling of green threads and, at last, a touch of red, a fiery red to humans, a blood red to the wolf.

"We should keep that one for ourselves," Des added. "Maybe hang it with the rest on the wall in here."

Indeed, the wolf noticed the small dwelling's walls were decorated with brightly colored tapestries. They picked up the firelight and threw it back in glowing colors.

Kat snapped at both of them. "What are you talking about, saving the damned thing for a decoration? We need every sesterce we can raise. You know those Romans will come wanting tribute again and that old fool, Mir, will have to pay them. What's wrong with you? Imona, playing about for three days with that stupid loom, trying to warp it properly. Who cares any longer for the fancy stuff your mother taught you to weave? Make simple, sturdy cloth. It sells!"

Both Imona and Des cringed back at the fury in her voice. Even the old woman shuddered and tried to huddle into a smaller shape at her daughter's fury. Only Leon seemed unaffected by his sister's tirade. He continued eating, eyes fixed on the middle distance, and ignored her.

Des cleared his throat and tried to smile at Kat. "Beloved, even if we must sell it, fine weavings bring a better price than—"

"A better price, a better price," Kat replied, snarling. "Who, I ask you, has the money for luxuries now?"

"Even so," Imona spoke up hesitantly in her own defense, "it's a valuable skill I have. Kat, at the next fair I might be able to attract a few pupils . . . They'd pay . . ."

"Pay . . . pay . . . You talk about payment. How will you ever pay this household for what you've taken from us? All the cattle we sent to your father for you . . . and you never able to make a man-child. Two mewling girls . . . and all Leon got from the match when he went to help that brother of yours against the Romans was—"

Then Kat screamed as Leon, who hadn't even seemed to be listening, backhanded her hard across the face with his only good hand—the left one.

Leon stood over his sister for a moment, then quietly, viciously spat on her prone, sobbing body. He turned, went through the door, and vanished into the evening's gloom.

Horrified, Imona hurried to a pitcher and wet a clean linen cloth. Kat sat up, sobbing. She pushed Imona away as the blond woman tried to press the cold cloth to her bleeding nose.

"You," she sobbed, "it's all your fault. He wouldn't have lost his hand if he hadn't married you and gone to help that worthless brother of yours." Then she turned to her husband. "You're no man. You won't even defend your own wife—"

"Hush," Imona crooned, and pressed the cloth to her sister-in-law's nose.

"By all that's holy, Kat," Des cried, "I can't see that this is anyone's fault. Imona didn't cut off Leon's hand, Caesar did, and no one poked a spear in Leon's back and forced him to join in the revolt. He volunteered, hoping to get glory and loot. Well, he failed. As for the children, no one can predict how the dice will fall in that direction. As far as I can see, we're all doing our best, and your screaming and clawing at us only makes things worse."

Imona tilted Kat's head back to stop the bleeding.

The wolf eased away from the house wall. *Well, wolves have their quarrels, also,* he thought, *but not so bitter and long lasting.*

He watched Leon wander through the fields surrounding the house and away into the trees. The dark forest wasn't safe, not because of Maeniel's people—the wolves—but because it was also the haunt of bear, lynx, and most savage of all, wild boar. Head up, ears erect, the gray wolf watched him depart. *He should be more careful, but then nothing will bother him,* he thought. *He carries an odor of the grave with him. I wouldn't bother him, so why should any other?*

Far away, the pack rose and began their evening song. A silver glow from the rising moon crowned the snow-capped peaks. The voices recalled him to his duty. He felt an odd emotion, one so strange it took him a moment to identify it, then realized it was pity. He pitied her, trapped in the smelly house by night, while he was free to roam joyously in the moon glow beneath the multitudinous stars.

D RYAS AWOKE BEFORE DAWN, STILL WITH THE SENSE of being watched. She looked up at the stars. Her people had studied the skies for four thousand years. She knew that in a few moments the sun would be a glow on the eastern horizon. She threw aside the bearskin, rose, and began walking along the stream flowing through the mountain meadow. At its edge the land dropped off and the freshet fell straight down in a miniwaterfall into another granite basin, becoming a pool.

It was as if something had set guards on it. Blackberries, raspberries, and dewberries twined in thorny profusion at the edges. The long, twisted vines were denuded of leaves, but bore a profusion of fruit— black, blue, orange-red, and the deep purple of an imperial gown.

She remembered the girl's words. "No one eats them. No one can force their way through the vines."

Dryas began to strip—her blouse, then the divided skirt, the breast binder, then the white linen loincloth.

She swung out, clinging to the rocks leading down to the pool. The shock of water flow stiffened her muscles and pulled her hair loose, unbraiding it and sending it fan-wise down her back.

The shock wasn't one of cold, but heat. The water was warm. A warm spring must intrude into the mountain freshet somewhere close by. That also explained the fruit and the lush vegetation around the pool. It must be warm here winter and summer alike.

Her fingers pushed through the moss as she climbed down. A few moments later she stood hip deep in the water, making a breakfast of the berries that glowed like jewels on thick black canes. She found herself reveling in their sweetness.

The light grew around her, brighter and brighter until she could see the vines were only a thin, inner ring around the basin, though a cruel one. Beyond them, a grove of quince and rowan surrounded the water. The lush, yellow fruit of quince bent the still-green branches to the ground and the deep red rowanberries burned like scattered coals against the blue morning sky. Thickly grown with waterweed, the pond's bottom seemed composed of silk velvet.

The sweetness of the berries was as intoxicating as mead. It seemed she couldn't get enough of them, picking and eating them as fast as she could. She stretched, reaching for a branch thickly covered with fruit so black it glowed blue. The weed under her feet was as slippery as it was soft.

In a moment her mind was invaded by a vision of a woman with her face and hair smashing her skull into the rocky side of the pool. Her blood was a scarlet stain in the clear water until the falls from above carried it away and left her pale and drained, drifting down and down to the blue heart of the little reservoir, then vanishing into a pile of white bones.

In panic she snatched at a thick strand of blackberry vine. The thorns bit, but she hung on and righted herself. She realized she was breathing hard—gasping, really. She clung tightly to the rocky pool-side, then let go of the vine and washed her hand. As in the vision, the blood was a scarlet stain, then, diluted by the crystal water, it vanished, leaving the thorn wounds, angry red and white rips in her skin.

The light was bright now beyond the guardian vines, quince, and rowan. The open forest stretched out, long aisles of pale-barked beeches, the ground carpeted with their light, golden leaves.

Dryas was beautiful. She hadn't thought about that beauty in some years. But if she could trap the wolf with it, the smooth surfaces nature had given her would, at least, be of use to someone.

At that moment, she felt eyes on her again. She stood straight, twisted her long black hair in her hands, and wrung out the water. Her upraised arms lifted her small breasts, perfect cones tipped with strawberry nipples, as her eyes covertly searched for signs of the watcher.

Nothing, nothing she could see. The light was bright now, the water a pale, blue, wavering curtain falling from above, boiling into lacy foam in the pool.

For a moment, just for a moment, the water took on the outline of a woman's body as if it flowed over an invisible she standing in the sheeting flow.

Dryas' breath caught in her throat, then the illusion, if illusion it was, faded. She saw the ears on a rock ledge near the top where the waterflow plunged over. Ears, two pointed ones, pricked as if their possessor was absorbed in the view.

Yes, he had come. But Dryas remembered the woman's form outlined before her. *Something,* she thought, *someone doesn't want me to succeed.*

THE ROMANS CAME . . .

She was high up on the hill, harvesting flax with an iron sickle. He lounged on his belly in the shade of a broken pine. It was late summer and the scratchy tunic protected his human skin from the burrs clustering thickly in the dried grass.

She lifted the sheaves of flax, throwing them across rocks exposed to the sun where they could dry out and be ready for retting in a pond at the foot of the cliff.

She stood, sickle in hand, looking down at the rath below. She wiped sweat from her brow, then shook out her hair clinging at the neck, temples, and forehead, wet with perspiration.

The wolf saw her face change.

"No," she whispered, and threw down the sickle.

He reacted without thinking. On his feet in a split second, he had one massive arm around her waist and the other covering her mouth so she couldn't scream.

Riding up to the farmhouse below were three of Caesar's light cavalry and one officer. The wolf didn't know it at the time, but the officer was careless and sloppy. The troopers carried their weapons, but wore no armor and were without their shields. A cart, with the horse led by a woman camp follower, brought up the rear.

Kat and her mother were working in the farmyard. The troopers herded the women to one side and began robbing the granary at the back of the house, filling improvised bags made from clothing and such cloth as they found inside.

Imona bit Maeniel's arm. He ignored her, but slid his arm back and placed his hand over her mouth. She kicked and squirmed.

Leon came out. He shambled over to Imona's loom and stood quietly. Des arrived on the run, but stopped when he reached his wife, and made no attempt to interfere with the foreigners.

When they'd loaded up the grain, the troopers began going after the livestock, tying chickens and ducks by the legs and throwing them over the high wooden sides of the cart.

Imona stopped struggling. Maeniel removed his hand from her mouth. "Be quiet," he told her, "or I'll knock you out. You can't help them. All your running down there will do is get you into trouble."

One of the troopers hurried toward the pig wallow. One of the sows was suckling a litter. He jumped the fence and snatched up two of the piglets, then leaped back as the sow reared up to defend her litter.

They whooped with laughter when the trooper, piglet under each arm, cleared the fence with the infuriated sow on his heels.

The laughter ended with shouts of astonishment as the sow charged the fence and it splintered. The trooper put on a burst of speed. The sow was really dangerous.

His two fellow soldiers spread out on either side, Roman cavalry spears at the ready.

The first cast his, but missed. The second made a run at the sow, but she was too fast for him and the spear skidded harmlessly along her ribs.

The still-mounted officer swore savagely and leaped to the ground.

At that moment, the trooper carrying the piglets looked back. He tripped and fell. The piglets let out almost human shrieks of terror and pain as they went flying from his arms.

The sow was a vicious four-hundred-pound juggernaut, saliva spraying from a tusked mouth with teeth that could inflict a fatal wound in seconds.

The officer got between the sow and the trooper. The spear he carried was the Roman battle spear, the pilum. The spearhead was mounted on a three-foot length of steel bolted to a beechwood pole.

The spearhead entered the sow's chest. The shock brought the officer to his knees, but he held on as the pig ran up the pole and reached the supporting beech handle. There, she stopped. The officer was strong, but her weight pushed him back several feet. Then she shuddered, blood gushed from her mouth, and her legs began to fold under her.

Maeniel was the only one who saw Leon move, and he didn't understand why.

Leon stood near Imona's loom. The officer's back was to him. He stepped forward, snatched the short Roman thrusting sword from its sheath, then, in an eyeblink, he plunged it into the Roman officer's back.

For a moment the world was still. A frozen tableau. Everyone stared at Leon in stark, unbelieving horror. Then the farmyard exploded into chaos.

The officer screamed, a cry so filled with raw agony that it made Maeniel's skin crawl. The spear pole fell from his hand as he clutched at the sword hilt protruding from his back.

Perhaps Imona screamed also, but if she did, Maeniel never remembered it. In any case, all other sounds were drowned out by the cries coming from the farm below.

The trooper who still held his spear drove it through Leon's body. To his credit, Des tried to defend his wife and mother. He turned, pushed them away, and shouted, "Run!"

The trooper who'd thrown his spear still had his sword. It was out of its sheath in an instant. Des was a farmer, not a soldier. All he had was a mattock he'd been using to chop weeds. The trooper's sword knocked the upraised tool from his hand, sheared through the arm holding it, and sliced into his chest, cut away the ribs, and entered his lung. Des fell, his hands pawing at the massive chest wound as his hammering heart emptied the blood from his body.

The old woman tried to run, but stumbled and fell after a few steps. Kat was able to run, and she did, but in the wrong direction. Instead of turning for the hillside where she might have been able to hide herself among the trees, she fled into the open field with two of the troopers in hot pursuit.

The woman camp follower, the one who'd been leading the cart, ran up. The old woman was still struggling to rise. The camp follower brained her with a rock. Then the remaining trooper and the woman crucified Leon on the dooryard tree that sheltered Imona's loom. He was still alive, kicking, as the trooper hoisted his body and the woman drove two knives they'd taken from the farmhouse into his hands. The spear hung from his chest. The whole front of his tunic was saturated with blood.

The other two troopers returned, dragging Kat by one arm.

Maeniel wasn't sure if the Roman officer was unconscious or dead. He didn't react when the woman pulled the sword from his back. She sliced off his linen tunic with her knife and began bandaging him. The wolf decided he couldn't be dead.

When the screams began to come from the house, the woman looked up from her task, an expression of disgust on her face.

Imona began to struggle again. "Kat! My God, Kat! They have her in the house."

Maeniel whispered, "What will you do? Give them another subject for their attentions?"

The camp follower went to a small fire burning in a pit in the dooryard. She lifted a flaming branch and began setting the low-hanging, thatched roof alight. In a few moments, fire began running up the roof blazing near the smoke hole.

Kat's frantic screaming stopped and the troopers came running out of the house, coughing, eyes tearing from the smoke.

"You piece of excrement," one of them screamed at the woman. "We aren't done with her yet."

"Pig's brother, dog's father. Yes, you are! My master's only wounded. If Lucius dies here, it will be your fault. I swear! I vow! I'll see you flayed alive if he dies because you wanted to see if you could fuck the little sow to death. Get him in the wagon. Now! There are physicians at the camp!"

The three troopers stood in the doorway of the house, undecided.

Maeniel got to his feet. He ran down the hillside. The noon sun burned his face and arms. He had only the rather poor protection of his ragged tunic. He felt, but ignored, the tearing of thorny vines and bushes and rocky ground cutting into his soles.

He reached the farmyard as the troopers were loading the Roman officer into the cart. The man lay in the bottom, leaking blood on the grain sacks.

They were leading their skittish horses. They gave Maeniel apprehensive looks when he jumped out of the bushes, shouting. The woman standing in the front of the cart laid her whip down hard across the backs of the ponies pulling it. One of the troopers made as if to go back and confront Maeniel, but the woman screamed and cursed him so savagely that he turned around and followed the cart as it bounced off down the deeply rutted road toward the valley.

Fire completely involved the house. The roof was blazing and flames were beginning to spurt from the willow withes that formed the walls.

Kat lay in the center of the room, naked, her body smeared with blood. Bundles of flaming thatch were falling around her. The long poles supporting the roof were on fire.

There was time only for him to snatch the woman up and carry her out, as the roof began to slowly fold down on him. He dashed out just as one wall buckled and the thatch slid into the center room like a blazing haystack.

Imona had followed him down and she threw herself to her knees beside her sister-in-law.

Maeniel looked around. Kat was bleeding, unconscious, and battered, but she was still breathing. The others were beyond all human help.

Des lay curled on his side. His wounded arm and chest were under him. He looked strangely peaceful. But for his pallor, he might have been asleep.

The old woman's head was a puddle of loose blood and thick brain tissue. In the noonday heat, flies gathered, their buzzing an angry whine in the air.

Oddly, Leon had the same indifferent expression on his face. His head lolled on his shoulder, eyes open. Whatever he found or hadn't found in death and revenge, it appeared to have left him unmoved.

Imona knelt, cradling Kat's head in her lap, sobbing. Maeniel stood, listening, hearing the sounds made by the retreating Roman foraging party as they struggled down toward the fortress in the valley.

Imona looked up at Leon and cursed him incoherently.

A breeze blew, cooling Maeniel's skin. The linden on which they'd crucified Leon was in flower. The heavy scent was almost able to cover the rank stenches of blood and fire hanging in the air. The loom, knocked over at some time in the struggle, lay at the tree's foot, under

Leon, his blood dripping down on this . . . the most beautiful of her weavings.

Imona screamed. She leaped to her feet. Kat still lay unconscious in the grassy dooryard. "They're getting away," she shouted.

Maeniel started, his whole body jumping with shock.

Imona ran toward him, caught him by the arms, and began shaking him. "You have to catch them, catch and kill them. If they return to the Roman camp and tell their story, they will attack and destroy us all." She clawed at her cheeks with her nails and began keening horribly. "Whatever you are, man or brute, go and kill them."

Maeniel backed away from her, horrified by the hysteria and ferocity she radiated.

She reached down and snatched up a stone from the fire pit. It flew toward his face and sliced across his cheekbone.

Still in shock, he reached up, touched the wound with his fingers, lowered them and saw she'd drawn blood. Another stone struck him in the forehead; a third hit hard on his ribs.

He turned and ran, following the path the retreating Romans had taken. He didn't have to follow them for very long. One trooper had hung back to cover their retreat. As a wolf, Maeniel was dangerous; as a human, a sitting duck. The road, no more than a cart track, ran along a high cliff on one side and a deep rocky ravine on the other.

The Roman pilum struck Maeniel's sternum and skidded across his ribs, failing to do permanent damage to his lungs. Maeniel staggered back, fell, and rolled down the rocky slope into the ravine. He landed facedown and lay still.

The trooper didn't care to follow him across the broken ground to be sure he was finished. *Much too easy to lose my expensive horse to a broken leg,* he thought. *Besides, a human who'd taken such a fall would be no further problem in any case.* He spurred his horse and followed the rest.

III

DRYAS HEARD THE VOICES BEFORE SHE reached Mir's hut.

"He knows she's alive and he wants her back!"

"Good God!" The second voice belonged to Mir. "Does he realize the condition she's in? Hasn't he done enough . . ."

Dryas saw a bush move a few feet away. Her hand dropped to her sword hilt, then she looked more closely and realized the girl, Mir's wife, crouched behind it. The sun sifting through the tree canopy above lit her face and shoulders. Dryas realized she was crying silently, tears sliding down her face from wide-open eyes.

"Tell him she's dead!" Mir shouted.

"He won't believe me! He knows it's not true. Now, where is she? Call her! She'll come to you. Don't give me any more trouble, old man!"

There was the sound of a scuffle, and a second later Mir emerged from the hut. He was pushed out by a large man. The interloper had his left hand on Mir's collar and the other held the Roman short sword, a gladius, to Mir's back.

"I warn you—"

Mir turned and spat in his face.

The other reversed the sword and smacked Mir on the side of his head with the heavy iron hilt.

The old man fell to his knees with a thread of blood running from his cheekbone to his jaw. He looked dazed.

Dryas gasped with horror. No one she knew would lay hands on a man of Mir's age and venerability. Even in her anger at Blaze she hadn't thought of touching Mir. The elder members of Mir's order had been known to stop wars by simply entering the field between the combatants, so great was the respect in which they were held.

Dryas had never seen such a one so much as manhandled by another, much less struck like an insubordinate servant. Even the mad girl looked profoundly shocked.

Dryas snapped her fingers to get the girl's attention. She turned a tearstained face toward Dryas.

Dryas signaled her to run.

She did, upslope on all fours like a frightened animal until she got her feet under her, then she scampered quickly into the trees.

The stranger was still shouting at Mir.

Dryas drew her sword, then charged the pair standing at the door to Mir's hut. The man bullying Mir didn't realize he was being threatened until she was almost upon them, but when he saw her, sword in hand, his response was astounding.

He gave a shriek more reminiscent of an angry and outraged woman than a man. The sword flew one way; he the other at a dead run.

However fast he was, Dryas was faster, rendered more so by the fact that while fleeing and screaming shrilly at the top of his lungs, he picked up the toga and tunic he wore, lifting them to keep his skirts out of the dust.

When he reached Mir's pole beans at the edge of the clearing, he glanced back and saw her, sword in hand, mantle wrapped around her free arm, only a step behind him.

There was a tree in front of him. He did a more than passable imitation of a terrified squirrel. She was certain he used toes and fingernails to reach the lowest branches. Once on them, he went up as if climbing a ladder.

Unfortunately for him, at some time in the past, the top of this particular scrub oak had been broken off in a windstorm and the terminal branches were only twenty feet or so above the ground. So he paused on the highest branch and successfully imitated a dog howling at the moon.

Dryas sheathed her sword and stared up at him. A second later Mir arrived next to her, wiping his face. An ugly purple bruise stood out next to his right eyebrow, but his eyes were clear and his hand steady. The individual in the tree continued screaming.

"Firminius!" Mir shouted. "Shut up!"

"Firminius?" Dryas said. "He's a Roman?"

"Sort of," Mir replied. "Somewhat. A bit. Occasionally. And at times." He reached down, picked up a pebble, and shot it with unerring aim at Firminius. It connected with the side of his head.

Firminius' next howl was cut off in midshriek.

"I said," Mir repeated, "shut up!"

Firminius was silent. He glared down at Dryas, did a double take, and almost fell out of the tree. "Oh, my goodness! She's a woman! Oh, my heavens. She's one of those *women*. Oh, by Zeus, by Apollo, by Minerva, by the Three Graces and Nine Muses . . . she's one of those *WOMEN*. Mir, you have to sell her to me now. Right now. Right now! She'll be a sensation in Rome. They will love her. Do they really fight naked? Tell me they fight naked. Will she fight naked? Dear me. Oh, my heavens, an Amazon. A real live Amazon!"

Mir gave a low moan and rested his forehead against the tree bark.

Firminius climbed to his feet, balanced on the limb. He began yelling, "Help! Help!"

Dryas was up after him in a second. She didn't know whom he was calling or even if there was anyone within earshot of his voice, but she couldn't take the risk.

Firminius saw her climbing after him. He ran out to the end of the oak limb and leaped blindly into the air, rather the way a diver commits himself from a high rock into a pool of water. His body crashed through the low branches of a small pine, continued on through a pear tree, wiped out a rather attractive hawthorn, and landed with a wild crackling in a thick pile of dried leaves. They flew up with a rush of dust and soaring flock of fragments, then settled, covering Firminius' inert body with a pall of last summer's autumnal leaves. He lay still.

F IRMINIUS NEEDED CARRYING INTO MIR'S HUT. They had both been relieved when he began moaning.

"He's excitable," Mir explained. "He didn't mean any harm."

Dryas grunted a reply that managed to imply a certain disgruntlement with the task of carrying Firminius and skepticism at Mir's testimonial to his good heart.

Inside, with Firminius drinking an herbal potion, Mir set him straight on a few things. He could not sell Dryas for the good and sufficient reason that he did not own her. His wife could not be sent to Rome. She was too crippled and too ill.

"I tell you, the man terrifies me, he absolutely terrifies me," Firminius moaned. "He terrifies me even when he's thousands and thousands of miles away, dallying with that Ptolemy bitch-witch Cleopatra. And that is where he is now. At least that's where I think he is. And, believe you me, my dears, she isn't one to let a lover like Caesar slip through her gilded fingers. Believe me, she isn't. I'll just bet they're at it night and day—on the floors, the beds, the couches. In the BATHS! Everywhere! Just everywhere!"

Dryas thought Firminius looked a mite envious.

He held out the earthenware cup to Mir for a refill. "What's in that? No, don't tell me. I wouldn't understand anyway. I'm sure I'd just get alarmed and refuse the rest of it. It's delightful and so relaxing. My headache's almost gone now. I can't thank you enough."

Mir refilled the cup.

Dryas began to believe Firminius' headache had been transferred to her.

"Now tell me again, Firminius, who are we talking about?" Mir asked.

"Why, Caesar, of course." Firminius blinked a few times. He'd become a bit glassy-eyed.

"Why does he want my wife?"

"Oh, didn't I say?"

"No, you didn't."

"Well, she is related to that awful hairy fellow. The one in Britain. Cunov . . . something or other. He's thinking—"

"He who?" Mir asked.

"Caesar, of course. He's thinking when he comes back from the east, he'll have to do something about Britain . . . You know, conquer it."

"NO," DRYAS SAID AS SHE PACED UP AND DOWN inside Mir's hut. "No, I can't let that happen. Caesar's been to Britain. You can't imagine the devastation he left behind."

"Oh, can't I?" Mir replied bitterly.

"He must be killed!" Dryas cried.

They were alone. Firminius had departed on a rope-woven litter a few moments earlier. Mir's potion had taken full effect.

"My dear, my dear," Mir whispered softly, "if you can think of a way to accomplish that, I would be very grateful. But so far I haven't been able to think of any plan that would surely accomplish his downfall. He is, as Firminius says, far away and powerful. We are here and very weak. Kill the hunter of the night for me, then go home and warn your people. We can do no more."

Dryas paused and stared into the brightness outside Mir's door. Perhaps there was a way. She didn't reply except to ask, "What will happen to Firminius?"

"Nothing," Mir said. "He will sleep for four or five hours, then awaken and probably eat a fine dinner provided by his slaves. As to my 'wife,' he will do nothing. Caught between the hammer and the anvil, he will find a way to fob off the hammer. But he was uncharacteristically truthful about his interest in you. Watch out. You don't want to end your career at the slave market in Rome. They would sell you as a woman gladiator. Some would pay a high price for such a novelty. They love novelty. You wouldn't survive long living such a life. Not long at all."

THE MAN-WOLF LAY IN THE RAVINE FOR SEVERAL hours. He drifted in and out of awareness. The sun high in the sky held the wolf at bay. He struggled to fully awaken and change, beset by the fear that the soldier might return and kill him.

As he slept, he dreamed. He lay on a beach and a gigantic comber towered over him. It seemed to pause at full height, then tilted and fell, foaming around his helpless body, dragging him out to sea. He was man, floating breathless in jade green water, then wolf, his pelt soaked . . . drowning, eyes open, jaws snapping hopelessly at the air and light above him.

The second wave lifted him high and let him breathe. The third dropped him—a heap of matted fur on the beach.

He sank into a deeper sleep and found himself wandering through the mountains. Above, two storms, one from the north, the other the west, came together above a green valley. From the high rock where he stood, the wolf could see the long, trailing rains, like a procession of dark priestesses garbed in gray gauze, moving over the green vales below, crags crowned with twisted trees and the very highest peaks streaked and mottled with ice and snow.

The two storms formed a V—the base at the overgrown valley, the apex open, lined with white cloud tops appearing to be mountains of the air and light, high and drenched with an alabaster purity no earthly mountain could ever know. Beyond, among the storm spires, birds drifted against the pale blue sky.

Suddenly, Maeniel felt self-awareness, thought, and knowledge contract into something so fine, so thin, it could pass through the eye of a needle or be compacted into an ever-changing crystal, its facets glittering in the sun.

He had wings and was an eagle. Wings spread, circling, riding the thermals up and up into the canyons of the stormy sky.

"I" vanished. Thought vanished. An unending joy filled his mind and he entered into a beauty as old as the world. A simplicity so stark, existence was all that was required or ever would be, world without end. Amen.

The wolf's memories were old, but the eagle's vastly more ancient. He soared confidently over a world where conifers with trunks ten times thicker and three times higher than the biggest tree any living bird had ever seen ruled the mountain crests, driving down roots that split the living rock like wedges and held their massive trunks like giant claws. Curiously nude, they were, with tiny barbed cones and thousands of small, feathery leaves. They held their place over flowerless, dank, wet defiles and valleys hazed with moisture, oppressed by a green gloom where monsters contended, roaring under a canopy of cycads and ferns.

Maeniel felt again the strange fear of self-loss and drew back from a simple but seemingly immortal consciousness that was older, older by far than the world.

He woke when shadows were pooling in the ravine. He was still a man, but as consciousness spread into his brain, the wolf shape covered him like a thick mantle.

He stood on shaky legs. A considerable quantity of his own blood lay dried on the rocks. He found, however, that the wolf was uninjured.

He climbed easily back to the road. During the day, summer clung to the mountains, but at nightfall, the temperature dropped and a sharp chill pervaded the air.

Even though the sun was gone, the sky was still bright. A deep confusion troubled the wolf. He sensed—no, knew—he'd been drawn deeper into these mad human matters than he'd ever intended to be.

He hurried back toward the farmstead. As the sky darkened, the moon seemed to grow brighter and brighter. It was the only light remaining when he reached the burned-out house and outbuildings.

A thin curl of smoke rose from a few still-smoldering embers. The grain fields tossed and whispered in the rising night wind. They hadn't burned and perhaps weren't combustible yet. Not yet brown and ready to harvest, but still green.

The living were gone: Imona and Kat. His nose told him Kat was injured but still alive when they took her away. A cluster of different scents told him that others had arrived to render aid after he left. The ruins had been searched and anything useful that could be salvaged by the rescuers was gone. They would not return.

Only one casualty remained: Leon, nailed by knives to the tree. In the moonlight, his still-open eyes glowed with an ugly counterfeit of life until, on closer examination, the wolf noted the pupils were invaded by the opaque clouding of death. Imona's cloth and loom remained at his feet.

Far away, the wolf heard the evening call of his pack. They were hungry. A few nights ago, they'd killed an elk and while the feasting had been long and rich, by today all that remained was a gnawed skull, a few long bones, and scraps of hide. Now they'd slept off their feast and their bellies rumbled again.

The wolf stood silent while the call reached a crescendo, each wolf adding its own echoing, unearthly identification to the message carried through the chill air.

In silence, he listened. The abandoned wheat fields whispered their vain message of a fruitful harvest—a harvest no one would come to reap. In the forested hills, owls called to one another. The last embers of the burned-out house flared in the night wind, then died. The tree bore its carrion fruit. The feet hung only a short distance from the ground. Why waste it?

He lifted his muzzle and called to the moon-silvered sky.

IV

IMONA HAD KNOWN HER FATE WHEN SHE LIS-
tened to Kat's ravings. The way she was being treated made
everything clear. Rescue, if it could be called that, arrived a few
moments after the Roman foraging party disappeared down the trail.

Neighbors, having seen the smoke, ran to help, if possible. When
they found out what happened, they were frantic with terror. The
Roman garrison would delight in taking savage revenge. They cursed
and spat on Leon's body and left it where it was.

They were discussing killing Kat and Imona when Mir arrived.
He brought a semblance of calm to the proceedings. He had the living
and dead carried off to the nearest oppidum not under Roman control
and sent out warnings in all directions.

It took two days for the Romans in the valley garrison to sort out
the situation. Then they marched, burning every farm and killing
every one of Mir's people they could catch. Luckily, Mir—no fool—
was prepared and had prepared his people for the attack. Most escaped
to the forests. In those places where the late summer crop could be
harvested, it was. In others, food reserves were cached in spots concealed from the Roman foraging parties.

When the first snows began to fall, the Roman cohorts had to
pull back to prepare themselves to meet the winter, a savage season
even in the comparatively sheltered area where the garrison was
located.

The storm of Roman anger passed. Mir's people survived . . . at
least most of them.

By that time, Imona was certain of her fate. Kat was living with her husband's people. Imona heard from her jailers that she lay with her face to the wall and wept most of the time. The only time Kat visited her, she cursed Imona viciously and then tried to rend her face with her nails. Imona was glad when they led Kat away.

The oppidum was only a small one. All of the large and important centers had been devastated during Caesar's Gallic conquests. It was like all the rest—a hilltop fort with a small settlement that supported the large gatherings that occurred when a dispersed, rural people met periodically to transact their business. It was located at the outer edge of Roman power in the Alps. Only a relatively few people resided there all year round. The Romans might not own it, but they'd managed to invade and burn it at least once.

Imona was penned in what had once been a large weaving shed, used to confine the slave women, captives from other tribes, who worked here. The windows were narrow slits, and because weavers must have light, there were a large number of them. In fact, if one didn't test the wall, the narrow beams looked almost like willowy slats. Actually they weren't, but hard like the bars of a cell. The room was a secure prison. No one could force his way past them. There was an enclosed hearth in one corner. A dip in the roof allowed the smoke to escape.

At some time in her journey to the oppidum, she'd been given a loose cotton tunic. Later, traveling at night, a householder had added a heavy woolen mantle. She was wearing both and squatting near the hearth when Mir walked through the door.

As he entered, she rose and came toward him. He was ritually dressed, wearing a loose white robe and a strange crown, a silver circlet decorated with golden birds. The birds were set off from the crown, each on its own separate mounting in such a way that they moved, and seemed to fly at each turn of Mir's head. A large, flat leather belt was tied around his waist. It held a sickle-shaped sword. The flat outer part of the sword glowed with the beautiful green patina of old bronze. A procession of figures, as an inlay of silver, marched around the outer edge. The inner curve of the sickle was filed to a glittering razor's edge.

He held a paper in his right hand, a golden torque with lion-head finials in his left. Wordlessly, he handed Imona the paper. She unfolded it and began to read.

"Dearest daughter," it began, "I hope this finds you well."
Tears pricked at her eyes as she recognized her father's handwriting.

One reason I hope this finds you well, is that the news I have to report is not good news. Tomorrow, we face Caesar. We have already lost one battle to him and, dear daughter, I greatly fear we will lose the next. Our trading ships are no match for his triremes, but we must fight. Better it is for a man to die quickly in battle than to see all he loves destroyed. No doubt he will write to his friends in the Roman Senate that I, King of the Veneti, gave him no choice in the matter. This will, of course, be a lie. I offered him full capitulation, hostages, tribute, all our gold if he would but spare my people. He offered us survival only as slaves for the profit of the greedy dealers who follow him everywhere.

Confronted with these "terms of surrender," the tribal council voted to fight. We have done our best to send off the women and children we could to Albion, the White Isle across the sea. Your sisters and daughters have gone to our allies there. Your mother, greatly to my sorrow, refused to go, saying only that she would find the world too empty a place without me. But she sends you her love and this memory of honor.

I say again, I think we will lose. As it is said, not even the best sailor can prevail without the wind and tide. Both are with the Romans. We will be lost. But, my daughter, remember the wind changes and the tide ebbs. But not, alas, in our lifetime. So, *ave atque vale*. Hail and farewell.

Imona stood silent for a moment. Outside, she and Mir could hear the shouts of children playing a chase game, the kind of game children have played for millennia and will play for millennia more.

Imona folded the letter and placed it in her bodice between her breasts.

He extended the torque with the other hand, but she didn't take it.

"How long have you kept this from me, old man?"

"Years," Mir admitted sadly. "It has been years since they died. But seeing you still had hope and a chance for some happiness among us, I believed that even if Leon never recovered, you would be able to carve out a life for yourself. And, for a long time, you did achieve some semblance of peace, and hope, even a faint one, played a role in this. Did it not?"

"I suppose so," she answered in a lackluster way.

Outside, someone called out to the children at play in a language with more gutturals than sibilants. And Imona remembered where she was, now driven forever from even the poor place she once held among Mir's people.

A woman's voice sternly ordered the children away from the weaving room and its shadowy guest, lest they be brushed and withered by the power crouching there.

"How did they die?" Imona asked.

"She took poison. He used his sword as a warrior should, sacrificing himself so that his power would go to those of his people who survived, and see them through the lifetime of slavery they faced, and beyond into another dawn."

She reached out and took the torque from his hand. "You will see that I receive wheat and oats so I may cook my daily meal and, of course, a fire on the hearth to keep me warm by night?"

"Yes, but rye bread and barley beer is likely to be more often found here."

"I'll make do," she whispered.

"You are the last, the best that we possess. All the great families are gone and the gods will never send down kingship to a dishonored people."

She placed the torque around her neck. "If that is what you fear, old man, I will do my best." She turned her back and walked toward the dead hearth. When she looked again, Mir was gone. She knew then she would see him only one more time and that would be the last for both of them. Perhaps even the last sight her living eyes would look upon.

DRYAS SLEPT AGAIN IN THE MOUNTAIN MEADOW. The path was quick and easy for her. She found when she entered the clearing near Mir's house that he again had guests. Dryas sighed when she saw Firminius, but was relieved to realize he was much calmer today. Sitting in the chair next to him and enjoying the fine morning was another man, a tall, blond, handsome youth dressed for hunting. He wore the tunic and trousers of a rider. Two horses grazed near a tree. One, a slender, long-legged gray mare with an elaborately padded saddle, obviously belonged to Firminius. The other, a big-boned, thick-bodied black with a leather saddle pad, must belong to the hunter.

And indeed, the hunt had been successful. A half dozen hares hung like a stringer of fish from a tree branch, and near them a young stag. All of the animals had been expertly field-dressed, entrails and scent glands removed.

Mir and his two visitors were speaking quietly among themselves as Dryas made her way silently to the edge of the sun-dappled forest.

The hunter's eye picked her out first. Dryas felt the stare lock on and hold her, long before he gave even the slightest indication she'd been seen.

Deadly, Dryas thought. A very keen mind resided under the fall of golden hair. She also took note that a half dozen light javelins were tied to the black horse's saddle.

Then Firminius saw her. "Oh," he squealed, "there she is—that's the one."

The hunter nodded. "I know. I thought so when I saw her coming down through the trees."

"Fulvia!" Firminius elbowed his companion. "You have sharper eyes than most men. Ah, what a soldier you'd have made."

Fulvia! Dryas thought. *A woman!* The young male image in her mind shimmered like calm water broken by a breeze. Yes, a woman. The soft outline of breasts, the slightly too-wide hips, and the soft facial skin all signaled female. *So are we all creatures of illusion,* Dryas thought. The woman dressed as a hunter rose to greet Dryas as she approached.

The hunter was beautiful, with a slender waist, a straight back, heavy breasts, and peaches and cream coloring. She also was the biggest woman Dryas had ever seen. Over six feet and, though she carried no surplus flesh, she probably weighed almost a hundred and seventy pounds. Dryas herself was not small, but the woman topped her by at least half a head.

The three—Mir, Firminius, and Fulvia—had been gathered around a low metal table almost lost in the grass. Fulvia reached out and touched Dryas' shoulder. "She chased you up a tree, eh?" The tall woman laughed.

"I think not a great victory," Dryas replied. "Usually I'm not so extreme, but he shouldn't have tried to bully Mir."

Mir's fingers brushed the fading bruise on his temple.

"An Amazon," the huntress exclaimed. "You promised me a real Amazon. So we don't know how good she is, not really? Do we?" she asked as she turned to Mir. "I'll bet and bet heavily any gladiator in Rome would have her on her ass or her back in the time it takes me to snap my fingers." Fulvia chortled as she suited the action to the words.

Dryas smiled. She knew she was being baited. "Possibly." One of Dryas' brows arched slightly and her lips curved. "But that would depend on what else he had. Besides a sword, I mean. Mortal combat isn't the only kind. It isn't even the contact sport that offers the most fun."

Fulvia laughed robustly.

Firminius looked sour. "Fine, just so you don't expect me to tame her. True, she'd be a novelty, but how long could she last? You can't tell me that woman—not a very big woman—is a match for some of those gorgeous killers you have at the Roman ludus. Besides, if you presented him with a woman, the lanista would be wild. Just wild."

"He'll do what I tell him to do," Fulvia said. "Nothing more or less. I really would like to see if you're at all possible."

Dryas inclined her head politely, thinking, *Gods, they're arrogant. It's as if they believe all the world exists for their pleasure and we should be grateful to be allowed to gratify their desires.*

Fulvia strode to her horse and lifted two javelins from her saddle. "I can throw a spear farther than most men. Let's see how you do." She hefted one and balanced it with her right hand. "See that black birch down there?" She pointed to a slender tree near the edge of the clearing. The papery bark glowed gray and silver in the sunlit morning.

The tree was almost thirty feet away. The lance took flight and ended quivering, embedded in the trunk. The tree shook, raining green-brown leaves onto the grass beneath.

Dryas balanced the spear, opening her palm, testing the weight. The head dropped only a few inches. *A fine weapon,* she thought.

Fulvia watched her critically.

Dryas' mind focused on the javelin still protruding from the trunk.

Her feet parted as she shifted into her stance. Her hand moved on the lance pole, seeking the perfect balance point. When she felt she found it, she let fly.

It arched higher than Fulvia's had, and then broke, flashed down, and the leaf-shaped head sank deeply into the tree trunk, slightly above Fulvia's.

"Amazing!" Fulvia exclaimed. "How I'd love to hunt with you. Your blade pierced the wood more deeply than mine. If that had been a deer or elk, it would be dying now. I must see your skill with swords."

"Only wooden ones," Dryas said. She unbuckled her sword as she spoke.

"Mir," Fulvia said commandingly, "have you any wooden swords?"

Mir rose and entered his house.

Fulvia, she thought, *has a bluff indifference to the pain of others, a brisk self-sufficiency that makes cruelty a casual reflex.*

Mir emerged from the hut with a half dozen wooden swords in his hand. He dropped them on the low, wrought-iron table.

Fulvia picked up a short, thick one shaped very like the heavy Spanish sword the legionnaires used.

Dryas looked at the wooden blades critically, then picked up a longer one.

Fulvia tossed the practice sword from hand to hand. Right to left, left to right.

She's going to pull some trick she believes clever, Dryas thought. She concentrated on avoiding accidents. She backed away from the two men seated at the table and found herself on low ground as the hill sloped away toward the creek. Fulvia followed and Dryas felt a prickle of fear. She was sure the woman wanted to injure her. She wasn't sure why. Natural aggression? Desire to humiliate Firminius? He had boasted of her prowess. Or simply the sheer, cold need to dominate that Dryas had found in so many men and women?

Injury was indeed a real possibility. The swords, though wood, could have doubled very well as clubs. A blow struck by an arm as powerful as Fulvia's could inflict a painful bruise or even break a bone. Dryas sensed she must end this quickly.

Fulvia tossed her sword into the air above her head. It arched, spinning, then began to fall. She clapped her hands together. "Which one, little warrior?" she shouted. "Left or right?"

Dryas steadied the wooden shaft in her hand, thinking, *Yes, it's about the size and weight of the light slashing sword I wear.*

Fulvia caught the sword in her left and, in almost the same moment, swung the edge hard at Dryas' left arm.

A beautiful maneuver and one that would have destroyed lesser opponents, Dryas thought. But even as she was being appreciative, Dryas was countering. She dropped to one knee. The sword passed harmlessly through the air above her head. At the same moment, she jabbed upward. Hard, but not too hard. Even if Fulvia was not concerned with the injuries she inflicted, Dryas was.

The sword point caught Fulvia in the abdomen just to one side of the floating ribs. The breath left her body in a loud huff. She'd overcommitted to her swing and her turning body drove Dryas' sword even more deeply into her abdomen than Dryas had intended. Fulvia went down, the wind knocked out of her, completely incapacitated.

Mir's face remained expressionless, but his lips twitched.

Firminius burst into shrieks of laughter. He stretched out his arm, fist closed, thumb down, and shouted, "She has had it. Cut her throat, little Amazon."

Dryas wondered what he was talking about; she didn't recognize the way a Roman mob dealt with a defeated gladiator. She lowered the wooden blade and backed away, eyeing Fulvia as she did so. She was too well trained to approach a fallen foe, however lightly the combat had been entered into, before ascertaining his or her emotional as well as physical condition.

For a few seconds all Fulvia was able to convey was distress. Then embarrassment, chagrin, anger but not rage, and, finally, a kind of admiration chased one another across her face.

Dryas wondered if she hadn't made a mistake in overcoming the Roman woman. If she'd allowed herself to be bested, Fulvia would have brushed her aside as a creature of no consequence, but now . . .

Fulvia staggered to her feet. She directed a truly poisonous look at a still-chortling Firminius. "That was," she said when she finally got her breathing under control, "beautifully done."

"Thank you." Dryas inclined her head respectfully, then tossed the wooden sword back on the table.

"You are very, very good," she continued.

Again, Dryas inclined her head. "But then I've spent my life practicing. I began my training at six years of age."

"Amazing, so young!" Firminius contributed. "I think you were wrong about the ludus, my dear. In fact, I should like to see her matched against your lanista." He licked his lips with evident prurient enjoyment.

Dryas stood, quietly ready to make her escape. She had no idea that a ludus was, in fact, a school where slaves were trained to be gladiators, or that a lanista was the head of such a school and an instructor in swordsmanship. All she understood was the dark warning in Mir's eyes.

"Have you something to write on?" Dryas asked. Mir rose and returned with a clean wax tablet and a stylus. She wrote her list on the tablet and handed it back to Mir. Then she turned and went to collect her horse, stabled in a bower under the trees.

"Wait," Fulvia called. "Don't go. Sit down, enjoy this fair mountain morning with us."

"I'm sorry, my lady, but I must leave. I have pressing business."

Dryas left Mir's farm at a trot, down the rutted road.

Fulvia rubbed her side, gritted her teeth, and, under her breath, consigned Dryas to the Furies.

"Dryas is dangerous," Mir said.

Fulvia nodded, and Mir saw her eyes were bright with lust.

IN THE CAVE, THE WOLF STIRRED. OUTSIDE, THE SUN was at its zenith. He'd slept away the morning. High above, clouds were massing over the pass. The wolf lifted his head. He felt slight confusion as he smelled rain on the wind the way he had when he'd first taken her near the avalanche track. He lifted his head, scenting her, sure she was just outside the cave and then realized the scent came from the rags of an old mantle she'd discarded long ago near the entrance. The wind stirred it, bringing about the change in the air.

Wolflike, he turned quickly 'round and 'round, remade his bed, and returned to sleep.

He'd searched for her that night, following the track of those who'd taken her away: across the mountain and down into territory strange to him. He'd stopped only to feed on an unwary brace of ducks he surprised sleeping at the edge of a valley lake. He took the first so quickly it never awakened; the second only just managed to get its eyes open and began to extend its wings when he broke its neck.

The rest of the flock rose in a whir of flashing wings and loud alarm calls. It was one of those situations when a wolf's ability to eat quickly was a saving factor. He'd killed in another pack's territory. He knew the behavior of the surviving ducks would alert the pack to his presence. But he'd gulped his meal and was on his way so quickly that all they found were paw prints when they arrived to investigate the ducks' late-night alarm. He'd crossed the valley by moonset and had reached a thick, dark wood when the cries of his own pack called him home.

A crack of thunder woke the wolf. He raised his head. A gust of wind blew into the cave, creating a miniature whirlwind on the dusty floor. The wind was cold, and the wolf realized that the deceptively beautiful autumn weather was coming to an end.

He was tempted to warm himself by snuggling into the tatters of Imona's mantle, but a dark, inchoate sorrow deep in his heart forbade it. So he withdrew toward the back of the cave, found a sheltered niche and curled up again, his bushy tail over his muzzle, and slept.

He'd known then, when he returned to the pack, that he might never find her. For the first time in his life, he'd felt war in his own soul as he struggled with ideas, concepts a wolf's brain was never designed to understand.

He'd already broken one ancient taboo by calling the pack to feast on human remains. Not that there weren't wolves who did it. They, and birds of prey, had been familiar scavengers on battlefields since the beginning of time, but not powerful, independent packs like his. They left such behavior to those garbage eaters who slunk and scavenged near human dwellings, those semidependent on human offal—the occasional unburied corpse or sick, unwary outcast who could be killed with impunity.

His kind usually encountered human aggression when confronted by young warriors seeking to prove their manhood in single combat with the strongest male wolf they could find. Sometimes the humans won and walked away from the battlefield wearing a wolf skin, upper jaw and face hooding their heads, forepaws dangling at their shoulders. Sometimes it was the wolves who walked away, maybe licking their wounds, maybe not.

He and his comrades learned about humans ages ago, when both hunted together across glacial plains: summer was a brief, halcyon season and winter a grim, ten-month ordeal. The fire people took their prey with wooden spears and butchered it with stone knives. They hunted in packs as the wolves did, and everything, even the giant bear, feared them.

Countless times, his gray people yielded up their kills to roving human bands when they attacked with stones and javelins. Humans were pitiless to all creatures, even each other.

A male not strong enough to hunt with the rest of the warriors was killed at his first testing. A woman not strong enough to bear a child, then rise and follow the band, was abandoned to the ubiquitous scavenging opportunists who haunted the bleak, freezing tundra. Yes, he and his kind learned to fear humans long ago, as had everything else.

The humans had changed only a little since then. They were smarter now and lazier, but just as darkly tainted with cruelty. He feared for Imona.

Pack law said he must not abandon his own. His inner voice told him Imona was as important to him as the pack, and deserved his regard just as much as they did.

He solved the problem by being faithful to both. It was autumn then, as now. The wild herds moved down in much the same way as the shepherds took the tame ones to the sheltered valleys for winter.

Countless animals were on the march. The wolf took only a brief nap when he returned to his fellows at dawn. By midmorning he was up, the rest following irritably along behind him.

At some time in the late afternoon, he saw his opportunity. The chamois were migrating. The small, antelopelike creatures of the highest and steepest slopes seldom fell to the wolves. They were fleet runners, traveling on ledges where only hawks could nest, where they left the surest-footed predators behind. But they, like their larger cousins, wild and tame, who felt the winter moving in, were searching for new feeding grounds in the high meadows.

The bachelor males were gathered away from the females and their young. There were about ten in this group, grazing on an intimidatingly steep slope covered with thick evergreen bushes that seemed to spring from the broken orange rock itself. Below them, rocky ledges covered with new snow projected out over the unstable surface left by one of last year's avalanches. A death trap if the wolf ever saw one, but if he was to find Imona, he had to provide for the pack.

The chamois themselves were so sure of their own security that they ignored him as he walked several yards down the slope. A few lifted their heads, studied him, and then returned to their search for dried grass tufts and the occasional green shoot left on the winter-bare bushes.

When he leaped, even the wolves thought him mad. They were astounded by his loss of good sense, since madness is not usually a condition that affects wolves.

The chamois bolted, the most agile to shelter on the steepest part of the mountain face, but inevitably about a dozen landed on the snow pack overlooking the valley.

Enough, the wolf thought.

The lower slope was not as steep as the upper, but it was still deeply inclined toward the cliff overlooking the valley. Had it been later in the winter, the snow would have been frozen hard and supported the hooves of the small, light animals. Had it been earlier in the year, these mountain gazelles would have been able to find purchase on the scree that formed the floor of the ledge. But it was just the right time of year for disaster.

The snow had drifted atop a layer of frozen slush. It let go, sweeping loose rock, chamois, and wolf up in a spray of white, sending them tumbling into the air over the hundred-foot drop into the valley.

The most primal terror, even for animals, is falling, but it is also fast. Fear wiped out all semblance of thought in the wolf's mind, and then he hit the ground.

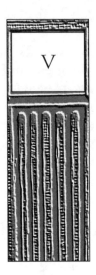

V

FULVIA RETURNED TO HER VILLA WITH FIRMINIUS for the light collation that constituted the Roman lunch. She ate standing in the shade of an open colonnade that marked the division between the luxurious owner's quarters on one side and the working farm on the other.

The colonnade had folding doors that could be closed along its outer edge. They could shut off the private world of affluence and comfort from that of drudgery and discomfort, but at the moment they were open. Fulvia watched her men butcher the deer.

Firminius sat with his back to the dusty courtyard, looking into a magnificent peristyle garden, the central court of the master's residence. "I can't see how you stand such sights while you're eating. Close the doors, I implore you."

Fulvia stripped a bunch of deep purple table grapes. Her lips were stained by the rich juices. "It doesn't bother me."

"It may not bother you, but it quite deprives me of my appetite," Firminius moaned.

"A fine catch, sister mine, but why we're watching this completely escapes me." The speaker was a slender young man, seated apart from the other two in a heavily cushioned wooden chair equipped with carrying poles. He was pale and leaned crookedly against the heavy pillows around him. His face and body were in deep shade, but the early afternoon sunlight just touched one sandaled foot.

"I'm making sure they don't spoil the meat," Fulvia said. "And they won't if they know what's good for them. The buck was in wonderful condition—fat with autumn fruits. I'm sure he gorged on sloes, crab apples, and blackberries. He died with a minimum of fuss; no long chases for me when I want good eating. I took him with one throw of the javelin as he was feeding on a thick waterweed. I want to be sure he's properly skinned and disjointed, and the meat is hung in a place well away from heat and damp. And, as long as my eye is on them, I know they'll do a good job."

"Naturally." Firminius poured himself some chilled white wine from a glass pitcher. "It's probably as much as their lives are worth if they don't."

"I don't know about their lives, but their hides . . . certainly," the young man in the chair sighed.

The men in the courtyard finished their bloody job. The stag had been a large one and they departed with the joints of meat over their shoulders toward the nearest of the thatched structures surrounding the cobbled court.

Firminius signaled a servant who came in and drew the big louvered doors shut. The room darkened. The servant went to Firminius and spoke to him in a low voice, then departed.

Fulvia sat down in a chair next to him and helped herself to some of the wine and a slice of bread and cheese. "I'm convinced," she began, "that the cheese from cows pastured in these high alpine meadows is superior to meat. A meal of it is more satisfying than roast pork or—"

Two men entered the room. One was the dark-clad servant who'd shut the doors. He led a smaller man by the arm and by a short chain attached to an iron collar around his neck. He stopped in front of Firminius and said without preamble or explanation, "Here he is."

"He doesn't look like much." Firminius squinted at both men. He and the rest were in deep shadow, and the two were backlit by the bright light in the peristyle beyond.

Fulvia stood and opened two sets of the small wooden slats in the doors. A pale light filled the room. "He still doesn't look like much."

He didn't. He was short, not more than five feet, maybe a little less. He had dark curly hair, closely cropped; large brown eyes; an olive complexion, one that appeared as if he'd been out in the sun a lot; and a small, compact body not muscular enough to be that of an athlete or fit for manual labor of any kind. The expression on his face didn't help matters much either. He looked distressed, very frightened, and a little lost.

"What am I looking at?" Fulvia asked Firminius. The man in the large wooden chair looked as if he'd settled down to try to catch a nap. His head was sunk on his breast, his eyes closed.

"Your brother's new physician!"

"What! That?" She gestured violently at the small man with one very large arm. She was almost as tall as he was . . . sitting down.

The eyes of the man in the wooden chair flew open.

The object of their scrutiny looked, if possible, even more frightened.

"You told me—" Firminius jabbed his finger at the arm of his chair with every word as though to emphasize his irritation. "—to send an order to my agent at Cos to buy the best Greek physician. Spare no expense, mind you, the best that can possibly be had—everyone knows Greeks are the best physicians—and send him to you, because you were very dissatisfied with Hippos. He wasn't curing your brother, and besides, his fees were exorbitant. And he was not attentive enough and 'complain, complain, complain' until the roof rafters rang. And now I've spent the mother of the gods knows how much money. He cost the earth, I'll have you know!

"He's said to have a wonderful reputation in the town where he apprenticed and practiced. And now you can't even remember all the hell you gave me! I could weep. I will weep. It's not enough that you drag me away to this repulsive barbarian place, filled with repulsive barbarians, where my delicate sensibilities are daily affronted by their wretched grossness, but you can't even have the good sense to re-member the orders you gave me in the first place."

Fulvia threw up her hands. "All right, all right. Before all the gods, I do swear. I do apologize. I'm sorry. Now, please calm down."

"The real reason you were displeased with Hippos is that he gave you very little hope that I would survive," the man in the chair snapped.

Firminius blubbered. He pulled a lace-trimmed handkerchief from the sleeve of the tunic and began wiping his eyes.

Fulvia jumped to her feet, her color heightened, a murderous look in her eyes. She rounded on the man in the chair. "Shut up, Lucius. Hippos is a self-important, greedy moron. I wouldn't want him caring for a dog I liked. At best, he's incompetent. At worst, a practitioner of black magic and a procurer of abortions—"

"My, yes," Lucius added, "and to the first families of Rome. I was wondering when you'd notice."

"Very well. You're agreed on the need for another doctor?" Fulvia asked. "The way you cling to your ridiculous popinjay made me afraid to search out a medicus of greater ability."

"He clung to him," Firminius snarled angrily, "because he could bribe the bastard to do anything he wanted."

"Is that true?" Fulvia's voice could have sawed through a marble column.

"More or less," Lucius admitted, a bit shamefaced.

"Well," she hissed, pointing to the man still standing in the servant's grip, "you have a new physician now and you are his only responsibility. You hear that?" She glared at the slave. "You, skinny whatever-your-name-is. You better be as good as advertised because the day my brother dies, I'll have you crucified."

He blanched.

Lucius pulled himself upright in the chair. "You'll do no such thing," he roared.

Fulvia drew back, staggered for a second by the tone of Lucius' voice. It rang with the authority of the old-fashioned paterfamilias, the head of the household with the power of life and death over women, children, and slaves.

"Fulvia, I haven't crossed you because I haven't had the will or the energy, but I won't sit here while you terrorize someone who might one day have my life in his hands. Do you hear me?"

Fulvia's eyes blazed into his. "Then you're willing to accept another physician."

"Yes, if you'll only calm down and behave like a rational woman, I will. I will do as you wish."

Fulvia sniffed, then turned cold eyes on the slave. He quailed visibly. "Very well. Remove that collar from around his neck and, brother mine, I'll leave you here with him to establish an understanding between you. Now, Firminius, as I was saying, I believe these cheeses to be superior in both flavor and keeping qualities. I hope they are because I've bought ten wagonloads of them."

"Ten wagonloads!" Firminius shrieked. "Woman, are you mad?

Taken leave of your senses? Possessed by some wandering evil spirit? Have you a buyer in Rome?"

"Certainly, I have a buyer." Fulvia picked up a handful of spiced black olives and strolled toward the door. "I even have the money on deposit with a banker in the Forum. Now, how do we ship? By land or sea?"

"By sea, by sea. A long land journey would absorb most of the profit from the transaction. It's rather late in the season, but . . ."

Their voices trailed off as they entered the peristyle and began a walk along the ornate pool in the center.

The chain came from the man's neck with a clatter.

"Sit down," Lucius said, pointing to the chair Firminius had just quitted.

The servant hustled the small man to the chair and seated him so forcibly that he gave a little squeak of distress.

Lucius sighed and waved his arm at the servant. "Leave us."

The man hesitated.

Lucius said, "Go!" and the servant left. Then he turned his attention to his new physician.

He sat, watching Lucius alertly. His hands were on the table. They were shaking.

"Please," Lucius said, "pour yourself a cup of wine. The silver pitcher contains a tolerable Falernian, the glass one a pleasant white from somewhere nearby. Either one will do for a bracer. Your hands are shaking."

"No, my lord—" The small man spoke for the first time. "—my hands aren't shaking. My whole body is shaking."

Lucius grinned suddenly, looking much less forbidding. "My sister has that effect on people, but don't worry. I'm used to frustrating her little plans when I want to. I'll see she never gets to carry out that threat she made. Now tell me. Do you have a name you'd care to communicate to me?"

"Philo, my lord." He poured himself a cup of wine.

"Very well, Philo. In the short conversation we had about your origins, before all the shouting started, I believe Firminius indicated you were freeborn."

Philo nodded, his nose in the cup.

"Then what brought you to the biggest slave market in the world?

I've found that one of three things is usually responsible—debt, capture in war, or politics."

Philo thought this over. "Politics," he replied. "Not mine, though. My father's."

"Ahhh," Lucius said.

"Just so, my lord. My family was of only middling wealth and rank in my home city. At sixteen, I was apprenticed to a physician. And my sister went out at fourteen to a tapestry weaver. Unfortunately—I say unfortunately because that's the way it turned out—we were both wildly successful. At twenty, my sister owned her own shop, and I was one of the most popular physicians in the city. As it was, the wealth gave my father leisure to dabble in politics."

"He picked the wrong side?" Lucius asked.

"Oh my, yes, my lord. Like any fall, my family's was quick and dizzying. The next thing I knew, I was standing in the slave market at Cos and Firminius' agent was looking at my teeth. Though what they had to do with anything quite escapes me."

"Well, of all the reasons that will bring a man down, I believe I like politics the best. It means you haven't an excessive devotion to the more annoying vices: women, the dice box, or the wine cup. However, you might be given to intrigue."

Philo shook his head. "No, I have no expertise in it at all. Had I any inkling of what was going on, I'd have kept my father on a shorter leash and I wouldn't be in the extremely uncomfortable situation I'm in now."

"Fine! Then be warned—stay away from my sister, Fulvia. She's one of the few people I've known whose bite is far more dangerous than her bark. And when she runs out of cruel, underhanded, and devious ideas, that nasty little poison mushroom Firminius will soon supply her with fresh material to continue her career of crime."

Philo looked taken aback. "She is your sister and I attributed her threatening behavior to anger at the physician's consigning you so casually to the Shades at so young an age. After all, she loves you."

Lucius chuckled. "I don't know if she loves me or just wants an heir, a male one, to the family fortune. Roman law favors men. At present, she has so—intimidated, dominated, bribed, frightened, terrorized: take your pick—all of our father's brothers that they jump to attention when she snaps her fingers. But who knows what will happen when they die off and are replaced by some less malleable individuals. A nice posthumous boy-child many years from maturity would suit her perfectly. He could easily be controlled by his pedagogues and tutors until she has to decide when he comes of age . . . or not."

"Sounds ominous, my lord." Philo's reply was carefully couched.

"She keeps sending women to my room. Fortunately, or unfortunately, I can't do anything about them."

"Hmmm." Philo searched the table, found a lump of cheese and some bread. He pared them and began to gnaw. "But, my lord, you know there is one's duty to one's family and ancestors."

"Don't start," Lucius snarled. "I get a lecture every week about our family's death masks."

Philo gulped some wine to wash down the bread and cheese. "Would this avoidance of the female sex be a matter of inclination, my lord?" he asked delicately.

"No. I have plenty of inclination, but also a lot of pain and fatigue. And you don't have to 'my lord' me every sentence. If you skip one, I'll understand."

Philo began to search around on the table. He found several clear wax tablets and a stylus. "Do you suppose I might use these?"

"If there's nothing written on them, help yourself."

"There isn't." Philo picked up the stylus and set a tablet in front of him. "Now, what seems to be the trouble?"

Lucius sighed deeply. "Little Greek, I think you might be a very good physician. About a year ago, I was an officer in the Fourth Augusta stationed near here. One fine day I led a foraging party . . ."

THE WOLF AWOKE LYING AMONG THE ROCKS AT the foot of a cliff. He knew he was badly hurt, perhaps dying.

The world grew dark around him. The fir and spruce pines clustered around. Man or wolf, he knew this had to be wrong. The trees that hemmed him in and frowned down on him so darkly didn't grow at this altitude.

He struggled to move and pain overwhelmed his mind, washing out thought in a torrent of red. He lay still and the pain receded. He knew he must call the change or he would die.

He opened his eyes and again looked into the shadowy, frightening trees. The darkness increased. Beyond the forest a waterfall fell from a great height. From where he lay, the wolf couldn't see from whence the pour-off came, but only a sheet of white water, so brilliant it seemed to be lit from within, a pale shimmering glow against the deepening forest gloom.

Spray rose high at the foot of the falls, drenching beds of moss and fern. They glowed like emerald sculptures in the water's light.

The wind blew and the ancient trees sighed . . . a profoundly timeless sound. It spoke to corners of the wolf's brain the man hardly comprehended. "You belong," it said. "We are one. We have been here for eons before there was man and will be here for eons more when he is gone."

The trees were quite dark now, the waterfall a dazzling curtain of light. The wind blew again. A mist of droplets covered the wolf's face, blinding him for a moment. He sat up a man.

He could see himself. It was as if he were separated from the muscular figure outlined against the silver light, watching from behind. As a human he was impressive. Short, brown curly hair. Skin on the dark side. A strong face filled with resolution. The figure of a person in his first youth.

Then the spray whipped out again. The forest spoke its ancient cry of earthy possession, and the wolf woke, shaking himself and coming to his feet by day among the scrubby second-growth forest and barren rocks of an old avalanche. The dark forest and waterfall were gone.

The prey he'd sought were lying among the rocks. At least a dozen of the chamois had failed to clear the falling snow. Enough to feed the pack for a week.

He raised his muzzle to the sky and called them. The wolf found himself ravenous. As pack leader it was up to him to choose his portion. When the rest arrived, they found him feeding.

He'd expected to be mobbed. The most usual response to the reappearance of a beloved companion is a greeting: licking, noses touching, the kisses and recognition of friends and family. But the gray was surprised and disappointed. The risk he'd taken had passed beyond those expected of the sane. And deep suspicions were aroused in their hearts.

He was offended and then indifferent. His thoughts were taken up with Imona and her fate. So, when twilight came, he left the pack sleeping off the burden of meat they'd gorged and set out across the mountain.

He passed through the territory of the other pack where he'd killed the ducks. The food he'd taken allowed him long travel without the necessity of killing.

When he was beyond the ken of the neighboring pack, he began to cast about for human dwellings. The first he found was abandoned, home only to an angry badger living in the tumbledown remnants of a mountain farm. The Romans had burned it long ago and, besides the badger scent, the wolf's nose could still detect the faint effluvia of blood and fire from the battle.

The badger reared on his hind legs and challenged the wolf. The badger is a tough and dangerous little animal. Not even a wolf cares to quarrel with one without cause. The gray wolf took his leave.

The light was brightening in the east and it was almost morning. The wolf found a narrow ledge close to the tree line. He fitted himself into the spot between the stone and the ground and fell asleep with his brushy tail over his nose. So well hidden was he that no one passing nearby would have seen him. He awakened at dusk. The trees were brown sentinels caught in the evening mist.

He traveled on as the day turned into night and light faded from among the pillared pines around him. Above, a hazy overcast darkened the moon and stars. The soaring pinnacles of higher mountains glittered above, sheathed in ice.

He left the tree line behind, moving through a wilderness of scree slopes and mountain meadows, their grazed-down stubble glittering in the cold. These high pastures were empty now and would be until the shepherds who inhabited them moved their flocks back up in the springtime.

THE HOUSE THEY'D LEFT BEHIND WAS AN EMPTY, fireless hole, abandoned to the wind, with ice already forming on the walls. But she'd been there. Her scent was faint in the sleeping hut, but stronger in the barn and sheepfold where some warmth still lingered under damp straw glittering with frost crystals.

The wolf went downhill, following the herds driven to lower pastures to escape winter's icy grip on the heights. This farm was a big one, almost like the villa in Mir's valley.

The weather here was not so balmy as in the sheltered valley. The houses were stone, the walls chinked with mud against the cold. The roofs were tall, steeply pitched, and heavily thatched. The wolf paused, looking down at the gathering of buildings huddled as if for warmth in their niche in the mountains.

The animals—cows, sheep, and goats—were gathered in close pastures or folds around the houses for protection. Dogs barked in the yards. It was the biggest human settlement the wolf had ever encountered. True, the Roman fortress in the valley was larger, but the wolf, mindful of the fate of the lowland pack, had not cared to ever approach it.

The fur of his ruff lifted. A snarl muttered in his throat.

Below, a dog barked again and then was joined by a chorus of yelps and howls. Wind ruffled the wolf's ruff again. It was at his back, blowing toward the lowlands as the tall rock spires above gave off their day's heat. The wind brought his scent to the dogs.

The gray wolf had a choice. Lie down now and wait until the lights glimmering faintly through the parchment windows of the house flickered out and men and dogs slept, stupefied by the thickest, darkest slumber of the night. The wind would drop and the air be as motionless and silent as the star blaze above. Then he could slip soundlessly from his perch, moving as elusively as a wisp of smoke or the low clouds settling over the mountains, and investigate the farmyard and the barn, and cut close to the dwelling to find out if she'd been there.

But though he'd learned a great deal from human beings, those he met had not taught him the superior virtue of the beasts' patience.

He ignored the wolf and let the man have his way. The gray dropped into the underbrush to circle the farm and approach with the wind in his face.

He was successful at first. Moving up quietly on a large, open yard, he eased past a cow byre without alarming the beasts. Most were milk cows whose calves had been slaughtered, their bodies going dry in the bitter autumn, weary after their journey from the heights and grateful for their winter rations of hay and oats.

The sheep were a different matter. They were coming into their thick winter coats. Most were ewes with half-grown lambs. They were much closer to their wild relatives than the later, rather stupid breed.

A half dozen dogs were chained in the yard, including two who gave the wolf a distinct frisson of terror. They were huge, each fully two hundred pounds or more with massive teeth and jaws. Each outweighed him by at least forty pounds.

One of the sheep saw him, but the yearling didn't know what he was and gave him a vacant stare through the wicker side of the fold. But she nudged her mother, an older ewe who gave a soft mutter of alarm; the sheep began to mill uneasily in the enclosure.

The wolf drifted away from them toward one of the barns. The gray knew as soon as he entered that she'd been there. The barn was drenched with her odor. But from here, where?

There was a noise behind him. The wolf turned. Smoothly and silently, his belly pressed against the straw, he crouched, motionless.

A woman stood in the open doorway, her hand shading a taper from the wind. It had very nearly been blown out. All her concentration was on nursing the tiny, wavering flame back to health.Once inside, out of the wind, it flared again behind her hand, illuminating the barn.

"Aaah," she said, pleased, and then she saw the hulking, gray shape crouched against the tumbled hay on the floor.

The resulting scream was enough to waken everyone and everything for miles around. Horses neighed wildly, cattle lowed, the sheep chorused in fear and displeasure.

The wolf tucked his tail down, laid his ears back, and fled. He bolted past the girl in the doorway and the livestock pens like a stone flung out into the night.

But before he was completely out of earshot of the hornet's nest he'd stirred, he heard the shout, "Loose the dogs!"

The wolf settled into his run, fast but not fleeing in fright, sure he would be able to outrun the most powerful dog ever born. No cruelty had awakened in him yet and he didn't know his own strength, but then he didn't understand what pursued him, either.

These were the dogs of war, man killers, meant to be loosed on the enemy in battle and used to harry and murder retreating forces or create chaos in the enemy's baggage train.

The gray fled upward, sure the steep slopes, the poor footing, and the increasing altitude would take their toll on the dogs. They were, after all, creatures belonging to men, lazy and dependent on their masters.

He was the one inured to flight and pursuit, tested by nature since the day of his birth.

So, inadvertently, he trapped himself. He topped the last rise and looked down into a rocky moonscape that gave no hope of any quick escape. The footing was treacherous. The clouds that wrapped the peaks had settled moisture on the long, downhill slope toward a misty valley. The moisture had begun to freeze. It would be like walking on glass. The wolf turned and ran along the edge of the escarpment.

The two dogs far ahead of the pack sensed he was slowing. Bloodlust quickened their pace. He realized they were only a few steps behind and, practiced killers as they were, they were coming up on either side of him.

Just ahead, he saw that the open grassy area ended in a blunt point with a steep drop on either side. If the two dogs caught him in the open, they would kill him. He might have run on blindly, turning onto the icy, uncertain footing of naked rock where the two war dogs would have pulled him down and dismembered his corpse.

But the man in him spoke. For the first time, words echoed in his brain. *Stop! Fool! Turn at bay. Remember what you are! Remember what you know, what you learned on the dark, frozen continent long ago.*

He stumbled forward a man, his right hand groping as if it had a life of its own for the first advantage the shambling half-ape from long ago knew—the first advantage the dark, ancient mother of life gave him to be his and his kind's forever more—the weapon.

His right hand closed on a rock.

The two massive dogs came, one from the right, the other from the left. He dropped forward to one knee, his left arm lifted to protect his face.

The one from his left overshot him, skidding away on the frozen grass stubble. The jaws of the second closed around his forearm. He expected to feel the bone crumble, but oddly it didn't. He realized no matter how strong these dogs were, they couldn't match the power of a wolf forged in the fiercest fire of all: survival.

He brought the stone down with all his strength on the dog's skull. It splintered like rotten wood. The jaws slipped free of his arm as it died.

But the other one had regained his footing and was charging in, its target the softer belly and groin.

His right hand was numbed by the blow he'd delivered to the dog's skull. The stone fell from his nerveless fingers. *Wait until he leaps,* a cool voice in his brain commanded.

The dog's forequarters left the ground. Maeniel, the man, pivoted, dropping his leg over the massive animal's back. He stood it straight up, one arm around its body, his left hand buried in its throat. His fingers found the delicate rings of cartilage that form the air pipe to the lungs and . . . crushed them.

The animal fell, dying, and Maeniel, wolf again, struggled down the rocky slope toward the dark, forested valley beyond.

PHILO TOOK OVER LUCIUS' LIFE. HE DIDN'T DO IT with loud, shouted commands or nasty aggression. Lucius found his new slave was a master of tact, suggestion, and indirection. He was gentle but firm; polite, but he could give a mule lessons in obstinacy; and he could never be distracted from his objectives by threats, tantrums, pleas, or even outright bribery and gentle or violent evasion.

Lucius' maid was Alia, who had saved his life by returning him quickly to the Roman encampment. She'd also become a free woman at that time, a token of Fulvia's gratitude for having saved her brother's life. She was a good servant, humble and hard working, but Alia had the intelligence of an oak stump, the personality of a bronze lamp, and a face like a snapping turtle. To Lucius' utter and absolute astonishment, Philo got on beautifully with her.

After lunch on the day of Philo's arrival, the bearers who carried Lucius' chair returned him to his cubiculum. The room was luxurious—the furniture ornate and decorated with gold—but it stank and was absolutely filthy.

The sheets on Lucius' bed obviously hadn't been changed or washed in weeks. No one had bothered to empty this morning's deposit in the chamber pot and it also lent its contribution to the fragrant air. The most overpowering odor was one of rotting meat and burnt charcoal from the braziers in each corner of the room.

Alia stood in the center of the floor, looking embarrassed. Two of Fulvia's maids stood giggling in the opposite doorway. The bearers set Lucius' chair down and straggled away toward the servants' quarters to begin their afternoon siesta.

Lucius snarled at Alia, "Get me some wine!" She rushed to obey. The two girls continued to stare at Philo and Lucius and continued to giggle. "They're supposed to take care of me, but one's an Egyptian, the other was captured in some godforsaken place in Arabia. Neither of them speaks a word of Latin, and I don't speak much else, just Latin and a gentleman's smattering of Greek. Alia's a Gaul. I can speak enough of that tongue to ask for water, wine, or sex. Beyond that, I haven't a clue.

"Every night I pollute one of the pools in my sister's elaborate baths, then return to my room and drink myself into a stupor. Most days I can persuade someone to change my bandages, usually one of the chair bearers. But sometimes I don't care and just lie here and stare at the ceiling. The worst is, I'm rotting away alive from the stinking, open wound in my back. Fulvia knows it, that hyena, Hippos, knew it, and so do all the servants."

Philo didn't reply. Instead, he spoke to the two girls facing him from the opposite doorway. They gasped. The giggles died, then they ran into the room. One began to strip the bed; the other lifted the chamber pot and left with it.

Lucius' jaw dropped. He'd never seen such a change so quickly wrought in two human beings.

"They speak excellent Greek," Philo told him quietly. "One is a hetairai from Alexandria and I recognized her at once."

The chamber was transformed before his eyes. The window was opened, the room aired out. The braziers, needed now because of the nights' increasing cold, were emptied and refilled. The floor was scrubbed, the bed remade with a fresh mattress, sheets, and pillows—all with the clean scent of sun-dried linen. Then Philo helped him to the bed and changed his dressings.

They had their first quarrel about the wine Lucius wanted to drink before his siesta. Philo favored a well-watered beverage mixed with honey. For Lucius: Falernian, neat.

Lucius lost. He gave up when he sounded querulous, even to his ears.

His first loss was the harbinger of more to come. His breakfast was no longer red wine spiked with opium and a few figs, but hard-boiled eggs, soft cheese, fruit, and well-watered white wine. Lunch was more of the same.

At dinner, Philo firmly placed the emphasis on food rather than drink and replaced the late-night wine with a sleeping draught he mixed himself, composed of valerian he'd gathered in the garden.

Somehow he always managed to persuade Lucius to take a turn around the garden with him after each meal and, in time, the one turn became two, three, or even four laps around the reflecting pool. Finally, Lucius could walk for long periods quite comfortably and no longer needed the carrying chair.

But the nights were the worst. Lucius' fever rose. He shivered, and pain, forgotten by day, hemmed him away from sleep. He tossed and turned in an agony of physical and emotional suffering.

Alia would call Philo. He came with medicine to relieve the pain and bring down the temperature; fresh sheets for the perspiration-soaked bed; and he often sat up with his charge till dawn, reading to Lucius from the villa's well-stocked, though rather dusty, library.

Though Lucius didn't care to admit it to himself, Philo's regimen was working. Lucius was feeling better. The simple, natural, painless things Philo did for him were far superior to Hippos' more exotic tortures. Bleeding, for instance, left him dizzy, nauseated, and weak for days at a time. Savage purges had sent him to the pot all night until he was emptied of everything but bloody mucus and left with stomach cramps that continued for days. Hippos also used hot irons. He'd never used them on Lucius, but by then Lucius had ended up bribing him to do nothing when he came, or to stay away as much as possible, all much to Fulvia's annoyance.

But what Lucius feared most, and the one thing he went in terror of giving way to, was . . . hope. Because hope unfulfilled is, after all, the final torment of the damned. Those in his situation, condemned to die slowly, yield it up so that their remaining existence can be borne with fortitude and without grief for what must inevitably be lost. He had long ago abandoned hope, but now it came to him, came back on the wings of morning.

It came on a day when he awakened realizing he'd slept through the night without being battered by pain or fever. He lay quietly, breathing deep draughts of clean, cold, mountain air. Air fragrant as springtime, sweet as the perfume of a thousand flowers and gentle as the first flush of dawn's light stealing through a forest.

And he knew he was going to live. He might end with a terrible scar and always limp a bit, and surely he would never be the strong, heedless young man who'd ridden out with the legions. But he would live and, in time, the world would open its bounty to him. Yes, he was forever changed and it remained to be seen in what way and how much. But he could accept that as part of his life and go on. Above all, he was going to live and be well. What had been hope would, in the coming days, harden into a certainty.

Then he closed his eyes and drifted away into a dreamless slumber, his soul at peace.

VI

STILL SHAKING WITH FEAR AT HIS NARROW ES-
cape, the wolf passed across the rocky slope. Beyond were close-
cropped, high pastures with grass stiff, brown, and lightly dusted
with frost. At length, he emerged into the forest. A greenish light filtered down through the trees.

Dawn. The wolf was exhausted. More than anything else he
wanted food and sleep, but a climax forest wasn't a good place to find
either one.

He moved through what amounted to an ancient, many-pillared
hall. High above, the interlacing branches effectively shut out the sun,
creating a cool, green gloom beneath. The wolf ran over a brown
carpet of dead and decaying leaves forming the almost incredibly rich
substrate supporting the towering giants—heaven and earth come to
an agreement, but a desert to the wolf.

On and on he traveled. Not even birdsong rang out above him.
Occasionally a breath of wind stirred the high-crowned giants and
they sighed out a deep song of lives incomprehensibly long and peace
so deep. It made all of mammalian endeavor seem as brief as the falling star creating a streak of light across the heavens at sunset.

You, even your kind are latecomers to the earth, the trees told the
wolf. *And man, an aberration in the long, slow warp and weft of time, a knot
in the thread woven by the Gray Ladies.*

So be it, the wolf thought. He was tranquil. *I am content to be what*

I am. And, besides, there are things that make you seem young as children: the rocks, the sea, and the stars.

Yet even as the forest announced its eternal and inevitable triumph, it began to break up. The ground grew increasingly rocky.

Eventually the wolf reached an escarpment, a spur of rock where he could look over the whole valley. The forest stretched out for miles and miles; at its center, a giant river. A blue and gold strip shining in the first light of sunrise, it curved and twisted through the tapestry of green, brown, and scarlet trees.

How to cross? A human might have been discouraged, but it isn't wolf nature to borrow trouble. Instead, he turned and continued his journey.

It was near noon when the wolf reached the river. He entered a narrow man-made trace along its banks, then trotted as close to the shore as he could. It was broad, brown, and deep here. He was a powerful, bold creature, but he was not completely foolhardy. It might be something akin to suicide for an animal his size to try to swim something its size.

Ah, well, he thought, *water.* He waded in up to his ankles and drank. As he did, numerous small swimming things shot away from his muzzle and into deeper water. He continued to drink while eyeing them. Little fat bodies with small, fingered forelimbs and big back legs: frogs. Aaah!

When he quenched his thirst, he moved quietly, tail gently waving high above his back. Umm, the swimmers were slow and awkward, the penalty they paid to the growing cold. One was lying on the bottom. Snap! *Not bad!* Not a familiar food to him, but really not bad at all. And there were lots and lots of them, clustered in the yellow-flowered greenery, the bare, sloping muddy bottom, hanging under lily pads. Everywhere. *How nice.* Snap! One might wish for a dipping sauce. Imona was corrupting him. When he found her, he hoped she'd corrupt him some more. Snap! *Umm, not very filling for a hundred-and-eighty-pound animal, but there are plenty of them. Rather like the wild artichokes she served me.* Snap! Snap! Snap! *Very good.*

The wolf went on, moving slowly downstream, dining after the manner of his kind, until he heard sounds of battle on the trace following the river. Someone began screaming.

The gray hovered for a moment between wolf and man. The

screams were compelling, cries of pain and distress. A nurturing creature, even human distress cries roused him.

Fifty or so yards down the road, one man was on the ground. He
was being kicked into submission by two others.

The wolf turned human and briefly considered matters—matters
such as the width of the river and the difficulty of crossing without
assistance—and decided it might be worth a try. But he'd best hurry
because the man on the ground was definitely in trouble: he'd stopped
shouting and was now curled into a ball, trying to protect his vital
organs.

He dashed toward the pair, shouting as he came. One stopped
menacing the victim, turned, and drew his sword. The two wore bits
and pieces of Roman armor and looked as if they might be deserters
from one of Caesar's cavalry companies.

The soldier crouched and Maeniel could read the contempt in
the man's eyes. He was naked and unarmed.

Maeniel was determined not to be taken as easily as he had been
in his first fight with humans. He closed with the soldier. *Right about
now,* the hunter's brain told him. *He has to commit.*

He did, aiming a vicious, downward slash that would have split
Maeniel's skull to the teeth.

The demiwolf simply increased his speed slightly, ending up
inside the downstroke just as it fell. His left hand snapped shut on the
wrist of the sword arm. His right fist slammed into the man's face. It
hurt. He had not known it would cause him so much pain. Still, he
managed to tear the sword from his opponent's hand.

A second later he realized why the sword came loose so easily.
The man he'd just punched in the face was dead.

The one who'd presumably been his partner left off kicking the
victim. He stared goggle-eyed at the red ruin that was all that
remained of his confederate's face and at the giant naked man holding
a sword in his hand.

Then he ran. Three horses and a heavily laden pack mule grazed
beside the rutted track. The brigand leaped into one of the saddles with
the ease of long practice, snatched up the pack mule's rein, and fled.

The robbery victim staggered to his feet and began screaming at
the fleeing man and mule. Then he took out after both at a hopping
run, still yelling imprecations, objurgations, and downright curses in
what sounded like three languages.

Maeniel, anxious not to lose his investment in time and energy, brought up the rear, waving the sword.

Up ahead, the muddy track had been flooded by a recent rain: tough going for the brigand's horse and the even more heavily laden mule. The horse slowed in the mud, but the mule sank in to the fetlocks.

The fleeing outlaw slowed the horse. The lead rope stretched out and the mule went to his knees. The mule did not suffer this tamely. He gave a braying outcry of anger and distress, leaped to his feet, planted all four legs, threw his head back, and jerked the lead rope out of the horseman's hand.

The thief pulled up his horse and gave Maeniel and the infuriated merchant one apprehensive look, then clapped spurs to his mount and ran.

The merchant caught up to the mule and stopped running. The mule brayed again and strolled out of the mud onto more solid ground.

The merchant spat in the mule's face and screamed, "Traitor!" in two languages. The mule was unruffled, so the merchant slapped the animal across the face.

The mule complained again, rather mildly, Maeniel thought. The merchant punched him in the nose. Mules are tough, but the area between the large nostrils of any equine is sensitive.

Maeniel arrived barely in time to sweep the merchant out of the way just before one of the mule's fore hooves raked through the air where his head had been only a second before. Then the merchant staggered over to a convenient fallen tree, sat down, and had hysterics.

Maeniel saw a loaf of bread and what looked like a piece of cheese protruding from one of the mule's saddlebags. Despite a few threats and foot stampings—the mule didn't care at all for the way he smelled—he was able to help himself.

The cheese was old and hard; so was the bread. Maeniel, who was usually interested in human food, decided he preferred his interrupted frog snack.

He ambled back to the fallen thief and stood over him, chewing the bread and cheese, puzzling about the reasons for his death. Surely he hadn't hit him *that hard,* but there he was, undeniably dead. Maeniel sighed. He hadn't wanted to kill his adversary, only stop him. At length, he removed the swordbelt from around the fallen man's waist and placed the sword in the scabbard.

The merchant's hysteria was subsiding. "What are you going to do? Rob me the same way your two friends did?" He screeched the accusation.

Maeniel looked at him. The long, steady gaze was the sort the pack leader gives a low-ranking wolf caught in an act of insubordination.

The merchant abruptly realized his accusations might be inappropriate or even dangerous in this situation.

"They are not my friends," Maeniel said. "No, I wouldn't rob you. The only thing I want is safe passage across the river. If you know how to accomplish this feat, instruct me now. If not, say so. I won't waste any more time talking to you and I'll leave."

"Cross the river? You want to cross the river?" the merchant gabbled.

"I just said so," Maeniel replied patiently.

"There's a ferry only a few miles down the road."

"What's a ferry?"

The merchant's jaw dropped.

Noting the dead man's horse was still grazing nearby, Maeniel began investigating a bundle on the saddle pack. He found a clean tunic, a dirty blanket, more bread and cheese, and a hard sausage that reeked of garlic. He put the tunic on. The thing was a bit small for him, barely covering his knees. He kept the food and threw away the blanket. He ignored the tunic and trousers on the corpse. They were far too over-ripe for his animal nose.

The merchant tried to explain the concept of a ferry to him and succeeded fairly well. Maeniel had seen boats. "You mean, it's a boat that doesn't go anywhere but from one side of the river to the other?" he asked the merchant.

"Yes, but that's enough places."

Maeniel nodded and the five set out together, Maeniel leading the brigand's horse, the merchant mounted on his own horse and pulling the mule's headrope. The mule had gotten over his bad temper and accepted the situation philosophically.

The merchant's name was Decius. A human might have been irritated by his unending flow of chatter, but as far as the wolf was concerned, he was a font of useful information. The merchant talked and, except for an occasional prodding question to direct the flow, Maeniel listened.

It transpired that Decius had not simply been set upon by the pair of thieves, he'd hired them at his last stopping place to protect him.

"Sometimes it works," he told Maeniel in a shamefaced way. "You hire a few of the wolves to keep off the rest of the pack."

"I suppose," Maeniel replied noncommittally.

"And speaking of wolves, there are supposed to be real wolves around here."

Maeniel was tempted to reply, "Only one," but he decided he'd better keep his mouth shut.

Decius craned his neck and anxiously looked up and down the road. "Do you suppose there are?"

"No" was all Maeniel felt he could trust himself to say.

"No wolves? You're sure? How do you know?"

Maeniel decided to give his companion something else to think about. "No wolves here, only bears."

Decius started so violently that his horse shied. "Bears!" he squeaked.

"Yes! Big ones."

"Where?"

"In the forest."

"Well, even I know that," Decius said condescendingly. "Where in the forest?"

"Right around the next bend in the road."

Decius began laughing. "How could you possibly know?" They were, at the moment, rounding the bend.

Above, clouds were piling up. The wind was rising. It whipped at the nearly naked tree branches around them, sending a flurry of brown leaves across the road.

Maeniel paused, his nostrils distended. He took a deep breath. A whole complex of sensations from the wolf flooded his brain. The air had a sharp, wet smell: rain or possibly snow before morning. An old smell of burning; fresh bear—he'd been nearby only a short time ago. Why? The wolf didn't fear the big animal and doubted Decius had anything to fear either. If the bear was stalking them, he'd be after the horses—the bony gelding Maeniel was leading or the heavier-fleshed mare ridden by Decius.

Around the bend, the road swung close to the river.

Decius laughed nervously. "Well, friend, where is that bear you were talking about, and how do we know he's here?"

Maeniel pointed to a muddy spot near one of the deep ruts. "There!" he said.

The paw prints were fresh. The mud that had gushed up between the bear's toes was still wet.

A fair-sized beech stood near the tracks. The claw marks on the bark were a good three feet taller than any man.

Decius startled, frightening his horse again. The mule brayed loudly in the sudden silence. "Does *he* know we're here?" Decius squeaked.

"Keep moving, and yes, he knows; you stink of it."

"Of what?" Decius seemed to be on the verge of panic.

"Fear!"

Decius obeyed. They passed the tree; the horses ambled on.

The sky was gray now. The wind shifted. Decius' horse caught the bear smell. She began dancing along sideways, throwing her head up—in other words, showing incipient symptoms of equine panic. Every one of Maeniel's senses, human and wolf, was at full stretch. What was a bear doing here at this time of year? They were usually fat, lazy, sleepy, and ready to den up. Then he heard the hum of bees. "Of course. Keep going," he urged Decius, but the frightened horse was no longer making forward progress.

Some of the bees arrived and began buzzing around them. One shot into the distended nostrils of Decius' horse. The confused insect obeyed the million-year-old command: *When skin-to-chitin contact with an enemy occurs, commit suicide.* He drove his stinger in to the hilt, maybe or maybe not screaming, "Die, horse!"

Decius' horse bucked. Decius took to the air, showing a lot of space between his rear end and the saddle, but he came down with a yell and a loud slap of flesh on leather just before the horse bolted.

This time the horse's forward motion was completely unimpeded. She thundered down the road at an astonishing pace. Decius dropped the mule's lead rope. He needed both hands to cling to the pommel of the saddle.

"Yi, yi, yi, yi, yi, yeee!" This last as the horse left the road and vanished into the scrubby forest bordering the river.

Maeniel stood quietly as both hoofbeats and Decius' cries died away. He examined the alternatives and decided there was little he could do in good conscience except take hold of the mule's lead rope, follow Decius, and hope for the best.

The trace was overgrown. Weeds, furze, and thistles filled the deeply rutted track. Maeniel got the impression that the road had once been heavily traveled. Now, for some inexplicable reason, it had been abandoned.

The hooves of Decius' galloping horse had torn raw, brown wounds in the grassy, weed-grown surface. Overhead, tree branches almost blotted out the sky. The knotted trace twisted and turned, drawing Maeniel deeper and deeper into the forest.

He looked up and noted that the sky was growing darker. The storms at the heights were extending their reach down into the valleys.

The road grew worse. Here a large rock blocked the way. There a cluster of thick-trunked oaks sheltering a dark pool caused a detour. Beyond the oaks, a lightning-blasted fallen beech completely blocked his path.

The mule snorted and backed, trying to plant his feet and refuse further progress. Maeniel wouldn't allow this. He dropped the lead rope and, taking the mule by its bridle, forced him past the shattered branches of the fallen tree. His own horse followed him in a docile way, as if used to the mad caprices of his human master.

He found Decius on the other side of the tree, lying sprawled on his back under a low branch. He was unconscious, a livid purple bruise across his forehead. Five yards father down the road, his horse stood grazing on the scrubby growth.

Maeniel knelt next to Decius. Yes, the man was breathing, but deeply unconscious. What now?

The sky was very dark.

If he turned wolf, he could be gone. Leave this fool here. Powerful as they were in a group, individually humans were weak. Left at the mercy of the oncoming storm, Decius would probably die.

But Maeniel was warm and sympathetic by nature. Many wolves in the pack, seeing the penalties and problems of leadership, ignored their opportunities to take command. Only those like him willingly accepted its burdens.

He sighed and lifted Decius in his arms. As he did, he saw a small snowflake land on his wrist. To his surprise, the horses and the mule followed him, trusting in human protection.

More snowflakes swirled through the air as the wind rose. It swept some of the scrub trees near the road aside, and beyond Maeniel saw open fields, arousing his hopes that human dwellings might be ahead.

He could leave Decius there to be cared for while he pressed on. But when he passed the last bend, he realized the road led only to a burned-out villa.

It wasn't nearly as elaborate as the one in his valley, just a large house surrounded by a scattering of outbuildings, protected by a palisade fence.

The house was a pile of blackened rubble. The other outbuildings were visible only as charred timbers nearly lost in the long grass. Only one structure of any size still stood. The raiders had set it on fire when they left, but only one side had been consumed. The roof had collapsed, turning it into a lean-to. That might shelter the injured Decius and the livestock against the winter night. The wolf had no survival problems. He was armed with all the necessities of life. Once they were safely inside, he need only leave, turn skin, and abandon them.

Maeniel shivered. He was barefoot and the wind cut through the thin linen tunic, freezing his skin. The snowflakes were falling more and more thickly.

He hurried on. The half-collapsed building had once been a stable. The stalls were gone, but there was a manger against one wall and a thick coating of straw covered the stone floor. He laid Decius in the straw and unsaddled the two horses and the mule.

Decius was breathing, but showed no sign of regaining consciousness. So Maeniel pillowed his head on one of the saddles and covered him with a blanket he found in the pack. In the fields, patchy stands of wheat had resown themselves. It took only a few minutes to harvest enough to give the stock a good meal. Then he lit a fire. No problem about fuel; deadfalls lay among the trees, and fallen timbers from the house and shed were scattered among the ruins. The only problem was keeping the rising flames from setting fire to the sloping roof.

Now he was at a loss. The horses and mule munched; Decius slumbered. As Maeniel peered through the broken wattle and daub wall of the shed, he shivered. The snow was falling fast now, blurring the outlines of forest and weed-grown fields in the dying light. Wind gusts tossed the trees, taking down the last sere leaves and spreading frost across the branches of evergreens, sealing their dense green.

Far away, a wolf howled, another answered, then a third added a comment. A whole chorus replied. Maeniel chuckled. Apparently the weather was even worse among the high mountains and some of the passes were already choked with snow. He'd crossed just in time.

A few wolves who lived along the river had been in the chorus answering the mountain pack. They were hunted by humans more frequently than the others among the peaks. They were wary— something about the humans on the other side of the river.

But wolf speech is laconic and Maeniel couldn't gather much more than that from their songs. That and they would not hunt tonight while the storm was at its height, but wait till dawn. Some animals were certain to be trapped by the snow. Pickings would probably be good.

He eased back to the fire. The lean-to was comfortable now. The north wind battered the sloping end of the roof. Ice and snow collected on the walls, sealing in the warmth. The thick layer of straw insulated the ground.

Maeniel had no need to search Decius' pack. His nose located flour, salt, sausage, and oil. He'd learned quite a few things from Imona, so it wasn't long before an oily flatbread puffed on a smooth rock in the fire. Maeniel made a meal of the sausage, hard cheese, and bread.

Imona! He stood and pulled off the tunic and sword. An instant later, he was wolf and he vanished into the snowy darkness.

VII

IMONA! HER DAYS PASSED. SOMETIMES THEY SUR-
prised her with their passing, seeming to flow quickly from
dawn to dusk while she was lost in her memories of the past.

Other days stumbled along on leaden feet. Her mind drifted from
grief to grief, each sorrow bringing with it floods of scalding tears that
did nothing to relieve her pain, but only left her with reddened eyes
and headaches.

Women came, servants usually directed by a well-dressed lady who
would never, by any means, meet Imona's eyes. They prepared food,
changed her bedding, and even sometimes bathed her when despair
overcame her willingness to care for herself. But none ever tried to
communicate with her.

Our memories of happiness don't comfort us when the great
darkness yawns, waiting for our souls.

There were things Imona simply refused to remember: her parents, for instance, and her childhood on the Breton coast. But she
would allow herself to remember the sea. Emerald water, thundering
and raging at the rocks, crashing its way into white foam.

Or the way the light changes at daybreak over the water, a splendid rainbow of subtle beauty making no sunrise or sunset quite like
another.

Sometimes she could sit, close her eyes, and smell the salt air. She
even fancied she could hear the cry of the wheeling gulls or taste the
moisture of the pale fog drifting in from the ocean, stilling all activity

along the coast, wrapping the whole world in its somehow sacred silence.

She didn't care to think of her husband, especially of the first few years of her marriage when they had been happy and she'd borne him two children, before he'd gone, at her family's behest, to fight the Romans. She didn't care to think of it because her mind would twist and turn, trying to find ways she could have foreseen his fate and prevented the mutilation that so devastated his body and soul—so emptied him of hope that he committed the act that brought ruin to them all.

When she thought of him, those were the worst days and the ones when she refused to eat or bathe, covered her head with her mantle, and wept without ceasing for him, for herself, for poor, half-mad Kat, her dull-witted but kind Des, and even the old woman. Except for Kat, they were dead in the ashes of what had once been their home.

But some days she could purge guilt and regret from her mind. On those days she would think of the mountains and how she'd first seen them.

As the daughter of a noble house, she'd been sent to her new husband in a skin-covered cart drawn by four white oxen. They were intended to be sacrificed at the wedding ceremony to content the gods of her husband's household and to feed the guests.

At first, traveling in the cart had been an adventure. Besides, the journey was broken often as they stopped to be feasted at the homes of her father's liege men. But after they left familiar territory, the cart became something of a prison. She lived there, eating and sleeping among her maids, only allowed out briefly at dusk, under heavy guard, to relieve herself and possibly, if they were near a lake or stream, bathe. When she complained, the older women who accompanied her shushed her and told her to be patient.

So on the morning when she heard a stir and increased talk among the men-at-arms near the wagon, she'd boldly crawled past the sleeping women, pushed aside the leather flap, and plunked herself down beside the driver. She looked up, gasped, and heard the gray-bearded man chuckle.

"It's a sight to behold! The mountains!" he said. "They seem to hold up the very sky."

And so they did. It was not long after sunrise. The snow-clad peaks were washed in golden light. The long, sinuous spines of the slopes were still wrapped in blue shadow. A wave of green softened the high meadows and mist flowed down between the snow-capped giants like rivers of cloud.

"Am I going there?" she asked.

The driver nodded.

"Then I will love it. I know I will."

And so she had. The brief, but beautiful summers—long, lazy days tending flocks of cattle and sheep in pastures beyond the tree line. The incredible autumns when fruit of all kinds seemed to vie for the attentions of humans. Peaches, plums, and cherries weighed down the orchards in the high valleys. Apples—green, red, blush, and even white—created such an abundance it could hardly be believed. Hedgerows were dark with raspberries, blackberries, and rose hips. Venison, elk, ibex, and chamois wandered in the high forests. When the snow flew, everyone hunted boar in the thick coverts.

They led the life of heroes: hunting, fighting, playing chess, entertaining visitors with song and story until, at last, full fed with beef, venison, ham, cheeses white and yellow, breads leavened and unleavened, all washed down by Italian wine, honey mead, and barley beer, she rested her head on her husband's shoulder, and her eyelids began to close before the guests were gone, or the last torches flickered out.

Sometimes she would wake and he would lead her to their chamber. At others, he would pick her up and carry her like a child. A world of delight surrounded her before . . . before the Romans came.

Her mind turned from the suffering that followed. Why torment herself? It simply didn't matter now.

Her only other visitor was the ruler of these people. Chieftain, magistrate, call it what you would, he came, accompanied by his warriors, as if a company of armed men could stave off the grim darkness that surrounded her and hovered over her days and nights.

She had been at the hearth in the back corner of the room. As the end of the year drew near and the harvest was hurried into the barns, the nights were becoming colder and colder. She had been building up the fire, trying to drive off the chill in her body.

He knocked.

She called, "Come in," and heard the key turn in the lock.

He stepped in, his men behind and flanking him. A blast of cold air followed them.

Imona stood up. Even though she was clad in a heavy linen dress and a stout woolen mantle, she shivered in the draft.

"Shut the damn door," the chieftain roared. "Where were you bastards reared, in a stable? It's freezing out there."

The door slammed loudly.

"Damn it! I didn't ask you to deafen me, just close that dishonorably born door!"

"The wind—" someone started to explain.

"Oh, shut up! Just shut up! Don't interrupt me again!"

Complete silence fell.

Imona wiped her hands. She had been mixing flour and flat beer to make her morning meal. To her, the flour was deeply suspect. It was filled with bran, and she often detected acorn and cattail root starch in the mix.

The chieftain harrumphed and cleared his throat, then harrumphed again. "I am Cynewolf, leader of the people here. I came to ask how you are, my lady, and if you need anything." He had begun strongly, but ended his little speech rather lamely.

Imona was darkly amused. She took no pity on him. "When I was a farm wife living in the mountains, no one remembered that I was the daughter of a king. Now, here, with my fate upon me, I am recognized and honored for my family's rank. Thank you, Lord Cynewolf, for your compliments and respect. They are one with the cold wind blowing through the door. The wind has more kindness in it. Go away, my lord. Leave me alone."

Cynewolf looked uncomfortable. *His discomfort does him credit,* Imona thought. It demonstrated that he didn't want to do what he was going to do in a few days, but she suspected his discomfiture would not stop him. No, not for one moment.

The expression on his face was bleak and sad. But, as is proper for a leader, it was filled with resolution. He half turned to the men around him, and said, "Go. Go away. Leave us."

They fled, clawing at each other, treading on one another's feet in their haste to escape.

The chieftain strode across the room and stood next to Imona. He knelt on one knee beside her feet and peered narrowly at the flames. The flour for Imona's breakfast was mounded in an open bowl on the hearth.

Cynewolf lifted a handful, then tossed it into the flames. A searing smell of burning filled the room.

"The flour tells the tale!" His voice was harsh with anger and desperation. "Our good farms across the river are gone. He burned them out years ago . . . when I wouldn't send riders for him to lead against my kin in Gaul. In the end, he got his cavalry. But we have never been able to return. The Roman garrisons drive us back. This year the women gathered cattails and acorns by the bushel. Last winter we stripped the bark from trees, but even so, many died. I lost my eldest son last year, my youngest daughter the year before."

The chieftain brushed his hand across his eyes as if to banish an evil vision, then rose to his feet and stared down at Imona. "I would be merciful, if I could, but I can't. I dare not. He, the haggard, sunken-cheeked Roman, has been a calamity to your people."

"They are all gone," Imona said softly.

"Yes, but mine still survive. This Roman must not cross the Rhine. Must not!"

Imona said. "Ask the Lady! I will abide by the answer." She removed the golden torque from her neck and handed it to Cynewolf. "If 'yes,' return the torque. If not, I'll go to the home of one of my daughters. I won't be welcome, but I will go. I'm an expert cloth worker. I'll find a niche somewhere."

Cynewolf stood silent. He turned the torque in his hand. "You are the daughter of a king. I owe you that. Yes," he sighed. "I suppose I owe you that." Then he turned and left.

THE ROMANS. CYNEWOLF WALKED TOWARD THE river. The oppidum was mounded high. People were gathered, camped in large numbers on the slopes that led up to the chief's hall and the workshops that clustered around the seat of power. He trudged down the muddy street between the tumbledown, burned-out dwellings wrecked by the Romans during their last incursion.

He paused and looked up. The sun was bright, but the wind was out of the north. The gusts that tore at his mantle and assaulted his ears had an icy bite. The sky was flocked by high, rippling clouds, in some places thin and hazy, letting the azure blue glow through, in others thick gray and striated like river ice.

Yes, he thought, *the river.* He hurried on. There must have been a light freeze last night because every so often the mud crunched as the ice crystals shattered beneath his feet.

He could remember from his long-ago childhood, the settlement around him buzzing with happy bustle in springtime. Not one, but three blacksmiths worked there, making armor, swords, farm implements, and much else needed by the people. A goldsmith and his family labored, the most beautiful of his creations worn by the warriors and women of Cynewolf's family—the ruling family.

Women, slave and free, clustered in the weaving sheds, creating magnificent fabrics. Some traded as far north as the legendary Pict land, lost in the hyperborean mists, and some so far south they warmed Romans against the damp misery of the Mediterranean winter. Ham, bacon, and sausage stuffed the smokehouses, darkening in the thick, cool clouds from banked fires, or salt cured in cellars, cold even in high summer.

Now, no more. Once, yes. Once I had sons and daughters, too. Once. The gods must be wood and stone. I had not thought it would hurt so much.

He'd reached the edge of the settlement and could look down the long sweep of green to the blue-gray shimmer given off by the smooth surface of water gliding between the banks.

There were a great many family groups clustered around tents and lean-tos made by draping awnings from the heavy wagons.

Yes, once these people had looked happy. They drove herds of horses, cattle, sheep, and goats. Their wagons were laden with cloth, beer, dried apples, pears, cherries, more hams, and cheeses from the mountains. At night, the fires leaped high as marriages were arranged, bargains concluded, and everyone caught up on the doings of everyone else. And the nights ended with feasts, storytelling, poetry, and song, all against a background of flame and so many flying embers that they rivaled the stars in the night sky.

Now the men he passed wouldn't meet his eyes, and the women, seeing the gold torque in his hand, drew their children in toward their skirts, touched amulets at their throats, and tried to pretend he did not exist.

Even where the sun shone, they were gray-skinned, pinched-faced, and afraid. The carts, once overflowing with produce for sale or trade, stood empty.

He strode down the slope toward the trees at the riverbank. When he reached the water, he wrapped his mantle more tightly around himself. The wind blew briskly, making the air seem colder than one would expect so close to midday.

The sun's glow came and went. Willows hung out over the stream, the long, trailing branches dropping blade-shaped, yellowish green leaves into an eddy pool at their base. When the wind stilled and the sun shone, the tan branches and yellow leaves found perfect reflection in the still water, as if the half-drowned willow was twinned by the strong, silent river.

Somewhere a child laughed.

The gods were wood and stone. They neither knew nor cared what more transient flesh and blood suffered. Throw the torque into the water. Let Imona go. Let her grow old as other women did, standing before the tall loom, weaving, throwing the shuttle back and forth in the shadowy light of a clay lamp. He could close his eyes and see her standing there, breasts sagging, hips thickening, hair streaked with gray, then silver, laboring until time dissolved her skin, then bones, and carried her away as the river did the willow's golden leaves.

The child laughed again. Sunlight sparked on the torque and the eddy pool beneath the willow.

He saw the child who laughed reflected in the sunlit pool. What child? Then he chuckled as he realized the child was his. His youngest daughter. And then he remembered where his youngest daughter was.

When he came to his senses, he was kneeling halfway up the steep slope of the green mound, clutching the torque with both hands.

One of his wives stood before him. Alix, the eldest and first. Not the mother of his daughter. No! She was gone. She left not long after . . .

With trembling hands, he gave the torque to Alix. "Take it to . . . the woman."

"And say?"

"Say nothing. Nothing need be said. She will understand."

After she left, he knelt there for a long time, trying to convince himself he hadn't seen what he'd just seen, and failing that, to explain it away. But in the end, he could do neither. So he rose slowly, thinking his joints were stiffening as he aged, walked to his dwelling, and called for wine. Lots and lots of wine.

As for Imona, the torque was delivered, held out to her with one hand, even as Alix used her other to cover her face with her veil. As she had been instructed, Alix said nothing. Alix, the willow.

Imona did as Cynewolf did. Drank all the wine and beer they would give her. She watched the sunlight come and go. Not tonight, but tomorrow. A day not in the world. Dawn and dusk, not day, not night. Beside the sea, not water, not land. The hinge of the year. A day not belonging properly to either one, ordained time out of mind, to exist and not exist. Most holy night. Sacred night. The door to forever. Imona shivered and, because there was nothing left to do now, idly watched the sun come and go as the wind pushed the clouds from the north.

THE WOLF WAS PREPARED FOR THE COLD. HIS TRIPLE thickness of coat repelled water, and the coarse, outer guard hairs wouldn't support ice even in the coldest, dampest conditions. The wide-splayed paws were self-insulated against the icy ground, and the claws and pads offered good traction even on slick ice. Sheer size gave him an advantage over most of his kind. Few, if any, wolves bulk as large as a human. He did, fully one hundred and eighty pounds. The thick overlay of fat on his muscles—the dynamic energy that fueled his change from man to wolf and back again—also served as insulation against the freezing winter night.

He had some misgivings about leaving Decius in his helpless state. The bear or other wolves might find him. So he cast about in circles, exploring the burned-out farm. He soon found it had been the scene of a savage battle. Many died. A wolf's nose, even in the bitter cold, found the remains of countless men and beasts.

The villa had not been alone here. Beyond its fields, a village once stood. The only traces of the structures inhabited by small farmers were a few weathered house posts and a rank smell of char and mud. They also left their dead. Mostly gone now, reclaimed by the earth, the dry smell of old bone and rusting iron told the wolf where they lay.

It was dark. The snow fell more and more heavily. Still, the gray wolf continued circling, trying to be sure the woods held no threat to his human charge; and he found nothing.

The wolves would not hunt tonight. The bear? She had only one interest here—the bee tree. Her senses warned her of oncoming cold even more quickly than his. She'd long ago sought her den. She was padded with fat and heavy with the cubs that would be born in the deep winter. The honey tree was in the nature of a bedtime snack.

His last circle took him to the road. Even the bees were quiescent. They had repaired what they could of the damage done by the bear's depredations. Now they hung deep in the hollow tree, insulated by at least a foot of bark, wood, and sawdust chippings. Each bee clinging to at least three others, they hung in a dark curtain covering their remaining larva and honey-laden comb. They were warm and they sang. Very softly. The wolf paused to listen.

They were content. The queen was alive and uninjured. Most of the larva they would need to replenish the colony had also survived and the remaining honey was more than enough to carry them through the cold months.

Above the bees' head, the branches began to clack and clatter as the snow melted then turned to ice in the north wind. They sang also of the tree's strength, though rotten and lightning blasted. They were assured that it was strong enough to protect them for at least another year. *Sleep now; sleep as the outside world is covered in white death. Sleep.*

The wolf drifted on, ignoring the strange lullaby. Here in the cold dark night, he was at home.

Where was Imona? He believed she had been taken across this river. Though he knew little of human doings, he was aware that it marked the boundary of Roman power.

Even to a wolf it made sense for her people to carry her away to a place where she couldn't be punished for her husband's actions. But once beyond the river, where had they taken her?

He hurried along the river road. He saw into the blurred, snow-filled darkness better than a human could. He avoided the still-wet puddles that might soak his feet. They wouldn't bother him much, but having to stop and gnaw away the ice between his toes would slow him up. His stomach gripped at him a bit.

A wolf wanted more meat than a human customarily ate. He craved something better than the bread and cheese he'd just eaten, but he could put off a hunt for several days if he had to.

However, he was growing discouraged. He'd been traveling through wilderness for several days and it had been close to a week since he'd found the last traces of her in the mountain fastness. He had no proof she was here.

The temperature was dropping rapidly. He no longer splashed through the puddles when he was inattentive. Ice was forming fast on everything in the forest, including the road. He was a very disgruntled wolf and almost ready to turn back, feed, and, if possible, reach the lean-to and sleep, when the smell of wood smoke drifted to his nostrils.

He increased his pace and, when he passed the next bend in the river, saw the faint lights of a settlement ahead, only a few buildings clustered around a landing for a rope-propelled ferry. The ferry was up on the shore, already half-buried in icy mud and snow. The few squalid huts that comprised the settlement were battened down, tightly shuttered against the blizzard outside.

The wolf paused, baffled. What now?

He looked at the river. It rolled black, its oily gleam misted by the thick flurries of snow steadily dappling its surface.

The wolf sat. *Damn!* This from the man who shared the wolf's brain. Then he looked up.

The low, rolling overcast was flurried with snow and sleet clouds. The encampment across the river advertised itself by the red glow its fires cast against the boiling clouds.

The wolf rose and trotted through the screen of brush cloaking the banks. Some bushes were still green and the torn leaves and broken twigs gave off an overpowering fragrance. Bay? No. The canine sense of smell is twenty times more powerful than is the human's. The wolf was capable of making fine distinctions no mere man could begin to sort out.

His nose touched a berry. Blue, it had the essence of blueness, nestled among leaves shiny, dark green. His tongue swept out. The berry tasted of blue, green, and gray. Powdery blue, almost violet; green the leaves' sharp fragrance, half incense, half cold bite and sweet bay. And then the gray, creeping like cool mist flowing from the heights into mountain valleys as the last sun blazes against the peaks, painting them with an almost unbearably beautiful golden light.

His nose found another berry and another and another. The man would have been trembling in terror. He, the man, might have fled. But the wolf looked into the other world and let it claim him. To the beast, to the wolf, tomorrow and yesterday are illusions. Now is all that exists: now and the taste of berries on the tongue.

He was in a garden, visiting in the magic moments between dawn and sunrise. Or was it the pale twilight between sunset and night? Even the wolf couldn't tell. Usually he could. Sunrise and sunset have a different fragrance. But not here where the air was drenched with the perfume of the berry bushes.

The cold was gone, replaced by a comfortable coolness. The river was gone, replaced by a narrow brook hardly deep enough to cover his paws. But beautiful, reflecting, as it did, the blue-violet and faint rose of an opalescent sky.

He had been given many maps when he was born. One of the heavens telling him how each day, month, and year wore away. Another of the mountains and the secrets of the seasons. Trails and all but invisible paths that could be followed in sun and starlight, rain and snow; ways to lead him to all he needed in life and, yes, in death. He had never been granted a map of this place; yet he took the gift it offered and so perhaps bound himself forever.

He pushed through the living green standing firm against snow, ice, sleet, and death, and drifted down a shallow, grassy slope through the creek, his careful wolf feet raising not a splash, and climbed another shallow slope until wind-driven snow and sleet slashed him across the face. And he found himself looking down from a bluff on the other side of the river at an encampment crowning the hill. The oppidum just across the river from the ferry landing.

VIII

THE WOLF WAS UNTROUBLED BY THE SNOW, wind, or cold. This was because the wolf is, par excellence, a bad-weather animal. His feet will not freeze because his body can lower their temperature almost to the level of frozen snow without impairing either activity or circulation. Maeniel didn't know this, but he felt no discomfort on even the coldest surface.

The undercoat of a wolf is a sort of insulating fleece. The outer guard hairs shed moisture from rain or snow and, as all circumpolar peoples know, it will not become coated by frost. He was, in fact, quite comfortable even in a semiblizzard like this.

But he was aware his other self wouldn't be so fortunate. So he set out for the encampment he saw ahead of him. The wolf wanted to run, go find Imona, and—if she was here—change and carry her away. The man told him not to be a fool. As a human he would die before morning without the protection of clothing and shelter.

No, he'd best think a bit about how to accomplish his objective. First, find Imona! She might not be here. If he hadn't found the path opened by the blueberries, he might have turned around and given up. But then again, probably not. More than likely he would have tried to swim the river and killed himself.

As he entered the human encampment, he found he could move about quite freely. His gray coat made him difficult to see in the blowing snow, and those humans sharp-eyed enough to spot him took him for a large dog.

At first, he was a bit furtive, slipping from shadow to shadow, but he quickly realized this only made the humans suspicious. So long as he trotted along, head down, tongue lolling and looking harmless, he was ignored. No one would believe a wolf would wander among humans so casually and without fear.

Not bad so far, he thought until he reached the gates of the oppidum, the settlement that crowned the high mound itself.

A tall palisade with heavy, iron-spiked wooden gates surrounded it. They were closed. On either side of the gates, torches flared in iron baskets, giving three armed and formidable-looking guards a good view.

He sat down in the darkness where he could not be seen to consider matters. Was she there? He couldn't tell. The number and variety of odors generated by humans, their livestock, hide tents, and cooked food was almost overpowering to his animal senses.

But just then a hard gust of wind whipped the snow into swirls of white, forcing the gate guards to turn their backs to protect their faces from the icy blast, almost extinguishing the torches hanging from the gateposts.

Yes, there it was. Her perfume. Her living body. A warm, memory-laden scent belonging only to her. She was here. This wasn't something left behind like a footprint in damp soil or a bit of hair or fur caught on the wicked projections of a holly bush. This was the message imparted to the air by a living, breathing being whose heart beat, lungs filled and emptied, and mind thought and dreamed beyond the cold night, the wooden gates, and the palisade that shut him out.

He felt a deeper sense of relief than he'd expected. He hadn't realized how fearful he'd been, or allowed himself to comprehend how much sorrow it would have caused him if she'd simply disappeared from his life and he'd never seen her again. How big a place she'd made for herself in his heart.

To the naïve human and the innocent wolf in him, everything seemed simple. He would pass the gate, greet her, and she would come with him. He was certain he could manage the pack and care for her at the same time. He could hide her not only from her own people, but the Romans if necessary. Now, how to get past that gate?

At that moment, he heard the hissing sound of wagon wheels, creaking and groaning, compacting the new snow underfoot. The shadowy shape of a large wagon drawn by mules emerged from the darkness and pulled up to the gate.

One of the guards looked up at the driver. "What is it?"

"Salt fish."

The guard shook his head. "Salt fish? Leave it out here. Go in the linch gate." He pointed to a smaller door in the big gate.

"What, are you a fool? You'll be a damn fool if the lord of this place catches you leaving a wagonload of food where it can be stolen. Leave six barrels of salt fish here and that rabble down there—" He pointed to the scattering of fires burning on the hill behind him. "If they get wind of the fact that there's food here for the taking, there won't be a scraping of salt on the barrel bottoms by dawn."

The guard sighed in a very loud and windy way. "I can remember when that wasn't so."

"Yes, so can I," the driver replied, "but it's true now, so open the gates before I freeze my balls off. I've been keeping company with this stinking fish so long, my hide smells like bilge water and even my piss reeks. I want some beer, a warm bed, and, if possible, a woman who doesn't mind the smell of fish."

The wolf saw what he considered his opportunity and drifted toward the wagon, sliding under it just as one of the guards began to swing the big gate back.

But the wolf reckoned without a cur already crouched under the wagon. He was taken aback by his first sight of the creature. It was small, white, liberally sprinkled with liver-colored spots, short coated, and shivering violently. It began to yap loudly as the wolf stuck his nose under the wagon.

The man swore mentally. The wolf snarled. A more intelligent animal would have been silenced, but the wolf reckoned without the power of stupidity. The small animal simply yipped faster and more loudly.

"What's that?" the guard asked.

"Stray dog, I think," the driver said. "The little one's mine."

The guard picked up a clod of ice and mud. He hurled it at the wolf. It caught him painfully in the ribs. The wolf squealed.

"Get out of here! Go!" the guard shouted.

The angry wolf lunged toward him.

The guard carried the rectangular Celtic shield, a wood frame reinforced with hide. As the wolf closed, the man brought the edge of the heavy shield down hard across his back and shoulder.

The wolf gave vent to a sound more like a scream of pain than a cry of anger, then scuttled crabwise back into the snowy darkness.

By the time he brought himself under control, the cart was inside and the gate closed and barred again.

The pain in his neck and shoulder receded from excruciating to bearable, but it was a long time before he could put his foot on the ground again. And longer before he was able to walk without a limp.

At length, he managed to free his mind of anger, frustration, and pain, by then convinced that nothing about dealing with these mad human creatures was ever as easy as it seemed on the surface.

Deep in every canid's heart lurks a con artist. He stood in the darkness and strained his ears, listening to the conversation of the guards.

Somehow they'd managed to erect a lean-to near the gate. As it grew later and colder, fewer travelers interrupted their drinking.

The snowfall had grown heavier as the night wore on. The flakes, which had started as a fine powder, were now so thick it was difficult to see more than twenty feet in any direction. True, the wind—a vicious blast earlier in the evening—had dropped, but as it did, the snow sifted straight down, flakes the wolf could hear tinkling faintly as they began to wrap the earth and every structure standing near the oppidum in a thick blanket of white. The wolf sidled toward the guard hut until he was close enough to see the three huddled inside.

The eldest, a bearded giant, was already unconscious. He was leaning against the wall, snoring. The other two sat at the table. One slept, head in his arms; the other, a rangy, ginger-haired one, was the problem. He was still awake and in a truculent mood. The wolf eased closer to the door.

"Get out of here!" the redhead snarled, and began looking around for a missile.

The wolf went down on his belly, whined, and produced what he hoped was a submissive canine grin.

"Bastard! You tried to bite me. Now that I kicked your ass, you want to be friends."

The wolf whimpered softly and eased forward on his stomach, tail wagging.

"Now you wanna be my buddy. Real sweetheart." The guard's

speech was slurred, but slowly a nasty grin spread over his face. He refilled his wine cup. "Come here." He beckoned the wolf with one hand as he lifted the cup with the other.

The wolf's muzzle was just inside the guards' hut. The wolf calculated the probable effect of a full cup of wine being dashed into his vulnerable eyes and tender nose. Not good. But he was sober and Ginger Hair was not. Nor was the wolf a human distracted by sleight of hand. Still, Ginger Hair was fast and almost got him.

The wine was in the air, coming, but instead of hitting a wolf's eyes, it splashed on human legs. Ginger Hair found himself looking at a man's face: a strong man's face, but with eyes exactly like those of what he'd mistaken for a stray dog.

It was his last sight for a time because, a second later, Maeniel's fist connected with the side of his jaw.

The other two in the guard hut not only didn't wake, but only one of them stirred. The one sitting at the table grunted, moved, and then went back to sleep. The other, resting against the wall, simply continued snoring.

Maeniel took Ginger Hair's tunic, leggings, and mantle, charitably leaving him with undershirt, shoes, and stockings.

He paused for a moment to make sure Ginger Hair was still breathing; he'd been unhappy about his killing earlier in the day. Then he went out. The palisade presented no problem. He was able to vault it quickly and began his search for Imona.

S HE WAS SITTING IN THE DARK, WRAPPED IN HER heavy mantle, when the lamp wick guttered out. She hadn't either the energy or the courage to brave the icy room and relight it. Instead, she lay in a half doze, burdened with both emotional despair and physical misery. The temperature inside matched the blizzard outside and ice was beginning to form on the walls.

All that remained of the hearth fire were red, glowing splotches. They brightened and darkened as the wind sucked at the air in the room.

At first, even the sounds on the street didn't arouse her. It was only when she heard *his* voice whispering her name that she got to her feet and scrambled to the slats forming the window: one nailed to the inside, one on the opposite side to the outside. This created as solid a set of bars as he'd ever seen. Only one little problem, though: they were rotten.

His big fist tore one loose on the bottom. Then he smacked the one on the other side and it flopped back. He saw Imona's face peering at him from the darkened room. He reached in and she took his hand.

She pressed it against her cheek and he felt a warm wetness. For a moment, he wondered at it because the snow had ceased blowing and was falling straight down, and then he realized she was crying.

"I thought no one remembered, no one cared. But you came, you remembered and cared. I do so love you." Her cheek and then her lips were like velvet and silk against his big, hard fingers.

He was a man. He blinked into the darkness of the snow-covered street. True, he was wearing the gate guard's tunic, leggings, and mantle, but he was barefooted. His toes were already freezing and every exposed inch of skin on his body was cold.

"Come," he said, tightening his hand on hers. "Come away. 'Love' is . . . love is something you crave. I can't understand it well, but if it's always falling asleep with a full stomach, staying warm at night, or finding sheltered, safe, cool spots to rest by day, I can lead you to all of these things. I'll hunt and kill for you. I'll carry you far from any of your own kind who want to harm you, and I will defend you against any who threaten you. Come with me, Imona. Come . . . be free. Forget these strange, contentious humans. Come. It will only take me a moment to break a few more of these bars. I know a place where I can take you. It's warm there. Come with me now!"

He pulled her hand past the broken slats. "Come! I'm afraid we may not have long. I had to hit the man at the gate and take his clothes to get here. He or one of his drunken brothers may raise an alarm."

He pulled her hand free of his and drew back. He could see only the outline of her face. Her eyes were shadowed hollows.

She saw his profile. *Gods, he's young,* she thought. *Whatever he is, he's young. What have I ahead of me in his wild home? Every morning it's a little harder to rise. Each time I have a session with comb and mirror, I find more gray hairs.* "No," she whispered softly. "No."

"Why no?"

His voice was so loud in the deserted street that she was afraid for him. "Sssh! They will raise an alarm and find you."

His arm groped through the window to try to catch hers again.

She took his hand, laced their fingers together, and pressed them against her forehead. "Hush, for the life of you, my love, my very dear. Please be quiet. I will come, only . . . only not tonight."

"No?" His voice was lowered again. "Why not?"

"Because . . ." She groped for an explanation, some excuse. "There's something I need to do before I go. Something that must be done. By me. Tomorrow."

Nearby, a man's voice shouted.

A torch flared.

"Wolves! Outlaws!"

His hand was gone and Imona saw the wolf shape where he'd been kneeling only a moment before.

Quickly, she pushed the barring slats closed. Then he was gone and the moment was past; Imona understood she had chosen, and what she had chosen.

Outside, the small settlement echoed with the hue and cry of what she was sure was a vain pursuit. She added tinder to the few live coals on the hearth. They flared. She set the last wood on the fire. It warmed the room and filled it with flickering, yellow light.

She sat staring into the flames for what seemed a long time, feeling a strange peace. Then she sought her pallet bed and, still staring into the flames, she slept, without dreaming of life or death. Only of the mountains and how they soared, lifting clean, knife-edged snowfields against a deep blue sky.

THE FIRST FEW MOMENTS FOR THE WOLF WERE busy ones. A javelin landed and went several inches into the mud where he had been standing only a moment before. For a terrible few seconds, he rolled, trapped in the tunic and mantle, and then he was free and running through the icy slush between the houses.

He trotted along, disoriented, lost in the circular settlement. He blundered, and almost got himself caught, when he suddenly became aware he was trapped in the middle of a street with hunting parties at either end. He turned away from the torches on one side only to find himself face-to-face with those at the other.

Being a wolf, he wasted no time dithering. He leaped for the roof of the nearest building, his paws managing some purchase on the frozen thatch. When he reached the ridgepole, he saw the toothed outline of the palisade through the blowing snow. He leaped.

The red glow glaring into his eyes showed his pursuers scrambling over the palisade behind him. He could run on a crust of frozen snow. They couldn't, but floundered and sank to their knees. He was gone.

He tried in vain to find the gateway to his passage over the river. He hurried along near the shoreline, but he found the gate closed, the strange green bushes encased in ice, the berries frozen dark pebbles among the branches.

Moving with the wolf's bicycling gait designed to cover distances on the hunt, he followed the riverbank a long way, but could find no ford. At length, he stopped at a spot where the stream narrowed between high banks.

The wind was blowing hard again, but the snow was ending. The flakes were fine, powdery, as they had been at the beginning and, high above, every so often the fast-flying clouds parted, showing glimpses of a star-filled night sky.

The ice along both shores was growing thicker. He committed himself to the river and found he had not a long swim or a very bad one. He shook himself dry on the other shore.

Guilt tugged at the edges of his mind as, for the first time, he thought about the Roman merchant. He stood, silent, as his brothers of the mountain began to sing. They were on the hunt now that the storm was ending, and Decius was injured and defenseless. The man might not interest them, but the two horses would and, in the process of taking them down, the pack would make short work of him.

The wolf stretched himself out and began to run.

IX

WHEN THE GRAY ARRIVED AT THE HUT, THE
snow outside was still falling thickly. When he rose to
his feet a man, he found himself freezing cold. Shivering,
he pulled on his tunic. The makeshift hut was dark. The fire had
burned down to coals. He added some kindling, then a few blackened
but not completely burned timbers he'd picked up outside in the
weeds. The fire flared, lighting the hut, and he saw that the spot
where he'd bedded Decius down was empty.

Maeniel hunkered down next to the fire for warmth. Not yet
human enough to swear, he was beginning to understand why humans seemed addicted to this curious custom.

He rose to his feet, ducked his head to keep from cracking his
skull against the roof, and peered through the door.

Nothing, only darkness and pale clouds of blowing snow. Over in
the corner of the hut where he'd stabled the two horses and the mule,
one of the animals stamped and whickered softly. He looked; the
mule moved. The bridle fastened him to the manger where they'd
been eating. He backed powerfully, testing the strength of the tether,
his eyes rolling.

Maeniel moved toward the door. *They are out there,* he thought.
He stripped off his clothing, ran into the darkness, and changed.

He found himself no longer blind. The odor was strong and coming from the open fields. He ran toward the faint sniffing sounds they
made. He saw their eyes first, glowing in the dark, casting back the dim

firelight from the hut. Then the slinking lethal gray shapes. They were investigating something on the ground. Probably Decius.

The wolf wondered if the man was worth worrying about. There was a good chance he was already dead. But he also knew, once having appointed himself Decius' protector, he felt an obligation to continue in that role. *Such is my mind,* he thought, *and how am I different from the cur under the wagon?*

A fragment of memory came to him. Memory or only a dream? They were the savage hunters of the dark tundra. Sometimes, when the winter seemed without end and hunger was not a titillation or pleasant encouragement to hunt and dine, but a savage agony lodged in the gut, an obsessive greed, these cruel lords of the chase turned on each other.

So it was when the wolves encountered the small, doomed band of women and children fleeing through the frozen night. There were only four shes and three boys not yet old enough to hunt. From the smells rising from the fire pits behind them, he was sure the meat cut from the bones of their men roasted in the cooking pits of another band.

These few were the only survivors fleet enough to escape the attack. The wolves spread out behind them in a semicircle, ready to trap their prey. Even though only shes and children, the wolves still feared them and waited until they took shelter in the shadow of a fallen spruce in the hollow between the trunk and the ground, kept clear of snow by the branches of the fallen tree. The humans dared light no fire for fear of pursuit, but lay together in the darkness, trying to keep warm.

In that, the night was against them all. The worst blizzard of the season swept down from the glacier. Even the strongest felt the bite of cold. Some like the musk ox formed a circle to block the wind and protect the females and young in the center. Deer, even the giant ones, died frozen where they stood, as did horses and giant elk and caribou. The old and the very young perished in the freezing darkness.

Even the well-protected wolves knew that to stay in the open was to die. So they slowly drifted into the shelter with the humans. The wolves bared their teeth at first, but the human she who led the escape spoke the command for stillness.

The male wolves were uncomfortable attacking anything so saturated with the female scent as these humans were. To the she-wolves, the children reeked of the den, warm milk, and soft skin.

In the darkness, a child began to cry. Its mother put it to the breast. This was something both wolves and humans understood. The heavy wolf pelts kept off the cold as well as fire would have, and the humans found the touch of the living consolation in a world of icy death. For here, the beast was kinder than kin.

When they awoke at dawn, the woman—or perhaps she-being, not quite human yet—knew that something new had happened. Something new had entered the world. Men might have ruined it. Men often ruin things by trying to find out too much about them, or worse, by distrusting an unusual event. But acceptance is woman's lot and so she accepted the wolves that surrounded her as she trekked off over the snow followed by the others, animal and human.

In a short time she found, as she had known she would, a small herd of elk trapped by the deep snow near a riverbank. They all ate well that night. The new band of wolves and women traveled together for a long time. And the wolves remained wolves, but were always welcomed at the fires of the women.

Then the memory trailed away as he approached his comrades. The tallest and largest of the pack eased toward him, walking slowly, stiff-legged in the blowing snow.

Maeniel approached Decius' body. Yes, he was warm, still living and, what was more horrific, he was conscious, eyes staring up in terror at the encircling wolves. Maeniel positioned himself next to Decius and snarled into the other pack leader's face.

The others, including the leader, looked undecided. Was the half-frozen rag of human flesh lying in the snow-covered ruts of the field worth the trouble? Worth chancing getting wounded if the big stranger really decided to put up a fight for what he obviously considered his prey?

Maeniel advanced a few steps. The others drew back, almost disappearing into the swirling white.

Maeniel crouched, lowering his head and hindquarters. Surely an attack from behind was imminent, but he found he wasn't the other pack's objective.

The animals he'd left stabled in the hut screamed. A split second later, the pack leaped toward him, closing in.

One chance. Maniel turned human.

But it was perhaps Decius who saved the day. He let out the most horrible scream the gray wolf had ever heard in his life.

The terrified wolves exploded, running in every direction.

Maeniel snatched up Decius, threw him over his shoulder, and bolted for the hut. As he reached the doorway, he was pushed aside as Decius' mare crashed into him, knocked him sprawling, and took part of the wattle and daub wall with her. One wolf was on her back; another hung from her throat. She jerked, twisting to one side. The wolf on her back lost his footing and fell, thrashing into a snowdrift. Then she reared, bucking, sunfishing, and the one clinging to her throat fell free, leaving a line of bleeding gashes on her neck.

She made it, Maeniel thought. *Now I'll have to fight all of them. Good, very good chance they'll get us before dawn.* Leaving the still-screaming Decius struggling in the snow, he dashed into the hut and snatched up the sword, then ran outside again.

The mare stood at bay, facing the wolf pack. In one bound, he leaped to her side and drove the sword in, just where the neck joins the head. She died instantly, blood fountaining from her throat. Then he turned, snatched up Decius, and dove into the hut.

It took him a few moments to block the door, then build up the fire. He was shivering violently again as he donned the tunic.

Decius sat, teeth chattering, extremities blue, crouched near the mule and the remaining horse at the far wall. His hair was standing on end. Maeniel had never seen a human with his hair standing on end. He knew, in theory, they were able to manipulate their follicles in the same way as cats or dogs, but he'd never seen it happen.

Outside they both could hear the snarls, growls, and wet slurps as the pack began to feed on the dead horse.

"Eeeee!" Decius screamed. "What are you going to do? Eat me, too? Eeeee!" he wailed again.

"No," Maeniel snarled, sounding very much like his confreres outside. "We don't eat each other. We leave that to you."

Decius blinked at him, not understanding the statement.

"I killed the horse to save both our lives," Maeniel said.

"You're one of them." Decius' teeth were chattering so hard, Maeniel had trouble understanding him.

"No," Maeniel said, almost dropping with exhaustion. "I'm no more one of them than you are." He was surprised to realize he was telling the truth and found tears were running down his cheeks. Found himself grieving deeply, in sorrow over something lost that he could only barely comprehend and never explain.

His tears as much as anything seemed to calm Decius. He could not believe that whatever Maeniel was, he could seem to suffer so much pain and then commit an act of cruelty.

They shared the remaining food and wine. The heat of the fire inside the shed melted the snow and ice on the walls outside, but it refroze quickly, forming an insulating covering for the hut. In time, between the fire and the snow buildup, it began to be almost cozy.

Maeniel didn't ask Decius what happened. The Roman seemed to be a bit fuzzy in the mind and that was very much all right with Maeniel. He decided he would probably need him to get across the river tomorrow and gain admittance into the oppidum where Imona was imprisoned.

He was still determined to rescue her. He believed she had not understood him. He had to get in again and make her listen to reason. All male creatures believe they have a corner on reason. Maeniel was no exception. He had no idea what the inhabitants of this particular settlement intended to do with her, but knowing humans as he did, he couldn't believe their intentions were good.

In the meantime, he had to keep this silly Roman alive and, hopefully, sane enough to help him reach his objective.

Maeniel thanked the universal powers that the wine seemed to have calmed Decius. He huddled in the straw, covered by his mantle, very near the fire, while his extremities returned to their proper pinkish color and, for a time, the pain of recovery from frostbite distracted him from the sounds feeding wolves made.

He asked Maeniel, "In the morning, will they still be there?"

"No."

"You're sure? Do you know them that well?"

Maeniel was doing his best to knock a small hole in one of the wattle and daub walls to keep track of what was actually going on outside. He turned and gave Decius one of his long, slow looks. "No, in answer to your question. They are not friends of mine any more than the brigands were, but I know the habits of wolves well."

"This I can believe," Decius murmured.

"Yes, do so. I am an authority. This pack was driven down from the mountains by the blizzard. Likely they had not fed in several days, otherwise they would not have risked coming so close to human dwellings or anywhere else a fire burned."

Finally, with the help of a sharp stick, he was able to drive through the ice-crusted wall and create a small opening. He peered out. Shadowy gray shapes still lingered near the scrappy horse carcass, and the snow was dying down. Indeed, only a few small flakes still fell. Above, the moon rose among ragged high-flying clouds and, from time to time, the glow of a few stars could be seen.

"No, the snowstorm is past. When they are full fed near dawn, they will leave and probably not return."

Decius let out a deep sigh and then began to snore. Maeniel curled up on the other side of the fire. The hut was comfortably warm now. The surviving horse and mule slumbered in the corner, standing over the manger. Maeniel watched the smoke from the fire rise to the steeply pitched roof, seek the highest spot where the roof was joined to the only surviving wall, then curl and eddy, looking almost liquid before it escaped into the air outside.

Yes, once we were welcomed at their fires. He remembered the face of the woman by whose side the ancient one had rested under the tree. Her eyes had been open and looked into his. The wolf then had seen a heroic vision in them. True, her brows were not as high as these humans' now were, but he had seen in her face the vision of what a world directed by intelligence might be. That and the knowledge they were both allies, warm living things, flesh and blood, feeling hunger and love. And outside, in the bitter icy night, the dark, eternal cold of a lifeless wasteland reached out its claws to take them and lock their aspiring souls in everlasting darkness. In entering a compact to defeat it, they would both achieve the highest of victories. The ancient wolf had understood and now, so did he. He slept wolflike, lightly, waking when the mountain pack circled the lean-to just before dawn, then headed back to their dens near the tree line.

THEY SET OUT WELL AFTER DAYBREAK. DECIUS TORE through his packs and found some clothing for Maeniel, a clean tunic and some trousers, and leggings for both of them. Decius had boots, but Maeniel made do with socks and sandals. He was tolerably comfortable since the sun was up and the temperature was rising.

Decius repacked the baggage and saddled the horse and mule. He didn't mention anything that had happened last night. Once or twice he said he felt dizzy, and was sure the blow to the head had addled his wits.

Maeniel did not contradict him. When they left the hut, neither man looked over to the drift where the horse's head, hooves, and a few tumbled bones lay.

Decius was mounted on the brigand's scrawny gelding. Maeniel followed on foot, leading the mule.

The sun was high in the sky when they turned off the overgrown road to the path along the river. They reached the ferry landing after a half hour's travel. The boat was on the other side of the river. The two men paused on the landing and waited. Decius avoided looking at Maeniel.

The sun shone in the clear sky. Ice formed in the night was melting, creating a patterlike rainfall in the stark woods. Except for places in shadow, the snow had melted, and the river shone sparkling like a diamond, but the wind was still cold.

Decius shivered a bit at the breeze from the river. He drew back to share the shelter created by the big bodies of the two draft animals. "I can . . . not remember what happened last night, but I know you probably saved my life."

"More than once," Maeniel replied.

"I thought so." He still didn't look at Maeniel. "I'm surprised you didn't go and leave me or at least take the packs. They have valuable things in them."

"Not to me."

"No! Yes! But then, I can believe, after what I didn't see last night, that a few golden trinkets might not impress you. But if not gold, what do you want?"

"I need your help to get across the river and enter that settlement."

"And what do you plan to do then?"

"Steal a woman."

"Oh, no," Decius moaned. "Don't you realize it's as much as both our lives are worth to offend that chieftain over there? Oh, help me, father of all the gods. If Cynewolf doesn't kill me, Fulvia certainly will."

"Who is Fulvia? Stop whining and explain."

"Fulvia is my mistress. I'm one of her freedmen. Oh, sisters of Zeus, I was happier when I was a slave and a bath attendant, before that louse Firminius decided I had a nice ass." He gestured at the river. "Do you think I'd come to this godforsaken, frozen, muddy ditch of my own free will? Do you realize how much wine these turd holes drink?"

"Probably not as much as the Romans." Maeniel was exasperated.

"Well . . . maybe not . . . Oh, in Isis' name, what does it matter? It's enough to line the Basilian family and Fulvia's pockets with gold, not to mention the commission I will get and my continued freedom."

"But you're free now!" Maeniel uttered the words through his teeth.

Decius' laugh was hollow. "Oh, yes, probably in law and in theory! I can't imagine Fulvia or Firminius paying attention to any known law. No, depend upon it: if I don't maintain Fulvia's monopoly with these ghastly Gauls and please that big, hairy chieftain across the river, they'll recoup part of their losses by selling me at auction. I've seen her do it before to other men unfortunate enough to blunder at the wrong time. Please, please, I beg you, don't drag me into the kind of trouble flouting this chieftain's hospitality will cause me."

Maeniel uttered a snarl that set Decius' knees to shaking.

"I'm beginning to believe all the things I didn't see last night are true." But when Decius looked around, he found himself alone. "Maybe he's gone," he muttered.

He was just beginning to feel relieved when a large gray wolf trotted out of the forest and took his place at Decius' knee. "No," Decius whispered. "He's not gone."

Across the river the ferry departed the opposite shore. A man driving a small flock of sheep, perhaps eight or ten, joined Decius at the landing. He was followed by a lady on a fine strawberry gelding and accompanied by two footmen.

The sheep didn't like the gray wolf at all. They huddled into a ball around the shepherd.

The lady dismounted and took up her position next to Decius. She was obviously of noble birth; a glance at her jewels made this clear. Add to them the fine carriage of her horse and the two well-armed warriors who followed her, and it was obvious she was no ordinary person.

She wore a heavy cloak with the hood back. She was magnificently beautiful, but it was plain she was no longer in her first youth. Her hair, dressed with gold chains and coiled in braids at each ear, was threaded with gray. Fine lines could be seen in her cheeks and there were crow's feet around her eyes.

She ignored Decius and stared off pensively into the middle distance, watching the ferry making its laborious way toward them. One hand held the cloak at the neck, the other hung at her side.

The wolf poked his nose into her hand. *Ahhh,* the wolf thought, *sweet, clean, perfumed flesh. Woman flesh. Woman smell. Woman, woman, woman softness. Ahhh.*

She felt the nose in the palm of her hand and looked down. "Oh, my, what a magnificent animal. Is he yours?" she asked Decius. She offered her hand to the wolf. He sniffed the soft fingers enthusiastically; one doesn't want to give up one's dignity completely, but he waved his big, plumed tail gently.

Then she stroked his head and scratched properly behind the ears. The wolf's mouth opened and he gave her a big, happy, doggy grin. "So beautiful, so well behaved," she told Decius. "You're lucky to own so fine an animal."

The wolf turned his head and gave Decius a more ironic version of the same canine smile.

Decius got control of his throat and answered, "Why, yes, my lady, he—" Decius' voice squeaked involuntarily and he was forced to clear his throat. "He's been no end of help to me on my journey."

"Yes, well, maybe, but the sheep are afraid of him," the shepherd commented.

The lady bestowed a charming smile on the shepherd. "I'm sure they have no reason to worry with a strong man like you to look after them."

The shepherd looked bludgeoned. Decius sighed.

She scratched the wolf behind the ears again. To Decius' jaundiced eye, his companion gave every appearance of ecstatic delight. "Oh, you're a fine fellow. I'm sure when we reach my brother's stronghold across the river I can find you a nice, big, meaty bone."

"Your brother!" Decius exclaimed. "Then you must be the Lady Enid."

"I am," the lady replied.

"How delightful to meet you," Decius gushed. "I'm here to bring your brother greetings from the Lady Fulvia and the Basilian family. Greetings, salutations, and presents from his Roman friends."

"How very kind of you," Enid purred. She responded well to the proffer of a gold bracelet, offered with respect when they reached the other side of the river.

Thus it was that the wolf found himself under the table in the chieftain's great hall, occupied with the promised meaty bone, while Decius flattered and bribed the man before his own hearth.

Things such as two exquisite wine pitchers in silver and bronze with animal head finials on the handles and lids. A service for six, wine cups, a platter for cakes, cups embossed with nude men and maidens, a tray embossed with the same men depriving the maidens of their right to be called maidens.

"Ooh, how naughty," Enid snickered.

"How valuable?" the chieftain muttered as he turned and weighed them in his hands.

"They are pure and heavy silver," Decius said.

Cynewolf dug his thumb into the bottom of the tray and found it unyielding. "Not really. Pure silver is very soft."

"Well," Decius fluttered, "some baser metal has to be mixed with the precious one in order to render it useful at all. Perhaps you will be better satisfied with these." He presented him with a dozen golden torques.

The chieftain bent one and grunted, apparently satisfied with its flexibility.

"To be sure," Decius said in an oily voice, "we will expect the same—or even perhaps a larger—order for wine this year."

Two other men sat at the table with the chieftain. One wore Roman dress and even a toga—an affectation for him, really, as he was not a Roman citizen. The wolf didn't know this, but the chieftain and the rich and successful farmer seated on the other side did.

Under the table, the wolf examined the bone from top to bottom. All of the meat was gone, completely stripped off by the canine fangs and the shearing rear molars. There always is a risk to bone cracking and this was a large one, but the wolf gave the equivalent of a mental shrug and bit down.

Crack! The sound echoed loudly in the silent room. All of the men in the room started, as did the only woman, Enid.

Decius shivered. He didn't know quite why. The hall, round after the ancient custom, was covered with a high, cone-shaped roof. The hearth, also after ancient custom, was black and dead. The only light was supplied by hazy daylight streaming in from the smoke hole at the apex of the roof. A still-higher cone, which prevented rain and snow from entering, protected the smoke hole, so the light that did enter was rather indirect and dim. A large round table, also after ancient custom, surrounded the hearth.

The chieftain pushed the gold aside. "We can't talk business today. It's unlucky."

Decius cleared his throat. "Tomorrow then."

Mir entered. He was dressed in a long, dark cloak that covered his body and hooded his head. None of the three men sitting at the table would look him directly in the face. He walked quietly to the table and sat down beside the rest.

From the other side of the room, Decius and the wolf stared at him across the dead hearth. The bone cracked again as the wolf cleaned out the marrow.

"Tomorrow," the man beside the chieftain said.

"Tomorrow," the man in the toga said.

"This is not an auspicious day," Mir contributed.

Decius found, for some unguessable reason, his mouth was dry.

"Enid," Mir said. "Go and make sure she bathes and eats the porridge."

The look of sweet amiability faded from Enid's face and she looked pinched and drawn. She had been examining one of the silver cups in a desultory fashion. Suddenly, she banged it down on the table and directed a look of fury at Mir.

He met her stare without flinching. She turned away first.

For a second, the wolf thought she looked old. Then she rose and, without a word, exited the hall.

Decius shivered again and remembered he had not seen a single fire in the entire encampment despite the cold. He felt as if something old and dark had entered the room and sat coiled, waiting like a serpent in the shadows.

Under the table, the wolf whined softly, almost inaudibly, and Decius knew his peculiar friend felt it, too.

"It's very close to evening," the chieftain said to Decius. "Go to the rooms we have given you. Light no fire. It is forbidden. Bar your door and don't come out until morning."

"Ye-ye-yes," Decius stammered. He rose. There was bread, cheese, and a flagon of wine on the table. He took them with him. "I'm leaving . . . I'm leaving. I'm leaving now." And then he was gone.

The wolf lay crouched, silent now, the bone forgotten, his belly pressed close to the floor. He regretted he hadn't come sooner and that he had bothered with that miserable Decius. He regretted he hadn't been able to persuade her to leave with him last night.

What! Had the storm frightened her? He didn't know. What was happening all around him? He didn't comprehend human purposes and their strange and sometimes contradictory ends. He only knew he distrusted them—distrusted them to the bottom of his heart and the marrow of his wolf bones.

"When?" the chieftain asked Mir. He didn't look at him.

"At sunset, between the day and the night. When it is neither day nor night, in a place neither dry not wet, neither rock nor soil. Then . . ." Mir glanced up at the smoke hole. The hazy light was fading.

The wolf eased back out of the hall and into the muddy street. The sun had fallen below the palisade wall and, because of the lack of torches or even candles, everything around him was in deep shadow.

Where was Imona? This time he realized he couldn't find her. Last night the wind had been blowing, sweeping away the fetid smell of the muddy streets strewn with kitchen garbage or the rank out-house effluvia that clogged his nostrils, a smell that always reigned wherever any large group of humans congregated. Among this maze of human sign, she was as much lost to him as when Mir had taken her away from her farm in the valley.

Then the wolf had to dodge to avoid being stepped on because suddenly the streets were filled with people. They were all dressed as Mir had been in the hall, wrapped in black cloaks, hooded and cowled. They didn't look at each other and, after a few moments, the wolf realized why: some of the gliding shapes weren't really there, but only shadows that passed through walls without any discernable difficulty.

Near him, a woman was sick or very afraid because the heat her body gave off was visible to him. The woman moaned softly, "The dead. The dead are here."

The wolf's hackles rose as another of the hooded figures passed next to him, radiating a thick, stinking, deadly cold. He was at the bottom of an icy river and the fish were stripping the flesh from his bones. No mind was left. The raw fear of death dissolved all reason. Only a lonely vortex of terror, bitter rage, and despair remained.

Imona, the wolf thought. His thought was an image, a woman's face smiling into his.

The crowd moved in the direction of the gate. The wolf followed. When he reached it and passed through with the rest, he saw Imona.

She stood not far from the open portals, Mir on one side, Enid on the other. She alone of all the company wore a white gown.

The wolf threaded his way among the legs of the throng, trying to get close to her, but he was too slow. Before he could get near to her, she, Mir, and Enid began walking, attended by a knot of men, prosperous men of middle age, their cloaks of heavier material than Mir's, their faces closed. The wolf caught the scent of hostility, a stench between hostility and fear.

It forced him back. Something in black. Something whose draperies the wind could not move. It stank and had no more mind than the first he'd sensed. It gibbered brainlessly. Hating, hating, raging at the yawning abyss trying to claim it. Clawing with fleshless fingers at anything it touched, even itself.

The breeze blew and the caped and hooded humans clutched at their clothing, holding it down against the wind. The blast was icy. Despite sun in the daytime, the night would be cold. The snow of last night had melted and the path Mir and Imona took led them around the walls toward the back of the stronghold.

The grass under their feet was brown and sere. Mounds of even darker, withered clover dotted the sward. As the procession reached the back of the hilltop stronghold, they turned downhill.

The wolf was closer now and he could see the gown Imona wore wasn't truly white, but rather woven of sheep's wool left its natural color, a mixture of white and gray, here and there streaked with rust contributed by wild mountain ewes.

The sun was very close to the horizon now and the long, red slanted rays poured a last fire-gold light into the scrubby woods at the base of the hill.

Imona wore a torque around her neck, and the incandescent last light burned it to brilliance. Enid's hood was back and the wolf could see her coiled braids. Otherwise, the pale-clad Imona seemed flanked by two black figures, very like the ones who surrounded the wolf.

Imona and her companions entered the forest. The last sunset light was a red haze in the naked forest. The night's storm had swept away the tattered remains of summer. Branches that might have held yet a few scarlet, yellow, and dusky brown leaves a few days ago now lifted bare against the glowing sky. Even the last straggler oaks were nude.

The odd-eyed phalanx crowded Imona and the two attending her past one giant trunk that stood like a pillar of the world. The branches above were decorated by fans of mistletoe, green against the brown of barren wood, covered by sprays of white berries gilded by the sunset.

Except for a few of the giant oaks, the forest was low and scrubby. The trees were small, second-growth types. In places, thick brush almost blocked the path and the group had to push their way through.

Then, abruptly, the path dipped into a hollow, partially filled by a dank pond. To the wolf, the water had a peaty, tannic smell, the tannin partially contributed by the leaves of another huge oak leaning over the pool.

Imona spoke loudly in the silence of the winter-blasted forest. "Here!" She paused, then turned, walked to the edge of the pool, and raised her arms in invocation to the last light.

The sun, its orb on the rim of a hill directly in front of her, shone on her face.

The wolf blinked, but Imona stared steadily into the flaming ball as it slowly sank below the rim of the hill.

A terrible moan rose from the black-clad figures around the wolf, a cry, a sobbing cry from the living and the dead.

Imona's arms fell. The sun was gone, but not the light above the hill. The sky glowed and a clear blue twilight filled the hollow.

Enid proffered a cup to Imona.

The wolf moved up. He was close now, no more than a few feet higher on the sloping bank behind them. It was almost dark. He would challenge anything, living or dead, to find him in the night, in the full dark, under the trees.

His eyes probed the faces around the woman in white. Resolve on some, and sorrow, hope, fear, and awe. A few pulsed with something darker; he marked them. What were they doing?

"No!" she said, pushing it away. "I drank the porridge. That's enough." Then she removed the pins from the shoulders of the dress and it fell at her feet. Her body was pale white in the blue gloom.

The chieftain stepped forward from the shadows behind her.

She removed the torque from her neck and handed it to Mir.

Then the chieftain hit her as hard as he could on the back of the head.

The wolf stood frozen, paralyzed by the swift and, to him, senseless brutality.

Mir produced the curved bronze knife and slit her throat.

In the second that the knife passed through her throat, the wolf saw she was doomed. Before blood flooded the wound, he clearly saw the white tendons and larynx, which held the head up and gave shape to speech, part, then the long, dark hoses, which sent blood to the brain and back, swiped in two. Old though he might be, Mir's stroke was true, and perhaps merciful, though Imona was still moving when her body vanished into the pool at her feet.

Enid turned away, hood up, hiding her face in her cloak.

The chieftain was down on his knees, forehead pressed against the damp earth. The others fell back, the living and the dead, the guilty and the innocent.

Only Mir still stood, his hand shaking now, the bloody sickle sword still clenched in his fist.

The wolf moved down like a piece of the darkness until he stood beside Mir, looking into the tarn.

Enid uncovered her face with a sigh of relief, a relief that didn't last because Imona's face reappeared a few inches below the surface of the water. Enid screamed and covered her face again.

A few bubbles trailed from Imona's lips, drifted up, and broke near a stand of waterweed. Then, her eyes, those gray-green beauties he had looked into so often, opened. They looked into his, just for one second, seemingly in farewell. Then they closed and her face was blotted out by the spreading black cloud of blood from her torn throat.

SINKING DOWN IN THE POOL, IMONA HAD ONE last plaintive thought, *It takes too long to die.* But it didn't, because that thought was her last, and she was swept across the bridge of starlight into the final silence.

I T WASN'T LONG AFTER IMONA'S DEATH THAT THE wolf visited Mir. When he returned from the oppidum the pack accepted him back, but not as leader. The she-wolf—mother of the pack, now heavy with her pregnancy—ran with a survivor of the lowland pack the Romans had wiped out.

This wolf, though battered, was gigantic. One ear was torn and a patch of white fur on his shoulder marked a scar where a Roman legionnaire's gladius had been driven into his body. One of his front fangs was broken. He was nervous, vicious, and quick to take offense. As a result, he was distrusted and feared by the rest of the pack.

He seemed to see all of the yearling males as rivals. In situations the gray would simply have handled with a look of disapproval, White Shoulder lunged and snarled. In more serious encounters, he slashed and bit—bit hard.

The new leader nearly crippled one of the yearling males over a few scraps of hide. The offender limped for a week after being bitten on the upper leg and neck. After that, the yearling males began to desert the pack, drifting away in search of more amiable company.

The bitch was little better among the females. This was a much more serious matter. They were the best and most effective hunters and responsible, collectively, for most of the kills.

They remained virgin for up to four years: lean, powerful killers who could outpace, when necessary, even the ibex and chamois.

They, too, were slowly being alienated and the gray knew some of them would leave, also. He couldn't bring himself to care. He could easily have challenged White Shoulder. Once, he would have, but even his pack's destruction couldn't seem to move him now.

One night he decided to visit Mir and kill him.

Winter had come to the heights, and the high forest of fir and spruce was choked now with several feet of snow. Game was growing scarce. The day before, the pack had taken a half dozen hare, a few marmots, and several nests of field mice dug from beneath the snow. Not enough, and the wolves knew it.

At this rate, they would starve. Only the gray had an inkling of the real problem: the Romans. It took a lot to feed the three hundred men Caesar had lodged there permanently. There was plenty of bread wheat in the commissary, but meat was in short supply.

The soldiers held hunts. They were not interested in fair play, but efficiency. They constructed an arrangement shaped like a large funnel and stationed pikemen and archers at the lower, narrow end.

The legionnaires then took their positions as beaters, driving game toward the narrow end where their executioners awaited them.

The wolf had watched while hidden in a cover of thick blackberry canes.

They killed, laughing and competing with each other for every creature that came through the opening of the makeshift corral.

Nothing was too small and, certainly, not too large. They stamped to death the smallest mice and drowned dormice in a pail of water. They were a delicacy intended for the officers. The slaughter of the deer was sickening because they came through so quickly. They couldn't all be killed cleanly.

The white snow became a trampled mass of red where the cripples lay screaming or trying to run, intestines dragging until they were felled with an ax or club. The fawns were ignored until last because they would not leave their mothers, not even when the does lay stiffening in the bloody snow.

The tender young animals were another delicacy intended for the commander's table. They were hung up by the heels while yet living and their throats cut to drain away blood from the delicate meat.

At some time in the long afternoon while he watched, it had begun to snow again and the small icy flakes began their work of purification on the killing ground, slowly turning the red-stained snow to white. The animals were all dead and the only sound that remained was the cursing and complaining of the butchers as they gutted and skinned their harvest.

Shuddering, the wolf crept away. He returned to the place where Imona's family had their home. The valley and the forest around it were a white waste.

The wolf eased into the cave where the two of them had enjoyed their summer's lovemaking. He slept. He woke long enough to drink and relieve himself, then went back to sleep.

Yes, indeed. They were definitely the lords of creation. He didn't think too much about what he'd seen. He decided he didn't want to.

On the third day, he came down, ready to rejoin the pack. He circled the area where the house once stood. The old smell of charred wood blotted out other scents. He went to the linden tree. Enough traces remained for him to tell that Leon's bones still lay tangled with the ruined cloth of Imona's loom. The loom poles themselves had been carved cedar. They lent their strange, clean odor to what was now a grave. Then he rejoined the pack.

That evening White Shoulder rose from his bed in the snow, shook himself, and headed for the valley. The rest followed. When Maeniel saw the direction of their travel, he paused and laid his ears back.

His thoughts weren't the thoughts of a wolf. He already knew how dangerous humans were.

He could have settled back in the snow and returned to sleep. Or simply gone somewhere else and hunted. All members, subject to their fear of hunting or surviving alone, were free agents. No one gives orders to a wolf.

So the wolf's ears flicked back, then forward. A few other members of the pack drifted past. They looked deceptively and equally bored. No one watching them would have believed they might be dangerous.

The wolf flicked his ears again, then shook himself to clear the last of the snow from his coat, gave the equivalent of a mental shrug, and followed the rest.

A few hours later, the wolves rested together in the snow under a canopy of tall conifers clothing the shallow slopes surrounding the fortress.

Had it not been winter and the ground covered by a thin skin of snow, the wolves would have been visible to the sentries walking the platforms along the palisaded walls. As it was, the white and gray snow camouflaged them almost perfectly.

The big gray chewed ice out of his soft belly fur and decided the Romans weren't stupid. They'd felled all the trees closest to the fortress to build the walls and the stout dwellings inside. This made ambush practically impossible. The soldiers protected anyone entering or leaving the fortress.

So, the wolf thought, *why are we watching it?* Then he turned 'round and 'round, draped the brush of his tail over his nose, and went to sleep.

He awoke a few hours later because White Shoulder had risen and was stealthily following a small party of soldiers leaving the fortress in a wagon. The weather was growing worse. Even though it was rather late in the morning, the sky grew darker, not lighter, and a few vagrant, tiny flakes drifted down from above. One burned the tip of the wolf's nose with an icy sting, and he could hear the soft crunch as his paws pushed into the snow, kept loose and fresh by the deepening cold. All the trees left standing near the fortress were tall, longtrunked silver firs, carrying their lowest branches very high up. The tops were caught in the misty cloud mass rolling through the pass.

The wolves followed the wagon, moving near the trail but not on it. The wagon passed a bend in the road and turned downward. The trees crowded in closer. They were out of sight of the fortress and the undergrowth grew thicker.

The wolves moved in closer. They did nothing menacing, but if they took advantage of the cover, they could not be seen and were able to travel alongside the cart.

The snow grew thicker; fine, almost infinitesimal flakes seemed almost a mist in the air.

Prey! The gray had been a leader too long not to want to study whatever he hunted. He increased his pace, staying just out of sight of the cart. He was a bit afraid of being seen, but as he drew closer, he realized there was nothing to fear from the men.

The four legionnaires sat in the back, trying to play at knucklebones, no easy task in the swaying cart, and refreshing themselves liberally, if surreptitiously, from several clay flasks and a heavy wineskin they carried with them. Occasionally they broke off long enough to curse the old soldier driving a cart.

He was a centurion, so called because he was the commander of a hundred men. They were the backbone of the Roman army. Most were hard enough to break rocks with their heads, but not this man.

The legionnaires he ostensibly commanded did as they pleased now. Once, he'd been a magnificent warrior, but now he was an old man and the younger soldiers, out of sight of the camp, treated him rather like they did the horses drawing the cart. They didn't dare do this in the camp. Too many of the other noncoms remembered Drusus' prime and would have savagely punished any insolence.

Drusus drove and privately thought the men with him today were fools. He himself was uneasy and was sure they were being shadowed. By what, he couldn't be sure, but he'd seen furtive movements from the corners of his eyes.

Hirax, a German from the allied tribes, was pretty much the ringleader among these men when any mischief was in the offing, and obviously today he had decided to use a short trip after firewood as an excuse to get stinking drunk. The other three—Marcus, Statilius, and Scorpus—would likely follow blindly because they hadn't one good brain between them. Once impaired by drink, the average bush was smarter.

Drusus checked his sword. This much remained of an honored warrior. He always kept it sharp and clean.

Another bend in the road passed and Drusus pulled the cart to a stop at the edge of a clearing. Here, during good weather, a large party of men had felled a dozen trees and cut them into sections ready to be loaded on carts and taken to the fortress.

Drusus shivered. The soldiers stood up, lowered the tailgate, got down, and started toward the house-sized pile of logs.

"Build a fire," Drusus said.

They ignored him.

"You sons of whores! I told you to build a fire. Do it and do it now! If you don't—" His sword cleared its sheath. "—I won't bother with a tribunal. I'll kill the four of you myself." His eyes locked with his men's. Theirs strayed away first.

The clearing was filled with deadfalls under its thin skin of snow. It took only a few moments to build a fair-sized fire near the cart. Then the soldiers attacked the woodpile. Each log had to be snaked from the top of the pile, then placed on crib supports and sawed into lengths small enough to be loaded into the wagon.

Drusus climbed back up and sat down on the driver's perch. He knew what was shadowing them now and felt better. One of the wolves had entered the clearing and left tracks in the snow—big tracks. He'd had them follow him before and knew they probably wouldn't attack unless they saw an opening that favored them . . . greatly favored them.

He'd met them on battlefields as a young man. The Romans had their own medical units, but they didn't extend this courtesy to their enemies.

Sometimes the screams from the battlefield lasted almost all night. Horses fell, too, and it was sometimes very difficult to tell if the cries of agony were animal or human.

Drusus wore a heavy mantle, but not the red, uniform cloak of the Roman officer. His was a heavy brown wool mantle edged with embroidered green willow leaves that he'd bought from a Gallic woman a few years ago. It was very warm. He wrapped it around himself more tightly.

His mind kept presenting him with images he'd seen as a young man. He thought then that he would grow harder with age, but he hadn't. Instead, the horrors he'd experienced over the years—and he had a large collection by now—seemed to disturb him more profoundly than they had in his youth.

He sighed and turned his mind away from the past. His service would be over in a few months, finally and forever. He'd re-enlisted twice and was due a large sum in pay and bonus money. He'd already used some of his gains to buy a small farm in the hills near Terracina.

There were ten acres in vines and olive trees. Enough to give him a good living if he remained frugal. His cousin, Festus, would do the actual work of cultivating and harvesting the trees and vines. Festus and his sons would be more than willing to do this in return for being made his heirs.

Once, Drusus had had a woman, but she and her two children— he was none too sure they were both his—had died while Caesar was campaigning in Britain. He had thought he would learn to stop regretting her as time passed, but he found this wasn't so. As he aged, he wished more and more for her company. She'd been shrewish, but funny and oddly solicitous about his health and comfort. He missed her constant joking and sharp remarks about his fellow soldiers.

And oddly enough, he missed the child, a little girl, the one he'd been pretty sure wasn't his. She was the one he missed most. Like her mother, she was always chattering and laughing. She'd been fluent in gobbledygook even before she knew how to form words.

The little boy had been less interesting: quiet, persistent, hard-working even as a very young child. He was olive skinned with the thick, curly hair of a true Latin and he showed signs of being stocky and muscular, as his father was.

But since they were gone, the only family that remained to him was Festus and his two sons. He didn't care much about the farm now, but he did want to sit in the sun on his own hillside and look down at the lapis and emerald sea swirling around the rocks. The foam was white, white as the snow drifting down . . .

Drusus was suddenly jerked fully awake by the realization that the sound of sawing had stopped. He opened his eyes and saw rotund little Scorpus moving away toward the trees.

"Where do you think you're going?" he snarled.

Hirax leaned on the saw. "He has to take a dump and pee."

"Well, go behind a tree. Don't stray off. There are wolves about."

"Wolves." Hirax snorted. "Are they a good reason for letting him stink us all out with his gas and turds? Besides, I don't see any wolves."

"No, and you won't. Not until they want you to, and then it will be too late."

Scorpus studied the centurion and Hirax with a rather foggy-eyed stare. His nose was large and red and he rubbed it vigorously with one hand, making it look still larger and redder.

Hirax watched Drusus narrowly. The old man's eyes closed and his chin dipped toward his chest. "Worn out old fart," Hirax said under his breath. "Go where you want to, Scorpus."

Scorpus sniffed and started walking toward a denuded group of oaks on the edge of the clearing. He didn't really want to relieve himself. He had another flask hidden in his mantle and was looking for a quiet place to finish it: someplace where the rest wouldn't see him and demand their share.

Holly and large bunches of mistletoe grew among the oaks. The forest was like a big room in some unearthly house. The mist was so low, the treetops were lost in it. The light was bright, a diffuse glow reflected from the snowy surface of the ground and the clumps of white covering bare limbs and the few evergreens that remained.

The holly leaves and red berries glowed against the omnipresent paleness. The mistletoe branches nesting higher with their delicate green boughs and gray-white berries seemed ghosts of summer fruitfulness caught in the tracery of small, slender trees.

To Scorpus, they were an added inconvenience. They grew so close together, it was difficult for him to push his way past them. The sharp spines on the holly leaves drew the occasional drop of blood from his arms and hands. It was as if they were trying almost consciously to bar his way. But, at length, he got through them.

A few yards ahead, a finger of the mountain stretched out, just a jumbled pile of gray rocks, wet with the fine snow and crowned with a tangle of white birches, their paper-white bark only a little darker than the almost glowing snow around them. There were several sheltered spots where he could sit and finish his wine without being interrupted.

Of course, the wolves had seen him. They watched from their holly coverts as he left the rest and struggled through the trees. To them, an animal that quit the protection of the herd must be sick or seriously disabled in some way.

Scorpus hadn't an inkling that White Shoulder was only a few feet behind. Maeniel flanked White Shoulder on the right, the mother of the pack on his left.

Maeniel still had misgivings. Was this the sort of hunting White Shoulder envisioned? And, if so, did the new pack leader understand the possible consequences of killing a man? The rest of the pack apparently felt the same because they dropped well back of the three leaders.

Scorpus paused.

So did the wolves. White Shoulder drew his lips back from his teeth in a silent snarl. The mother of the pack bumped White Shoulder as if urging him forward, but he didn't respond, only stood frozen with a look of murderous ferocity on his face.

Scorpus lifted his tunic and with a shiver—the air reaching his bare skin was cold—took his penis in hand and began to pee. The stream arching away from him created a yellow-rimmed hole in the snow.

You didn't kill them, Maeniel remembered. *Oh no, you didn't kill them, not even if they took your kill. After all, you could always kill again. But if your skin formed a parka, the fur surrounding a man's face to keep off the chill, you were not going to be doing any killing then.*

When they came to rob you, the first thing their women did was make a fire out of whatever was available. Then the whole band advanced with flaming brands in one hand and fire-hardened spears in the other. Occasionally, a wolf pack would stand its ground. It always lost. It was a disaster for a winter pack if its strongest members ended by coughing out their lives when their lungs were pierced by those wooden javelins or dying slowly in agony, infected and unable to eat when they were disembowled.

No, these creatures were not legitimate prey. Standing against them was simply too costly. In victory or defeat, the pack that did faced ruin.

Scorpus finished, shook his organ and tucked it carefully away, then pulled the clay flask from under his mantle and lifted it to his lips.

The she-wolf whined.

Scorpus went ice-cold with fear. He turned, flask still in his hand, and saw the three wolves only a few paces behind him.

White Shoulder lunged toward him. Maeniel dropped back. So did the mother of the pack. She'd given the game away and they both knew it.

Maeniel's shoulder slammed into her, sending the bitch flying head over heels.

Scorpus smashed the clay jug down on White Shoulder's head. In and of itself, it wasn't enough to do permanent damage or even stun a wolf the size of White Shoulder. But when it connected with the wolf's skull, it broke and the wine splashed all over White Shoulder's eyes and nose.

For a few seconds, he was blind and in terrible pain as an involuntary reflex caused him to sniff the acidic wine into his very sensitive nose.

Scorpus ran. He ran as he had when he joined the legions fifteen years ago as a young man. He ran as he didn't think he could still run, like an eighteen-year-old.

Just ahead, he saw a fissure in the broken rock. He thought—no, hoped—it was narrow enough and deep enough so that the wolves couldn't reach him after he squeezed himself in. He didn't scream, almost instinctively knowing it would be a waste of breath.

White Shoulder was down, ineffectively pawing his eyes and nose. The she-wolf slunk back to the rest in terror of what they had almost done.

Maeniel plunged after Scorpus, but the delay had been enough. Scorpus squeezed into the crack sideways as deep as he could get.

Maeniel was right behind him. He drove forward, almost reaching Scorpus' right hand. The man did scream then, but the groping fingers found a stick, a thick heavy branch fallen from the trees above. He transferred it to his right hand and, on the gray wolf's second attack, he got him across the skull with it.

Maeniel staggered back, dizzy. Scorpus pushed himself deep into the fissure and clung to his shelter the way a drowning man clings to a plank.

By then it was clear to Maeniel and the rest of the wolves that Scorpus was not to be dislodged. In fact, from the expression of stark terror on Scorpus' face, it appeared he might not relinquish his cover until sometime in the spring.

Maeniel wasn't disposed to waste any more time with him, not at present.

White Shoulder had shaken off the worst effects of the wine, though from time to time he still whimpered and pawed at his muzzle.

Maeniel melted into the holly and oaks and vanished with the rest. He had to think and by now he was much better at it than most wolves.

He felt they should leave at once and head back for the mountains. With luck, the officers in the Roman garrison might not believe the tale told by that idiot who remained crouching in that crack in the rock, especially if the still-falling snow filled in their tracks. But White Shoulder and his bitch weren't having any, and the gray realized they intended to stay until they killed.

Drusus remained dozing on the high seat of the cart. He hadn't noticed that Scorpus had wandered off. Drusus finally fully awakened when the other three legionnaires began loading lengths of logs into the cart. He yawned and counted his men. "Where's Scorpus?" he snapped to Hirax and Statilius.

The two legionnaires dropped the log they were carrying and looked around. "He said he was going to take a leak," Statilius said.

"Do any of you dimwits know which direction he went in or how far?" the centurion asked.

They didn't know. Even Hirax hadn't noticed where Scorpus had gone.

Alarmed, Drusus climbed down from the wagon seat and threw some more kindling on the fire. He checked his sword to be sure it was loose in the sheath and would draw easily. Then he began circling the clearing, looking for tracks.

At length, he found a few shallow depressions he felt sure were left by Scorpus' feet. The problem was the humidity was low and the snow was so dry it didn't take tracks well. The powdery stuff that was falling quickly filled in any mark made on it.

Drusus briefly considered the footprints. He looked up. The overcast was so low the treetops were hidden in the hazy whiteness. He himself could not see far into the increasing snow fog. He loosened his sword in the sheath again, a nervous gesture.

"I'll go find him," Hirax said in his thick, accented Latin.

"No, no, you won't!" Drusus snapped. "If something out there picked him off, it'll get you, too."

Hirax made an obscene reference to Drusus' ancestry, then accused him of being a coward.

Drusus didn't reply, not at first. The only sign of emotion he showed was that his eyes narrowed slightly, at least in part because he noticed Marcus and Statilius were watching both of them intently. He sensed this was the final assault on his waning authority over the cohort. If he allowed Hirax to get away with this, his men could make his life so miserable he might end it by falling on his sword before the expected bonus and discharge came through. This would certainly happen if he allowed Hirax to draw him into swordplay here and now. He was no match for the younger man and was certain to go down in humiliating defeat.

"Very well." Drusus nodded. "It isn't a test of courage, Hirax, but if you want to make it one, go ahead. Suit yourself." Then he turned away, an expression of complete indifference on his face. "Shape up," he shouted to the two other soldiers. "Get the cart loaded. It's late and I believe this three-times-accursed snow is coming down harder every minute."

Grumbling, the two legionnaires complied.

Drusus ignored their complaints, walked over, and stood near the horses at the front of the cart.

Hirax vanished into the forest.

Drusus remembered again how the blue, deep water turned to emerald as the combers approached the shallows near the coast. The last time he'd been able to visit, he climbed the steep slopes, walking among the trellised grapevines until he reached the abandoned stone farmhouse like the one where he'd been born and brought up. Day or night, winter or summer, the air was cool and clear here. The wine, laid down in a limestone cave near the house, yielded a drinkable beverage in a few months.

He could almost taste and smell it, even now. It reminded him of salt air, sweet marjoram, and the wild oregano and thyme growing on the hillsides.

He'd wrapped himself in his toga and spent the night alone there, his only company the sigh of wind in the stone pines. The silver-clad full moon floated among the long-needled branches as the distant sound of the sea lulled him to sleep.

How and why, in the name of all the forgotten Tuscan gods, did he end up in this miserable frozen forest, freezing his backside off and worrying about wolves?

He mentally cursed Hirax. *Fortuna, send the pushy, barbarian, fatherless offspring of a pig to Hades and let him whine and moan among the unburied ghosts along the Styx.*

Next to him, one of the horses threw up her head, whickered, and stamped a foot. For these horses, short cobby drays trained to behave calmly even in battle where they drew siege engines, such behavior almost amounted to hysteria.

Yes, Drusus thought, *the wolves are on the prowl, but it remains to be seen if the elusive gray predators are dangerous.*

HIRAX FOLLOWED SCORPUS' TRAIL INTO THE thickets of holly and holum oaks, cursing him all the way. "Where did that boneheaded louse go?" he whispered, then shouted. "Scorpus, where are you?" His voice echoed in the snowy silence. It seemed to bounce around directionless among the surrounding trees.

"Scorpus!" he shouted, then added, "You bastard," in a whisper between his teeth. Twice he thought he heard answering cries, but the sounds were too muffled and distant for him to be sure what he heard wasn't his own voice thrown back by the frozen forest around him.

Then he noticed something dark, half-buried in a snowdrift on the windward side of a fallen tree. He turned and walked toward it. Yes, Scorpus' clay flask. He bent down to pick it up. As his fingers closed around the neck of the flask, he tried to straighten up so he could see it in a better light. *How odd,* he thought as he realized there seemed to be a huge weight on his back . . . then he knew or thought nothing more.

MAENIEL WATCHED AS THE REST CLEANED HIRAX'S bones. They were furtive, swift, and uncharacteristically silent. But then they shared the same drift of memories he did and understood as well as he that they were doing something forbidden.

IN THE CLEARING, DRUSUS AND THE TWO REMAIN-ing legionnaires built up the fire. He noticed with some satisfaction that they were becoming more and more nervous about Hirax's failure to appear with the errant Scorpus.

The cart was loaded now with big logs destined to be sawed and chopped into more usable lengths at the fortress.

"Likely they're somewhere arming themselves against the cold," Marcus said.

Statilius glanced up at the sky. If anything, the overcast seemed to have increased. The clouds moved lower; the formerly bright light was growing dimmer. They all knew the short winter day was drawing to an end. It went without saying that none of them wanted to be caught in the forest after dark.

"If one of you wants to go and see if he can find them, you have my permission," Drusus said almost sweetly. He climbed to the top of the box in front of the cart and picked up the reins.

"Are we leaving them, then?" Marcus asked.

"No," Drusus said. "There's a better way to search. Come, we'll use the road."

THE GRAY WOLF SLIPPED AWAY FROM WHERE THE rest were feeding and went back to where Scorpus had taken shelter.

It was snowing more heavily now. He looked at the legionnaire through the veil of small flakes.

Scorpus' body was wedged between the rock, but his head was turned facing the wolf. His eyes were partially open. His cheeks, nose, and neck were scummed with a thin membrane of ice. An expression of mortal terror remained fixed on his face, but the eyes didn't move and neither did any other part of his body.

He is dead, the gray thought.

THE TWO LEGIONNAIRES PEERED AT THEM.
"I don't know," Marcus mumbled.

"Well, go and look. It's only about fifty yards from the road." Drusus sounded completely exasperated.

"No!" Marcus replied. His hands clamped tight on one of the crossbars of the cart where he and Statilius were riding. Insubordination was savagely punished in the Roman army.

"Come on," Statilius said. "I'll go with you."

The two men jumped down from the cart. They were wearing their swords. The forest was silent except for the crunch of dry snow under the two men's feet.

Drusus watched them advance toward the black specks near the trees.

As they drew closer, both men realized they were looking at a flock of ravens resting on the snow, feeding on something. Then, just before the men reached them, the birds took flight with a sudden loud flapping.

Bones lay scattered over the snow, red bones newly cleaned of meat. The bones were tumbled and broken. Neither of the men could tell much about what sort of animal they had come from, but then Statilius saw something that looked like a skull half buried in the snow.

He reached out toward it and at once pulled away his hand. The bone was slick and cold. He drew his sword and turned the thing over with the tip. He found himself looking down at a human skull. One eye socket was empty, but a single blue eye glared up at him from the other. He had a second to reflect that they had certainly found Hirax.

From somewhere not far away, a terrible scream rang out.

THE GRAY WOLF CONSIDERED SCORPUS. EARLIER he'd pitied the man, but if he was dead, well, the wolves were hungry. Scorpus' mortal remains might as well be put to good use— at least good use from a wolf's point of view.

So he jumped up, placed his forepaws on either side of the fissure Scorpus had thrust himself into, set his teeth in the soldier's tunic, and pulled.

Scorpus' body was wedged tightly in its refuge, so he pulled hard, arching his back once, twice. Nothing happened. The wolf growled, about all he could do with his mouth full of cloth, then he yanked hard.

Scorpus blinked and came to life the moment he was pulled free of his sanctuary. He landed in the snow, next to the wolf. He screamed, giving vent to an unearthly cry of despair.

The man the gray had thought dead only a few seconds ago staggered to his feet and began clubbing at the wolf with his almost-frozen hands. The wolf ducked and backed, Scorpus caught him across the top of his head. The wolf yipped.

AT THE SOUND OF THE SCREAM, MARCUS BOLTED, running toward the cart on the road.

The wolves flowed out of the small grove the way a stain spreads through water. They were both silent and deadly.

Marcus was down and dead before he knew what hit him. Statilius already had his sword out. This saved his life . . . for a moment. He drove his sword through White Shoulder's body. The pack leader was busy tearing off Marcus' face, but the bitch got Statilius, fracturing his lower legs. As he fell, his head cracked hard against a stump, splitting open his skull.

On the cart, Drusus had just seen two of his men die in less time than it took to sneeze, but he was an old campaigner and didn't lose his head.

The road was narrow; the cart pointed the wrong way. His life depended on the horses. He raced them forward, away from the killing ground. The narrow road dead-ended at the finger of rock where Scorpus had taken refuge. Drusus' fingers were locked on the reins. He pulled the two cobs to a rearing, strangling halt.

A clearing lay on his right. He swung them into a turn into the clearing and back toward the road. Everything seemed to move with glacial slowness, but Drusus didn't dare push the already terrified animals to any greater speed. One of them might fall and break a leg, not only finishing the horse, but him, too.

The cart swung around. In a few seconds, he could feel from the traction the horses' hooves were getting that they were back on the road. Then the cart tilted as one back wheel went down into a ditch hidden by the snow.

Drusus nearly despaired, but he stood, throwing his weight to the left to counterbalance the right rear wheel. At that same moment, he heard a ghastly screeching. He looked back and saw Scorpus clambering to the top of the cart and crawling over the load of wood toward him. Behind Scorpus, chasing him, was the largest wolf Drusus had ever seen.

Scorpus was a vision of horror, his face and beard caked with ice and other sorts of frozen filth—Scorpus had vomited after he'd been chased into the rocks. His mouth was open, a red orifice in his frozen features. He screamed, howling nonstop as he reached Drusus and began clawing at him.

Drusus jerked his sword clear of the sheath and slammed fist and hilt into Scorpus' face. He felt his own knuckles break, but so did Scorpus' face and he abruptly went silent and tumbled off the cart into the snow-filled road.

The horses' hooves gained the road. Freed of Scorpus' weight, the wheel rolled out of the ditch. Drusus sat hunched over his broken hand in agony as the horses made the best speed they were capable of toward the fortress.

The wolf stood in the blowing snow beside Scorpus' body. He had not really wanted the man to die.

It was snowing harder now. The wolf shook himself to get the accumulating flakes from his fur, then he poked Scorpus with his nose. Yes, he was well and truly dead. The body lay on its back, legs slightly spread, arms thrown out on both sides, white now as the increasing snowfall covered it. White except for the still-seeping blotch of red where the face had been.

The wolf whined deep in his throat, then turned and trotted through the trees where the rest were feeding.

The bitch stood next to White Shoulder. The wolf was not yet dead, but the gray could see he was rapidly dying. His legs scrabbled, making running motions, throwing snow in all directions.

The bitch raised her head and howled. A wolf's howl is always eerie, touching as it does the upper register of audible sound, but this outcry was more uncanny than most, since it carried equal measures of sorrow and pain.

The other wolves paid no attention. They feasted on Marcus and Statilius. As it was, Hirax had been barely an appetizer.

As the gray watched, foam began to appear at White Shoulder's jaw. The foam grew thicker and then red. The wolf knew the sword must have passed through his lungs and, in the same moment, he watched White Shoulder cough out his life.

The words in human speech formed in his brain. *I am no longer simply a wolf.* He didn't ask the next logical question: *If I am not a wolf, what am I?* It was terrifying enough for him to lose his identity. He didn't want to know any more.

White Shoulder died. Blood continued to pool around his jaws for a time, then ceased.

The bitch didn't feed with the rest. She stood silent over White Shoulder's body. An outburst of snarling nearby told Maeniel that some of the other wolves had found Scorpus' body.

The gray was still reeling from his sudden awareness, but he had responsibilities. With White Shoulder gone, he was senior member of the pack and the strongest.

He snapped at the bitch's shoulder, nipping her slightly, breaking the skin. She rounded on him in a burst of fury, giving a snarl of sheer, mindless rage.

But he didn't back down. He simply stood, teeth bared, stiff-legged, glaring at her.

Her eyes were a furnace of white-hot madness, but then, as he watched, he saw the rage die away and sanity return to her gaze. She eased back away from him.

The gray turned and trotted away from the pack's feeding grounds, following the road toward the fortress. When he'd gone what he considered a sufficient distance, he stopped, ears up, alert, waiting, listening.

DRUSUS ARRIVED AT THE FORTRESS, HALF-FROZEN, incoherent, and moaning with the pain in his broken fingers. When he fully regained consciousness, he found himself in the thatched, low-ceilinged building that passed for a hospital at the garrison. He was surrounded by his friends, professional noncoms in the Roman army.

His memory of the afternoon was quite clear and he was aware his behavior did him no credit, especially at the last with Scorpus. Could he have helped the man? He had been in such stark terror of the wolves by then that he would have done anything, anything at all, to escape.

Well, he had escaped. He was here and safe, warm and safe. The farm on the coast near the blue sea beckoned him. Nothing must stand between him and it. Nothing.

"What happened?" someone asked. "You've been babbling about wolves."

Drusus licked his lips. "No," he said. "No wolves. That bastard Hirax and the rest . . . attacked me . . . deserted."

Yes, he thought, *that would do nicely.* If the commander found out he'd so lost control that they fell victim to wolves, he might be blamed for not maintaining proper discipline. He might lose the lump sum payment he was due to receive at his discharge from the army, the money he needed to support him for the rest of his life.

Who could blame him if his men plotted to desert, attacked, and wounded him? No, no one would blame him.

He was a hero. He was dimly aware he was alone now. His friends were gone. Gone, no doubt, to make up an armed party to hunt down those rotten deserters. Drusus chuckled, then he woke completely, really afraid.

They might find the bodies. His eyes, wide-open, stared at a candle on the bedside table dissolving into a pool of melted wax. Gods, what if they found the bodies?

But then he realized they wouldn't. Even through the walls he could hear the wind as it hammered the building. Outside, a storm was rising. Between the wolves, ravens, and the storm, he was sure they wouldn't find anything.

THE WOLF STOOD IN THE ROAD. THE SNOW INcreased. The sky grew darker. He felt the hoofbeats through his paws rather than heard them.

He wheeled and took off at a dead run toward the pack. They had finished feeding. He gave one low bark, then turned and fled uphill, deeper into the mountains. The wolves followed.

In due time, the armed party arrived. It was growing dark by then. The swift winter night was falling and snow covered the bones. Neither Drusus nor the wolves were blamed.

The gray found a sheltered spot among the scattered boulders and deadfalls left by the old avalanche track to den up for the night. It was near the place where he and Imona had dallied together, the place where he'd won her love. In a way, she was still there. The moss in the secluded glen amidst the broken rock was perfumed by her body.

The wolves found different places to take shelter, sometimes in twos or threes, but the gray noticed the bitch went off alone, as did he, curling his body in the hollow in the rock where they'd made love on that long-ago summer day.

Sometime after midnight he crawled from the hollow among the boulders. The snowstorm had blown itself out. The sky was clear and the stars sparkled like a spill of crystal across the black sky.

The air was cold, so cold he felt its bite beneath the long coarse guard hairs and the fleecy undercoat that protected him.

Slowly, very silently, he visited each wolf's sleeping place. They were all sunken deep in slumber, even the bitch, though of all of them she seemed most restless. Sometimes she whined deep in her throat and, for a second, her legs and paws twitched. Then she drifted down into darkness beyond sorrow and fear, sighed, and relaxed.

The snow was several feet deep now. The crust wasn't frozen yet. In the day there would be a slight thaw and, by tomorrow night, it would act as the wolves' road. They could fleet across it like gazelles ready to kill heavier creatures such as ibex, wild cattle, elk, or deer incautious enough to flounder into deep drifts and become trapped. The dead of winter is a feast for wolves. Not even the Romans would dare the high fastness now.

Tonight, though, the crust wasn't frozen and he encountered heavy going. That was why he was so late when he reached Mir's dwelling.

Nothing stirred in the snow-covered countryside. His footprints, and his footprints alone, marred the perfectly smooth, cold surface of the virgin covering as it rested in silence, glowing with an uncanny pale radiance beneath the glittering sky.

Mir awakened without knowing what roused him and found his uninvited guest, couchant, head on his front paws, resting on a bench before the fire. The eyes glowed with the opalescent shimmer of the night hunter's gaze. The wolf lifted his head and glared a challenge at the old man.

Mir glanced at the door. It was closed, the bar in position blocking it shut. No true wolf could have gotten past the planks and crossbeam.

The wolf lifted himself to a sitting position.

Mir shivered. The room was very cold. On the fire, the last log snapped loudly and blazed up, lighting the room for a second.

Next to Mir, his little wife sat up. She turned to the old man and clung to him as she stared at the wolf.

The wolf drew back and snarled deep in his throat. Shadows clustered around the scarred child protectively, shadows only the wolf could see. A voice whispered softly from the darkness, "She, alone, lives."

No, the wolf thought, the words rising from the jumble of images crowding his brain. *I am no longer a wolf. Mir would be easy to kill. A real wolf would have done the deed quickly and without further fuss, but I . . . I must look at him, into his eyes, and search for guilt, want, need, desire, fear. I want him to be afraid, the way she must have sometimes been afraid, because surely she knew what they were going to do to her. Why did she stay with them? Why didn't she flee with me? Did Imona prefer death at the hands of her own kind rather than life with me?*

Then the girl clinging to Mir began to cry, moaning and whimpering like an animal in pain.

The room darkened as what was left of the fire sank to coals on the hearth.

When Mir's eyes adjusted to the darkness, he saw the room was empty, the wolf gone.

XI

WHEN LUCIUS FREED PHILO AFTER THEY RE-
turned to Rome, Fulvia kicked up a violent ruckus.
"He cost the earth, I'll have you know!" she screeched.
"What?" he answered. "You consider my survival a minor gift? I
hate to tell you, my dear sweet sister, I'm glad to be alive and I consider I have the right to show some well-deserved gratitude to the
man who saved my life."

"You stupid bastard. You always were a stupid bastard. We could
have made a fortune with him. He's being spoken of as the finest
physician in Rome. People from the first families resort to him now.
One-third of the fees we charge for attendance is plenty for that
scrawny little twit. He thinks he's well off getting that much. I had
my eye on one of those big villas along the coast near Ostia. I could
easily have put aside enough from his fees to . . . Where did everyone
go?" she asked, puzzled.

Lucius glanced around. The magnificent garden was empty.
Only a few moments ago a gardener had been digging near one of the
columns supporting the porch, preparing to plant some bay bushes.
Now only the shrubs remained, roots soaking in a bucket of water.
Farther down the walk, two of the cooks had been gathering rosemary for the chicken at supper and one of the housemaids had been
picking figs from a heavily laden tree shading the path. They, too,
were gone.

"Sister mine, very few people care to encounter you when you're in a bad mood. By the way, don't insult my late mother the next time you fly into a rage over something I've done, not unless you want Philo to have to carve you a nice new set of teeth out of ivory. Don't cast aspersions on Silvia's virtue."

Fulvia took a step backward. A month ago she wouldn't have bothered, but now she wasn't sure what Lucius might be able to do. The bath attendants she paid to spy on her brother had told her the wound was healed and that he was easily able to swim a dozen or more laps in the big pool housed in the tepiderium. She was beginning to think she'd wrought too well when she bought Philo. The twitchy little Greek had pulled him back from the edge of death. She wasn't sure she was glad.

"I'm sorry. I apologize for my remark. I didn't mean to insult her. Actually, the insult was directed at you. Why did you go about doing something so extravagant and foolish without consulting me first?"

"Extravagant? Foolish? Fulvia, hadn't you noticed we're rich? Richer than most senatorial families."

"Yes, and we wouldn't be for long if I didn't spend my time scrimping, saving, keeping an eye on our living expenses. You men have no idea of the cost of keeping up appearances among noble Roman families. Why, monthly cost of this house alone—"

"Spare me!" Fulvia in a fury frightened him. Fulvia whining and moaning disgusted him.

Fulvia stepped back. He didn't catch the glimmer of satisfaction in her eyes. She gave a windy sigh. "I suppose what's done is done, but . . ." Her jaw closed with a snap and she spoke between her teeth. "That oily little Greek ought to be willing to come across with a percentage in return for the patronage of an illustrious family."

"Indeed, he should do so," Lucius answered smoothly. "And just what family did you have in mind?"

Fulvia exited the peristyle toward her own luxurious reception rooms.

Lucius flinched as a door slammed loudly. He sat quietly for a moment, then reached into a bag at his side and scattered some grain on the flags in front of his bench. Two doves fluttered down and began pecking at it. The sun was hot on his neck and back, but the autumn morning had been chilly and it was still cooler than was comfortable in the shade.

Philo appeared, then sat down on the bench next to him. A few more doves glided in and joined the first two.

"She sounded a bit angry," Philo hazarded.

"She's always angry when she believes she's lost money."

"Oh," Philo contributed, "and are you in . . . Is it possible that your family lacks . . ."

Lucius fixed him with a stare of absolute incredulity and burst into laughter. "No," he said when he stopped laughing. "Keep your money. Send it to your sister, the managing one. That's what you've been doing all along, haven't you?"

Philo colored and looked a bit guilty. "As a matter of fact . . ." He paused. "You're more perceptive than I thought."

"Yes, not just another Roman lout who believes that because he has a prick dangling between his legs and a proconsul as a grandfather, that the gods, Roman and otherwise, gave him the right to kick the rest of humanity around in whatever way he pleases."

Philo's eyebrows rose. "You said it. I didn't."

"Besides," Lucius continued, "I'm not a trusting soul. When it looked like I was going to recover, I didn't know what she might try to bribe you to do. So I had someone check into your background. I received a glowing report, the gist of which was that you sacrificed yourself to save your family."

"I warn you, my lord, many very bad people I have known were devoted to their families."

"Is that 'don't trust me too much'?" Lucius asked.

"In this city, I would not trust anyone too much," Philo said darkly. "Once you asked me if I was given to intrigue. I told you no, but I had no idea the levels of complexity it could reach until I experienced this queen of cities. I thought we Greeks were devious, but we are as children compared to the denizens of your Senate."

Lucius threw back his head and howled.

"In summer, recurring fever and dysentery carry off many citizens of your little garden spot, and in winter, a simply fearful amount of lung congestion haunts these drafty dwellings. But winter and summer, rain or shine, hot or cold, dreary or sunny, politics finishes off more of the wealthy and well-born than any significant or comparable amount of plague. Simply being elected to that august body seems to be a death sentence in many families and, I might add, their wives are no better off."

"Been to see Calpurnia today?" Lucius asked.

"Yes."

"Umm," Lucius said.

"Exactly," Philo replied.

"How about a game of draughts?"

"Not with your dice, thank you. It took me some time to figure out why I had such a long losing streak. I had, heretofore, considered myself a fair player."

"I'll let you contribute the dice," Lucius said.

Philo reached into his tunic. "I just happen to have—"

"I wonder if I'm going to start a losing streak."

"It's possible," Philo said.

"Fulvia is planning a career of public service for me. Such a career begins with election to the Senate."

"Were I you, I would find another profession. What say you to being a gladiator? It's probably safer."

"I was doing my military service in preparation for standing for election when I was wounded. You see, the career path of a young Roman of noble family begins in the army, then the Senate, followed by an assignment in—"

"I know the steps on the road to power," Philo interrupted. "I've been in Rome long enough. I also know every one of them is fraught with difficulty, peril, and enormous out-of-pocket expenses."

One of the doves near Lucius' foot pecked at his ankle.

"They're telling you they've eaten all the grain, and trust me, birds are a lot cheaper to feed and to keep content than the Roman mob, my lord."

Lucius dropped more grain. The birds reached it with greater speed than he would have thought possible. "Fast walkers, too," he told Philo. "My heart's not in it. I just don't want to become another Pompey, Cassius, or even Caesar."

"Then you will surely die," Philo said. "If you don't bend all your heart, intellect, and strength to such an endeavor, you will fail. I can tell you haven't sufficient low cunning or hysterical fear of death, not to mention the pure horse sense required, to achieve victory in the political arena. You will . . . pick the wrong party, become an inconvenience or possibly an encumbrance to one of the larger and more bloodthirsty denizens of the senatorial shark pool, be faced with some crime you haven't the stomach to commit, and . . . so . . . perish."

Lucius picked up the almost empty bag of grain and turned it inside out over the growing crowd of birds. "My, there must be a couple of dozen here."

"Just so," said one of the kitchen maids as she dropped a net over them.

"You leave them alone!" Lucius jumped to his feet and shouted at the unfortunate girl.

She backed away, looking really frightened. "But what's the difference," she stammered, "if I catch them here for the cook's pie or buy them in the market?"

"Buy them in the market," Lucius roared. "These are my birds and I won't have them taken while they're under my protection."

The girl began crying.

"Oh, immortal gods! Give her some money, Philo."

"As ever, my lord, I hear and obey," the Greek replied as he pressed some silver into the child's hand, then cooed a few words into her ear. She walked away as Lucius freed the doves from the net.

Philo turned to Lucius. "I'm going back to Greece. My sister will be happy to see me. My father will be happy to see me. I've never felt it was part of a physician's duty to help his patient commit suicide, and certainly not by jumping into a snake pit."

"Sit down and shut up," Lucius snarled. Philo sat down, but Lucius decided he wasn't ready for him to shut up. "Very well. Suppose I eschew politics. What then? And what do I tell my sister?"

"Tell my lady to go for a swim in the Styx," Philo said.

Lucius began laughing.

"It isn't difficult. In fact, I believe I heard you do something similar while I was concealing myself behind a convenient cypress just before she left." Philo shuddered. "Zeus dispater! I'm afraid of that woman. I believe it concerned loosening some of her teeth."

"I felt I had to defend Silvia, my mother. Her life was difficult enough while she was alive. Hortensus, my father, led her a real dance and not a pleasant one. That six-legged groin biter beat her whenever he was in a bad mood. He was unfaithful with everything but the keyholes, not that even they were beneath his notice. I remember Fulvia was Father's darling daughter; she spied on poor Silvia and reported her every move to Hortensus. Mother got a little tipsy at dinner with some lady friends. My darling father heard about it from that little sneak, Fulvia, and threatened the poor woman with the traditional punishment."

"What's that?"

"Death."

"Death?" Philo squeaked. "My, you Romans take your domestic arrangements seriously."

"No!" Lucius snapped. "Do you think he'd dare offend the noble Claudians? She was better born than he was. Father was only a knight. All my consular ancestors are in her family, not his. He never forgave her for it. That, and probably his first wife, Fulvia's mother, made his life such a hell and a misery for him that the old reprobate never had the guts to trust a woman, any woman, again. I don't know. I'd like to trust my wife. Tell me, Philo, can you make a career of marriage? If you find the right woman?"

"Are you thinking about women?" Fulvia asked.

Both men gave a violent start. She stood behind them, a speculative gleam in her eyes. "What do you like in a woman—fat, tall, short, thin, blond, redhead, brunette, dark or light skin? I can buy you something from Africa or Greece. Whatever you want."

"Fulvia, I'm not a bull, a stallion, or even a stag. These things require . . . they are matters of some delicacy."

"You're impotent," Fulvia stated flatly.

"Do you know," Lucius said quietly, "it's entirely possible that I am."

She looked like someone who'd bitten into an apple and found half a worm. "Worthless," she muttered under her breath. "The two of you." She snapped her fingers. "Philo, help him bathe and dress if he still needs it. We're having guests for dinner."

"Who?" Lucius questioned.

Fulvia chuckled. "Caesar and Cleopatra."

DRYAS CAME TO THE POOL, THE ONE WHERE MIR felt Imona must have first met the wolf. *Time to begin,* she thought as she slowly removed her clothing.

The idea of seduction repelled her. She'd had only one experience of sexual congress with anyone in her entire life and the memory was one of terror. But Dryas was first and foremost a warrior and, as any soldier, she had been trained to do what she must to prevail. But preparing to do battle was a serious business. She could easily lose her life if this wolf creature guessed her ultimate purpose.

She dropped her clothing near the rock where Imona used to sunbathe, walked out on the stone projection, and dove into the pool. It was autumn and the shock of cold poured through her body as she knifed through the water. Down and down. The pool seemed so innocent as its glassy surface mirrored the crimsons, yellows, tans, and, at last, deep browns of the forest. It was all that remained of an extinct volcanic fumarole, a memory of the shattering crustal convulsions that ages ago built the mountains.

She had expected to reach the bottom and swim along it as in a conventional lake, but instead she found herself diving down and down into the almost stygian gloom. Preserved in the darkness of its heart were traces of its fiery beginnings. It was shaped like a cone. She saw the sides begin to draw closer and closer together and, while the sun warmed the surface layer, the deeper one swam, the colder it got.

So Dryas turned on her back. Above lay a layer of silver light. The water was cold against her skin, but as in her youth, she seemed to carry some glowing fire within that moved along her skin like an invisible shield against the chill liquid around her.

She came to the surface, knowing the warming effect of the water wouldn't last, and swam toward the rock.

She'd always known when she was being watched and she had that feeling now. He was nearby, she was sure.

Since Blaze's unpleasant adventure, neither women nor men frequented the pool, and Dryas was sure the eyes watching her were not completely human.

She reached the spur of rock, stretched out her arms, and lifted herself from the water to the warm stone above. *This battle is a seduction,* she thought, then rolled over and lay naked.

To Dryas, her own attractiveness was only another weapon. She hadn't felt desire in a long time, hadn't allowed herself to. Until her son died, she'd been a queen, and the queen's body among the painted people belonged not to herself, but to the royal line. She was not allowed to give herself to just any man. No, he must pass muster at the Assembly. Show himself not only courageous in battle, but also wise and temperate in his behavior, both his body and his blood pure, without taint of madness or deformity of flesh. He and his son would be major candidates for kingship. True, there would be others. Many of the great families would have young men among them if her son was judged unfit.

Her breath caught in her throat and she pushed the memory away. *No, I am here to tame this killer, and if he will not be tamed, to end his life.*

She realized her memory had been about to present her with an image of her child, the way she'd last seen him before Caesar had invaded the White Isle. If she accepted the burden of that memory, for a long time she would only yield to the utter prostration of grief and be useless for all else.

Be still and I will banish him. The voice spoke in her mind.

Dryas' eyes flew open and she looked up at the trees marching up and up toward the ridge above.

Close your eyes, the voice whispered from what seemed an immense distance. *Then I can talk to you. I will help you to catch the wolf.*

They were so beautiful, the autumn woods. The unchanging evergreen and pines were a patchwork of green among the oaks' brown and the scarlet gold of aspen and poplar. The leaves of the slender birch were fallen and the pale trunks stood out among the rest.

Dryas closed her eyes. "I must capture the wolf," she said.

He watches you now, but he will not come to you.

"Why not?" Dryas asked. Her fists clenched and she was filled with frustration.

I don't know. Then the presence trailed away and was gone.

Dryas slept.

The wolf watched her. Yes, this one was beautiful and she came to the pool alone, almost as if she wished to meet him.

I have a taste for them, he thought. *Otherwise, I would not be looking at this one because, beautiful or not, she shows no touch of desire. She is as one apart, the way Leon was. But different in that she carries no aura of death about her, but is rather an ice form carved by wind and rain or a cloud shaped like a mountain or a wolf's head, a thing that deceives the eye into believing it is what it is not.*

He rested his head on his front paws and he also slept.

The cold woke them both. The sun was almost gone beyond the trees.

Dryas rose, stretched, and walked toward her clothing. She was wiggling into her shift when she saw the shadow among the trees.

A shadow alone as the thing she'd seen in the stone circle. A shadow not made by anything else. She froze, not out of fear, but caution. She had encountered them before, but this was the first time she'd been this close to one; and they could be dangerous.

The voice spoke in her mind again. *The wolf is here.*

Dryas looked around and saw him watching her from a rocky outcrop on the other side of the lake.

Do you want him? You must make the choice. Do you?

Dryas really never wanted to yield her body to anyone again. She sensed she could leave, change her fate, and abandon her useless quest, return to her people on the White Isle, return to the Isle of Women. Her heart hungered for it. The silence broken only by her sisters' voices or the cry of seabirds on the shore. From there, she could leave on her last voyage and not return, not for a long, long time. She could cleanse her abiding grief and drink of the river of eternal forgetfulness.

Her heart hungered for this. But she had her duty.

"I will dare the eagle's talon, the wolf's maw. No matter what the suffering, I will not commit my soul to sleep until my heart's blood runs red from battle wounds and my head is sundered from my body. Nor will I abandon my chieftain or my duty, living or dead, till I have completed my course and victory is within my grasp. This is what is asked and this I yield."

Eyes glowed in the shadow's face. *If you would have the wolf, make an offering.*

She fumbled among her clothes and found the poppy broach. She lifted the ornament and hurled it into the pool. It splashed once and vanished.

Physical desire entered her body the way water soaks a cloth and left her just as limp as wet linen. She fell backward. Her legs were weak with the compulsion and she sprawled on the pine needles. Her eyes searched the twilight for the wolf, but she didn't see him.

In his place was a man and he moved with the assurance of the great killer. In a few moments, he was bending over her.

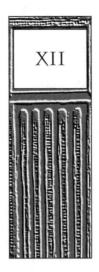

XII

H E WAS BACKLIT BY THE FLARE OF SUNSET above the trees. Long rays of pink and gold light streamed upward as the sun vanished behind the mountain.

Dryas tried to push herself away from the dark figure standing over her, but her hands slipped on the carpet of pine needles.

Almost casually, he reached down and scooped her up with one arm. She was sure he must be immensely strong because he held her easily.

He pulled her closer. "It's cold," he said. "Let me warm you."

She found herself pressed gently against the length of his body. He was warm. Being held against his flesh was rather like experiencing a conflagration.

To her terror, she realized his right knee was between her knees, rising, easing her legs apart.

"No!" she gasped, her hands pushing against his chest. "No . . . no."

"What's wrong? You don't want me? You knew I was here. I know. I can tell. You reek of desire. It's not so different for one of us. Even the odor is much the same. I don't understand. If you didn't want me, why did you come here? Why didn't you go hide in the old man's den with the . . . the mad girl?"

Then he had both hands holding her. "Come. Imona was afraid at first, but then she quickly realized I would do nothing to harm her."

Imona! Dryas twisted anew from him, trying to get herself under control. A second later she was on her feet, running uphill into the dark wood. She could move silently in the shadows. They were black, thick as velvet, but she found she couldn't escape him. No, not even for a moment. Though the air was cold, she saw the faint brush of starlight on his damp skin.

He embraced her, kissing her neck. Then he lifted the luxuriant spill of her hair and nibbled expertly at her throat and ears.

Gooseflesh erupted all over her skin as a thrill of pure lust poured over her body.

He laughed, then kissed her again, running his tongue between her lips and pressing his to her open mouth.

She found herself remembering that mouth in the twilight—firm, warm, seeking, searching. She moved toward the heat in him like a moth to a flame.

I want to die in that fire, she thought. But no, no, die wasn't the word she wanted. And then she remembered *die* was sometimes what that final pleasure was called . . . a kind of death. When the final flash of desire's lightning burns away all else, it is like death.

No, if anyone was going to die here, she must not be the one. She allowed herself to fall limply against him as if in total surrender. She could feel his arms close around her. The wish for that splendid pleasure, that burning delight, surged like some dark fire in her veins.

And then, abruptly, she saw her son's face—the pupils cloudy, but the irises still green and clear like shallow seawater in the sunlight. But he was dead, given into the hand of darkness. With a strange look of comprehension in his eyes and pale lips parted as if to speak, showing the small teeth of a child only seven or eight years old— Stop! And then came the filth and the horror, just as it had been when she saw her son and knew he was dead. He and the rest of the children he lay among. There was nothing left but darkness.

L UCIUS DIDN'T NEED PHILO'S HELP. THE HOUSE WAS acrawl with servants—slaves and freedmen and women belonging to his family. Mostly to Fulvia.

Both young men attending him were slaves, newly purchased from one of Caesar's gladiatorial ludi and thus slated for death in the arena at some festival or other.

They were very glad to have escaped that fate and fallen into a very soft life, and he was pretty sure they had been told to keep him happy at any and all costs. Beyond that, he had no illusions as to their loyalty. They would report to Fulvia.

It was a source of some puzzlement to him that Fulvia controlled all of the household slaves. How had it happened? When he'd left to take up his first command in the legions, she had not dominated the household so completely. But gradually, as the years passed, he found his mother's remaining women and his father's freedmen slowly being supplanted by those knowing no one's authority but hers. She was expert at picking individuals such as the two young Campanian Samnites, who knew their very lives depended on her favor.

She need not bother even with so simple a thing as a household execution. All that would be required would be to return them from whence they came, with a notification that their services had proven unsatisfactory, and the lanista would make sure they died in the next combat.

The same was true of the two Greek girls who saw to his chamber under Philo's direction. They were both beautiful still, and had been favorites of Fulvia in their time, but though no more than twenty-seven or twenty-eight, they were now growing a bit long in the tooth for their original profession. They would not survive long in the unhealthy brothels clustered near the Tiber. Thirty to forty men a night would destroy most women's health in a matter of a few years. Neither of them was very bright, both entirely unskilled and physically not very strong, so they went in terror of Fulvia.

He was, as it were, surrounded. He studied himself in a long mirror. Yes, it was a mirror, silver backing with a glass surface. True, the reflection was a bit fuzzy and one arm appeared longer than the other, but it was definitely him. He was decked out like a bridegroom or, as an even more sinister metaphor suggested itself to him, like the main attraction at a bull sacrifice: hair curled, horns gilded, freshly bathed, shorn and drenched in perfume. He sighed. His two servants were still fussing around him. He reached up to see if he perhaps had horns to gild.

"Don't do that, my lord," one of the young men said. "You'll mess up your hair and the divine Julius will—"

"Divine Julius!" Lucius broke in on him. "Has the Senate voted him divine honors? You mean he's not satisfied to be first man in

Rome, father of his country, consul for life, and whatever else those whimpering senatorial toadies can dream up, and he wants to be a god, too?"

The two young men busily arranging the folds of his toga kept perfectly straight faces. *At least Philo would have laughed,* he thought rather self-pityingly.

His bedroom cubiculum was another source of conflict between himself and his sister. She wanted him to move into the more spacious, luxurious, and newer part of the villa, but he was attached to his boyhood room. She considered his desire for privacy one of a number of unpleasant eccentricities that made him an unfit heir to the Basilian fortune.

She herself lived in what he considered gilt-edged squalor with two secretaries—Firminius was one of them—five dressers, two tiring women, three maids of all work, and several pretty little things, none of them out of her teens, ready and willing to snuggle with her whenever she felt amorous. She slept in solitary splendor on silk sheets in a bed of aromatic lemon wood covered by brocade.

Firminius enjoyed quarters of his own nearby, but the rest bedded down in concentric circles around her luxurious couch and, when he visited her, he could always tell who was in and out of favor by how close their present sleeping arrangements were to her bed.

In his cubiculum there was no real accommodation for servants. The Gallic woman who'd cared for him along with Philo and his two personal attendants had rooms nearby. Fulvia considered it scandalous that his room, at the corner of the house, was only a little bigger than his servants'.

He liked it, though. For one thing it was cool in summer. Two high, narrow windows near the ceiling were covered with heavy iron grillwork. They overlooked a strip of grass shaded by cypresses. A glass skylight in the ceiling admitted plenty of light by day and the windows near the ceiling drew cool air from the tree-shaded garden outside. In winter, the windows could be shuttered and the room easily warmed with a brazier.

His bed was narrow and covered with a feather mattress and linen sheets. The mirror was the only luxury in the room. It was a present from his mother, but he always felt she was encouraged by his father to give it to him, since they dealt in the things. To say Hortensus was close with a sesterce was a very charitable understatement. Even her secret drinking, uncorrected by his father's poorly veiled death threats, probably bothered his father more because she preferred to seek oblivion with the aid of expensive Falernian rather than the cheaper tipples stocked by the cook in tuns near the kitchen.

Well, his father had been rewarded by his single-minded pursuit of the almighty denarius, his two financially rewarding but unhappy marriages, and his obsession with saving something on every purchase. He was known, in certain quarters, as "Never Pay the First Price" Hortensus. His miserly ways meant he left a large estate when he died.

Now, Fulvia was expanding his empire. And these particular dinner guests were in a position to make her very rich.

The light coming in through the glass plate in the ceiling was growing dimmer. The two young men wanted to continue with the folds of his toga, but he felt that as much as could be done to improve his appearance had been done and any further efforts were simply foolishness.

He showed only too well the effects of a long illness. He was over-thin, rather pale, and he still limped a bit on his left side. The massive bundle of scar tissue left by the wound pulled at the big muscles of his buttocks and thigh.

He went out without locking his door. Why bother? If a thief could find anything of value in his room, said thief was more than welcome to it.

He met his sister near the big triclinium close to the front door. He hadn't seen the formal dining chamber fully lit since he was a boy, and its appearance staggered him.

The floor was decorated with a mosaic of a garden, a green garden organized as if the beds bordered the room. The tessera that formed the green plants and flowers were malachite and the petals of the flowers were cabochon semiprecious stones: crystal amethyst for the purple, bloodstone for red, citrine for yellow. The picture seemed to leap from the floor to the eye.

The walls gave the appearance of severity, being pure white marble, but each panel was set with onyx bordering violet porphyry, all inlaid into the marble.

The pale violet of the porphyry was picked up by the couches upholstered in the brightest shade of Tyrian purple velvet he'd ever seen. The room was brilliantly lit with hanging bronze lamps, all hissing away, doing their best to cast out the night.

He stood, gazing at it, awestruck. "Now I know what killed Father," he said, bursting into laughter.

Fulvia, resplendent in white gauze draped over white silk, all embroidered in gold, spoke without moving her lips. "No miser jokes, no entertaining stories about your exploits with Gallic whores. Don't tell him how you got your wound or where your scar is or discuss your low Roman or military friends. Don't, don't, don't embarrass me in front of this pair. If you do, I'll kill you."

Lucius didn't doubt it for even one moment. He opened his mouth, but nothing emerged because there was a sound of military movement in the streets—the tramp of booted feet, to be exact.

"They're here!" he finally whispered.

"Yes," Fulvia said.

Lucius found his mouth was dry. The closest he'd ever been to the most famous man of his time was a bust in the atrium of one of his mother's sisters. It had depicted a young, handsome man. Painted, as most statues were then, it showed him with slightly curling hair and light, rather piercing hazel eyes, a full, if firm, mouth, and a strong chin. The famous profile was that of an intelligent eagle, fierce but fair, domineering but just. The very epitome of all Rome brought to the world and the reason she had been chosen by the gods to rule it.

All of this was about to enter the front door.

In a swirl of draperies, Fulvia hurried toward the atrium to greet her guests. Chained to his usual place and as terrified of Fulvia as all the other slaves, the porter reached the door first. And so the rattle and clank of fetters announced the entrance of the most important man in the world.

Lucius felt an odd weight enter his stomach. *How is it that though I haven't eaten since morning, I have dyspepsia? I must ask Philo about . . .* That was as far as he got because, by then, he'd realized he was afraid.

A soldier entered first and bowed to Fulvia. He carried a torch that brilliantly lit the old entryway and was followed by others.

The shock of brightness blinded Lucius for a second, then he saw they were not in parade dress, but wearing the working armor of legionnaires on duty. Leather helmets stiffened with bronze, boiled leather cuirass and thigh protectors studded with metal, and greaves on their shins. All three looked around very carefully.

The Basilian villa, like almost all houses of the period, was a patchwork of old and new areas. The entrance was one of the oldest parts. No one knew quite when it had been built, probably as a farmhouse before the city surrounded it. Its tenants had been plebeian farmers nursing vines, olives, and the low, hard wheat that didn't rise any higher than a tall man's knee, and living by the sweat of their brows on an open, ancient hillside beyond the walls.

The door was very heavy, old oak reinforced with iron. The first room was an atrium where pour-offs from the roof filled a pool, once a water source for the whole family. The same stars still shone through the opening in the roof, but beyond, a magnificent peristyle garden, brightly lit by torches, beckoned.

Cleopatra preceded Caesar into the atrium through the doors. At first, she seemed but a shadow. Fulvia greeted her with as close to a curtsey as Lucius had ever seen her make, but then she rose and she and the queen embraced, kissing like old girlfriends.

The slave porter at the door bowed down so low, his forehead almost touched the ground.

And *he* entered the doorway. He also seemed a shadow until he passed the atrium pond where Fulvia and the Egyptian queen took his hand, one on either side, and led him into the light.

Lucius backed up quickly to get out of their way and saw the living man for the first time.

He was old.

This was Lucius' first thought: *He has grown old,* and he had. He was raising Fulvia's hand to his lips and bestowing a pretty compliment on her. Nothing trite. He compared her to a Praxiteles' Venus he had seen in Greece and ordered copied. The copy would be shipped to Rome to grace his peristyle when he finally settled down.

Being compared to the titular goddess of his house was high praise indeed. Lucius wondered irreverently how much it was costing her, but then she was her father's child and would do nothing without the hope of substantial gain.

At length, the old man with Caesar's face turned to him. Yes, he was old and the years had not been kind to the conqueror. His lips, once full and sensual, seemed to have thinned out and they were not rose, but pale in the torchlight. The aristocratic high cheekbones and bladelike nose were still present. But the cheeks were sunken; the nose jutted imperially, but seemed thinner now; the skin, yellow, drew tight across the bone. His neck, to put it bluntly, might have belonged to a barnyard fowl. Loose skin stretched in wattles from his chin to the midpoint of his throat, and below them, the masculine swelling was pronounced. Yes, he was old and the hounds of time hot on his heels.

"This will be your brother," the great man said, and offered him his hand.

Lucius took it and found himself blushing furiously.

The hand was hot and dry. The voice that charmed his legions into unimaginable valor and scourged the Senate like a whip was still beautiful. "I understand," the beautiful voice said, "that you have only lately been treacherously wounded by elements of the enemy while on patrol."

The bastard is a genius at his craft of managing men, Lucius thought. *He already has me cornered and soon will drag me off in triumph to worship with the rest of his followers. He had the sheer, cold-eyed efficiency to find out where and how I got my injury and has the ability to make a thoroughly stupid and lax officer, who managed to get himself almost fatally stabbed in the back, sound like a hero. Mind your tongue, and express your appreciation.*

Lucius never afterward remembered what he said, but it must have been satisfactory since he got a smile from Caesar; but he saw quite clearly that what happened to his lips didn't extend to the hazel eyes. They seemed as cold and abstracted as ever.

All this is business as usual with him, Lucius thought. *I wonder why he's here?*

After the compliment, he was, in effect, dismissed as Caesar turned his attention back to Fulvia.

A few more legionnaires trailed after Caesar. The last one in placed a torch near the gatekeeper's cella and stood with his back against the door. The others fanned out through the peristyle, personally checking all the entrances and exits and ordering the curious servants back to their posts. They quickly herded everyone without business in the kitchen or dining room away from the area.

"Very efficient," Fulvia commented.

"Yes," Cleopatra answered softly, "but they're Spanish mercenaries. My guards, not his."

"I beg you, Caesar, take proper care of yourself," Fulvia gushed. "So many like me depend on you."

Caesar laughed. "I don't need to worry about myself. There are so many others to take care of that for me." He entered the triclinium first, the two women followed, and Lucius brought up the rear.

He looked at Cleopatra. No, she wasn't beautiful, but she was something he had never seen before—a woman the equal of Caesar.

Tall and slender, her skin carried just a touch of the amber lent to her by her Egyptian forebears. In all other respects, she looked more Greek with her light hair, rather like autumn honey, golden brown. He was sure some rather clever bleaching and oiling must have been done, because it shone like a young girl's.

For a moment, she looked raw-boned, but then he saw she belonged to a completely different physical type than Latin women. Not for her the ample hips and abundant breasts. Her hips weren't wide. Her stomach was set between them, a round shape with concavities rather the way a pearl rests in a cup. She was long-waisted, the curve of her midsection rising, nipped in at the slender waist, up to two high breasts, small, but so perfectly shaped he was sure they were bare beneath their silken covering. The silk gown she wore was at least as revealing as Fulvia's. In fact, he was sure she was completely naked under the gown and it was soft as a scarf.

Yes, her chin was pointed, her nose showed the Semitic ancestry, but her eyes were pure Greek, wide, pale with tawny lashes. They reminded him of Alexander's—those portraits, statues, and paintings he had seen. But then all those Macedonians had probably been related to one another, whether they admitted to the relationship or not.

Fulvia looked green with envy. Cleopatra was older than she was and had borne a child, but she managed somehow to look better than Fulvia or most Roman women ever would. If the Egyptian queen reached seventy, she would still make most Latin women look fat and frowsy beside her.

"My lady," Lucius said, "before we met I felt the poets were too fulsome in their praises of you. Now that I have seen you, I know that even the verses of Homer in which he praised the Cyprian goddess were inadequate to describe the beauty of your person or the charm of your manner."

Cleopatra smiled up at Caesar and gave Lucius a glance that almost caused his knees to turn to mush on the spot.

"The mother of my house was Venus and she bestowed the fairest of her daughters on me," Caesar said. He and Cleopatra reached one of the couches and they reclined together.

Lucius chose one couch and Fulvia took another.

His sister wore enough jewelry to raise a new legion for Caesar. Gold bracelets, gold necklaces, gold armlets, and enough rings to make it difficult for her to eat.

Several wines were brought in and offered to Caesar; reds directly from glazed clay flasks and whites chilled in snow. He rejected several, then accepted three to be shared by him and the queen.

"My, what a beautiful room," Cleopatra said as Caesar began tasting.

"Planned and executed by my father, as are the more modern parts of the villa," Fulvia replied, giving Lucius a warning glance.

Lucius did his best not to allow his sister to catch his eye and to look innocent. "But surely," he said smoothly, "the Queen of Egypt is used to more luxury than this. I heard the palace at Alexandria is—"

"A drafty labyrinth," Cleopatra broke in. "Many parts of it are of immense magnificence, other parts are haunted by both great and bloody legends generated by my forebears, but nowhere do I find the comfort and relaxation created by the inhabitants of Rome. These villas are wonderfully suited to the climate of your great city."

Lucius chuckled. "Most began as farmhouses, surrounded by open fields, housing livestock—horses, mules, cattle, and sheep—alongside people."

The queen laughed, a deep, throaty sound that caressed Lucius in all sorts of places. He found himself wanting to make her laugh again.

"What have we here—a historian, an antiquarian, or . . . ."

"A troublemaker," Fulvia interposed. "He knows very well that however beautiful some parts of the house are, this villa displays its commercial origins a little too publicly for me. I had my eye on one villa at Baiae, but he tripped me up by his careless disposal of a very valuable piece of property. But," she sighed, "what is a poor woman to do when she finds herself in opposition to the men in her family . . . except obey."

"Poor darling," Cleopatra said in mock sympathy. "I wouldn't worry if I were you. I'm sure you'll find any number of villas everywhere at your disposal after tonight's dinner." She laughed again.

Caesar glanced down at the wine in a golden cup encrusted with pearls he was holding and joined in the laughter. "Ah, the Basilian family," he said. "I know I will receive nothing but the best in your household."

The slaves arrived with the first course, the gustatio, just then, serving the powerful pair across from Lucius first.

The night was cool and the louvered doors separating the torchlit garden outside were partially drawn, but Lucius found he could smell the men and women serving dinner, even above the odor of garlic, ham, and pear, apple, plum, and quince preserves.

Caesar, Cleopatra, and Fulvia inspired mortal terror in the slaves. One of them was the girl he'd chased away from what he considered his personal pet doves. She was pretty and he liked her because she sang a lot while she was going about her work and he thought she had a beautiful voice. But at this hour, she was gray with fear.

Lucius found he had no appetite and Cleopatra didn't seem beautiful anymore. *I must be going insane. The wound must have afflicted my mind,* he thought. *Why should I care what these people feel or think?*

But when the girl started to pour his wine and the gold pitcher she held rattled against the lip of his cup, he was alarmed. She looked as if she might faint.

He reached out and grabbed her wrist. She seemed to awaken with a start. Color flooded her cheeks and her lips parted.

Fulvia glanced at them both and her lips thinned with wrath.

"Would you get me some lettuce, arugula, and chestnuts and bring some of that fine oil we got yesterday?" he asked the girl.

Caesar and Cleopatra helped themselves to melon with a dressing of vinegar and oil spiced with a bit of pepper.

Fulvia ate dormice with honey. "If I'd known you wanted a salad, I'd have had the cook fix one for you, brother dear."

"Oh, I like to do my own. You should try one. The mixture of chestnuts, bitter cress or arugula, and nuts with oil and a little salt is wonderful."

When the girl returned, he took the things she brought, on a gold tray no less, and mixed them himself.

The curiosity of both of the distinguished guests was piqued and they tried his concoction.

"My doctor feels sweet and bitter greens, oil, and nuts are the best way to arouse the appetites of his patients," Lucius explained.

"I think I particularly like this one," Caesar said. "Philo would be the doctor, of course. He treats my wife's headaches and has done wonders with her. To calm her, I mean."

Lucius, who felt sure he was looking across the small circular table at Calpurnia's worst headache, agreed blandly.

At length, the slaves cleared the gustatio. White wine and a bread made with pine nuts and hard cheese were served.

The wine rocked Lucius' senses. He'd never tasted anything like it. It was subtle, fragrant with the flower of the gray sage, and intoxicating at the same time. Over Caesar's shoulder, in the shadows of the garden, he saw the cellarius and Philo both wearing triumphant smirks.

"Ah," Caesar whispered, "incomparable. My dear, I count my acquaintance with your family the greatest of good fortune."

Fulvia smiled and offered a toast with the wine. "To our continued success."

Then the slaves brought in the mensa prema. The food was all of the plainest variety. They had their choice of five or six, including a roast of wild boar with prune sauce; a rare treat of a beef stew cooked with mushrooms; grilled liver wrapped in omentum or caul fat; a whole roasted suckling pig seasoned with pepper, bayberries, rue, silphium, and olive oil; and last but not least, a young, unweaned goat with a sauce of pitted damsons, wine, garlic, and oil.

"Parthian kid," Caesar remarked. "Is that a hint, my dear daughter of Hortensus?"

"Are the Parthians next on your menu, Caesar?" Fulvia asked as he and the queen helped themselves to small portions of the tender meat.

"I don't know," Caesar answered. "If I can raise enough money . . ."

"There is not even a need to ask, Caesar," Fulvia said demurely.

"No," he replied. "I owe your father's daughter a great debt and I haven't been able to repay most of it."

"No need," Fulvia said. "What I propose will make both of us rich beyond dreams."

"What?"

"Wine," Fulvia said. "Gaul is prime vine-growing country."

"What!"

"I know, I know," she said, waving her hand, "but I have hunted over much of it and, I tell you, with the right investment, you will reap a twenty-fold reward. No, more than twenty-fold. Fifty-fold."

Lucius was about to laugh when he realized Caesar was taking her seriously.

"What would you want? How much land? How many men?"

"I leave that to your generosity," Fulvia said. "In my study, I have maps prepared. All wars generate slaves. It doesn't matter where they come from. My people can train them."

"I think it's a perfectly mad scheme, but I've learned to respect your judgment. After all, both you and your father had the courage to bet on me."

"There's one other thing I would ask you." Fulvia positively simpered.

"What?"

"Not for myself, for my brother. Before you march to Parthia, please assure him of a command in your army. Make him one of your legates, if possible."

Caesar gave Lucius an opaque look. "I believe he is the last male of his line, isn't he? It would be a shame if the very notable Basilian family were to die out."

Lucius hoped his fear—abject terror, actually—didn't show on his face. The last thing he wanted now was another military engagement. He wondered if even the most redoubtable soldier didn't want to come home at last.

But then, he was looking at one who had just finished a brutal war but was now ready to march out and begin another one: Caesar himself.

Lucius wasn't the only one doing some staring. Caesar and Cleopatra both gazed in his direction, looking faintly amused.

Cleopatra saved the situation, an embarrassing one for him, by saying, "I doubt if a man having just recovered from a nearly mortal wound wants to contemplate an immediate return to combat. Your wound *was* nearly mortal, wasn't it?"

"Yes, nearly mortal and very painful for a long time, nearly a year."

"Yes," Caesar said, "and a legate has to be able to perform his duties, be strong enough to carry out the orders given him by his commanding officer. In any case, worries about any new campaigns must wait until next summer . . . when the Senate is finished honoring me."

Cleopatra laughed at the heavy irony in his voice in the last statement.

"And very gratifying honors they are, too," Lucius said.

"Yes, if one were only sure they were bestowed with perfect honesty by truly loving friends." Again, Caesar's statement was laden with the same ironic detachment.

"Some do honestly admire you. Marc Antony, for instance."

Caesar and Cleopatra both laughed and exchanged glances of perfect, limpid understanding.

Caesar continued, "I met a centurion in the Forum the other day, a veteran of my Gallic wars. He has only one leg, but was provided for so well that he doesn't have to beg. He lives with his grandson as an honored guest. That's the way it should be for old servants of the state, but often isn't. The other day I ran across another who was begging. He had the grace to try to avoid my eye, but I recognized him and had my servants bring him to me. Seems he is much the worse for women and drink . . . but . . ." He turned to Cleopatra. "I have lost the thread of my discourse."

She gazed at him somberly. "The first soldier, I believe, my dear."

"Oh, yes." Caesar brightened. "We spoke together as old friends will. Then he drew as close to me as he could. I had to bend my head down to hear him for he wished for private communication. He whispered into my ear, 'Watch your back, Caesar. Watch your back.' "

"Probably some of the best advice you'll ever get," Lucius said with deep conviction.

Caesar and Cleopatra burst into uproarious laughter at the same time. Caesar laughed till the tears came, then got himself under control.

"It seems I amuse you," Lucius said rather stiffly. "One can't but be—"

Caesar sobered. "Oh, yes, one can't but be concerned given the record of fidelity to friends and even relatives among our conscript fathers and considering the deaths of both the Grachii, and the murders of Clodius and other close friends and associates of mine, not to mention the fate of such worthies as Cicero's son-in-law at his own father-in-law's hands."

"Not at his hands, exactly," Cleopatra said.

"No, our model senator simply led him to the executioner and stood nearby as a witness, while he was beheaded—or was it hanged—then and there. He believes it evidence of his integrity that he would sacrifice his nearest and dearest to the state.

"But don't worry, my dear boy. I'm not as big a fool as I look and it would be very dangerous for anyone who took me for one. Very dangerous for them."

During the last words, something entered Caesar's voice that frightened and chilled Lucius.

Cleopatra shot Caesar a warning glance and Lucius thought, *He's planning something.* Suddenly, he felt as if the four of them were not alone in the room. Ghosts were there with them and they clustered thickly around the pair opposite him.

The lamplight shone in Cleopatra's eyes. She'd had a brother once . . . . hadn't she? And Caesar . . . at least a couple of legions of both friends and enemies had died cursing him.

Lucius felt dizzy and remembered, and the memory found its voice before he thought, as if it were a thing meant to be said. "The man who stabbed me, he used my own sword. He took it from my scabbard with his left hand because his right had been cut off. He had no right hand."

Fulvia's dining couch was close to his and he felt her nails bite into his shoulder. "Are you mad?" she whispered. "Have you gone completely mad? The greatest lord in all Rome is a dinner guest—"

"And a very satisfied one, too." Caesar spoke up loudly. "Now, you promised me a surprise, an enticing surprise. Bring it on."

Lucius stammered, "I'm . . . I'm . . ."

"No," Caesar said as he rose and the rest followed. "Don't apologize. You're a brave young man who has been very close to death and it's marked you. It marks us all. In different ways, that's true, but it marks us all."

Then, with torch-bearing soldiers in the lead, they strolled through the labyrinthine complex of buildings, old and new, that formed the Basilian villa.

Lucius proceeded from embarrassment to mortification and then from mortification to chagrin. By the time he reached the third feeling, he was beginning to wonder what his sister had in mind, because they were walking toward an old warehouse at the edge of their property, where wine had been stored at one time.

They paused in an archway built of terra-cotta brick. For a moment, it was as if they looked into a cave. Then, high above in a dome, Lucius saw the stars. A torch flared in the darkness before them.

Fulvia said, "Behold!"

His eyes, shocked by the sudden brightness, took a few seconds to adjust. When his vision cleared, he became aware they were looking at an arena, a miniature version of the one across the city where gladiatorial combats took place.

"My gift to you, Caesar." Fulvia made an expansive gesture, indicating Caesar should sit in one of the fine marble chairs on a high dais that overlooked the sand-covered circular space in the center.

Caesar threw back his head and laughed. "How perfectly wonderful. I cannot thank you enough." He kissed Fulvia's hand. Cleopatra smiled and gazed at him adoringly.

Lucius noticed that some of the servants, one of them Philo, were lighting pitch-covered torches on the walls surrounding the arena.

With the exception of the seats taken by Caesar, Cleopatra, and Fulvia, there were no other chairs in the gigantic room. Instead, the arena had concentric circles of marble steps that led up to the door where they entered.

The marble chairs were upholstered with downy cushions in a rainbow of colors and shapes. Caesar relaxed in his copy of the consul's curele chair. The soldiers took up positions around the walls.

Philo made an imperious gesture and two servants carried in a wooden chair filled with cushions. They placed it on the top step of the amphitheater. Lucius sat down and felt, rather than saw, Philo come up to stand behind him.

Without further ado, Fulvia snapped her fingers.

The gladiators entered from passages below floor level, up a low flight of brick steps. There were two individuals. One Lucius recognized immediately. His face was scarred by a puckered line that ran from the top of one ear in a diagonal slash almost, but not quite, to his lips on the right side of his face. He was famous. His appearances in the arena were now infrequent and he was highly paid to fight when he did.

He had become notable in a contest where he faced ten opponents in succession, not only defeating them all, but killing three and wounding two others so badly that they later died. It was said that the then-lanista hated him and was determined to see his death. But the lanista's hatred was only equaled by the love the crowd felt for him at the end of his contest and the ensuing riot they caused when it was announced that he would be forced into an eleventh bout. It was so violent that he was given his freedom then and there and, in time, was said to have become a wealthy man.

He wore only the subligaculum and a simple legionary helmet, boiled leather reinforced with brass. He carried a somewhat shinier version of the standard issue sword carried by legionnaires, the so-called Spanish sword.

A younger man, dressed in the same way and holding the same type of sword, followed him.

"Gordus," Caesar said in satisfaction. "I have never seen him fight. Of course, I've heard of him. Who hasn't?"

Gordus, the older, scarred man, raised his sword hilt near his lips, blade up, and saluted the group on the dais. The young man bowed, then the two turned and faced each other. The sound of steel on steel rang out.

At first, Gordus seemed almost passive, negligent before the attack of the other. The youngster was very good. To Lucius' experienced eye, it looked as if he twice came close to wounding the older man. The youngster came in aggressively, his steel a whirl of fire in the torchlight.

Gordus seemed barely to move his blade, but he fended off each of his opponent's strokes without difficulty, without even the appearance of exertion.

At first, the younger man simply hacked. He looked strong and was. Lucius would have been afraid of him on that account alone, but his strength didn't seem to matter to Gordus.

When the younger man saw he was getting nowhere, he stepped back and showed there was more to him than brute force. He attacked again, this time with intelligence, coming in with a slashing attack low, then using the hacking blows to draw Gordus' arm out to set up the wounding or killing thrust. But he failed here also.

Gordus' footwork was beautiful and he never allowed himself to be drawn out far enough to be threatened. At length, the youngster drew back. The evening was cold, but he was perspiring freely.

Lucius felt sure Gordus would press the attack, but he didn't.

Instead, he waited for the youngster to get his breath, circling him slowly, the tip of his sword pointed down.

The young man's breathing quieted and he closed with Gordus again, this time showing great skill and coolness. Lucius had never seen such adeptness with the short sword, certainly not in a legionary encampment.

But, as before, Gordus fended off each attack. Only now he took more trouble, one foot thrust forward, catching his opponent's sword almost before the blows landed.

The end came quickly and unexpectedly. The young man swung hard. Gordus didn't parry, but stepped back. The swing missed. The youngster recovered, but before he could get his guard up, Gordus' sword, just the tip, entered his right arm and sank in between the two forearm bones.

Lucius gritted his teeth and shivered as one sword edge grated on bone.

The youngster stepped back, the sword dropping to the floor of the arena from his already blood-soaked fingers. The blood, red on the cord-wrapped sword hilt, spattered on the white sand beneath.

Behind him, Lucius heard Philo sigh. The Greek physician stepped past him and down the four shallow steps to the pit. There was no question of a killing. This was purely an exhibition match.

Philo examined the youngster's arm. He stood, clutching the bloody wrist, supporting it with his other hand. Then, with a look of reproach at Gordus, Philo led the younger man away into the opening beneath the seats.

Caesar leaned over the railing of the dais in quiet conversation with Gordus. The gladiator listened to what Caesar had to say, nodding and occasionally making what were obviously laconic comments as he cleaned his sword with a napkin.

Some of the slaves who'd waited on them at dinner came in with wine in a glass pitcher and sweet cakes of various kinds on a tray.

Lucius, who was a little dizzy from the wine and excitement, declined further drink. From somewhere under the floor, he heard feminine giggling.

Caesar, Cleopatra, and Fulvia partook freely of the wine and sweets. The Egyptian queen and his sister had their heads together in whispered conversation. Caesar continued speaking quietly to Gordus. Lucius looked at the blood drying on the sand and felt queasy.

A slave Lucius recognized as one of the gardeners came and raked the sand clean.

The volley of giggles came again and then, almost hesitantly, a small figure entered the arena wearing the subligaculum.

Lucius forgot his stomach. Unless he was losing his mind, this one dressed as a gladiator was a woman.

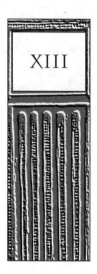

XIII

DRYAS AWOKE ON THE GROUND, LYING IN A dense forest. She rolled over on her back, looking up at the lofty canopy above, and felt leaves and twigs pressing against her skin. She realized she was naked. She tried to rise, but fell back and looked at the forest giant near her shoulder.

It was the biggest tree she'd ever seen. As her eye followed the trunk skyward, she saw that the branches bore needles and cones. Some sort of conifer and it wasn't even the largest tree around. Others nearby were bigger.

Somehow she got to her knees, her mind staggered by what she was seeing. She'd been in forests, but she'd never seen anything like this forest. The very smallest tree here dwarfed any she'd ever seen before in any wood in Alba, or anywhere else for that matter. The ground was covered not with grass, but with fern and moss.

She felt something sticky on her hands and stomach. Was she wounded? Was she dead? Had the wolf guessed her purpose and torn out her throat?

"No!" she cried out loud, and the word echoed away into the silent forest. Then the moment of fear passed and she forced her mind to come to grips with the present. She looked at her hands and down, then shivered. She must have vomited as she lost consciousness.

She got to her feet and saw water. It welled from the ground near where she had lain in the center of a veritable pool of green moss. The ground sloped away toward it. She rose and stumbled forward.

She found a fountain. The water bubbled up from the earth and formed a stream whose rocky bed was almost drowned in thick moss and fern. The mosses were of more than one kind. It ranged from a delicate green fuzz on rocks, carpets of brown needles and deadfall branches to thick, almost furlike covering at exposed tree roots, small boulders, and the lower tree trunks. The ferns ranged from a lacy spray of small chartreuse circles borne on almost invisible black wiry branches to stately olive-green arrowhead-shaped fronds with thick midribs bearing hundreds of parallel leaves.

She knelt and washed her face, hands, and body. Where was she?

When she rose upright on her knees, she found that the tree nearest to her clung to a cliff and she was looking past its trunk into a deep valley drowned in mist.

In the distance, the sun was only just rising. Half masked by the drifting fog, it glowed like a gold coin, shedding a clear yellow radiance into the drifting vapor wreaths still stained blue by darkness.

But as she watched, the dawn wind began to rise, slowly at first, only a breath against her naked skin, then blowing more and more briskly, driving out the moist azure shadows.

She found she knelt on the side of a high mountain, even higher than those she'd seen in this part of Gaul. It looked down on lower, older hills and mountains clothed in green that stretched out until her eyes lost their power to focus into the violet haze of distance.

She breathed deeply. The air seemed to demand deep breaths, being fresher than clear water and laden with the fragrance of cedar and pine. It asked to be drawn in to fill the lungs with the energy of its pure essence. To burn away the rooted sorrow in her heart and carry her to everlasting forgetfulness and peace.

Again, she remembered her son's face—the open eyes with clouded pupils gazing up into hers—and the knowledge, black as an abyss, that for all her training, her wisdom, even her love, she had chosen wrongly and, at last, come too late.

She screamed, "No!"

Then she was on her knees beside the lake. It was morning. The pines around her were ordinary trees. Here the sun had not yet risen. The light was gray and Mir stood in front of her with a white shift over his arm. He looked shocked and her knees were sore as if she'd fallen from somewhere else and landed in front of him.

In fact, she learned later, she had.

He handed her the shift. "You are not catching him."

Dryas pulled the shift over her head, rose to her feet, and looked at him narrowly. She remembered she had been a queen. "Who is Imona? What happened to her and why? And I will want the truth. No lies or evasions."

Mir nodded and looked off over the mountains. The sun was just beginning to glow on the snow-capped peaks. "Imona," he murmured. "Imona. Imona is a dead woman . . . Imona is in . . . no, not in the earth. She is where it is not water or land, not day or night, not cold or warm . . ."

"Yes," Dryas said. "I understand, but tell me who she was and . . . why."

"Come," Mir said. "Not to my house because the . . . my wife will be there. Higher up under the trees. I have some bread, cheese, and a little beer there. You will refresh yourself and I will tell you everything you wish to know. The story is a long one, long and rather sad."

I T WAS NEARLY NOON WHEN MIR FINISHED. DRYAS was very tired. Mir departed and Dryas, still clad only in the shift, walked back toward the lake to rescue her clothing.

She found them not where she'd placed them but scattered, as if he must have investigated the cloth after she left for whatever strange destination she'd reached. There were wolf paw prints in the soft earth near the water. She was exhausted and must sleep. Now, before she could do anything else.

She decided she would return to the same mountain meadow she'd investigated earlier. She stood, for a moment gazing out over the sunlit lake. *If I go, he will come, follow me, and I will lead him to the standing stones.*

Oh, but she was weary. Her head bowed, she wondered how she could find the strength . . . the will to do what she must.

She looked into the sunlit water. She could see down, and down and down.

Shapes moved in the gloom rising from the perpetual darkness at the center, then, stroking slowly with almost no movement of fins, into the sun-struck level just below the surface.

Near the shore, a water bird cried out. A frog plopped and she saw the long-legged shape, the head a nub on the surface of the water as the amphibian kicked his way along, swimming across the pond.

Something on top of the rock at the shore flashed in the corner of her eye. She walked toward it and saw her poppy broach resting on the stone, the gold gleaming in the sunlight. She was sure she'd thrown it into the water last night.

She went over, climbed up on the rock, picked it up, and weighed it in her hand. Yes, she *had* thrown it into the water last night. She remembered the splash it made. Odd, it was almost as if she were being asked to choose again. She hesitated, bone tired and deep in grief.

The frog reached the midpoint of the pond. He didn't see the dark shape beneath him, the dark shape with scissorslike jaws armed with long, needle-sharp teeth. No more than her son had seen it. No more than she had seen his pursuer in the dark wood until it caught him. She came too late.

The frog saw or sensed something because he zigzagged frantically, looking for escape. Almost without her volition, the broach flew from her hand toward the striking pike. He was lightning fast, but it almost looked as if he hesitated for a split second. The broach hit the water next to the swimming frog and, given his choice between two targets—one dark, the other bright—the deadly fish chose the shining one.

The jaws snapped shut and he vanished with his prize into the black realms.

And the still-swimming frog vanished into the shadows covering the other side of the lake.

O N SEEING THE GIRL ENTER THE ARENA DRESSED as a gladiator, Caesar looked astounded.

Lucius passed his hand over his face. *By the honey-dipped tits of the queen of the dead, it's one of her sex kittens.* Mellisa, by name, somewhere between fourteen and sixteen.

Even the subligaculum looked good on her. On most men, it was sweat stained and had more than a suspicion of hair protruding at the groin. On her, it wrapped around her waist. One end was drawn up decorously between her legs and over the top of the waistband to dangle seductively between the thighs.

For a moment, he thought she was bare to the waist, then saw he'd been mistaken. She wore a camisole of very fine silver chain mail that hung to just below her breasts. Very fine mail. He could see the shadows of her nipples through the shirt.

The sword she carried gave him pause. It was one of Caesar's silver-plated weapons and it flashed brilliantly in the torchlight. The thing was sharp.

She was followed into the arena by another of the sex kittens, Vella, by name. She was dark; Mellisa was fair. Otherwise, they were the same weight and size and dressed almost alike.

They joined hands and bowed to the company seated on the dais.

Caesar burst into laughter, turned, and whispered into Cleopatra's ear. She blew into his and bit his earlobe. He chuckled again and turned his attention to the two combatants and smiled indulgently on them.

The two girls began something that might be called a duel and, after the first few passes, it was apparent they had some training.

Gordus remained in the ring. He folded his arms and leaned against the lower half of the podium where Caesar was seated along with Fulvia and Cleopatra.

The blond Mellisa was the more aggressive of the two. She had a better reach and so began chasing the dark-haired girl around the ring.

At this point, Gordus stepped in and broke the combatants by lifting their swords with a bronze and ivory rod. They separated, the dark girl throwing angry glances at the blond one.

Gordus looked up at the dais. "Shall I declare a victor, Caesar?"

"Not yet," Caesar said. He looked vastly amused.

"Oh, no," Fulvia said. "I should think at least another passage of arms. Let them get their breath, though. Neither of them is addicted to exercise in the palaestra and they're short winded."

Gordus visited both combatants with towels and wine mixed with water.

Caesar's eyes devoured them, and yes, they were an enticing spectacle.

It was hard to tell which was more attractive, but Lucius was more interested in the dark one. The exercise brought a flush to her cheeks, chin, and forehead and a light film of perspiration oiled her creamy skin. The dark hair was slightly curly and it clung to her cheeks, forehead, and the nape of her neck in soft, damp ringlets.

The mail outlining her budding breasts left a tightly muscled but downy abdomen bare. The material of the loincloth was red and it set off her olive skin to perfection.

Lucius was glad he was wearing his toga. He'd managed to fool his sister into believing the worst about his manhood, but now his own treacherous body was making a liar out of him. In addition, he was already plotting and planning how to transform and transfer his sister's little sex toy's affection from women to men, and from her to him.

Fulvia didn't deserve to have all the fun. He was entitled not only to his share of the family's inheritance, but also to influence, luxury, and power; he'd let Fulvia cut him out for too long.

But he'd have to be careful. Tonight he'd played into her hands by making a fool of himself in front of Caesar. A lot of ugly and unpleasant things were said of Caesar and, in all probability, every one of them was true, but no one ever said he betrayed those who trusted and helped him. He paid back injuries with interest and would do the same for favors and loyalty.

At this point, Caesar dropped his napkin and the combat, if it could be called that, was renewed.

Lucius entertained himself by watching the play of light and shadow caused by the flickering torchlight on the somewhat-less-than-athletic curves of the dark girl's body.

Mellisa was beginning to develop what, to Lucius, was an ugly flush, whereas when Vella perspired more freely, the moisture began to give her skin an oily tinge. Now she was fighting back and not allowing herself to be intimidated as she had been at first.

When she came close to the edge of the arena, the two women closed, swords locked against each other at the hilt as they pushed at each other's faces with their free hands.

Gordus moved toward them.

"No," Caesar exclaimed. "Don't stop them. I believe their blood is up. This is a real fight now."

Evidently it was, because Mellisa reached out suddenly, seized Vella's nipple, and twisted it savagely.

Vella screamed. They broke and faced each other across the arena.

Tears of rage streamed from Vella's eyes and she touched her breast tip gingerly. "That wasn't fair," she sobbed. "We weren't supposed to really try to—"

"Oh, stop whining," Fulvia snapped. "You promised to give us a good show. Now, get to it."

Caesar clapped his hands. "Just so. One thousand sesterces to the winner and her freedom."

Fulvia laughed. "Caesar, it's not a real battle."

"It is now," he said.

And so it was. For at least a half dozen passes, they each had a two-handed grip on their swords. The two women rushed together and the amphitheater rang with the clangor of steel on steel. They hacked at each other with a will.

Lucius felt desire drain away. He felt he should do something to stop this, but Caesar and Cleopatra were both watching avidly.

Both women were drenched with sweat. The moisture plastered their hair to their scalps and streamed down their faces.

Lucius knew more of practical battle matters than the rest. Even Caesar had others do his fighting for him. But Lucius knew both women would soon be blind when the perspiration ran into their eyes. Neither of them had the modicum of protection real gladiators did—shield, helmet, or armor.

Lucius struggled to rise. He had to get in the arena and stop this. Then he felt a hand on his shoulder, pressing him down, and knew Philo had returned and was standing behind him.

Vella went blind first. A similar thing had happened to Lucius once, and he knew how helpless it made him feel, and must be making her feel. Aside from being blinded, she probably was in pain, a lot of pain, her eyes feeling as if they were on fire.

Mellisa, in no good shape herself, on the next swing caught Vella's sword below the hilt and knocked it out of her hand. The blade went spinning, striking the marble at the edge of the arena with a ringing sound.

But now Mellisa was blind. Vella managed to clear her vision.

Lucius gave a sigh of relief.

Caesar was laughing, Cleopatra was pale with disgust, and Fulvia looked annoyed.

Vella gave a screech, charged the blinded and backing Mellisa, and grabbed a handful of her hair.

Mellisa shrieked and tried to fend off her attacker . . . with the sword. The weapon entered Vella's body easily, the way a knife cuts soft butter, up to within about three inches of the hilt.

Vella looked down blankly at the sword in her body. She raised both hands as if to clutch the hilt, but it seemed as if she didn't quite dare. Then she said, "My legs." And indeed, they were without strength, because she slowly folded to her knees. Her eyes were empty by then. Lucius saw because, for some reason, she turned her head toward him. From her knees, she fell to the side, and a thin trickle of blood flowed from the corner of her mouth to the sand. She tried to breathe once, twice, then a third time. Her legs stretched out straight, quivered, and then relaxed, her knees in a slightly bent position. She was dead. The color drained from her face, leaving a waxen, yellowish pallor behind.

Lucius was sick with horror. Mellisa screamed and screamed and screamed. Philo was down the steps into the arena. He knelt for a second near Vella. No more time was required to confirm what he knew already. Then he and Gordus each seized one of Mellisa's arms and marched her out of the amphitheater. For a few moments, Lucius could hear the screams continue, then they faded into sobs and, at last, stopped.

The gardener who'd raked the sand clean came out and stared at the corpse. Blood was still flowing from it, from the terrible torso wound. The man looked at a loss, but Gordus joined him, and he knew what to do with the dead.

They picked up what remained of Vella by the legs and under the arms. Gordus propped her head against his stomach and together they carried her out of the ring. The gardener returned with his rake.

Only then did Lucius look over at his sister, Caesar, and Cleopatra. Fulvia seemed a little pale, but Caesar smiled at Cleopatra and they bantered in low tones, like lovers.

The two royal vipers were completely unperturbed.

XIV

DRYAS DRESSED IN FRESH CLOTHING—A WHITE
tunic without embroidery and the loose leggings of a
rider—but she left horse and baggage at Mir's home. Before she departed, she spoke quietly to the girl Mir called his wife.
This time she couldn't draw any speech from the girl, though there
were some tears. Dryas was glad to see the tears and she hoped the
child might find peace and, if possible, healing.

Before she started up the mountain, she spoke with Mir. He
nodded when she told him about the tears. "She will die now," he said.

Dryas was taken aback. "Die?"

"Die," Mir repeated.

Dryas looked over at the girl. She had crowned herself with blue
wild asters and was dancing among the fading autumn sunflowers,
humming a tuneless tune to herself. "You're sure?" Dryas asked. The
wisdom of a man like Mir wasn't to be taken lightly.

"Yes, I've seen the look before. She only waited for you to come.
Now, she can to go to join the rest. She has lived, suffered enough.
Catch the wolf and take him to hunt Caesar. Now there's a quarry
worthy of such a beast."

Dryas nodded and started up the mountain alone.

It was near sunset when she reached the mountain meadow.

The shadow awaited her. The voice spoke in her mind. *He is a
powerful creature and you will not conquer him without help. What you plan
is not enough. Bind him. You have the power. You have the will. Bind him.
Or certainly one of you will die!*

Dryas disdained to ask which one, but then, possibly even the spirit couldn't be sure. On the Isle of Women, among her fellow students, they had debated the ability of her and her kind to seek the trance and sometimes know the final results of a course of action. Were the results of these rites more accurate than those allowed by the vagaries of chance? Had beings from beyond the world a greater ability to acquire foreknowledge of the workings of destiny?

Her teacher, Lyssa, believed they did. "Knowledge is one," she told Dryas. "The ability to predict the future is rooted in our knowledge of the past and present. Assuming they are attentive . . . an assumption others have quarreled with . . . they of the worlds beyond death are in a better position to assess the virtues and failings of humanity as a whole and the strengths and weaknesses of individual men and women. Thus, their knowledge of past and present may be broader and deeper than ours could ever be. So we feel it wise to consult them in moments of doubt, and their advice should be weighed and considered. Such wisdom as they offer us, even if it is not perfect, is still not lightly cast aside."

Dryas smiled. How dispassionate, how logical, how objective Lyssa had been. But one could be all of the above and still be very, very wrong.

The shadow remained. She could see the darkness where it stood was not made by anything visible to her eyes.

It warned, but it didn't command, and she would not ask its permission for anything. The burden of choice was on her. She, and she alone, must set her course and abide the consequences, for good or ill. In a sense, her whole life was a preparation for this moment.

The shadow was silent. It did not speak again.

Dryas turned and walked over to her bedding. The thing was in a small, soft leather pouch. She emptied it out into her hand. When she felt the cold links against her skin, it was as if she had inadvertently placed her hand on something wickedly hot. A pot that looked cold, but had been heated in the fire almost to the point of melting, a heat great enough to sear the flesh down to the bone.

She felt the jolt of pain flash through mind and body as if her loss had only been a few days, a week, a month ago. The sense of loss drenched her mind with an agony of grief. An almost mortal sorrow washed over her like a breaking sea.

But then this grief had been long ago, and also like some monstrous wave, it failed to drag her into the depths. She kept her footing in the refuge of now until the suffering ebbed, tamed by time and distance.

Odd that something so beautiful could be the source of such sorrow.

It glimmered in the deepening twilight with a metallic sheen, a chain formed of gold in the pattern of rowan leaves, flowers, and berries. Or rather, the rowan leaves were gold, the flower corymbs ivory, and the berry clusters garnet.

The tree was in leaf, flower, and fruit, and Dryas thought, as she always had, that it was wrought with more than human skill. She lifted it up, high up, so that it caught the last sunset rays and it seemed she held fire, snow, and sun dazzle in her hand.

It is forbidden to make such a thing because it might capture the rowan spirit in it or at least a splinter of the tree's life. It could capture part of the life of any being, and this was what she wished to do.

I have been tested, she thought. *I have been tested and not found wanting.*

She bowed her head as one bending it to accept a yoke, and slipped the chain over her head.

It was never intended to be worn by mortal woman. She could just barely see the shadow. It was part of the trees looking down at her from the slope behind.

She felt desire rise as it had last night. She understood it was the fire of creation, a cascade of light illuminating the world like another sun and sweeping all before it as does the wind when it pulls the waves to higher peaks and deeper troughs until they crash at last, falling through the spectrum of gray, blue, jade, emerald, and then, at last, white—white as the clustered flowers of the elder and rowan in the springtime.

LUCIUS WAS AWAKENED BY HIS TWO PERSONAL slaves a little after dawn. He debated cursing both of them, but knew they wouldn't have ventured to call him without strict orders from Fulvia and, if he gave vent to his displeasure and crawled back under the covers, she would probably undertake some really poisonous course of action. No, he had better find out what was on her mind.

He raised his first finger and thumb, leaving a small space between them, and said, "You're both about this far from the auction block."

They accepted this threat with equanimity. Well, he hadn't expected them to cower and cringe.

One of them handed him a folded piece of paper. He squinted at it, but for the life of him, he couldn't make out what it said.

He rubbed his eyes and finally realized he was holding a fragment of one of Cicero's nastier speeches about Catiline.

He gazed at it, mystified. "Una?" he asked.

"On the inside," one of them said.

Lucius decided he'd name them Castor and Pollux, but he hadn't decided which one to name Castor so the other would be Pollux. He wasn't even sure if it was Pollux or Castor who spoke.

He unfolded the paper. Scrawled on the inside was an invitation. He could make out enough words to be clear on that, but otherwise the message was unintelligible.

"Unan," he said.

"It's from the Lord Marc Antony. He would like to invite you to breakfast."

Lucius said, "Brrette," blowing through his lips. "Brrreakfast." Breakfast or a reasonable approximation of the word. Then he decided he'd best halt these proceedings before he descended into complete and utter, irrevocable idiocy. "Get Philo," he snarled.

They did.

Philo strolled in looking fresh as an April morning. Lucius handed the note to him. "Get my lord fresh clothing, his toga, and some warm water," Philo told Castor, or was it Pollux? Lucius didn't know, but they both disappeared and that was comforting.

"Hmmm," Philo said, and stroked his chin. "I imagine your sister's request to Caesar has already borne fruit."

"How did you know about that?" Lucius asked.

"Because I, like every other member of the household—slave and free—was standing in the kitchen, listening avidly to every word said."

"Nonsense. The kitchen is a tiny room. They couldn't all fit."

"You'd be amazed how many people can get into a very small space if they all cooperate and besides, there's always the roof and the garden."

Castor and Pollux returned just then, carrying the indicated articles of clothing and the warm water, ending the argument. "Will you want a bath, sir?" one of them asked.

"Why, in the name of Charon's ass, should I bathe at this hour of the morning? Antony wouldn't notice if I was dripping perfume or stank like an unflushed latrine."

Antony didn't.

When they reached his house, the porter admitted them without difficulty. One of Antony's freedmen was in the garden, setting a table for breakfast.

Lucius asked for Antony. The man rolled his eyes at both of them. "My lord is in the tepiderium," he said.

Antony was. He sat in a cloud of steam, sipping something that smelled disgusting from a silver cup. He moaned loudly when they opened the door and daylight struck his eyes. He was a big man and, though running a bit to fat, was still handsome. He was dark with thick curly hair on his head, chest, arms, groin, and thighs.

He looked at Philo the way a drowning man looks when someone throws him a plank. "I'm reluctant to thank any god for anything this morning," he murmured, "but I'm glad to see you, Philo."

Then he transferred his bloodshot gaze to Lucius and looked at him as if he were limbless and had just crawled out from the damp area under a boulder. "Do I know you? And, if I don't, what could you possibly want? It had better be important or your next stop will be a tour of the Tullianum."

"Oh, you know me," Lucius said. "I just don't know if you remember me. How many of the people you meet do you remember?"

Antony began to laugh, then choked, gagged, and vomited over the raised edge of the marble pool he lay in. "Oh, oooh, ooooh. Don't make me laugh. It hurts too much. My skull is going to split and my brains will run out of my eyes and into the hot water and I'll be out of my misery. Please, please, please." He extended one arm to heaven. "Immortal gods, let this happen," and then added, "That bastard Caesar will be sorry. No. Correction. Caesar's never sorry about anything. The answer to your question is probably one in ten."

Just then Philo re-entered the room. Lucius hadn't noticed he was gone. He carried a glass of rather murky crystal, decorated with spirals of drawn gold wire, and a rolled towel. He placed the towel on Antony's head where it resembled a rather thick crown and handed the glass to him, cautioning, "Take it slowly."

Philo removed the silver cup Antony had been sipping. It stank of the sour wine, more vinegar than wine, called posca. It was made for slaves on rural estates. The vile beverage was considered a sovereign remedy for hangovers.

Antony cautiously tasted the contents of Philo's glass. "Ahhh," he sighed, and allowed himself to sink deeper and deeper into the water. "Philo, I never know what's in your concoctions, but I don't care. You can poison me anytime."

Lucius looked around the room, found two stools, and brought them to the edge of the pool where he and Philo sat down.

"Spearmint, white wine, valerian, and a touch of opium for the headache," Philo said. "It's no secret. Spearmint settles the stomach, white wine is a hair of the dog, in your case Cerberus, valerian calms the nerves, and I've already explained the opium."

"Cerberus, eh!" Antony rumbled.

"You are reputed to engage in some ferocious drinking bouts. In your case, I believe Cerberus is appropriate. No lesser dog would dare bite you."

"True," Antony said, his nose in the cup again.

"It's nice to be admired, isn't it?" Lucius contributed.

"Snow in the towel, I suppose?" Antony asked.

Philo nodded. "There was some left over from last night's party."

"You've come up in the world, haven't you?" Lucius said cheerfully. "Last time we met, I believe you'd fallen out with your noble friend. You and Caesar weren't speaking. What happened?"

"What happened to cause the rift or what healed it?"

"Both."

"I don't think I'll answer that," Antony said. "Some time when I know you better, maybe."

Lucius said, "Ummm."

Antony yelled and pounded on the floor. "The water's getting cold and I want more steam. Gesses, tell those lazy sons of stray mongrels to stop feeling up the kitchen maids and throw some more fuel in the furnace or I'll have their hides off in strips before noon." Then he clutched his head again. "Oh, oh, oh." He snatched the wet towel from his forehead and handed it to Philo. "More snow!" he roared.

Philo wrung out the towel. It diluted not one, but several puddles of an unpleasant substance, all near the tub.

At this point, Antony contributed another offering of the same material, then drained the cup and yelled at the departing Philo, "More hangover cure, too."

Lucius, almost compulsively neat, found the condition of Antony's baths appalling. Yes, they were luxurious—white, black, and yellow marble. The floor showed serpentine waves in yellow, black, and white mosaic, all surrounding the black marble tub—big enough to have submerged a horse—where Antony floated.

But the place was a mess. Linen towels, sponges large and small, perfume flasks, oil jugs, combs, brushes, tweezers, and other nameless miscellany were scattered everywhere. Not to mention sticky puddles of vomit, wine, and hunks of discarded food lying scattered around the central tub.

"I said," Antony yelled at the top of his lungs, "this water is getting cold. Don't make me come out in the chill morning air to—"

This was as far as he got. Flower-shaped black marble fixtures on the wall hissed loudly and steam began to pour out of openings in the center, filling the room with warm fog. At the same moment, a black marble statue of a Nubian beauty clad in ivory and bronze began to pour water from a pitcher in her hand into the tub.

"Aaah." Antony settled back and relaxed. He had a bowl of walnuts near his hand, so he picked some up and began cracking them with his thumb.

"Caesar woke me at the crack of dawn with a list of things he wanted me to do today. I can't see how he stands it. I can't and never could do half the work he does. If I tried, I'd die of exhaustion before the calends of next month. He goes home with that Ptolemy bit—. . . ah, Egyptian queen—and porks her. Then he goes home and has to prove to Calpurnia that they're still married, and here he is at first light, with a list of all he wants me to do and tells me—me!—to get up! Don't sleep till noon! And do it! Or risk his grave displeasure. Smiles at me with the grin that shows all his sharpest teeth and leaves for the Senate.

"We had a party last night. Fulvia—my wife, not your sister— took a horsewhip to me. Seems I got it up, but couldn't get it down. Wine will do that and a horsewhipping always does the trick. But here I am, it's dawn. My ass is sore. My stomach is upset. My skull wants to explode, and he's telling me to get you into the Senate."

"No," Lucius said mulishly. "I have no intention of—"

"Don't argue with me," Antony roared. "Not unless you really want a room in the Tullianum. Let's see what bread, water, and a week in that hole in the ground will do. I'll wager you'll sing another tune then."

Lucius sighed. "I'll wager I will, too. All right, but don't try to convince me he's doing it out of the goodness of his heart. Tell me what he really wants."

"I will if you shut up and stop interrupting me. He wants you to spy on the other senators."

Lucius stood up so quickly he knocked over the stool he'd been sitting on. It clattered loudly on the marble floor. "You . . . you! I may not be a patrician the way you and your ass-kissing friends are but . . ."

Philo walked in just then carrying another towel and a second cup.

Antony slammed his fist down on the water. As a gesture it lacked force, so he snatched up the bowl of nuts at his elbow and threw it at Lucius' head.

The bowl was a heavy molded stoneware piece. The rim connected with Lucius' forehead, opening a cut about three inches long. After a few seconds, it bled profusely.

Lucius saw stars. Not only stars, but comets and maybe a few small moons. He staggered and his knees turned to water for a moment.

Philo caught him by the arm, flipped the stool upright with one foot, and assisted him into a sitting position. He pressed the snow-filled towel to the cut on Lucius' forehead and handed the hangover cure to Antony, who gulped it down. "May I ask what happened?" Philo asked calmly.

"Yes, you may ask," Lucius snapped.

Antony climbed out of the pool and threw a gown with a hole in the middle over his head. He explained Caesar's request to Philo.

Philo gave Lucius a sympathetic look. "The man is . . . what and who he is. There is no appeal, my lord."

Lucius gave Philo a poisonous look and snatched the snow-filled pack from his forehead.

"Shut up!" Antony roared. "Shut up before you commit treason and I have to report it to him! Your man's no fool and he's right. There is no appeal. And besides . . ." He ground his teeth. "Once you've put up with that gang of liars, thieves, grafters, whores, slobs, windbags, idiots, bumfuckers, thugs, leeches, six-legged bloodsuckers, adulterers, bores, panderers, blackmailers, extortionists, murderers, and—have I missed anything? Oh, yes, snakes—for a few months, you'll be delighted to pour your frustration and rage into my willing ear."

He raised his finger. "Trust me, Caesar has lots of spies and you don't have to tell me anything you don't want to. Your sister will be happy and, by the way, they tell me she's a worse harpy than my wife—I'd stay clear of her—and Caesar will leave for Parthia, and you can do whatever you please. Hear me?"

Lucius was tight-lipped with rage, but he managed a "Yes."

"Fine." Antony rubbed his hands together. "I'm feeling better all the time. What say you to a few hours at the palaestra and then some lunch?" He slapped Lucius on the back. "My cook is butchering two wild boars for me." He added gleefully, "My wife will be out of town. Come have supper with me.

"Hey, do you remember our first meeting? We were sitting up late over the wine with that little Alexandrian dancing girl. You remember her. She had two big gold hoops in her nipples. Do you remember the suggestion she made?"

Lucius did and he colored a little at the memory.

"Amazing," Antony continued. "It shocked me. Imagine that. I was shocked."

"Indeed," Philo said, "that is difficult to imagine."

Antony looked at Philo for a second through his eyebrows. "In any case, at about that point in the . . . ah . . . evening—"

"I think it was closer to morning," Lucius interrupted.

"Yes," Antony continued, "at about that time my memory gets a little hazy."

"I should think it would," Lucius said. "I didn't know anyone could drink that much wine and remain upright and moving."

"Yes, yes, but what I want to know is, did we act on that, um . . . suggestion?"

"I don't think I'll answer that right now," Lucius said. "Sometime when I know you better, maybe. Then I will tell you, but not right now."

"Ha!" Antony said. "So, turnabout's fair play. Well, I asked for it."

"Beautiful room, this," Lucius said. It gave him an excuse to look away from Antony. He needed one.

"Crap," Antony answered. "It makes me feel bilious. Now, all you have to do there in the Senate is keep your mouth shut and your ears and eyes open. Go in, sit down if you can find a seat. Or if you can't, lean on the wall."

"All the Senate does is dream up new honors for Caesar," Lucius snarled.

"Yes, Caesar packed it so nicely. Don't you know anything about politics at all?"

"It seems not."

"Well, my boy, the members of law-making bodies are helpless until they can form factions, cabals, conspiracies, cliques, parties, associations, or, in other words, find partners in crime. Now, what Caesar did was add three hundred members to the Senate who all owe their elevated rank to Caesar. So all our indigenous criminal class—the patricians—can do now is mill around and talk. Not that they aren't dangerous enough when they do that.

"But no one faction is big enough to vote down three hundred new members—need I add all loyal to Caesar—so at present they're harmless. He's drawn the adders' teeth."

"Yes, but they grow back."

"Not just yet." Antony gave Lucius and Philo a hooded glance. "You go to the Senate and make your sister happy. Don't give me any more trouble." He strode out the door and was gone.

D RYAS RETURNED TO THE MEADOW. SHE SAT IN silence, watching from high up as night claimed the world. The shadow of the mountain stretched out over the plain, sliding over hills, forests, and the villas and pastures of the people.

Her people and the Romans were indistinguishable because of their distance in time and space.

As the sun sank lower, its last rays rose higher, drowning the world in shadow, enriching the heights with golden light. The long, soft, shining green grass in the meadows around her tossed, whispering in the evening wind. The tall blades caressed her ankles, calves, and thighs.

I must love him, the wolf, the man-wolf, the way the grass loves the earth whereon it grows and the autumn wind that blows and kisses it to brilliance.

I must teach him to turn his fire to me. Not the way he burned the wheat fields of those who he blamed for her death, but to allow me the fire of desire that weds the fruitful earth to sunfires that draw from the soil the manifold shapes that form the kingdoms of life. The tree bending in adoration before the wind. The tall white barley, yellow wheat, orchards adorned with the multitude of flowers that become the pomes, apples, plums, pears, and downy peaches. The flowers of the waste raising their faces, pledging fidelity to the sun by day and the moon by night.

The stormfire lancing across the sky, sending its blow to earth to bless eternally the sacrificial toil that calls fire from the gods and places it in the hands of man.

Then she took her iron ring and kindled the fire from among the deadfalls littering the grass.

The sun hovered for a moment at the edge of the world, then descended into darkness. This high, her fire was balanced against the light of the ghostly crescent hanging in the clear autumn air, rather like a nail paring discarded by an eternal deity. And, as the last orange and green glow of sunset faded from the horizon, the stars peered in their myriads from the darkness above to look down on Dryas standing alone.

She drew off her shift and threw it into the flames. The fire flared very high, illuminating her flesh as she stood in proud nakedness before night and the stars.

Will he come? she wondered. She reached for the chain around her neck and her hand made a fist around the golden leaves.

A blasphemy. The thing was a blasphemy.

No one had the right to make such a thing and include in it all the stages of a tree's life and all the parts, making it share the human universe. There, among the leaves, fruit, and flowers, she felt the dark secret roots twisted into the pattern formed by the artist. The tree informed the earth and gaia. The earth formed the tree. To include all in the circle was dangerous. Her people didn't usually do it, always leaving something out or breaking it in spots even in a fortress or a crown.

Will he come? she wondered. *Because his is the choice now. I have already chosen.*

Then she heard a movement in the grass and a pair of strong male arms closed around her. She shivered for a second and then yielded to the body, warm and strong behind her.

He kissed her on the throat and ear. Then asked innocently, "Do you like this? Imona did."

"Yes," she answered and forbore comment on the fact that he spoke of one woman while in the arms of another. *No,* she thought. *He is not yet a man. I must make him one—tonight.*

His hands roamed over her body, searching, testing, exploring until, at last, caressing. "You are made as she was. The first time, I never knew her name; the second was Imona. I have had only two of you. Are you all made so?"

"Yes." Then she made a small sound. His explorations were now intimate and she found herself electrified by some of the places he found to investigate.

"What does that mean? Is it a word?" he asked. "I thought I knew most words, but I haven't heard that one . . . before."

"No, it's not a word, but an indication of pleasure."

Then, very gently, he turned her around.

For the first time, she felt afraid. There was an awesome and beautiful innocence in his face. And, for a second, she had the pleasure and guilt of a ravisher who holds helpless, forbidden fruit in his hands. But then no, because there was no sense of theft. It was rather as if he were the cowering, yet eager, virgin bride and she the bridegroom burdened with the duty of initiation into the mystery, and yes, the cruelty, of creation.

But then he kissed her and pressed his body against hers and the illusion vanished. He was male, compellingly, totally male and, for a second, she was only an animal with the freedom from responsibility only an animal knows. Now she'd passed the point of no return.

She'd spread a clean linen coverlet on the ground near the fire. It was padded with the blanket she used when she slept in the open.

He moved her toward it, saying, "Yes, Imona liked to lie on something. In the opening in the earth where we coupled, she said the floor was cold."

He moved her backward until she was standing on it. "I can touch you. I can smell you." He bent her body back over his arm and buried his face between her breasts. "Now I want to taste you."

She stood. He knelt before her. He parted her thighs with his hands.

"How do I taste?" she asked.

"Of yourself, alone." He did something, she wasn't sure what, but it made her gasp and she found her fingers tightening in his hair, urging him on.

"Yes, only this is you. The first didn't taste the way Imona did and you don't have her flavor."

"Are women then wine, that each forms a separate kind of cup?" she asked.

But he didn't answer. He was . . . preoccupied. A second later, so was she because her sex had begun to pulsate in time to the beating of her heart.

She found herself on the ground in his arms without quite knowing how she got there.

"You vanished from my arms last night. How can I hold you here?" he asked.

"I don't know. Try."

His weight shifted and she found her body's pulsations increased. Only now the throbbing was delightful, so delightful in fact that she was sure this must be forbidden. But she could no longer resist it, no more than she could have resisted a current that sucked her down. She wanted more of such joy and she was getting it. It entered her body the way a sword enters a warm padded sheath, penetrating her more deeply by the second until she was sure it would become unbearable and then it did.

The sheer flow of raw pleasure drowned her will, her intellect, and, at last, her very consciousness of self.

The reflexes—back arching, fingers clutching, final outcry—were all no more under her control than the extinction of self in an abyss of surrender. It is the power of creation; she knew it then finally, and struggle how we will, we are all its slaves.

She didn't know how long she slept in his arms, but when she woke she read the sky and could tell by the position of the stars that it was almost dawn.

Not a man, but a wolf lay beside her. He was a giant, even as the mountain wolves went, and she knew he had but toyed with Blaze. No mere man could stand against this creature.

The chain at her neck moved, making a soft clinking sound. One of his ears flipped back and she knew that even in his sleep, he heard the sound.

For a moment she was afraid, but then she dismissed the fear as unworthy of a warrior. In a duel where one must prevail or die, the acceptance of the mortal alternative is a precondition for beginning it. No one who is willing to join battle fears death.

He truly might kill her. Emasculation would be kinder than what she planned for him.

The fire flared for a moment in a freshening breeze, then sank to coals. The wolf slept on, muzzle on his paws, eyes closed, dreaming.

The darkness pressed around Dryas like a living thing. She heard the voice in the wind or perhaps it *was* the wind—for *she* is not simply mother of the earth, but queen of the winds as well. *Do not tarry. You have not much time.*

Dryas rose. She would swear she only looked away from the wolf for a second, but when she glanced back, he was a man.

The black wind hissed over the grass. She walked toward the invisible ladder up to the stone ring overlooking the valley. The long grass blades were tousled like the hair of a sleeping child.

In the night, ice had formed on their edges and burned Dryas' feet as she strode toward the stone footholds that led out over the valley and up to . . .

Odd, Dryas thought. *It has no name, but everyone knows what you are speaking of when you talk of one.*

He caught her halfway across the meadow. He embraced and tried to kiss her. "Come back. You must be cold. Come back and I will warm you."

His voice was like velvet; his lips silk.

Dryas thought of all the tales she'd heard of women who betrayed men. In the end, they were easy to fool, but to take advantage of such splendid innocence was as cruel an action as Dryas had ever contemplated. Her teachers had demanded the highest standards from her. Absolute truthfulness; the courage to lay down her life, if necessary, not only without complaint, but without a second thought.

What would they think of her deeds this night? But she knew they, like she, would weigh them against the safety of Mir's people and, however reluctantly, accept her choice.

But they would also believe he, too, should be given the right to choose.

"I have drink above," she said. "It will warm us."

The black wind died down and it seemed the whole earth was still.

"It's near dawn," he said. "Tell me where it is. I watched you climb up there before. I'll go up and get it. I don't like that place. It smells and looks wrong to me. If you fall, you'll be dashed to death against the rocks."

"So will you," Dryas forced herself to say.

"No, I can bring myself back from the edge of death. I have that power. Anything that doesn't kill me instantly doesn't hurt me at all. I am not a wolf."

"And you are not a man." She kissed him again, molding her body against his, spreading her legs at his hips as if asking for his heat.

"No, and I don't want to be one. You of all beasts under heaven are the cruelest, the most malicious and merciless. You spare nothing in your wrath. A wolf understands anger. But you don't kill to live, but for convenience only."

She kissed him again, running her hands over his body. "If you despise us so, then why take our shape?"

"Because I'm tempted by . . . women. Women and power."

"Then come with me. Come drink the honey mead. I put some up there near the stone circle."

"I have had wine. I don't know as much about mead."

"Then come," and her voice was subtle as the serpent's when it spoke to Eve. "Don't you want me again?"

"Yes," he answered. "Yes and yes and more yesses. One for each night and then however often I can persuade you to yield to me on each and every night."

"Come, and I will show you magic, enchantment. Come taste of love perfect and everlasting."

"No," he said. "Perfect and everlasting is too much to ask of . . . anything."

He drew back. In the distance far away, a wolf howled. He turned away, listening.

"Are they calling you?"

"No." He shook his head. "That's . . . They don't have names . . . I'm trying to think of a way to tell you. He has white on his muzzle, four claws on his left forefoot and very worn teeth. He is telling me where they will den today after the sun rises. Why do you ask me these things? Imona never questioned me this way."

"I think she didn't want to know too much about her lover."

"No," he said. "I don't think she did either."

Another chorus of howls ran out. To her shock, he answered. She hadn't known such a sound could come from a human throat.

She looked at him questioningly.

"Imona would have been frightened out of her wits."

"I'm not Imona," Dryas said. "What did they tell you?"

"Nothing. These were only polite greetings. Now, be sensible. Come with me."

"No," Dryas said, turning toward the edge of the meadow. "I want to greet the sun and I'm cold. The mead will warm me."

He watched her draw away from him for a moment, then shrugged and followed her through the grass.

For a moment Dryas thought she'd lost, but her ears were sharp enough to detect the whisper of his tread on the ice-crusted grass blades. A few steps brought her to the edge of the meadow. She was feeling for the first handhold when he came up behind her, took her hand in his, and placed it in the first niche in the rock.

"You see well in the dark," she commented.

"I am a wolf. I do a lot of things better than a man. You are a clumsy kind. Your talents lie in other directions."

She felt no sense of insult. His tone was matter-of-fact, neutral. She understood he was simply stating the truth as he saw it.

They climbed together.

Below, the meadow was somewhat sheltered, but here it was as it had been the first time she came. The wind seemed to blow almost constantly.

But she'd hidden another blanket and it was wrapped around a clay flask. It was surprisingly heavy, glazed on both the inside and outside. The stopper doubled as a cup.

She knelt, poured some mead into the cup, and tasted it. Her stomach was empty and the drink rocked her to her heels.

In the spring, the mountain flower crops succeed one another. First, the lowland orchards bloom with wild cherry and crab apple, then the tame fruits—peach, plum, almond, quince, and clover—begin to spread white, yellow, and scarlet.

But there are other more sinister growths: orange henbane; the ghostly white poppy; and, in the shadows on streambanks, nightshade, blue and gold, which scatters its first blossoms among the yet-green lavender hidden by the grass.

Then the oak, ash, and beech drip with male flowers, scattering pollen into the spring winds and, mixed with tree pollen, drifts that of mistletoe, carrying the key to otherworldly paths.

The bees don't discriminate. Some things are lost. Some things will be lost, Dryas thought. For only those of Mir and Blaze's order knew when to collect the honey and how to brew the mead, and neither would have any real successor. They would take this secret to their graves with them.

She drank, seeing that mysterious, gentle innocence in his face. He sipped.

"It has a good taste," he said, and drank some more. And, without quite realizing it, he'd finished the jug.

Gently, she kissed the last few droplets from his mouth.

He reached out and touched her breast and a savage hunger awoke in her. She wanted him. She wanted him to wipe out her consciousness, her will, as he had the first time. But she knew with a deep sadness that he couldn't. She was cursed by what she'd done and would now do.

He was more demanding and impatient now and she sensed the mead had done its work. It was all she could do to keep him from forcing her to the ground then and there. But she was able to lead him to the flat stone in the center of the circle.

Once there, lying on the bier, the place of the dead, she found herself afraid and her desire began to ebb. All around, in each opening in the circle, she saw them standing. She could see each clearly for only a second, then they shimmered as does a reflection in a still pond when an insect or a fish breaks the surface and the picture of trees and sky flies into a thousand scattered shards.

A skull-eyed woman in coarse, brown homespun held a child by the hand. Both woman and child had their eyes burned out. A young warrior, too young, his beard only fuzz on his sallow skin, eyes closed, tears on his cheeks, one leg a mass of blood, a scarlet stripe across his throat: he'd been wounded, his throat cut while he lay helpless. Another woman, faceless, a winding sheet wrapped tightly around her, trying to hide the fact that her skull was crushed and she'd been gutted like a deer.

They are shadows, Dryas thought.

She looked up and concentrated on his face. The wind was rising, blowing low clouds across the edges of the clearing. She could see the vapors glow whitely because the light was growing, the dead were being drawn into the boiling clouds, rising from the valley, and vanishing.

He forced her legs apart with his knee and, a second later, she felt a stab of pain and knew she hadn't been quite ready when entered.

Then she wondered if she'd been right because the slight pain was tonic and cleared her shadowed mind. She was drawn into the exquisite contemplation of the excitation of quivering flesh on flesh. *Rather like being in a swing, being pushed high,* she thought.

Oh, how does one describe this feeling, even to one's self or even remember it? Higher. Don't let this ever stop. Then highest.

Just then, the sun's rays poured golden light into the mist. She studied his face, intent and beautiful above her, and her body was drawn into worship, submission, and an ultimate realization of absolute peace by his.

P HILO AND LUCIUS STOOD QUIETLY ALONE IN Antony's bath.

"I'd like to . . ." Lucius raised a clenched fist.

Philo rested a hand on his arm. "Don't." The word was the closest to a command Lucius had ever heard Philo utter. "Don't!" he repeated, this time more as an entreaty. "Don't! Not even in front of me. Antony meant everything he said about treason. And sit down. The cut on your forehead is bleeding again."

Lucius allowed himself to be pushed into a sitting position on one of the stools near the tub.

"Let me get a clean bandage on it." Philo picked up the heavy bowl that held the nuts. Water was still pouring from the statue's pitcher. He rinsed the bowl and filled it with warm water. One corner of the room held a stack of clean towels. He fetched two, washed Lucius' face with one, and tore the other into strips to use as a dressing. "Before we talk, let me look around," Philo said.

He left and returned with another glass of something. He handed it to Lucius. "Drink!"

"You mixed it yourself?"

"Yes! It goes without saying."

Lucius drank.

"Now," Philo said. "I believe we're really alone."

"How do I get out of this?"

"You don't. I meant what I said. There's no appeal, but you can develop a lingering illness, an ague, tertian or quartan fever. Go one day, then the next, wrap a cloth around your neck and tell everyone—including your sister—that you have taken a chill. I'll support you, saying I believe you have a fever. Then you can spend several weeks lounging around on a velvet couch in the library, reading . . . whatever takes your fancy."

"And when the several weeks are up?"

"I'll think of something. I was coming to see you this morning to talk to you about a very important matter. The girl, Vella . . . her lover . . ."

"She had a lover?"

"Yes. Not a man, a woman: the kitchen maid you sent out to get a salad." Philo reached up and ran his fingers through his hair. "This girl is very distraught. She . . . she . . . made some threats."

"Oh, no, you didn't leave her alone? Where's Fulvia?"

"Easy, the girl is sleeping and the other slaves are watching her. They are afraid of the punishment if one of the household slaves kills their owner. Every man, woman, and child belonging to the family will be executed. They are in terror of such a massacre. They might kill her if she gets too violent. But your sister's safe enough. She's off visiting the Egyptian queen."

"And blissfully unaware someone wants to cut her heart out, if she has one."

"Just so. I was coming to intercede with you for the kitchen girl. Or at least to try . . ."

Lucius shook his head, then winced. His forehead was sore. "Is everyone, no matter who, indispensable to someone else?"

"Almost always," Philo answered sadly.

"Get the praetor. Do you know someone who will take her in?"

"You're sure you want the praetor and not the carnifice?"

"I can remember when a noble house could command the loyalty of its servants without calling in a torturer, an executioner. No! I will not have my home dishonored by such an individual or his actions. No! That was horrible enough last night. I don't want any more blood on my family's hands. Get her out of my house. No! I don't want her executed. No! Give her her freedom; tell her to get out and never come near the Basilian villa again. You know someone who will take the girl in?"

"There's a woman who—"

"No! No! No! Don't tell me. I don't want to know. Just get rid of her—and make sure Fulvia never gets wind of the whole affair. Did you get any sleep last night?"

Philo shook his head. "No."

"Well, let's go home and get some."

"I can't," Philo said. "I have to call on Gordus and make sure his son—"

"The other swordsman was his son!"

"Yes. Martinus by name."

"Why, for heaven's sake?"

"The boy hero-worships him and wants to follow in his father's footsteps," Philo said.

"Oh, he wanted to discourage him."

"Just so. He'll cripple the boy if he has to, to keep him out of the arena. And I can't say I blame him. I think were he my son—"

"If he were your son, you'd probably bring him up to have better sense. What's Fulvia up to with that Egyptian . . . trull?"

"I don't know and I wish I did. Firminius is with her. She's up to some mischief, all right."

"Well, let's go and free that girl before my darling sister gets back. Tertian or quartan fever?"

"What?"

"Your memory is worse than mine. What kind of disease do you want me to get?"

"Tertian. It's less serious. We wouldn't want to get your sister's hopes up now, would we? And, by the way, what did that Alexandrian dancing girl suggest you do?"

"Never mind. You don't want to know."

"I don't?"

"No."

WHEN MAENIEL WOKE, DRYAS WAS SITTING ON the edge of the stone, plaiting her hair.

The valley was filled with mist. So thick were the vapor clouds that they concealed even the mountain meadow.

He sat up, knowing he hadn't slept long, and shaded his eyes with his hand against the light. His head hurt. He was unfamiliar with the classic hangover. He tried to call the wolf and panicked when he found he couldn't.

Dryas stood there, wearing only the necklace, her hair braided to a coil at the back of her head.

Her eyes met his and he knew his wolf senses remained. They told him men were in the high meadow. He heard the clink of fetters. He wondered why they hadn't killed him. The mountain's bones weren't far below his feet and he clawed up a rock, but then he met her eyes again.

They were dark blue, not like water or the sky, but lapis or sapphire. The blueness was like that of the berries he'd tasted when he crossed the river to try to rescue Imona. A blueness that tasted and smelled of the color itself. Then they were wells and the black pupils expanded the way a hawk's will when it looks into distance or profound darkness to snare its prey. Or the raven's wing mantling bloody meat scraps.

Yes, he thought, *I killed when I should not.*

He remembered them as the fire people, when his kind, the dire wolf, first met them as hunters across the frozen plain. Poor things. At first they were only scavengers of the frozen carcasses abandoned by the gray, his people; the yellow, cats and their ilk; and the brown, the giant bear.

They were weak. Perhaps their very weakness was what made them strong. Desperation was in their cries, and in the blows of rocks and sticks they hurled at their rival killers.

Yes, a pack that fought back might take one, but always they took two or even three. They blinded the yellow tribe with fire and often blinded them in earnest, taking their eyes with sharp sticks, leaving them to wander in agony and starve because they could not see.

The brown, the bears, held them back the longest. Even after, everything in the frozen forest and tundra feared them. But they fell also because, in spite of their great strength, they were solitaries and slept through the dark months.

His wolf's mind had no concept of the time from the moment of the battle's inception till its end. No one counted days, months, years, or even millennia then, or marked the brief summers and those times when the ice withdrew and the world was kinder.

Always, always the cold and darkness came back. They died under the fangs of wolves. They died of disease, shivering, their lives burning away during bitter nights in places where they could barely shelter from the killing wind and cold. Cats took their young on the stalk when the shes let their children stray too far from the band. And the giant bear disputed his caves with them.

A hundred times they failed, a thousand. So many times one might spend a lifetime simply counting their defeats, but they never yielded. And it was this fearless spirit that brought the wolves into the gully to lie and warm the few women who were trying to save their own and their children's lives.

They had forgotten these things and ruled where they had once been outcasts, even among the killers. But their flesh, every ounce of it, remembered every drop of blood in their veins, kept faith with their struggle, as did every atom of bone.

He saw all this in Dryas' eyes. Like each of them, she was formed for desire and, like each one, for murder, also.

He fell into the darkness he saw there and was swept away.

XV

WINTER WORE ON AND THE COLD DEEPENED. The glaciers reached down from the heights, sending their messengers of snow into the valleys. Rivers froze, except the pool where the wolves gathered. They searched for him there and, for a time, called him, their voices making the mountains ring with their unearthly summons. But he did not either reply or return. So, in the end, as both beasts and men do, they forgot him.

Another leader emerged and the pack went on as before. The days grew shorter and shorter and sometimes the northern lights flared over the mountains. The wolves ran like demonic shadows over the frozen crust and prospered amidst the winter desolation. When all other beasts struggled with hunger, cold, and even thirst as the streams and river froze, they took their apportioned tribute—the young who would never see springtime, those who had been strong now weakened by hunger, and those showing the first traces of age.

Even the Romans were loathe to stir out of their fortress in the valley because the days were so short, the cold so intense. So the powerful silver predators roamed even the deep valleys by sun and starlight.

Dryas remained with Mir and his wife.

"No one can remember a winter so harsh. Even I, who am much older than most, would have difficulty remembering one worse than this."

Dryas sat at his table, spooning a bowl of soup into his little wife's mouth. The girl sometimes forgot she was eating, and Dryas would have to tap the wooden spoon against her lips to remind her to take the food into her mouth and swallow it.

"You are very patient," Mir said.

Dryas nodded and continued her task.

"And not just about the girl. Do you think he will ever come around?"

"I don't know," Dryas said. "I know because of what I have done that I must try."

"Perhaps we should have killed him. I wanted to. I tried."

And he had. Dryas remembered when they brought the man who had been the gray wolf back; they chained him in the lean-to where Dryas stabled her horse. He wouldn't speak. A wolf, he had behaved as a man; and now a man forever—or for as long as Dryas wore the chain—he seemed more like a wolf.

He made no objection to wearing clothes. He knew human skin was tender and the human body lost heat quickly. They chained his leg to a staple on the wall. It had about six feet of play. One thing she knew, he didn't foul his bedding. The chain left him enough room to visit a silt trench in the back among the weeds.

It was dangerous to come near him, though. One of Mir's people got too close, and the unfortunate man was put out of action for the rest of the winter with a broken arm and ribs.

After this, food was placed on a piece of bark and pushed toward him with the Y end of a forked stick. Sometimes he ate it, sometimes he didn't.

No one knew why the final shattering blow to both Dryas and Mir happened, or even quite how. Mir tried to poison him, mixing opium with the mishmash of meal scraps and vegetables he was fed every afternoon.

"I hoped that he would simply go to sleep and never awaken," Mir said.

But Mir's little mad wife got the food. They didn't know that she was the only one he would tolerate near him. They didn't know that every day she joined him in his makeshift cave. She ate the food. Neither Dryas nor Mir knew until he began pounding on the shed wall with his fist and it began to disintegrate.

They found the child struggling, trying to breathe. It took most of a night and a day to clear the drug from her body, but when she recovered, she seemed worse than before. Now she wouldn't feed herself. Sometimes she didn't sleep.

Every evening Dryas went to bring him his food. She pushed it toward him with the stick and then sat on the woodpile at the low end of the lean-to and tried to talk to him.

He ignored her, refusing to speak or to acknowledge her presence. He certainly never met her eyes. They had felled him once and he remembered her power.

There was a window at his end of the lean-to, partially boarded up. Through it and the door so low he had to crouch to crawl through, he could see the wind-barren winter woods.

The skeleton trees' bare limbs lifted against a misty sky. On the clear days, the snow-capped peaks mantled by the high forests—spruce, pine, and fir—were visible, their summits draped with mists of snow, fog, and sometimes before it grew too cold, long, trailing veils of rain.

Ever after, he remembered the first days of his captivity as the worst of his life. And often throughout his life, he refused to revisit them in memory or imagination. He felt part of himself had been destroyed—as it had. And he had never known that any creature, brute or human, could ever feel such pain or be sunk so deeply into despair.

Only in dreams was he free. Only in dreams could he don his gray coat and wander again with his friends, those he loved. He knew guilt that he had been seduced by the warm, sweet flesh Dryas represented, and a regret so profound it came near to sending him insane in the long, cold watches of the night.

But then Mir's little wife would come and he would find her huddled against him for warmth and he would stir in the rags that were his bedding and place her small body between himself and the wall. She was seldom quiet when she slept. It was as if she must replay some long, tragic, and unbearably painful story in her mind over and over again.

Sometimes when she moaned or cried aloud, he saw the shadows coalesce into forms of darkness, come to keep watch over her. It seemed that whatever she saw in her dreams caused her so much pain, it summoned the dead from their graves that they might share her grief.

Mir worried about her. "Do you think he might . . ." He wouldn't finish the sentence, the idea was so terrible to contemplate.

"No," Dryas said. "I don't think so. I found in my hunt and when I brought him down, certain signals must be present for him to . . . bring his love to a woman. She must desire him in return. The little one's injuries are such that I don't think it's possible that she could ever present herself to him as a woman. And besides, what will you do? Chain her as he is chained? Imprison her as he is imprisoned?"

Mir didn't say, "You should have killed him." He felt he'd said it often enough, but, at such times, he thought it.

So Dryas would go each day and sit on an oak trunk that had proven too tough even for ax and wedge and she would try to reach him. After a time, she ran out of words and they both sat quietly, accepting the vast abyss between them. Sometimes the mad girl would come and share his food while both he and Dryas watched the sunset.

He knew, but she had been too busy all her life to notice, each sunset is the same and all are different. She watched the sunsets come and go, and found that every day they presented some new beauty to the human mind and spirit. Perhaps to the mind and spirit of every living thing.

After the first few times she saw Mir's wife approach him, she ceased to be afraid for the girl. She felt he treated her rather like an unweaned cub, casually but protectively. He did. She posed no threat to him or, for that matter, to any living thing larger than a mouse or lizard.

When she caught live things and tried to put them into the pot, Dryas gently removed them from her hands. But she boiled pine needles, dead leaves, broken sticks and branches, old bones left scattered in the woods, and the occasional shed antlers of elk or deer.

Periodically, Dryas emptied the pot, cleaned it and washed Mir's clothes and bedding, then did the same for the girl. On days when it was warm enough to dry them in the sun, she threw them over tree limbs and bushes. She cooked and hunted. Deadly with crossbow and spear, she brought in enough meat to feed the four of them.

On one of the darkest, coldest, and shortest days of winter, the wolf tried very hard to kill Dryas.

Every day she split logs for Mir's hearth. One day a heavy section of ash rolled to within his reach. He took it and hid it in the tumbled scraps of his bedding. She was too preoccupied with the manifold responsibilities she had undertaken to notice it was gone.

The cold was bitter. The sky had been overcast for a week and there was a smell of snow in the air. She paused before she entered the lean-to and saw the heavy gray clouds hanging over the pass. Their edges were touched with rose as the sun's ebbing light brushed them with its dying fire.

She went into the lean-to and set the bark trencher on the floor and reached for the forked stick.

The stove wood flew out of the darkness, hurled with the force only a strong man's arm can give a missile.

He had calculated coldly how best to kill her. Throw it at her head? No, the thing was too heavy and he might miss. The secrets of human battle were a closed book to him. He'd never practiced flinging anything and he wasn't willing to risk losing the one opportunity to repay her for the pain she'd inflicted on him.

The legs? He'd observed that though wolves were beasts of the foot, humans weren't. He'd seen them survive truly horrible injuries to the legs—injuries that would have condemned a wolf to death within days or even hours.

No, the legs were no good, but her body was slender, almost fragile. He turned away in shame from the memory of how much he'd desired the slim waist and soft breasts. If he could drive those tidy ribs into her lungs, she would die even as White Shoulder died on the gladius of the Roman soldier.

The flying wood caught her squarely in the chest, breaking two ribs and bruising six others. It flung her turning body back onto the woodpile. Her forehead cracked against the oak trunk that served as her seat. But she wasn't knocked unconscious or even stunned.

She wore her sword. She was almost never without it, even when she was involved in mundane tasks such as cooking or mending. In a second it was out of its sheath. She advanced toward him, feeling her own mind giving way under the twin burdens of hatred and rage.

He stood facing her, wearing the faded tunic she'd made for him from a worn-out blanket. The dark hatred burned from his face into her mind.

In the last light of day, the sword blade traced a shimmering arc in the air. She aimed to cut his throat.

But Mir's little wife was standing in the door and she saw the blood on Dryas' face and the sheer murder on his. And she screamed, a scream of such pain and terror as had to be heard to be believed. It punched through Dryas' skull the way an awl punches through soft leather. She deflected the sword. It sliced across his chest, leaving a six-inch gash across his flesh and tunic. Dryas, set for a killing stroke, overbalanced and fell, slamming her right hand into the muddy floor.

It took several hours to calm Mir's wife. In the end, they resorted to opium. Other simples, valerian and sage, didn't touch the agitation and terror the girl displayed. When, at last, she drifted off, hiccuping with the aftermath of her hysteria, and her breathing quieted, the two sat together and talked. Or rather, Mir talked and Dryas wept.

"I'm at my wit's end," Mir said. "I don't know what to do. Yes, I think it would be wrong to kill him, but I believe that, in the end, we will have no choice. Consider the alternative: turn him loose on the world as what he is, half-man, half-animal."

"He wouldn't be a wolf. As a butterfly in a spider's web, he is caught in man shape. I have changed something that once had a certain beauty about it into a monster. And I have crippled him forever. The only way I can make amends is to try to teach him to make the best of his enslavement to his human half."

"No, you can't make amends, if that's what's in your mind, Dryas. Cripples seldom prosper. Caught forever in the man shape he would be just as dangerous as a wolf. Perhaps more. He could become a brigand. Ask yourself, do my wretched people, already wracked by Roman taxation, deserve to have his kind prey upon them? I've seen enough of him to fear him greatly. He is, even as a man, majestically strong and quick. Once initiated into the use of weapons, anyone within reach of his sword would be in mortal danger. As most would be even within reach of his bare hands."

"He's not as strong as he was when I first captured him. He's losing weight. He doesn't eat and, at times, sleep. It's not yet midwinter. Your 'wife' gets worse and worse. I have come to believe he is the only thing keeping her alive now. No, Mir, I am certain we will have to dig two graves before spring."

Mir leaned back in his chair and covered his face with his hands. Then he dropped them and they rested on the table before him. "I'm against letting this evil tale play itself out. Often and often, as a youth, I had such stories told to me. The Greeks collect them: Oedipus, Jason and Medea, Agamemnon. They have an unnatural affection for these hideous narratives. You positively know when the stories begin how they will end. You hope someone will hand a friendly cup of poison to Tiresius, the seer. Or that Medea will show some compassion for her own children. Or that Orestes and Electra will be content to let the murder of their father be punished by the gods, and they will go forward and live their lives in peace. But no, they don't. None of them do. And this difficulty we're in strikes me as holding no hope for any of the four of us."

Dryas understood little of this tirade. "I've never heard any of these stories."

"Well, my dear, if you continue on your present course, we're going to be keeping each other company for some time to come. So I'll start telling them to you. And, when you finally decide this is a lost cause, let me know and I'll try to help you end it with dignity for both you and our erstwhile wolf. But, for now, do as you like. I don't think either of them can live, neither my wife nor the wolf. But if you must exhaust yourself in a futile struggle, I suppose there are worse ones you might have chosen."

L UCIUS HATED TO ADMIT IT, BUT HE FOUND CAESAR and Marc Antony were right and he and Philo were wrong.

He found the Senate absolutely fascinating. Not pleasant, not safe, not comfortable, and not even really totally comprehensible, but nonetheless fascinating.

Caesar had, as Antony had been at pains to tell him, packed the Senate. In theory, the surviving patricians could have controlled new legislation, but they seemed to Lucius to have lost heart. Or perhaps they were too much at odds with each other, even now that they'd had their knuckles firmly rapped by a man who now made no secret of the fact that he despised them. The layering that was occurring as a result of the obvious snobbery of all concerned wasn't helping to put what had been a distinguished and influential body back in order.

But whatever they might be, Lucius found himself mightily entertained as he tried to find his own level. The haughty patricians snubbed even most of the plebeian old families, who were almost equally socially prominent. They, in turn, looked down on those they considered foreigners—newly created senators from Gaul, Greece, Africa, and some of the Latin states—trying to pretend these gentlemen didn't exist.

Mill around and talk. That's how Antony described it and it was an apt description of what went on. They gathered at about the third hour, milled around and talked until Caesar or his acting representative arrived. He was, by then, dictator for life and that's what the Senate did—took dictation. It was their function to give immediate, enthusiastic approval to every law or decree Caesar proposed. And, in their few idle hours, to vote him new and unprecedented honors.

It didn't take Lucius long to discover the old ruling class loathed Caesar, but were now powerless to halt his complete administrative overhaul of the Roman state.

"If Antony thinks I'm going to find out anything he can use from the Gracchi, the Schipoes, the Metelli, or any of the rest of our exalted first families, he's got softening of the brain," Lucius told Philo. "None of them speak to us new men, and we're lucky if they acknowledge our existence at all. The other day Tillius Cimber shoved me out of the way as he was pushing through the door to the gardens in front of the Curia. I think if I'd fallen, he'd have stepped on me as if I were a lumpy paving stone."

"Did you just take that?" Philo asked.

"No, I got him in the instep and shin with one of my old military boots. I think he knew who kicked him and why. One of those small victories we were talking about. And the new senators are an interesting lot. I do have about seven dinner invitations so far. Tonight, it's two Greeks, Manilius and Felex. We met yesterday. They saw what I did to Cimber and enjoyed it to no end."

Lucius had been standing there and nursing his sore ribs from Cimber's elbow when they walked up beside him. It was misting rain and the gardens looked sadly denuded by the early winter chill. All but the stone pines were leafless, and none of the public slaves had been out to sweep the walks between the flowerbeds. They were coated with wet, brown, soppy-looking fallen leaves.

"Nicely done," one of them said, and they introduced themselves.

"Where are you from?" Lucius asked.

"Greece," Manilius said.

"Africa," Felex told him. "Actually, Alexandria but . . . Caesar, or someone in his huge entourage, appointed us to represent Greece."

Manilius was a conventional-looking Greek with brown, curly hair and a delicate, pale complexion, lightly built and strong looking. Felex was black: ebony skin, dark eyes, short, tightly curled hair, muscular, with a cheerful face and a magnificent ivory smile that set off the darkness of his skin.

"Greek," Lucius repeated. "If you'll excuse my saying so, Felex, you don't look . . ."

Both young men laughed. Felex said, "I'm African. My father speculates, sending wild animals to the games in Rome. He made a lot of money and sent me to Alexandria to get a liberal education."

"His father," Manilius contributed, "began to feel, after a time, that his education was turning out to be entirely too liberal and wanted to call him home."

"Yes," Felex said. "In fact, I picked up a few habits in Alexandria that Father didn't approve of at all. In truth, his disapproval was so great that I had to flee in my nightgown to escape being turned into lion food."

"Luckily, his mother wasn't as tediously narrow-minded as his father, and she managed to warn him in time," Manilius commented, "and as long as he stays away, his father won't become difficult, and he is even able to act as his family's agent here in Rome."

"Yes," Felex said. "I receive nice quarterly payments. A commission for placing my father's shipments with Caesar's purveyors when the games are celebrated."

"So he put you in the Senate," Lucius said.

They both giggled girlishly and Manilius lifted his friend's hand and kissed it gently. Felex patted him on the cheek. "So sweet, my adored one."

"And Manilius, what do you do for Caesar?" Lucius asked.

"Oh, spices. I'm a broker, don't you know? My family has been in the business since before the Peloponnesian War."

"Oh, for longer than that," Felex said. "Far longer than that. Since the Trojan War, at least." Then they both laughed.

"Come have dinner with us tonight," Manilius said to Lucius, then turned to Felex. "Imagine, my dear, a Roman who will actually speak to us publicly. We have the most charming Attic poet. He will give us a reading tonight, his newest eglactic ode. We have a truly excellent cook and you may have your choice of a girl or boy for dessert."

"I'm afraid I'll be a disappointment to you," Lucius said. "I'm not a patrician, though my mother was. She married beneath her. The Basilians are only knights."

"So charmed to make your acquaintance," Manilius said. "What in the world is a knight?"

"We are allowed to stoop to make money from commerce. We're the Roman business class."

"I'm still happy to know you," Manilius said. "And do come visit us."

"Perhaps we can compare notes on our experiences in trade," Felex said.

"Or perhaps you're in the market for some spices?"

"In any case, " Lucius now told Philo, "I believe I'll accept their invitation tonight."

"They're probably a good pair to cultivate," Philo said.

"Do you know everybody?"

"Felex has hemorrhoids."

"Felex? I would have thought Manilius would be the one, or maybe the soldiers who handled my education were wrong. I was always told the woman in the pair got the sore ass."

"The soldiers have no room to talk," Philo said. "I see at least three a week from Cleopatra's personal guard, same problem."

"I'm not surprised. They can't marry. Not that regulations would stop any of them if they could afford to keep a wife. But, as a rule, below the rank of centurion they don't have enough money, and they're moved around too often to maintain a family. That leaves the local whores and they're most likely to be dirty, drunken, and ugly, if not downright diseased or dangerous. Sure as you run into some sweet-faced, innocent young thing, five will get you twenty-five, she'll have a pimp hiding somewhere ready to cut your throat for a copper coin or your military issue sword and boots. So they more often than not make do with each other, and I can't say I blame them. I can't say I'm enthusiastic about joining the army again, either. Why should I cultivate those two? I can't think we have much in common."

Philo smiled mirthlessly. "First, they're as harmless as pet rabbits. Second, no, a number of the aristocracy won't speak to them in the Curia, but they damn well will at those banquets they give. Just about all the spices that get to Rome pass through Manilius' warehouse, and Caesar has made something of a pet out of Felex.

"Three, they're both inveterate gossips. I wouldn't doubt that either one of them would climb down from his funeral pyre to hear or tell the latest, really salacious tidbit stemming from the activities of the magnates of our fair city."

"Umm, Philo, is Caesar . . . ?"

"No, and don't repeat that old lie about King Nicodemous to his face. Not a few people who twitted him about it in his younger years wound up with a very final invitation to visit the Elysian Fields courtesy of Rome's most distinguished general."

"Philo, are . . ."

"No. I could possibly have bribed my father out of trouble, if I hadn't been besotted with a charming little article named Roxanne."

"Dropped a bundle on her, did you?"

"Yes," Philo answered morosely.

D RYAS RETURNED TO THE HUT AT DAWN. SHE found him sleeping. Mir was right about one thing: he did still show unnatural strength and a strange kind of power. The cut her sword inflicted on his chest was only a healed red line and she knew in a few hours that would fade, also.

As she watched, he awoke. "Have you anything else hidden?" she asked harshly.

"No," he said. "I only wish I did. I should have aimed for your head, but I was afraid I might miss."

Dryas, her ribs hurting, limped toward the oak stump and sat down.

He noticed she had difficulty breathing and that she was in obvious pain. "At least I hurt you and you will remember me and my pain for a long time."

"Yes," she answered. "I will." She sat upright for a moment. It was painful to do so. Then she tried to get him to look into her eyes, but he avoided her gaze and, instead, sat back and stared through the open door at the growing light outside.

"You have taken away my life. It would have been kinder to kill me."

"No!" she answered. "And I didn't take away your life, only half of it. I was charged by my duty to do so. I couldn't let you run the woods as a wolf and kill Mir's people. Now you cannot take your wolf form and you must live your life as one of us."

"I told you I don't want to be a man!" he shouted.

"Well, now you have no choice!" she shouted back. Then she was knifed by a spasm of pain in her chest. Her body and face twisted, until she managed to get pressure with her hand on the place where the broken bones' ends grated on one another. The pain eased to a tolerable level.

"You can be proud of yourself, and you're right. I'll think about you a lot for the next few weeks," she said. "Perhaps even for the rest of my life because I don't like the thing I did to you. I didn't want to destroy the wolf, but it was the lesser of two evils. My order is charged with the care and protection of our people. That was why Mir sent for Blaze and why Blaze asked that I come here."

She looked up at him. This time he met her eyes and again she saw the beautiful, primal innocence of the beast in them. Then she bowed her head, feeling defeated by his absolute assurance—so much freedom from doubt and complexity.

"I suffer and will for a month or more, and your injuries heal in a few hours. I grieve for years, but you ease your sorrow with murder, and then you reproach me with restraining you."

"Yes, and what of Imona? How much care and protection did you offer her?"

"Imona had a duty. She was born to it. She was a noble woman, daughter of kings uncounted. In happier times, she wouldn't have been asked for her life. But a catastrophe has befallen our people: she was called upon to sacrifice herself that the Romans and their Caesar might never cross the Rhine. And they never will.

"Even so, I was offered. I bore a child. He should have been a king, but the Romans killed him. He was my son."

The wolf spoke contemptuously. "Your people make up tales about gods. The stories you tell are about *yourselves* and *your* fears. I know what walks near the wooden image rotting in the sacred grove in the valley. I have seen her or what she allows us to see. Because we are her children and paid homage to her long ago. Sometimes she travels with us and sometimes sends us to guard her minions. Why would she demand Imona's life? One human life is nothing to . . . them.

"Have they intentions? Do they will actions or care about wolves or men? I cannot say. I was the wolf then; I came to the grove where blood sacrifice was being offered. Blood, but not death.

"The mead was in wooden bowls resting in the grass. Bolder than the rest, I drank, and then felt the touch of she who intoxicates. She in whose dreams we see all our desires. So she made me a man and called me Maeniel. And I took a woman in the grove, one of the chosen ones, they who yield their blood in the spring that the water—blood of the earth—is to be set free. Not locked in ice, caught in cold stone forever." He stopped speaking and sat down in the straw and rags of his bedding.

Dryas glared at him with a murderous accusation. "You chose to be a man and now you refuse the responsibilities of your state."

"I desired the girl—woman—whatever she was," he said.

"Girl when you went into the grove, woman when you left, I'll wager," Dryas answered with fury. She stormed out of the shed.

Maeniel found himself shaking with fear. He had given the one he thought of as a sorceress his name. And a name was a word of power. How might she use it to further bind him? But nothing of his fears materialized. Dryas did not return.

Instead, the mad girl brought him his food at the usual time in the late afternoon. She brought hers with it, more than enough for both of them. A pannikin of soft freshly baked breads, venison—a big chunk—and a cobbler made with dried apples and honey. They both ate well. He was enjoying his food more and more. Wolves had nothing like this in their lives.

He watched the girl eat. She was dainty. Her hands were still beautiful, graceful and long-fingered, though the nails were dirty and bitten to the quick.

She had table manners, always chewing with her mouth closed. The morsels of meat and vegetables were wrapped in flat bread and she conveyed them to her lips without dripping gravy on her clothing. She always left the hut or house to wash her hands and face before and after meals.

Today Dryas had been convincing about his need to accept his humanity. But a look at the maimed and crippled child convinced him again that he wanted no part of the human journey. Then he thought, if he wanted to live, he might not have a choice.

L UCIUS FOUND MANILIUS AND FELEX'S HOUSE RESO-lutely Greek. There were no frescoes. The walls were plain stucco decorated with a white baseboard and a red stripe, broad, shoulder high. Above it, the wall was white until it reached the ceiling, beamed with cedar.

Everything in the house showed the same sparse elegance. From the exquisitely carved chairs, stools, and banquet couches to the statues in what Lucius recognized as a very Roman style peristyle. Only a wealthy Greek could afford a Roman house. There were expensive copies of priceless Greek originals.

The Attic poet lived up to his reputation, looking very like a bust of Pericles. Lucius was unable to develop an opinion as to whether the poet had any talent or not because he declaimed the verses—suitably accompanied on a kithara, of course, played by a tall, horse-faced young man—in a somewhat more archaic Greek than was spoken by the Hellenes at present.

Lucius' Greek was weak at best, and being asked to follow an ode in old Greek placed an intolerable strain on his rather precarious abilities. He said as much to Philo the next day.

"Dionysus, you say that was his name?" Philo asked, then snorted. "If he's the one I think he is, his name is Septimius and the kithara player is Priscus, his brother-in-law. Septimius was a pedagogue, but found tutoring didn't pay enough, so he bought a few scrolls of Attic verse and set up shop as a poet. He's about as Greek as you are. He was born in Pistum. Manilius and Felex are businessmen. They're completely overawed by the literary pretensions of this mountebank."

"The food was as good as Manilius promised."

"Yes," Philo said. "That would be Felex's aunt Myrtus. She owns cookshops across from the Circus, the public baths, and near the Forum."

"Ah, I did notice a very un-Greek amount of feminine company at dinner."

There *had* been and, at first, he was rather bewildered by them. They were well dressed, impeccably coifed, and beautifully behaved. But all they could seem to talk about were clothes, jewels, who had been taken as a mistress by some wealthy man, makeup or how to paint the face and perfume the body for seduction, what senator had found his wife with a gladiator or what wife had found her senator with a gladiator. Clothes, jewels, money, what patrician caught his wife accommodating six of her litter bearers, what knight caught his wife accommodating all eight. What wife caught her husband taking on all comers in a brothel that didn't employ women. Clothes, makeup, jewels, hair dressing: they all received free and, Lucius felt, sometimes cogent advice from both Manilius and Felex, complete with appointments for anything from demonstrations of the uses and abuses of white lead, kohl, and curling irons, to complete makeovers supervised by the expert on female dress—Felex himself—ably assisted by both his valet and his hairstylist, handmaidens dressed beautifully as women, but who both had, not so obviously, begun to shave some time ago.

As in conventional Roman homes, the ladies departed early and the men sat up late over their wine.

"You really should give one or more of them a tumble," Felex told him. "They are so amusing and, I tell you, most of them would fall right over on their backs for a boy as rich and handsome as you are. Unless they're not to your taste," Felex remarked archly.

Both men eyed him speculatively. There was a brief silence and Lucius felt he'd better explain himself.

"If you know Philo, you know he was my physician. I was injured rather badly . . ." He got no further. They both fell all over themselves to apologize to him.

"Oh, no! My dear, don't say another word. Oh, for heaven's sake, don't pay a bit of attention to our nonsense. We're the worst gossips in Rome, but we did invite the ladies here just to meet you." Manilius smiled charmingly.

Felex had slapped Manilius on the wrist. "Oh, for heaven's sake. Stop beating around the bush. Every one of those little birds of paradise can be had for a pair of fairly nice garnet earrings."

"I think describing them as birds of anything is a bit much," Philo said now. "You fall into their clutches and they will do the plucking. They expect men to ruin themselves over them."

Lucius laughed. "No, I don't think I'm attracted enough to any of them to go that far. But I wouldn't be averse to a fling if I weren't afraid Fulvia might find out about it."

"My lord," Philo addressed him formally, "what in the name of the gods above and below does Fulvia have to do with your love life?"

They were walking along a narrow street leading into the Forum. Lucius glanced back. Castor and Pollux were following at a distance. "Think they can hear us?"

"Not if you keep your voice down, no," Philo said.

"I think," he said softly, "that Fulvia would rather be rid of me than not. And, as I said at one time, a nice minor child would suit her perfectly, and if one of those professional graces happened to get pregnant, I'm sure she would lose no time at all in selling my descendant to the highest bidder. Who would be, more than likely, my devoted sister, Fulvia Camilla Basilian. Then how long do you'd think I'd live?"

Philo looked disturbed. "Heaven and probably the denizens of a lot of other places know most Romans, and not a few Greeks for that matter, are indifferent to the fate of most non-Romans or even those classes in their own republic inferior to them in wealth and influence. But most people value their own kin to some degree and most feel at least a little love and loyalty to them. In heaven's name, man, you're talking about your own sister."

"Philo, I never thought I'd have to say this to you, but don't be naïve. Fulvia probably hates me and I know I don't care for her at all. Remember, I warned you about her at our first meeting, just after she'd threatened to nail you to a cross."

"Yes, but I'm not her brother."

"I don't think that matters at all. What Fulvia wants is control of the family money. Complete control, and all that stands in the way of her getting it is me. In law, my authority in the household is greater than hers . . ."

Lucius swung around so quickly, Philo jumped; then he saw Castor and Pollux had drawn very close to them. They were bright eyed and listening intently.

"Do either of you have something to say to me?" Lucius spoke sharply.

"No . . . no," they stammered in tandem.

"Then get back to where you were. Nothing I have to say here is intended for your ears. I don't care much for eavesdroppers or spies, and if either of you makes the near acquaintance of a lead-tipped whip, you'll quickly learn to be both deaf and dumb when I want you to be."

By then they'd both scurried back out of earshot, but he made sure they heard the last few words.

Philo said nothing. He might be free, but he knew Lucius was very angry. In fact, he hadn't seen him this angry before.

"I didn't mean you," he said to Philo.

"I know and I understand better what you mean about the . . . other thing."

"Did you love your family?"

"Yes, I did. I do. I didn't have to allow myself to be sold to protect my father and sister. Slavery is difficult enough for a man, but a complete nightmare for women or the elderly. And if I hadn't been an improvident fool, I would have had enough money to pay the bribes the Roman provincial governor demanded and save my family, but as it was I didn't."

"Oh, but you're free now and you could go back . . ."

"No, I couldn't, not just yet. Sometime, maybe, but not just yet. Besides, I'm doing well here."

"Yes. Don't let Fulvia steal too high a percentage of your fees."

"One third!"

Lucius stopped. "That's extortion!"

"Shush." Philo laid his finger on his lips and glanced back at Castor and Pollux. "She gets one third of all the ones she knows about. You know they don't call us Greeks sneaky for nothing. We were learning sharp dealing from the merchants of Sidon and Tyre before Romulus ever figured out what a wolf's tit was. I can take care of myself."

THE GIRL CAME BACK TO JOIN MAENIEL FOR THE night. He didn't mind her sleeping with him. Nor did she stir his blood any more than a wolf cub would have.

A whole succession of signals had to be right before his body would be aroused. In that, Dryas had understood him perfectly.

In spite of the terrible scars that marred her face and body, the girl was young and she heated up like a stove. Wolf cubs did the same and, used as he was to sleeping with his own kind, he found it terrible to feel so isolated and alone.

It was going to snow tonight and be very cold. A myriad of factors informed his senses: the humidity, low clouds, the smell of the wind, its direction; and he felt in his ears the minute changes in air pressure. At dusk, the wind began to blow and he could feel the storm moving toward them the way a human hears approaching footsteps and knows from the graduations of sound that someone is coming closer and closer.

The girl ran into the shed. He picked her up and placed her body between his own and the wall on a pile of straw covered by an old blanket. She would receive the most protection there. After a very short time, he slept. She woke him once when she slipped past his body to use the trench outside.

She didn't return. A man might have thought she'd simply gone to the house to join Mir and Dryas, but he wasn't a man. No matter what Dryas tried to do, he took nothing for granted.

He rose. The storm had been a mild one, leaving only a light snow cover over the meadow, Mir's house, and the shed. The moon was out and, by its pale light, he could see where she'd visited the trench. But then something must have frightened her and he saw her footprints cross the thin covering of snow on the meadow and vanish into the woods.

He eased slowly through the door, moving quietly as only a wolf can move, being extra careful because the chain was noisy and he was clumsy with the staple on his ankle.

There was little wind. He turned cautiously, feeling the direction on his skin until it was blowing on his face, directly into his nostrils. The odor was man, man and soldier, the combination of iron, leather, and woodsmoke peculiar to the legionnaires in the Roman camp. Not only soldiers coming, but soldiers who stank of the acid perspiration sent out by men who are on edge, aggressive, or afraid. To his surprise, he found he'd developed a new skill. He could count them, five fingers and one. Six.

He took a deep breath and tried to control the instant fear that odor roused in his brain, then remembered that he was dealing with men, not wolves, and he didn't have to worry about them scenting him.

At the same time, he froze in absolute stillness because he heard a sound. Footsteps, a whisper of motion, some animal or human walking in the snow behind him.

SEVEN INVITATIONS. LUCIUS WAS ON HIS FIFTH. This one was a senator from Gaul. He was only slightly more Roman than any Roman Lucius had ever known.

Lucius thought it was rather like having dinner with Cato the Elder, except that Amborux was a far less stingy fellow. The ladies sat at meals instead of reclining. A loom was highly visible just off the atrium, thus showing the industry of the ladies of the household. The larium was on display next to a wall painting of the household gods, Lares and Penates.

But Amborux was a lot less likely than the elder Cato to stint anyone when it came to food or, for that matter, wine. So Lucius had a comfortable glow on when he left the Gaul's house and began to walk home.

As usual, Castor and Pollux were with him, as was a powerful Gallic servant from Amborux's house.

Castor and Pollux walked ahead with torches in their hands. Amborux's servant followed. They'd left the narrow streets of the residential quarter behind and were cutting through the Forum.

It was deserted, after nightfall, and the torches lit only shuttered shops and locked public buildings. Usually in a residential area the presence of human beings comfortingly close was indicated by music, laughter, and the clatter of cutlery from balconies overlooking the street and behind garden walls. Romans loved visiting and feasting and, more often than not, in the early evening there were still parties returning from banquets and passing each other in the street before the late-night quiet set in and the roadways were abandoned to the carts transporting goods to and from the city.

But here in the public center of Rome, the streets were as empty and silent as the road full of tombs outside the city. Both Castor and Pollux looked nervous, though they were both armed.

The Gaul behind Lucius quickened his pace and drew alongside him. "How much my language you speak?" he asked.

"Some," Lucius replied. "I understand it better than I speak it."

"So, I speak yours. Good. We being followed, but don't think it trouble."

"Why not?"

"Too small. Only one footsteps."

"Walk up and keep those two company," Lucius said, gesturing toward Castor and Pollux, then, loosening his own sword in the sheath, he eased into an alleyway behind a group of market stalls.

Very good, he thought. Castor and Pollux were still walking along, passing the time of day with the muscular Gaul. *Fine guardians they are,* he thought sourly. They hadn't even noticed he'd dropped back and disappeared. He'd discovered while in the legions how easy it was to move around unobserved in the dark.

He'd been gifted with good night vision and most of the time, even when the moon was low, he could travel by starlight.

His pursuer's shadow appeared in the street beside the alleyway.

Lucius had hoped that was what would happen—the follower would chase the torchlight ahead and not notice he was gone. Yes, the Gaul had been right. The shadow was a very small man or a woman.

He saw and heard no one else around. She was carrying something in her right hand—a weapon? No, light leaked out around the shade. A lamp.

He reached out and caught her by the arm, pulling her into the alley while simultaneously snatching the lantern out of her hand.

She didn't scream as he thought she might, but only gasped until he raised the lantern and she saw who he was.

"Oh, oh, oh. You frightened me out of my wits. Don't you recognize me?"

He did. The girl from the kitchen. "I'm sorry. I never knew your name, Vella's lover."

"Lucrese. Your sister named me that when she bought both of us. After a time, I found she meant it as a form of derision, giving me the name of a faithful woman. Faithful unto death." Sudden tears shone in her eyes.

Lucius found himself reacting almost without thinking to a jibe of such cruelty. "Hush! Don't cry and don't be ashamed of your name. People who have no understanding of honor and no honor themselves are always the first to laugh at it. Lucrese was a person of great honor and honesty, and her actions brought her everlasting fame."

Just at that moment, Castor and Pollux clattered into the alleyway, torches in hand.

Lucrese turned her face away, covering it with her mantle.

Lucius glared at the two of them. "Smart boys," he said sarcastically. "You finally noticed I was missing. However, you never know when you're not wanted. Now get out and wait in the street. Not, I might add, within hearing distance."

Castor and Pollux clattered right back out, leaving them alone. The Gaul stood in the street also, his hands spread wide as if to say, "What could I do?"

Lucius nodded, jerked his head in the direction of Castor and Pollux, then turned and led Lucrese deeper into the darkness. "What's wrong? Do you need help? Money, perhaps?"

"Oh, no, no. I'm fine," she whispered. "And I wouldn't trust those two."

"Who? Castor and Pollux?"

"That's not their names," she said. "They're called Macer and Afer and they were among your sister's favorites."

"Favorites? What was she doing? Sleeping with . . ."

She shook her head violently in negation. "No, oh no, no, no. Your sister is chaste."

"Well, then, favorites in what way?"

She looked very frightened and glanced around as if afraid of being overhead.

"I don't see a crowd gathering," he said. "Now stop dithering and tell me what's going on in my house. Why are they her favorites? No one can hurt you now. You're a free woman, if Philo did as I told him, and safe from my sister's wrath."

"That's a lie and you know it. The powerful in this city do what they like to the weak and no one gainsays them. Look at this Caesar. Everyone fears him."

"He's not the worst of the lot." Lucius was exasperated.

"No, and that's why they're going to kill him. They're already talking."

Lucius clapped a hand over her mouth. "I don't want to hear this, and if you know anything of such plots, don't talk about them to anyone. Not your mother or sister or most trusted, beloved friend. Understand me?" Then he pulled his hand away. "Now tell me what that sister of mine is up to."

"But, I don't think the killing, the assassination, will happen. He, Caesar, is already taking steps to—" She was trying to reassure him, but he clapped his hand over her mouth again.

"Gods of war, destruction, and chaos . . . Shut up, please."

She pulled away, weeping, saying, "Stop. I can't breathe and—"

"Girl, get it through your head that if . . ." He took a deep breath. "There are people in this city who, if they get wind of such talk, will stop you from breathing permanently."

She leaned against the wall, hands clasped at her breast, eyes closed, trying to get herself under control by an effort of will.

"Lucrese, tell me about my sister's favorites."

"I don't know the polite words for it."

"Fine. Tell me in the impolite words. I'm a soldier. I've heard them before. I've heard them *all* before."

"She likes to watch people in . . . in . . . doing the act of desire. It . . . it excites her."

Lucius sighed. "Ah, well, that's not so bad, but *chaste* isn't the word I would apply to such conduct."

"Oh, she doesn't take part. No, she says her chastity is important to the future of the Basilian family."

"I suppose it is. Macer and Afer supply the male, ah, point of view at these little . . . soirees?"

"Yes."

"You're sure about this?"

"Oh, yes." Her voice shook. "I was there. They had a lot of fun with me. I'm afraid of men." She began to cry quietly, then turned around and began to give vent to what was a deep, hopeless grief. "Participation isn't voluntary." Her voice was thick with tears.

"Now, let me get this straight. You've been scurrying around Rome in the dark, putting your life in danger to tell me this ugly little secret about my sister . . . And while I, like you, deplore her actions, there's very little I can—"

"No!" She spun around, wiping away her tears with the dark mantle. "What I came to tell you is that Philo's been taken. He was at Gordus' house, the gladiator. Philo went there to check on the son's wound. Gordus' wife walked with him to the end of the street. They found soldiers waiting there. Marcia, Gordus' wife, tried to interfere, but they drew their swords and told her to get back home if she knew what was good for her. Then they took Philo away and no one has seen him since."

MAENIEL CROUCHED. THEN HE COULD SMELL HER. Mir's wife, the mad girl. "Come," he whispered.

She did as he asked and ran to him. He snatched her up and entered the shed. The chain clinked softly. He pulled the blanket away from the straw and pointed to the exposed bedding. She understood and burrowed down into it. He covered her with the blanket so that all a casual observer would see was a pile of straw covered by a ragged discard.

Then he raised his head and looked out of the window. Four men entered the clearing; two others were already at Mir's door. He struggled savagely and futilely with, first, a desire to change his shape, then with the fear of calling attention to himself in his present helpless condition. But in the end, he did what he knew he must do, and roared out, "Dryas!"

Dryas came awake at the sound of her name. Her sword hung from the bedstead. She drew just as the first man kicked open the door. He was silhouetted against the first faint mixture of moonlight and dawn outside.

She crossed the floor at a run and drove her sword into his throat, then she kicked his body into the man behind him. They both went down, the first man dying: she could hear the bubbling roar of his last breath through his laid-open larynx. The second shoved the first aside, trying to get his sword clear of the sheath.

Dryas went for the best target she could see. She drove the sword into his upper thigh, severing the big arteries that send blood to the leg and foot. He dropped his weapon and staggered away, trying to stem the brilliant red arterial flow covering his hands and spraying out onto the blue snow.

Four remained and they were afraid of her, but she hadn't even been able to get to her knife. She wore a blood-daubed nightgown and held only a sword. She knew that unless she could somehow cut down the odds, she was doomed.

They were backing her away from the house toward the forest. She had to keep on backing because otherwise they would encircle her and she would be taken down. All she could hope for was that she might lead them away from Mir, his wife, and Maeniel.

Mir staggered out of the house.

Oh, no, Dryas thought but then, *Maybe he will distract them.*

"What do you want?" he shouted.

They weren't distracted. They continued their advance. One held a spear—the long Roman pilum—and a sword; the rest had swords and shields.

"Give up," the one with the spear said to Dryas. "What we want is you. You're good, but we're better. You're overmatched. Surrender and we will leave the rest alone."

No, Dryas thought. She'd rather fall on her own blade than face such a fate. "What?" she asked. "Aren't there enough whores in the camp for you?"

The light was better. She could see they weren't Roman legion-

naires, but wore much better quality armor: boiled leather with muscled breastplates, metal greaves and arm guards, plumed helmets with
long, Greek nose guards. *Mercenaries*, she thought, *and well-paid ones at
that*. The one with the pike was the oldest. His hair was grizzled, as
was his spade-shaped beard.

"Give up," he told her again in rather accented Latin. "We have
orders to bring you to Rome. And strict orders not to hurt you while
we're bringing you there."

"I don't believe you," Dryas whispered between her teeth.

Gray Beard motioned his men to back off. He continued to stand,
pointing the spear at Dryas. "Get the old man and the mad girl," he
told one of his men. "You." He gestured the spear at Dryas. "Stand
where you are. If you run, this spear will be sticking out of your chest
before you get two steps. I want to deliver you to my paymaster unharmed, as she requested, but you've killed two of my men and, if I
have to, I'll take your head to Rome." He smiled. "Without the body,
Gallic bitch."

"No," Mir cried. "Leave my wife alone—" Then he doubled over,
trying not to cry out in agony as the soldier twisted his arm up behind
his back.

Another one of the soldiers entered the house, while the third
dragged Mir toward Dryas. There were sounds of a rough search being
conducted in the house, furniture being overturned, pottery breaking.

In a trice, the soldier reappeared. "She's not in here," he said, and
even while he was speaking, he started toward the shed.

Inside, the mad girl jumped out from under the blanket. She took
Maeniel by surprise. He was looking at the door, but he was so fast
that he nearly had her as she dashed past. All he got was her sleeve,
and it tore away since the cloth was rotten.

She ran toward the woodpile at the other end of the shed. She
reached it just as the soldier entered.

"No," Maeniel shouted, "No!" trying to distract the man, and
lunged toward him. The chain on his ankle brought him up short
and he fell on his face.

It took the soldier only a second to see Maeniel was chained and
he disregarded him. He snatched at the girl, but she had a big piece of
wood, part of an ash branch, a log of about three feet. She swung it at
his shin and connected, but he was wearing greaves. The wood
bounced off, but the blow was painful.

The soldier ran the sword through her body, but the wood continued to roll toward Maeniel.

On his hands and knees now, Maeniel lunged for the log. Again, the chain brought him up short, this time cutting into his ankle and foot. The tips of his fingers brushed the wood.

The soldier advanced on Maeniel, ready to dispatch him, too. It looked easy. His foe was down, freedom of movement limited by the chain, and he was unarmed.

Maeniel scrabbled backward as if afraid.

The soldier came closer. He had both sword and shield. He slammed his shield in Maeniel's body and raised the sword.

Maeniel dove under both sword and shield, got the man by both ankles, and pulled his legs up.

The soldier went down, cracking his head on the floor. But the floor was dirt and the soldier was wearing a helmet. He cursed and kicked, trying to break free. His helmet made a dull sound as it rolled away.

But there was nothing of the human left in Maeniel's brain. He was all infuriated wolf. Still holding the soldier by the ankles, he swung the screaming man around and dashed out his brains against the oak planks of the wall.

The dreadful scream from the shed and the thud distracted the man with the spear for a second. Dryas threw the sword into her left hand and leaped right. She felt the spear point graze her stomach, slicing through her nightgown as she cut for the throat left-handed. She succeeded better than she'd hoped. She decapitated him.

In the shed, Maeniel picked up the sword the soldier had dropped as he died. The log the child had given her life for was now within reach. He stretched the chain over it and swung the sword down with both hands. The blow destroyed the sword, but it sheared through the chain and set him free.

XVI

FAMOUS LAST WORDS, LUCIUS THOUGHT. "I CAN *take care of myself.*" *Ave atque vale. Philo, you idiot.* What had his Greek physician stepped in? He studied the girl. "I'm worried about Philo, but I'm also worried about you. Can you safely find your way home?"

"Well," the girl said, "I don't want to tell you anything you don't want to hear, but close by there is a place where I can spend the night. A shop I have to open in the morning, so . . ." She displayed a bunch of keys at her belt. "It's only a few steps away."

He nodded. "Good. I'll lead Castor and Pollux off. I don't think they saw your face, so they won't be able to run to my sister with any information, but I'd wait till we're out of sight, then dive for cover."

He hurried back to the street. As he moved past the line of shops he found he could overhear the Gaul talking to . . . he'd forgotten their names already.

"I don't like it," either Castor or Pollux was saying. "If anything happens to him, the mistress will—"

"What?" the Gaul asked. "You think he's some baby, needs his chin wipe? She lady's maid. Her mistress want him hump! Hump! Hump! Gave him message where to come when husband not home." Then he laughed raucously at his own humor.

"There's money in it for you if you know who the lady is," one of the unheavenly twins suggested.

Lucius paused in the darkness.

"How much money?" the Gaul asked, interested.

237

"Lots," was the reply.

"Want to see money first."

"He doesn't know anything." There was a certain studied contempt in the remark.

The Gaul refused to be drawn. He laughed again.

Lucius stepped out of the alley and brought the conversation to an end. "Get moving," he told Castor and Pollux. "I want to arrive at home sometime this year." When they tended to hang back, he ordered them, "Move! And get those torches up. I want to see my way, and I don't want to be treading on your heels."

The Gaul dropped back. Lucius found himself alone, thinking furiously. The worst of it was that freedmen, not being Roman citizens, had few rights, and there were a dozen places to which Philo might have been taken, including the dreaded Tullianum, the carcer or official prison and place of execution in Rome. As he walked, he felt his rage growing. He found himself struggling with the same frustration he'd felt when he was talking to Antony a few weeks ago, a feeling that somehow he was powerless to control the direction of his own life.

That feeling said that he didn't want the future being mapped out for him. Not by his own family, but also not by Caesar and Antony. He drifted, rudderless, because he didn't know what he wanted. Somehow the wound had changed him. He couldn't tell what about it had wrought the odd alterations in attitude and belief he was experiencing now. Once, the fate of someone so low in rank as Philo wouldn't have concerned him in the least. But now . . .

He knew that in Philo, he had a friend. He had drawn closer to the man. When and how it happened wasn't clear to him. Was it the nights when Philo read philosophy and he lay there, chilling and then burning with fever, eyes on the ceiling, watching the shadows created by Philo's flickering lamp, thinking about his own death? Struggling to pay attention to the convoluted arguments of some long-dead Greek trying to prove the immortality of the soul, and not believing one word, but knowing he was a lot closer to testing the validity of those propositions than the philosopher was when he penned the text . . .

He felt he had seen through the comforting illusions most people surrounded themselves with to hold back the darkness of the mind. A darkness deeper than the darkness of simple night. A bleak emptiness wherein the spirit doesn't doubt the gods are only pretty images created by artists and we humans are nothing but a better kind of animal allowed a small sojourn beneath the sun by the ever-distant and, perhaps, blind powers. And then, nothing more.

So far as Philo went, he would sell the whole Senate cheaply to get his friend back.

Because that's what Philo was, no matter what his rank—a friend. And whatever mysteries the universe may or may not hold, no one gets more than a very few of those in a lifetime.

He dropped back again and spoke to the Gaul. "Want some money?"

"A language everybody understand. Yes. What you want done?"

"When I reach my home, I'm going to ditch those two."

"Smart. They sell you cheap."

"You knew I was in the alley."

The Gaul chuckled. "How much?"

"One hundred aurei."

"Gold. Murder! Who?"

"You're a man with a fine grasp of essentials. When you reach my house, I'll go in with those two. You ease around back. There's a stable there; I'll let you in. Saddle two horses. Know anything about horses?"

The Gaul grunted. "Rode for Caesar."

"An allied cavalryman. Good. What's your name?" It was a jawbreaker and sounded more German than Gallic. Lucius whistled between his teeth, very softly lest he alert the two ahead. "Give me something I can call you."

"Cut Ear."

"Cut Ear?" Lucius questioned. To the best of his knowledge, both of the man's ears were intact and unscarred.

"Ya! Cut ear and hang around neck. Call me Cut Ear when in army. Cut off lots and hang around neck. No problem. Cut Ear."

"Certainly. Cut Ear, a nice name."

Cut Ear chuckled. "Not so nice, but you don't pay hundred gold coin for nice. Want nice? Go get women. Want carry big trouble with you? Get Cut Ear."

"Are you free?"

"Sure. Amborux say, 'Cut Ear, get Roman home safe.' Work for Amborux. Pay stinks. You pay better. For you, I kill."

"Not tonight, I hope, but when I ask someone a question, if I don't get the answer I want, you can kill him."

Cut Ear grunted. They'd reached Lucius' door. The porter opened it for him. Castor preceded him into the house, Pollux followed. Or maybe it was vice versa, he still wasn't sure.

They tried to follow him to his room. He told them he hadn't needed help undressing in about twenty-two years. He could tell they didn't know what to make of this, since few men dispensed with the help of attendants, but they departed for their rooms.

As they left, he had a brief vision of what they were used to doing for his sister. The images weren't salacious, they were repulsive. He decided he'd pick his own personal servants in the future.

Before he went to his room, he stopped by Philo's quarters. The door was ajar. The room was not only empty, but stripped bare. Even the cot where he slept was gone. Lucius walked out, then turned his back to the wall, closed his eyes, and clenched his fists. He felt helpless, sick, and enraged all at the same time.

Then he entered his room. His sword was in the corner. He drew it, hoping it was not rusted or the blade dulled. No, it was still as sharp as the day he'd last put it on.

He remembered he'd had a hangover that day. There wasn't much to do in a garrison. He and some of the other officers had sat up late. The others had done a little wenching, but he hadn't joined them.

He'd had a strong sex drive, but the last whore he'd had stank so badly of her first fifteen or twenty customers that when he completed the act, which was almost without pleasure, he realized that the dank reek of her body was her form of revenge, directed at the men who used and despised her. He stared into her cold, dark eyes, slitted like those of the feral cats that foraged in the refuse that the soldiers dumped outside the palisade. The look in her eyes was worse than that in the eyes of the cats because they, at least, were indifferent to him, whereas a cold hatred glowed in hers and consigned him to an eternity of suffering that would not be enough to compensate her for even one moment of the life she led. He staggered out of the whore's room and vomited in the ditch.

He'd never gone back to visit any of them again. He wasn't sure how isolated his experience had been, but a lot of other young men seemed to feel the same. So they drank and boasted and drank some more and then woke up like him, with a foul mouth, a raging headache, and a sour stomach. Not to mention cursing the prospect of foraging around the farms of the unfortunate locals on whose necks the heel of the conqueror descended.

But he was glad this night that he'd cleaned the sword and . . . but then, he couldn't have, because the man had driven it into his back, very nearly killing him. And so someone had come, cleaned the blood off the blade, and oiled it. So that now, tonight, he could go kill someone else with it.

He scrabbled around in the pile of military junk on the floor and found a dark, hooded mantle. He dropped his toga, the one decorated with the senatorial purple stripe, kicked it into a corner, and went to let Cut Ear in.

S HE WAS MORE DANGEROUS THAN THEY THOUGHT. The awareness was written on the two men's faces. Their commander lay dead on the ground. The one holding Mir quickly pushed him away. They had been six when they arrived. Now they were two and weren't sure how it happened.

They both rushed Dryas. She circled and backed, trying to separate the two of them or, failing that, get one in front of the other. But they were both practiced swordsmen and it was only a matter of time before they had her.

Number One swung hard. She parried and slipped the blade, letting his weight take him past her, but she felt something like a streak of fire on her arm and knew one of them had gotten to her.

The adrenal rush that had carried her along at first was fading, and she was in increasing pain. Crash! She parried another blow, but the second sword licked at her and she found herself backing faster and faster as they both pressed her. Another and yet another. Her feet were numb, but she still had a trick or two left.

She dropped to one knee and struck upward at her closest opponent's body, up under the breastplate. He jumped back as she'd wanted him to do, running into his partner. For a second, they got in each other's way, but she couldn't take advantage of their confusion. Her foot slipped and, to keep from falling, she had to catch herself with her free hand.

Just at this moment, Mir launched himself at one of the soldiers, landing on his back, arms around his neck. The man twisted, yelling with rage, slamming with the upper edge of his shield at the old man's arms.

Dryas managed to avoid a really dangerous thrust of the other's and opened a wicked gash in his sword arm, but she paid the price. He was able to slam his shield into her body.

Normally she would have ridden the blow backward and finally jumped clear, unhurt. But her ribs were broken and the raised metal shield bos dug right into them. The pain was blinding. She staggered back into something soft. The chain came out of nowhere, wrapped itself around her opponent's neck and, a moment later, Maeniel's fist slammed into the side of his head.

The one remaining soldier had just freed himself from Mir's grip. He saw the massive individual come to Dryas' help, threw down his weapon, and ran.

None of them pursued him. Maeniel and the rest went into the shed. They all knelt near the mad girl. Maeniel thought she was dead, but on closer inspection, he saw she was still breathing. One hand was over the dreadful wound in her body, the other lay on the dirt floor.

She gave a little sigh, smiled, and spoke. "Tell Dryas my spirit is free." And there was nothing more.

There was no question of chaining him up again. In fact, he had to help the two of them to the house. Two bodies lay across the threshold. Maeniel gazed at a pale-faced and staggering Dryas with respect, kicked the bodies out of the way, then picked up Dryas and carried her unceremoniously to the bed and covered her.

Mir began to build up the fire. "You both need to soak your feet or they'll freeze." But he paused for a second before throwing tinder on the coals. "Do you know, I've never seen her smile before, but she did then, didn't she?"

Maeniel paused, the faint glow of the firelight on his skin. "No," he said. "She had never smiled at me either. She saved my life. The one who came into the shed would have killed me, but she got in his way."

"She was glad to go," Mir said.

"Old man, nothing dies willingly."

"Sometimes we do," Mir said, scattering kindling on the coals. Then he rose and went to a chest in the corner. He pulled out a mantle of black silk embroidered with autumn leaves in scarlet, brown, green, and yellow, and trimmed along the edges with fur of a sable, deep brown, almost black. He handed it to Maeniel. "Take this and wrap her in it. We will make a pyre for her tonight. The silk came from far away, but the embroidery was done by her mother and sisters and the fur was from kinsmen in the north. It is all that is left of the nobility and beauty they brought to the mountains long ago. Let her wear it when she joins them."

Dryas said, "No! We have to get away from here. They came for something and they didn't get it. You can be sure the one who got away will tell the rest in the Roman camp and they will attack again."

Maeniel swung around and looked at her, an unreadable expression in his eyes.

Dryas felt the cold metal of the necklace against her skin.

But all he said was "No, they won't. The sprinkling of snow last night was only the advance guard of what will hit today. I know. I felt it before I went to sleep and I still feel the storm. My ears are popping. I don't know why, but they do before a blizzard. No! Soon nothing will move on the mountain or in the garrison camp below, and we won't either." Then he left.

Mir pulled some more heavy clothing from the chest and brought it over to Dryas, then began to heat water to wash her wounds.

Maeniel carried the mantle to the shed. He lifted the mad girl and placed her body on the silk, wrapping her carefully. Then he laid her on two of the wool blankets where he'd been sleeping and covered her with two more. He paused. When he was finished, he hadn't covered her face. It was just visible through the fine cloth. The precious wrapping softened her features and hid the scars and, for a moment, he saw the woman she might have been if the murderous destroyers of her family hadn't invaded her home.

He didn't think what she'd done was out of madness or fear. She'd given her life for him, to save him. She was confused in his mind with so many cubs he'd nurtured and protected. *Yes,* he thought, *for you, not the other one, for you I will sit by their fires.*

He didn't fear death; no wolf does. Even dogs are free of it, so that escape hatch was always open to him. But for him, like all other creatures, including the human ones, the ever-changing nature of experience is what keeps us alive. He was not afraid to die, but he would hate to stop living. And in order to keep on living, he would have to join with creatures who were alien to him, to learn their ways and their rules. But she had wanted him to have this gift so dearly bought.

He glanced again at her face, silent, beautiful, and at peace. So he would accept it and try to become one of them. But it was hard and left an abiding sorrow in his heart. He remembered pitying Imona, trapped in the smoky hut by night when he and his kind, pulsing with an appetite for food, friendship, and even love, ran in an unappreciated freedom by moon and starlight. Secure in the knowledge that, at birth, they had been endowed with all they ever had or would need to survive, or they would not have been allowed by the great arbiter of all life, necessity, to take their first breath and live at all.

But these incomplete creatures, so dependent on each other for the satisfaction of each and every need, were born to a thousand torments: fear of disease, hunger, a harrowing loss of the approval of their fellows, needing clothing against the cold and protection against the predatory instincts of their own kind. Each day was a struggle and, by night, they entered a cavern of fear and always, every day and hour, they looked on death, knowing that it would one day inevitably come to them or from them.

Maeniel picked up the ax and began to split the logs stored in the space between the roof and the wall. The sky, which had been clear at sunrise, was now clouding over and small flakes were beginning to fall.

A few minutes later, Mir entered the shed. He brought a pan of cooked cereal, some fresh-baked bread, and strips of cooked meat from the night before and gave it to Maeniel. Then he went to where the girl lay and stood over her. For the first time, he saw the mercenary Maeniel had killed. The man lay in a heap on the floor against the wall. Most of his skull and brain was distributed along the planking. Mir, who had been a warrior in his youth, sucked in his breath.

Maeniel ate the bread and eyed the cereal he held in the other hand.

"Use the spoon," Mir said.

Maeniel finished the bread, but still looked puzzled by the cereal. Mir reached over, picked up the spoon, and showed him how to scoop up the cereal. Maeniel tried some and made a face. "Hardly worth the trouble," he said.

"Eat it," Mir told him. "It will warm you." Then he returned to the back of the shed and stood gazing out the door. The snow was increasing, the flakes growing larger and larger. Mir heard the spoon scrape the bottom of the pan. "I wonder who they were," he said, glancing again at the warrior lying against the wall.

Maeniel resumed splitting the logs. "Romans," he hazarded. He was soon working up a sweat, and the droplets were freezing on his face. This was a new experience for him: no canid perspires.

"No," Mir said. "Armor and weapons are all wrong. These men didn't come from that camp in the valley. No, I believe they were after Dryas. Their leader said, just before she killed him, that he wanted to bring her to Rome unharmed."

Maeniel stopped chopping. "What is Rome and why would he want to bring her there?"

"Because she is unusual. She is what they call an Amazon, a woman who fights."

"She does that well." Maeniel stacked the wood. "And other things, too," he added darkly.

"Women like her are uncommon, even among us. In a way, it may be a pity we dispensed with them some centuries ago. They had a good grip on issues larger than winning and losing a few battles. A woman like her dealt with Marius, and another might have dealt with Caesar. She was right about you. I wanted to kill you and she refused. She and my wife believed you could be taught to be . . ."

"Human." Maeniel supplied the word. "Well, your admirable Dryas has somehow . . . I don't know what she did, but I can no longer summon the wolf. She has given me no choice in the matter. I hope you're a good teacher, old man, because I have a lot to learn."

Mir looked at the corpse resting against the wall. "Not the least of which is how to control that great strength of yours."

"What I did to him is what I intended to do. He killed her and cannot be excused for it. All he need have done was brush her aside, but she tried to give me a weapon, so he killed her."

"Not surprising," Mir said. "Most soldiers are so made, or perhaps being soldiers makes them so. They resort to force when other methods might accomplish their purposes more easily. Whatever evils he committed, he paid for them."

"Not enough!" Maeniel was splitting logs again with grim energy. "How much of this do you need?"

"What you have done now is probably more than enough. Come

in. We will have to devise some foot coverings for you. The temperature is dropping and your feet will freeze. We must prepare to flee when the weather breaks. While I don't think those men were Romans, they couldn't operate here without the permission of that garrison in the valley. And when they are again able to travel, they will no doubt be here to try their hand at capturing Dryas. We must go. All of us."

"To the town across the Rhine?" Maeniel asked.

"What do you know of Cynewolf and his stronghold?"

"Enough!" Maeniel answered, then buried the ax six inches deep in the oak butt where Dryas usually sat.

Mir considered that he'd probably asked his new protégé all the questions he should. Or, for that matter, certainly all the questions he wanted answers to. Bringing up the matter of Imona's fate could be both unfortunate and unwise, and Mir was neither. So he picked up the discarded eating utensils and led Maeniel to the house.

LUCIUS LET CUT EAR INTO THE STABLE. TOGETHER, they saddled two horses.

"We go now?" Cut Ear asked.

"No," Lucius said. "First, we ask questions and I will pay you. Come!" Cut Ear followed.

The money was in a chest chained to an iron bar set in the wall near the atrium. The lock opened when Lucius turned his key in it. He wondered if his sister knew he had a key. He'd never used it. His father had given it to him on his eighteenth birthday when he rode off to begin his military service, but he'd never ventured to raid the family strongbox.

He'd been given what, to him, was plenty of money. His horse, armor, and clothing were paid for out of family funds, and two old family retainers accompanied him. The female servant, Alia, had been recruited by the two servants, both freedmen of his father's, because they were basically lazy and somewhat status conscious. Washing clothes, emptying chamber pots, and sweeping floors were beneath them. As for cooking, after a week of eating their culinary disasters, Lucius gave up and took the line of least resistance—a popular direction with him—and paid Alia extra to cook.

This left the two old fussbudgets free to worry about his health, his morals, his spending habits, drinking habits, his eating habits, etc., etc., and so forth. After enduring two months of this, he found reason to send them back to Rome with orders to his father's accountant to pension them both off.

Thereafter, he made do with Alia. A lifetime of following the legions left her compulsively neat and constitutionally parsimonious. Since there was nothing to spend money on except women—he was too fastidious; drink—he was not addicted; or gambling—he was indifferent to it—his quarterly allowance was more than enough for him.

In short, he had never worried about money before, but he had seen his father putting it away in the form of various coin denominations.

He felt around in the open box. "Yes." A leather strap. His father had been an orderly individual. He had leather pouches made, ten spaces sewn up and down, a pocket for each coin. Ten up, ten across: a hundred golden aurei. He unfolded the leather. The glimmer of gold was apparent even in the dim light.

"Gold," Cut Ear said.

Lucius handed it to him.

It disappeared somewhere into Cut Ear's clothing. "Do murder?"

"Only if I tell you to."

"Ya!"

Lucius felt Cut Ear sounded enthusiastic.

There was a clank of chains and the old porter emerged from his sleeping space near the door. He looked up and saw two men looming over the strongbox. He crouched, frozen by fear. Then Cut Ear struck a light and an oil lamp flared, showing Lucius' face.

"Master Lucius!"

"Yes. Where does Firminius sleep?"

The old slave pointed one trembling hand to a corridor to the right of Fulvia's rooms.

Lucius nodded. "Go back to sleep."

Together, he and Cut Ear walked down the hall until they reached a door. To Lucius' surprise, light streamed out under it and there were voices in the room.

"Well, who was she?" The voice was Firminius' and he sounded exasperated. The answer was muffled, but the tone was exculpatory.

"Castor and Pollux making their report, no doubt," Lucius said in a low voice.

"That what you call them, eh?" Cut Ear replied. "I tell you, they sell you cheap. Want knock or kick the door open?"

"Kick it open."

Cut Ear kicked. The door flew open.

The room was relatively bright and more feminine than any woman's room Lucius had ever been in. There was a domed skylight in the ceiling set with glass panels. At present, all they showed were stars.

The bed occupying the middle of the chamber was the centerpiece. Lemon wood, curved at both ends, polished to a high gloss, plumped with a triple feather mattress and many cushions. Long swags of gauze draped from the ceiling, tented the raised dais on which it rested.

Two giant golden roses served as candelabra, one mounted on each side of the bed. The oil was in the base; the wicks poked up between the petals that served as reflectors for the flames. They were dazzling. The whole room was dazzling. The walls were painted to simulate pale white, yellow, and plum velvet draperies held up by cupids and swans.

Firminius gave a little shriek when the door flew open. "Oh, my." His hands fluttered like doves and he batted his eyelashes at Lucius.

Lucius stepped inside, followed by Cut Ear. He pointed to the door. "Go," he ordered Castor and Pollux. "I want to speak privately with my sister's secretary."

"Oh, no, don't you dare leave me alone with that . . . drunken wastrel and that terrible barbarian he has with him. In what gutter did you find that monster? He's not only badly dressed, but also unspeakably hairy—"

"Firminius," Lucius said, "I would like to keep this conversation within the limits of civilized discourse, but you're trying my patience. You two, go!"

"No, don't you dare go." Firminius seized Castor's arm. "Lucius, if you don't leave this minute, I'll have my two friends here expel you and your hairy friend from my chamber right now. I have a delicate constitution and I can't function if my sleep is disturbed . . . No, please, please, get them out of here. Mistress Fulvia will be ever so grateful if you sweep this trash out into the hall now—"

"They're both trained gladiators," Lucius told Cut Ear.

Cut Ear laughed.

The two "gladiators" advanced on both of them.

Lucius reached for his sword.

Cut Ear drew and Lucius found out why he'd laughed. In a movement so quick Lucius' eyes couldn't follow it, Cut Ear slammed the drawn sword into the side of Castor's skull. Castor stood looking stunned for a moment, then his eyes rolled back in their sockets till only the whites showed and his knees folded. He sank to the floor and lay still.

Cut Ear laughed again and flourished the sword at Pollux. "Him, I give a nice rest. You, I gut. Come on."

Firminius shrieked. Pollux ran.

Lucius kicked the door shut behind him. "Block it," he told Cut Ear.

Cut Ear did, pushing a big clothes chest in front of it.

Lucius found himself in the ridiculous position of chasing Firminius 'round and 'round the bed.

Cut Ear returned and settled the matter by kicking Firminius' legs out from under him and placing one large foot on his chest when he tried to rise.

Firminius began to scream. Cut Ear disposed of this problem by slapping him hard.

Firminius' head bounced against the marble floor and his eyes got a hazy look in them.

"Firminius, listen to me. If you scream again—"

"You give one ear," Cut Ear said.

"Very good," Lucius said admiringly. "Yes, Firminius. My friend here is called Cut Ear. Do you know why?"

Eyes now wide with terror, Firminius shook his head.

"Because he likes to collect them as souvenirs. He threads them on a chain and hangs them around his neck. He's starting a new collection and, if you scream again, one of yours will be his first one . . . or possibly two."

Firminius nodded.

"Now, I'm going to ask you some questions and I'd better get the right answers because if I don't . . . well, I collect eyes," Lucius said, drawing his dagger. "I put them in little glass bottles, preserve them in wine, and keep them under my bed. I need two more, to complete my set of ten. Yours will do nicely. Now, where is Philo?"

Lucius watched various expressions chase each other across Firminius' face. Fear, not of him but probably Fulvia. Anger, since he probably wanted to see Philo suffer. Rage, because he found the position he was in humiliating. Denial, since he was sure Lucius wouldn't do anything to him. Better break that up. Lucius tested the tip of his dagger on Firminius' cheek. A line of blood appeared.

Firminius huffed. "No—"

Lucius drew another line, this one deeper.

Firminius gargled, "Noooo . . ."

"Silence is not an acceptable answer, Firminius," Lucius snarled, and positioned the tip of his dagger over the man's left pupil.

He broke.

The answer dismayed Lucius even more than giving it did Firminius. "You see," he said spitefully, "nothing you do can help him. Not now."

Cut Ear picked up Firminius by the back of his nightgown and plunked him down on the bed. Then he patted Firminius' cheek and asked Lucius, "You want I come right now?"

"I could give you a few minutes. How long do you think it would—"

Firminius dove over the high back of the bed with a shrill scream and hid.

"You don't think it's unmanly?" Lucius asked.

"No!" Cut Ear said. "Same like woman, but hole tighter. Good! Fun!"

Firminius screamed again, this time at the top of his lungs.

"Apparently not as far as he's concerned," Lucius said.

Cut Ear laughed.

Someone was pounding on the door and shouting. Firminius' screams had roused the household.

"Too bad," Lucius said. "I think we'd best leave now, not that they'll do anything. This is my house. As the eldest male of the Basilian family, I rule here. Hear that, Firminius?"

The pounding on the door stopped. "Master Lucius?" a tentative voice outside asked.

"Yes," Lucius said. "Don't bother me right now. I'm talking to Firminius!"

There was a moan from behind the bed.

Cut Ear pulled the clothes chest out of the way. Fulvia's other secretary stood in the doorway. He was a freedman of Lucius' father, his steward or dispensator. He fixed Lucius with a disapproving eye. "My lord, I could hardly believe you capable of disturbing the peace of this household at such an hour."

"I apologize for awakening you, Aristo." The heavenly twin on the floor was still slumbering. Lucius pointed to him. "I don't want to see this pair again."

"Yes," Aristo replied. "Do you want them sold?"

"No," Lucius said. "It appears they're more devoted to my sister than they are to me. Enroll them among her servants. Prepare a chamber for Philo near mine."

Aristo's face remained impassive. "Your sister said he wouldn't be back."

"She was wrong. This—" He indicated Cut Ear. "—is Cut Ear and he will need a room prepared for him also, because he will be part of the household from now on."

Lucius left with Cut Ear following. They led the horses into the street.

"Alone?" Cut Ear asked.

"Yes," Lucius said, then they rode out into the night.

THE WOLF HAD THOUGHT LIVING AMONG HU-mans would be difficult and perhaps painful. In Cynewolf's stronghold, it wasn't. It was merely occasionally unpleasant and often puzzling.

Blaze's insistence that he bathe in the icy river every morning was both. Wolves didn't bathe. Why should they? The wolf pelt was water repellent, the dense undercoat self-renewing and clean. The outer hairs were shed in the summer and grew back in the fall. The wolf's tongue was adapted for grooming.

This idiotic compulsion to wash their skins in water might be understandable, but in cold water, in winter? As far as he was concerned, he'd just as soon not be included in this particular mad ritual, and Blaze's choleric insistence that he do so was equally puzzling.

When persuasion wouldn't move Maeniel, Blaze resorted to threats. They were equally ineffective. Blaze tried a whip. After two blows, Maeniel took it away from him, letting him know, in no uncertain terms, that the sensations it caused were unpleasant.

Blaze sat on his unmade bed, sucking a thumb Maeniel had inadvertently bent back too far during the struggle, and cursing him in not one, but three languages.

Dryas and Mir arrived, drawn by the uproar.

Mir took Blaze's side, but Dryas entered into negotiations, explaining why a daily bath in the freezing river water was good for him. He did have to break the ice to get to the water.

He said, "I don't believe a word of it." He then found out, when Mir and Blaze attacked him verbally, that humans are sensitive about accusations that they are fudging the truth, even though he knew from direct observation that they were guilty of this particular activity much—if not most—of the time.

But Dryas settled the matter by marching down to the river, finding a secluded spot, removing her clothes, and jumping in. She washed briefly, then donned her clothing with great speed.

He went ahead and followed suit, coming to the personal and private conclusion that they were fond of doing unpleasant things to themselves, for the purpose of proving unguessable things to themselves about themselves.

He imparted this to Dryas as they walked up the slope together back to the oppidum. Having seen her naked at the river bank, he again tried to persuade her to run away with him.

Dryas refused. He'd been certain she would, but thought it worth a try anyway. Sadly, she was now as a woman carved of snow to him.

Together they sat down on the log outside the gate. "Please try to humor Blaze more," she told him. "There are many things he knows and can teach you. I can't take you to Rome with me now. Neither of us knows enough. You must learn to ride, dress, to understand money—"

"You still want to go to Rome and kill this Caesar? What did he do to you?"

"He killed my son," Dryas said.

"How?" Maeniel asked. "You want me to help you and this journey may cost me my life. Give me your reasons."

"It's morning," Dryas said.

And it was a cold one. The river wasn't locked in ice, but the trees along its banks were bare and hoarfrost covered the remnants of vegetation remaining after the last cold spell. Beyond the mountains, the sun was just clearing the peaks. Though a striated gray cloud mass dominated the sky, there was just enough sky rim around the clouds for the sun to shed its vast golden light over the desolate winter landscape.

"It seems an obscenity that the sun rises on a world where my son no longer lives," Dryas said. "For this long time, I have felt the cruelty of his loss."

"Wolves do not grieve so," Maeniel said. "You pay a high price for your powers. How long has it been?"

"As humans reckon time, ten years," she answered.

"Longer than most wolves live. If pain is similarly lengthened, what of joy?"

"I cannot say," Dryas said. "I cannot remember any. I suppose there was some long ago while he lived, but I can't summon its image to mind. Odd, at first he was my duty. I only learned to love him when I put him to the breast. And, as he grew, he became a delight to me. But, as he was my son, he was doomed to be a candidate for kingship among my people.

"His hair was red and, when he smiled, my heart melted." Something almost like a smile appeared on Dryas' features, but then swiftly departed. "My heart misgave me to lay such a heavy burden on one so young, but from the first, he must be taught to rule. And before his hand touched my breast, before his lips gave suck, he must touch steel. I know I rose from the birthing stool among my women and, with blood streaming down my legs, I walked with the wailing babe in my arms to the walls where the weapons hung. I placed his hand on a sword hilt and pressed his lips to the cold blade. So he was consecrated to his people while yet wet with the fluids of my womb.

"He was happy, though, as he grew. Mischievous as red-haired children are and with beautiful, sparkling green eyes and a winning smile. I had to be stern. I tried to be. Perhaps too often . . . There were some harsh words, a time or two when he went supperless to bed . . . Oh . . . oh, but I loved him. My women spoiled him. From them, anything he asked for, he got. And I fancied, I fancy still, that it would have been so with women when he was a man. Not a good trait in a king, but that . . . turned out not to matter . . . I tried not to be too susceptible to his charm. He must, I told myself, learn discipline. So he quickly found he couldn't get round his mother . . . at least most of the time.

"But he had no difficulties with his studies. In many ways, he was naturally good. But all children must be taught to share, not to pick on the weak, and never to tamper with the property of others. He learned this well and, as he grew, I was proud but pained to know how popular he was among his age mates.

"Proud because he was shaping himself to be a leader among the men, but pained because each step a child takes away from his mother drags at the love she has rooted in her heart. But they must go. That is the way of it.

"So, when a sister of mine who lived among the Briganties asked that he be allowed to come and stay for a year, I agreed. I rode out with him, and a long journey it was. She and her chieftain husband entertained us royally, though. I saw many things that were only rumors in our mountains.

"I drank wine for the first time, saw war chariots and iron horse trappings, listened to bards sing long, incredibly complicated tales of wealthy kings and queens, their courage, ferocity in war, wealth, vanity, and cruelty.

"You see, my people live among the clouds, amidst the rain. It's always cool there. We pasture our flocks on the long green grass. We have four assemblies a year. At those assemblies, the queens, kings, and law speakers settle all quarrels, arrange marriages, buy, sell, and trade. At the assemblies anyone may speak. Man, woman, poor, rich, wise, foolish, free, and unfree. And if they have a dispute with anyone, we are bound to adjudicate it and to enforce our judgment.

"We sing beautiful songs, but they are old. About how our ships once plied the cold northern waterways and sailed beyond the pillars of the sky, skimming the warm blue sea the way the white-winged seabirds do. We sing the song of the stars, their changes; write the tale of summer with its flowers and fruit, and winter's struggle to fish the cold gray ocean. The lights of heaven that, properly read, point the way to the farthest corners of the earth.

"Our weavings are also very beautiful, but like the songs, the patterns are old, some so old we have forgotten the meaning of them. But their bright colors burn against the brown walls and gray sky. And, in them, we can trace the borders of our land and, for six times a thousand years, trace the lineage of our kings and queens. All have a meaning—the comb, the fish, the bird, the wolf, and the dragon. Woven in cloth and picked out in more colors than the rainbow. Each tribe has one. Each family, each man or woman has their own, and it lives and dies with them and no other will ever bear it. They are hung in my hall, mine among them. I will never return. Never return to see my son's tapestry with the events he lived woven into it.

"I shall not see the one representing my life, either. Another hand will complete it, cut the threads, and sew the border. I can only hope it will be the hand of a friend. I finished my son's before I left, and closed the border. Let those who can read the ending in the cloth. I cannot bear to describe it."

She was silent.

The wolf studied the river. The brief sun turned it into a glowing pathway sheathed in gold. The lacework of hoarfrost sparkled on the grass and trees like the jeweled coronet of a princess. Then the sunlight faded, as did the illusion of beauty, and the river lay gray as a polished sword taking its path between the icy glow of a metallic earth and sky.

"You left him with your friend," Maeniel prompted.

"Yes. And then Caesar came. We were late receiving word of the trouble in the lowlands. We rode at once. Though my people fight among themselves at times, we had many friends, allies, and blood relatives among the tribes Caesar preyed on.

"As I said, we are well versed in war, but this wasn't war. It was . . . extermination. Farms with the crops still standing in the fields were ashes, and the people who cultivated them corpses abandoned to the wolves and kites. The cows in the pastures, the sheep in the fields had their throats cut. The dogs and cats in the dooryards were clubbed down, trampled, and kicked to death. Where the wheat would burn, it was fired, and even in the orchards, the trees were girdled, wilting and dying in the autumn sun.

"Oh, yes, sometimes we caught up to these Romans. They had taken some things—gold and silver, for instance, and boys and girls not too young or too old to match the speed of their retreat. But everyone and everything else they murdered, spoiled, or destroyed.

"So I still had hope when we came to the place where my sister had lived. There were no children among the dead. Once sure, we vaulted into our saddles again, knowing they must have sent the children away, trying to hide them in the woods. And yes, so they had. We found them only a few miles away, within sight of the trees."

She was silent again for a time. At length she asked, "Do you know that what we call love can be perverted into an insupportable vileness? A horror so ghastly that the mind turns from it and gazes with longing into the abyss of death, and finds a kind of hope in the contemplation of eternal nothingness. A kind of comfort in everlasting sleep without dreams or fear of ever waking."

For a moment he didn't understand, and then did, but his mind turned from the grisly puzzle. "Wolves don't do such things. They don't even think such thoughts. I cannot imagine it."

"The children were guarded," Dryas said. "The guardians fought back, but were no match for the legionnaires. Before they were ridden down, they even managed to kill some of the children. Those were the lucky ones. My son was not among them."

"Did you and your friends manage to catch the soldiers who did this?"

"I am told we did," Dryas said. "I was effective as a commander. I was tried in battle as a young woman, but the last thing that I remember is looking down into my son's dead face. After that, my memories are as those of one who walks in darkness, under a sky veined by lightning, and sees the world around only for brief seconds when the clouds are lit from within by the storm's wrath.

"We caught them in the flat. We were wary of those long spears they carry, the pilum. They can use them to disable our footmen very quickly. The long shaft sticks in the shield, then bends or breaks so that the warrior can't use it any longer, and must throw the shield aside and fight without it. Fully a third of my force were women. Among us they are expert slingers and can bring down a bird on the wing. Indeed, many have to when the men are gone fishing for the big fish, deep swimmers of the bottomless ocean, or on long trade voyages where the winter sun doesn't shine and the gods do battle with each other in the sky, drawing fabrics of colored lights against the backdrop of countless stars.

"The lead shot my women carried was lethal, and when the Romans charged us, we opened our formations to let them by. If they were few, we slaughtered them then and there. If many, we melted back into the long grass or into the shadows cast by the groves of trees scattered across the open lands.

"When they reached the river there were only a few left. They tried to ford it in the night before moonrise, but we were waiting in the darkness under the trees.

"The chiefs called a meeting and we went. I spoke and tried to get them to burn this Caesar's ships, trap him on our territory, and kill him. But they were afraid. Afraid and thought it politic to be rid of this scourge. So he went his way and called this rampage a victory.

"Now I hope to follow him and kill him. I would like you to help, for I have the money, but I'm not sure I have the skill. And, if I fail, we will both die. Truth is, I have no plan," she ended lamely.

"Nor do we when we hunt. Humans make plans, have rules, play with logic the way a dog plays with a stick or a pup a piece of hide, but we don't. I cannot see how you could plan such an adventure. First, get to Rome, find out about this man, and then see if any possibilities present themselves. But to kill deer, you must know where they are likely to forage. So I had best learn what this Blaze has to teach me."

"So you will come?" she asked.

"I might as well, and besides, I have been listening to the people here talk. They talk a lot, especially the women. They seem to like to brush against me often. It seems I can't go anywhere without running into one or two of them and always the same ones."

Dryas looked him up and down. He was muscled like an athlete. Clean shaven? No, he simply never grew any sort of beard. He was slightly more brown than fair, but his complexion had a red flush under the tan that lent him an air of glowing health. His hair was the color of old polished wood. It curled freely and had auburn lights in it. No, she didn't think he'd miss her attentions for long.

"However, the people here do talk a lot about this Rome," he continued, "and I think it would be interesting to see it. But if Caesar is as contentious a fellow as you say he is, someone may kill him before we get there, and then all your trouble will be for nothing."

The ginger-haired man he'd punched in the head while trying to rescue Imona still did guard duty. He and Dryas passed him when they entered the gate. The wolf was sure the guard recognized him. But the look of hatred in the ginger-haired man's eyes puzzled the wolf. Yes, he'd hit the man hard, and yes, he had stolen his clothes and then abandoned them in the street, but why such anger about what he'd done? Why all the hatred?

Maeniel was puzzled, but he didn't have long to ponder the matter because he had to confront his two angry teachers and listen to their "blessings," then sit while the two elderly men fought about what course of instruction he should follow. He managed to find a small cask of mead and received a whispered message from one of his female admirers, the one who sent the mead, to meet her in the stable after dark. Her object was mutual "satisfaction." He was looking forward to an extended period of idleness while Mir and Blaze settled their differences when Dryas swooped down on him and dragged him off to a grueling afternoon of instruction with wooden swords.

He quickly realized that she, not Mir or Blaze, was going to be his chief problem from now on. Dryas was an indefatigable perfectionist of immense stamina and great skill. She managed to so exhaust him that when he met his inamorata in the evening, he was almost too tired for what she had in mind. But a short rest and two or three cups of mead found him quickly regaining his strength for not one, but three or four suggested procedures, one of which left him sore enough to be glad to jump in the river at dawn.

Dryas noted the look of relaxed satisfaction on his face. She was tempted to whack him in the throat with the sword to teach him a lesson, but the necklace at her throat moved of itself and clung oddly to her skin, reminding her of where she stood in relation to him.

After a month, she wouldn't have tried to smack him in the throat; he was too good. His hand-eye coordination was as perfect as any she'd ever seen. He had the stamina to run down a horse and the wolf's speed. His eyes were, as a matter of course, better in dim light than any human's she'd ever known, but his hearing was the marvel.

Once, when they were at practice outside the wall, he told her quite casually that Mir was coming because he was late for his Latin lesson.

Dryas asked him how he knew.

He told her he could hear him walking and was familiar with his step. In a few seconds, Mir appeared at the gate.

At length, the river froze and he wasn't troubled with ice-water baths any longer. There wasn't much snow, so he and Dryas were able to get in a lot of practice sessions.

She bore down hard and knew she was producing one of the most dangerous warriors who would ever fight a duel. She taught him not only the sword, but also the uses of a shield in combat and how it might be used by a skilled man, even one whose sword arm was incapacitated, to bring down an opponent. He learned the sling— which she previously thought required a lifetime of practice, beginning in early youth, to master. He was deadly with it, even against small targets like sticks and dried fruit. He was the object of some derision because he wouldn't let fly at anything not wanted for food.

But one afternoon, a cold, bitter, and gray one, he, Dryas, and a half dozen of the children went into the marshes to hunt. A feast was in the offing and there was nothing very special to serve. They brought nets, hoping to trap waterfowl feeding among the reeds.

It transpired they didn't need the nets. He brought down seventeen geese, mostly with head shots, in a little over an hour. The laughter ceased and the feast was a huge success.

But she found he excelled most at the hero's salmon leap, perhaps because, in his heart, he felt like a wolf again when he practiced this art. It centered on a form of unarmed combat now lost even in most of Britain and Gaul. But it was one that once served Dryas' people well, since it allowed one hundred percent of the adults in any community to resist an attack or raid launched against them, even when they could not immediately lay hands on their weapons.

A wolf's body—fang and claw, speed and weight. Maeniel's weapons were in his intelligence and agility, which allowed him to excel in unarmed combat. The sword, dagger, arrow, javelin, and the sling stone all came last. "Don't worship the weapon," Dryas told him. "If one turns in your hand, be ready to seize another. And, above all, teach yourself to be dangerous without anything but your two bare hands."

So it was, when the ginger-haired man, whose name was Actus, went after him with a knife. Maeniel was unarmed.

XVII

Y THIS HOUR, THE STREET WAS EMPTY OF ALL but carts. Lucius and Cut Ear threaded their way in and out between them without difficulty, hearing an occasional curse when they cut too close to a driver carrying a heavy load or one who had to slow his mules at a corner when they blocked the way for a few moments.

At length, they pulled their horses to a stop at the high gates of a large, walled villa near the Forum. The doors were wood, bound in iron. There was a bell with a hammer to ring it in a niche to the right of the door. Lucius whacked the bell with the hammer. It rang loudly.

In reply, there was only silence.

Lucius reached up and pounded his fist against the door.

From inside, someone cursed him.

"Let me in. I must see Caesar or the Lady Calpurnia."

A string of curses consigned him to a dishonored place among the dead. "Fool! Are you drunk or simply insane to demand admittance to the house of the first citizen at this hour of the night? Go home."

Lucius lifted the hammer and slammed it into the bell. It rang out loudly three times.

"Stop that, you stinking pile of dog turds. You'll rouse the whole neighborhood."

"Then let me in!"

Inside, he heard the rattle and snick of bolts being drawn and chains unhooked. Two legionnaires pulled the door back. They were in full armor, both wearing their scarlet dress cloaks and helmets.

One thrust a torch at Lucius' face while the other stood back, pilum in one hand, the other resting on his sword hilt.

Lucius blinked and lifted a hand to shield his face, but didn't give ground.

"Come in," the centurion with the torch said, "but leave your weapons here inside the door."

Lucius removed his sword and dagger. Cut Ear divested himself of a simply unbelievable amount of sharp-edged cutlery: one Greek sword sharpened on one side only, which was a first-class slashing weapon; a German broadsword slung at his back; the standard gladius of the legions; no less than three daggers, all different lengths; one sling, with lead shot; and, in case all else failed, a cestus, the loaded glove of a Roman boxer.

Even the tough-looking centurion seemed impressed.

Three more soldiers joined the first two and they escorted him past an ancient larium with over a dozen death masks, past an atrium pond older even than the one in the Basilian villa, and out into a peristyle surrounded by a columned walkway.

Everything here was intimidatingly magnificent and radiated not simply wealth, but also the assurance of nobility and whole lifetimes of distinguished service to the city and its most ancient institutions.

A woman stepped out into the light. She wore a green silk tunic that hung in long, straight, soft folds to the ground, fastened by buttons at the shoulders and arms. She was very beautiful and, for a second, Lucius wondered who she was. Then, as she stepped closer to the torch-bearing soldier, he realized that, though beautiful, she was no longer young. The voluptuous figure, only hinted at by the curves under the soft silk, was a bit thickened by time, and the auburn hair falling around and framing the heart-shaped face was threaded with gray.

When she spoke, her voice was low, her words and manner exquisitely courteous, and he felt at once that this woman would not know how to be shrewish, shrill, rude, or even haughty. Nor would she be able, by any stretch of the imagination, to whine or complain. She would be polite and considerate and careful never to give offence, or create a scene, even on her deathbed. He understood once and forever the meaning of the word *patrician*.

"My husband is sleeping at present. He is very weary and I am loath to disturb him. Have you an important matter to discuss with him? And, if so, are you sure there's nothing I can do to assist you?"

Lucius found himself going to one knee. "My Lady Calpurnia, a member of my household was today denounced as an enemy of your husband. He was arrested today by the Praetorian Cohort at the order of Marc Antony. He is a freedman of mine, a Greek physician named Philo. I believe you know him. I'm sure there has been an error somewhere. Philo has never been any man's enemy, least of all your husband's, and I'm equally certain he cannot possibly be even peripherally involved in any plot to harm him."

She moved closer to Lucius, stretched out her hand, and took his, indicating that he should rise. He did. "Yes, I do know Philo and no, I cannot believe he would harm anyone either, but couldn't this wait till morning?"

"Gracious lady." Lucius took a deep breath and tried to think of a way to convey the urgency of the situation to a woman whose life had insulated her so completely from the grim realities he was certain Philo was now facing.

"What he's trying to say is that after a night of brutal and intensive interrogation at the hands of Antony and the worthies of the Praetorian Cohort, Philo's own mother might not be able to recognize him."

Lucius saw Caesar standing in the shadow of the colonnaded porch. He looked both peevish and annoyed.

"Give me, please, one good reason why I shouldn't send you over to the same cell in the Tullianum to keep Philo company."

"Because then you would be punishing two innocent men instead of one."

"And you are willing to pledge your word to me that your friend is innocent of any and all charges that led to his arrest?"

"I am, Caesar."

"Even on pain of forfeiture of your own life if you should be proven wrong?"

"Yes! Yes, Caesar, I am."

"You are that certain of him."

"Yes."

Calpurnia turned her back to Lucius and moved gracefully toward Caesar. She paused at his side, rested one hand on his shoulder, and spoke quietly into his ear. Then, without looking at Lucius again, she glided away through a door on the porch. A maidservant met her with a lighted lamp in hand to escort her back to her chamber.

Lucius' eyes followed her almost against his will. When she was gone, he switched his gaze back to Caesar.

"Yes, she's very beautiful," Caesar said.

"It's not just that," Lucius said, as usual finding himself talking out of turn, admiring the woman about whose mind all Rome wondered. And, worse yet, in front of her husband.

"Yes, you're right," Caesar replied, then turned to one of the soldiers. "Bring me my writing case."

The soldier returned with a leather case that, when opened, folded into a small desk with a hard surface. The soldier held it in position while Caesar scratched a few quick lines on a sheet of paper, then folded it, and handed it to Lucius.

Lucius bowed and turned to go.

"Aren't you interested in what it says?"

"Should I be?" Lucius asked.

"No. It's an order for your friend's release into your custody."

"Thank you, but you will pardon me if I take my leave quickly. I'm a little afraid . . ."

"Of what might be happening to him while you're passing the time of day." Caesar finished the sentence. He spoke again to one of the soldiers, who nodded and left. Then Caesar preceded them to the door where Lucius and Cut Ear began to rearm quickly.

In the torchlight Caesar saw Cut Ear's face clearly for the first time. "Cut Ear, how did things go with Amborux?"

Cut Ear growled under his breath. "Eat, sleep, sacrifice to family gods. Eat, sleep, sacrifice to family gods. Every day all same. No end. No fun. No fights. All women old. Bed narrow, hard, cold. Pay stinks."

"So you changed patrons?"

"Ya!"

"What do you think of this one?"

Cut Ear looked Lucius up, then down, then up again. "More to him than shows on the outside."

Caesar nodded. Lucius was still in a hurry, but Caesar said, "Don't worry. I sent a soldier on ahead. Your friend won't meet with any more attempts at 'persuasion.' "

Lucius was belting on his sword. When he looked up, Caesar was gone.

A detachment of cavalry waited at the door. They escorted him to Antony's villa, but to an entrance for servants only, teeming with soldiers even at this hour of the night. Lucius rode into the courtyard and dismounted.

Philo, brought in by several soldiers, was a frightful sight. His tunic was splattered with bloodstains, old and fresh, as was his mantle. His nose had obviously been broken. One eye was purple and completely closed, the other purplish and only partially open, the lashes matted with blood. His lips were split and swollen. Worst of all, there was a horribly suggestive odor of burned flesh about his body.

Lucius handed the release order to the centurion in charge.

"Help him!" Lucius told Cut Ear. Both men supported Philo, one at each arm. "Can you ride?" Lucius asked.

"Yes," Philo replied. "I can crawl, walk, or even fly if the notion takes you. I will do anything to escape this dreadful place."

Lucius was inexpressibly relieved to realize it was, despite his injuries, the old Philo speaking, the man he knew.

However, Philo didn't have to ride. Caesar's soldier hired a carriage. It wasn't much, just a two-wheeled cart pulled by a very sullen mule with one small seat on each side and another in the back padded by worn leather cushions, with a canvas covering pulled up over hoops to keep the wind off. It was blowing briskly, as the night grew colder and colder. One driver sat behind the mule.

Lucius joined Philo in the carriage. Cut Ear declined the offer of a ride with a grunt and joined the soldier on horse behind the cart to begin the journey home.

"What happened?" Lucius asked.

"I don't know. All I know is that they were waiting for me near Gordus' house. Poor Marcia, she tried to object and almost got a nasty whack across the face for her pains. I told her, as sternly as I could manage, not to interfere. I was afraid to ask her to try to get word to you. I feared they might arrest her, also."

"They probably would have, but you didn't have to say anything. She knew. She found someone to deliver a message right away."

Philo nodded, but didn't ask for names. "In any case, they brought me to Antony. For a moment I was relieved. But he accused me of being a liar. I pleaded, begged really, thoroughly disgraced myself in a way that's painful to remember, but not nearly as painful as what happened a little later.

"Of course, he paid no attention. In fact, he told me not to make too big a fool of myself because it wouldn't matter. Then he turned me over to his friends. They didn't tell me their names and I didn't catch them. Later I was too, shall we say, preoccupied.

"First, they showed me all their little toys. That wasn't too bad, though they tended to knock me around while they were explaining their uses to me. But then they began to demonstrate how they worked, using me as their subject. I'd be in worse condition . . ." He looked down at his hands. They were swollen and badly bruised, but intact. "But they got careless with me and I managed to break loose. By then, you understand, I was hoping somehow to persuade them to kill me, because I had no idea if Marcia had been able to contact you, or if contacted, you could do anything to help me." Philo's voice grew more and more hoarse.

Lucius deliberately looked away from his friend's face.

They turned a corner and the wind caught them in the face. Lucius pulled Philo's hood down and the cloak tighter around his body.

"Do you know, that wind feels good?" Philo said. "It sort of numbs all the spots that still hurt. In any case, one big bruiser, who I think probably didn't know his own strength, socked me in the head and I became oblivious to the proceedings for what I believe was a rather long time—some hours, in fact. When I finally awakened, my mind wasn't clear. Not being a complete lackwit, I strove to give the impression that I was even more addled than I truly was. By then, Antony had returned and was cursing his assistants rather roundly.

"He was not taken in by my little deception, but he did order that I be given some sops of bread and wine. I can't put it down to kindness. I felt they were only preparing me for further inquiries . . . But I heard a messenger arrive and, thereafter, I was left alone. What did you do? How did you get me out? Incidentally, I don't believe I ever saw a more beautiful sight than you, and whoever your new . . . What should I call him? But I'm babbling. Don't pay any attention to me. I can't think clearly. It's possible I wasn't pretending I . . . was hurt by the blow to the head as much . . ."

"Be quiet," Lucius said, indicating the carriage driver sitting right in front of them. "We'll talk after I get you home."

When they reached the villa, the snowy winter moon was down, but the courtyard was ablaze with light. Aristo was waiting with Alia. She began clucking when she saw Philo and helped him down from the carriage and into his room.

Lucius hadn't been aware that she liked the doctor, but when he saw Philo's room swept, his bed made, and his belongings neatly arranged where there had been emptiness before, he realized Alia must be fond of the physician.

Aristo brought warm water and clean clothing for the Greek and linen for dressings. Alia, who'd had a lot of experience, cleaned and dressed the wounds, including some very ugly burns.

Lucius asked where his sister was.

"Gone," Aristo said. "To Gaul. She came back from visiting Cleopatra and said something to me indicating her dissatisfaction with some of her agents there, complaining that if you want something done right, you must see to it yourself. Then she added, 'She killed five of them. I sent six and she killed five. Can you believe it?' I asked, 'Believe what?' But she wouldn't answer, nor did she say when she would return. I've found you a servant, by the way: the doorkeeper. He's been chained in that alcove for years, ever since your mother died. I believe your father was angry with him for being a bit too loyal to your lady mother."

"Bringing her drink, you mean?"

Aristo developed a pained expression reminiscent of someone with an acute case of constipation and didn't answer.

"Fine," Lucius said.

"He's clean, quiet, and will carry no tales. And he will be grateful to escape what has been a long imprisonment for him. Macer and Afer are taking his place for the time being, at least until your sister returns home. Then she can make such disposition of them as she desires. Their behavior toward you was a serious matter, as was Firminius'. You are the ruler of this house, being the oldest male surviving member of the direct line.

"You are paterfamilias, patria potestas, the head of the family. All of those living in the household, free and slave—including your sister—are in your potestas, your power. They both threatened you in front of a witness. I have not acted before, since you did not assert your rights, but now that you have, I feel I must weigh in on the side of law and support your wishes. But I must say I disagree with your leniency toward Macer and Afer. I believe theirs to be a most serious offence, and they should remain in chains until your sister returns."

"Thank you," Lucius said with true and proper gravity.

"Now, with your permission . . ."

"Certainly."

Aristo departed, nose in the air, surrounded by his usual aura of polite disapproval.

Alia completed her task and left Philo's room. Cut Ear patted her on the backside as she was leaving. She flashed him a glance that verged on just the edge of irritation as if to say " 'Who are you to be familiar with me?' "

"I have gold," Cut Ear said.

"Ummm," Alia said, but there was no disapproval in her expression.

She was a bit old for Lucius, or at least he'd never thought of her in that context, but her body was firm, with wide hips and big breasts. Her face was not pretty—the hooked nose and snapping turtle jaw were too prominent—but she was apparently to Cut Ear's liking.

Lucius went in to see Philo, but paused at the door next to Cut Ear. "Alia?" he asked.

"Some 'women trouble.' 'Man trouble,' 'money trouble,' 'litters like cats trouble,' 'never work trouble,' 'bad temper, want to stick knife in you trouble,' 'jealous all the time trouble,' 'not looking and they steal trouble,' 'wine trouble.' This one take pay, shut up, no trouble. Ya, is good."

Lucius nodded.

Philo was lying on a bed, a more comfortable one than he'd had before. His upper body was bandaged, the lower covered by linen sheets and a down counterpane. There was a lamp in the room, but his pupils were contracted. He'd taken opium. "Did she mix that or did you?" Lucius asked.

"I did. I'm not fool enough to entrust that to someone else."

"I went to Caesar himself."

"Zeus thunderer. You took a dreadful risk."

"Yes." Lucius did not deny it. "What I want to know is, did I lie to Caesar when I swore on my own life that you were not involved in any plot against him?"

Philo paused for long moments, so long that Lucius thought he'd drifted off to sleep.

"Well?" he prompted.

Philo said, "No, you didn't lie. But . . ."

"But what?" Lucius glanced quickly around the room to make sure it was empty. Not only were they alone, but the only window was a light well in the ceiling, and the door was closed.

"I do know something."

Lucius kept himself from moaning by an effort of will. "What?" he asked between his teeth.

Philo told him.

"Why in blazes didn't you tell that to Antony in the first place?"

"Because it's a rumor. The sources from whence I got it are hardly unimpeachable and, if I had, our illustrious counsel would have decided that I had more information and I was concealing it. And gone right ahead with my . . . examination. I decided that a posture of complete innocence was the most sagacious one to adopt under the circumstances."

"Sooner or later they would have gotten the truth out of you."

"Truth has nothing to do with a man under torture. Sooner or later I would have invented something . . . just to make them stop. Now you know everything I do. Go to Caesar if you must, but tell me in advance so I can prepare poison."

"I must. I gave him my word," Lucius said miserably.

"Fine! I've had too much opium to care. You're a Roman citizen. You will be beheaded."

"Ah, mother of the gods." Lucius dragged his fingers down his cheeks. "Maybe he will let me commit suicide."

"That's not any more fun than being beheaded, Regulus."

"Regulus was a man of honor. Besides being who I am, I have an advantage in dealing with Caesar."

"The advantage is Caesar's," Philo said. "He's not stupid. I'm not sure you can say the same for his heavy-handed friend. I suspect that you will arrive home with your head still on your shoulders in no danger of having it removed in the immediate future. The ones I worry about are the conspirators. There seem to be so many of them and their rank is so high and they won't take kindly to little birds who carry tales to Caesar's ear. Or, as Caesar's veteran said to him, 'Watch your back, my lord. Watch your back.' "

IT WAS EARLY AFTERNOON WHEN MAENIEL ENTERED the barn. There were no windows and it was dark. He heard Actus before he saw him coming in on the left side, knife in underhand position, ready to drive it in below his ribs. He reacted the way Dryas had taught him, knocking the knife out of his opponent's hand with a blow of his forearm. He was pleased to see the technique worked well. So pleased, in fact, that he didn't think of making any other countermoves as Actus managed to sock him in the face. But the blow didn't even rock him. He simply picked up the ginger-haired man and threw him against the wall.

Actus looked stunned for a moment, then slid down the wall, sat on the floor, and began to cry.

"What's wrong with you?" Maeniel asked.

He didn't get a coherent answer, but then humans were mad. They would do the most peculiar things, usually at the worst possible times. He picked Actus up by the scruff of the neck, as he would have done a cub throwing a temper tantrum, and dragged him through the barn door to the half log that formed a horse trough. He punched through the thin skin of ice on the surface in two or three places to make a fairly big hole, then dunked Actus's head.

Actus came up sputtering and screaming. Maeniel dunked him again; he came up sputtering; then a third time. Actus came up an interesting shade of robin's-egg blue with purple lips, eyes set and staring, and water draining from his mouth and nose. Maeniel looked at him doubtfully.

Dryas came running up and helped him assist Actus back into the barn.

"I didn't kill him, did I?" Maeniel asked anxiously.

Dryas propped Actus up against a bale of hay. "No," she said. "There's color coming back into his face." Her foot kicked something and it slid across the floor. "A knife!" She looked at Maeniel. "What . . ."

"Don't look at me! I didn't do anything to him. Not this time, at least. He's still mad about what I did before when I hit him in the head, stole his clothes, and tried to get Imona to come with me. The very smallest slight will anger you, and then you are the worst creatures about holding grudges. Even an elk would forget after a week or two that I chased it . . . but not one of your kind. Besides, he tried to throw wine in my eyes. He missed because, as a man, my eyes are much higher up than when— Why am I explaining this to you? He tried to stick a knife in under my ribs. I took it away from him. I could have stuck it in him. In fact . . ." He reached for the knife where it lay in the shadows.

"No!" Dryas shouted. "No! No!" She pushed him away from Actus. "Please! Don't! He's helpless now."

Maeniel held Actus' knife, a long, dark, thin-bladed thing with a boar's-tusk handle. "So I see." He sounded truculent, and Dryas eyed him the way she might a big, vicious dog that had just slipped his collar. He caught her expression and then stepped back with a look of disgust on his face. "You're afraid of me." He pointed to Actus. "It should be that fool you worry about." He turned and drove Actus' knife into the doorframe, snapped it off just below the hilt, then stalked out of the barn.

Actus, who had never lost consciousness, staggered to his feet. His nose was running and his eyes tearing.

Dryas got a good whiff of him. She drew back. "You're drunk."

He spat in her face and called her several things in a low voice, most of them in Latin. The language had a fairly rich sexual vocabulary, much of which reeked of denigration and insult. Then he began weeping again and wove off down the street.

Maeniel walked toward the gate in the palisade. "Woman of the night" is how he remembered the queen of madness, the she-bitch of procreation, creation, and, at last, disintegration and destruction. "Woman of the night, I hate being a human!" The only answer he got was the bite of winter wind at his face.

Clouds were rolling in from the north, winging small blades of sleet and sharp, cold snow at him. He remembered the wolf with a deep, hungry longing that he thought he'd put behind him.

Would there ever come a day when he would forget the easy feel of fur, not skin, as he carried his warmth with him; the smooth way the big paws found purchase on the frozen ground; the stamina that gave and gave when he needed to run; the speed yielded by four legs as opposed to the clumsy struggle on two?

The beauty of silence broken only by the rush of water or the faint bell-like sounds of falling snow, wind sighing in the fir and spruce on a mountainside, the spring and summer birdsong as he ran along the river at dawn, as opposed to the endless babble, a constant assault of sound, leveled by these gibbering creatures at each other endlessly.

He paused and sucked in a long breath. The bitter wind burned his throat and lungs.

A wolf's muzzle is long and warms the air flowing through it. As a human, he hadn't even that minor comfort any longer. He longed for freedom beyond the walls of the half-ruined town. He hungered for a winter crossing on the ice-covered river and a journey through the frozen forest beyond. But if he attempted it without the wolf to call on, he would probably die. No, he was tied here. Tied as these cowering humans were, fearing the cold and snow, dreading the long dark winter night.

No, he was trapped here, enduring the labor of a slave. At first he hadn't been status conscious. Whatever needed to be done, he did. But it didn't take long for him to notice the same jobs he was so often given otherwise went only to either women or the lowest and most despised males of the community.

Separated from the most important part of himself, lonely among these unhappy creatures, he would be left to wear away his life as a servant among the remnants of a broken people. The atmosphere of despair that haunted this last refuge of what once had been a proud people wasn't lost on him.

He could feel their sorrow and desperation. The miasma of their tragedy was as palpable to him as the cold borne by the winter wind.

Mir called him from a spot under the eaves of the big, round, chiefly hall. The old man stood quietly watching the snow fall.

Maeniel walked over and stood beside him. Despite himself, he liked Mir. One reason was that when he had nothing to say, he didn't say it. Blaze seemed never to shut up. Dryas—well, Dryas was a mystery. Sometimes he hated her. At others he was afraid. He remembered the desire he'd felt for her, but as she'd said, she was now a woman of snow.

Mir scratched the bridge of his nose. "Feast tonight," he said. "Cynewolf is having trouble holding his people. Know anything about hunting?"

Maeniel looked down at the old man. He was deeply annoyed, then realized Mir was joking. "A little," he answered.

An hour later, he found himself on a horse, cantering along the riverbank, the wind in his face. He was warm enough. In his quiet way, Mir was the most efficient of the three.

Blaze drifted easily into esoterica. For instance, "Do the fixed stars move?" He entertained the wolf for three hours on the subject, beginning with what one meant by *move*. "Is the earth round or flat?" "What is the smallest indivisible particle?"

Dryas wandered into stories such as, "If a warrior is forbidden to drink mead after moonrise, but he finds that to save a friend's life, he must drink mead after moonrise, which is worse for him to do? Go ahead and drink the mead or sacrifice a friend's life to the letter of the law?"

The wolf considered this absolute, complete, and utter nonsense. He would drink mead after sunrise, sunset, moonrise, or any other rise to save a friend. But he did agree such a situation might be, all in all, a terrible conundrum.

Mir worried only about getting him dressed for the weather and finding him a reasonably steady mount. Some horses still tended to become unmanageable when they got a good whiff of him.

He had on a heavy tunic, loose trousers with cross-gathered leggings, a woolen mantle, hob-nailed boots, and heavy stockings.

He scanned the marsh and riverbank with an expert's eye. Deer were the most common game near the oppidum. As evening drew closer, they would leave their coverts in the marshes and enter the abandoned fields to feed on what grain remained among the furrows. In the thickets that served as windbreaks for the farms, they could still find fruit of crab apples and quince, hummocks of seed-bearing grasses, and even red, fleshy rose hips.

His saddle was only a triple thickness of blankets. He carried three javelins in a leather quiver hanging near his knee. Mir had given him Dryas' best. The poles were ash, the tips sheathed in steel. The blades were narrow, but sharp as razors and saw-toothed along the edges to keep them from being easily withdrawn.

To Dryas, this was the world of the hag, the winter queen. Brown, black, green, and gray—those were her colors. The demiwolf rode his horse through a kingdom of desolation arrayed with her symbols.

The wood and marsh were black—damp seeped into the tree trunks, staining them the color of wet mud—but the high branches were brown except where they were festooned with mistletoe's pale green branches and pearl-colored berries.

The dead grass was another kind of brown, a deep, rich color where it was interspersed with the second-growth scrub trees, but a silvery brown where water met land and hoarfrost coated the dead grass stems. The sky was the gray of rolling mist, staining the marsh pools and the river. Here, it wasn't frozen over, but bubbled and spat, racing among broken rocks. Only its edges were stilled by cold. The quiet pools and angry river both seemed one with the chill gray sky.

Man is the winner, he thought, *the winner in the ancient game of survival.*

When he was out of sight of the oppidum, he pulled the horse to a walk, keeping the animal near the marsh and away from the river. He was adept at helping the horse pick a route on solid ground between the low places, sodden mud, and standing water so the animal could move silently against the dark background of the scrub forest. The wind was still in his face.

The oppidum was located on a natural hill. Near it, the ground dropped away steeply, so steeply that, for a time, the wolf found it hard to keep his mount on solid ground. But then the land rose again. There had been farms here, when the town had been the center of a powerful tribe. They were still worked, but the farmers lived in the oppidum, fearing to dwell on their land any longer.

The marsh retreated and Maeniel entered the edge of a large holding, broken into ploughland and pasture. Now he rode more cautiously. The sharp-hooved tracks of deer were among the furrows. Then he saw them, brown shapes, a winter bachelor herd: all males, from spike bucks to six-pointers.

He eased his mount toward the forest, riding slowly. The wind was still at his face. The horse stepped along quietly and he drew closer and closer to the deer.

When he judged he was close enough, he lifted one of the spears from its sheath and nudged the horse into a run. The deer had been feeding near the river. They bolted up the slope for higher ground.

He loosed the first javelin the way Dryas taught him and scored a clean miss. Under him, he felt the horse gallop faster and faster.

Several of the biggest, oldest bucks disappeared behind a rise in the ground. He found he cradled the second javelin without even realizing that he'd plucked it from the sheath.

A spike buck darted just in front of him. He loosed the shaft automatically. Also without thinking he led the deer slightly, again as Dryas taught him.

He was sure he'd miss, as the deer rose with almost birdlike grace to clear a low stone wall. The javelin and the deer came together at midleap. The animal died at once, falling in a heap next to the wall.

The horse was up the hillock, running flat out. Maeniel's thighs tightened on the withers, holding his body set forward just above his mount's neck. Another javelin was in his hand. Below him, the herd was a semicircle, the two leaders just about to enter the marsh. The deer at the points were easy targets, but they were small, yearlings at most.

The closest deer to the trees was in his prime, a big four-pointer. Maeniel made his choice, not as a wolf, but as a man. He didn't even feel the spear leave his hand, but a second later, it was in the shoulder of the biggest buck as it vanished into the brush and small trees.

Maeniel vaulted, clearing the horse's neck, and hit the ground running. The blood spoor was clear, big, scarlet drops leading into the trees. Maeniel could hear the animal ahead of him crashing through the brush at the forest edge and then the drumming of hooves as it cleared the barrier of vegetation and flew into the open.

Maeniel lifted his mantle and covered his face to protect it from the thorny canes of wild rose, blackberry, and hawthorn and followed, slamming through the hole the deer made.

In a second he was past, just in time to see the buck leap a shallow ditch that led to the river. It didn't appear on the other side. Still, Maeniel didn't slacken his pace until he reached the edge of the ditch.

The buck lay on the downslope, stretched out, tongue protruding from its open mouth, eyes staring, dead.

Maeniel found he was holding his knife in his hand. He hadn't been aware he'd drawn it. For long moments he stood, still listening to the wilderness silence settle around him.

Yes, he thought. "Yes," he said aloud. "We are the very king of killers." A wolf would have taken one of the slow ones, tested the herd for the old, cripples, and weaklings. But not a man. He chose the best because he had the means and skill to take it, for himself and his kind.

Then he remembered others would have the first choice of the cooked meat at the feast tonight. The champion's portion would go to other men, not him. And right now, the barley gruel he'd had for breakfast sat sour on his stomach.

He walked down the slope, grasped the antlers, pulled the carcass to the top of the bank, and began the task of butchering it. Before he finished, he ate the heart and liver, hot and steaming in the frigid air. They had a good taste. He hoisted the dripping meat to the lowest limb of a tree and went to deal with the other animal.

When both were cleaned and dressed, he felt warmer and full fed. He'd also eaten the heart and liver of the second deer.

The horse, lather drying on his flanks, grazed in the open near what had been the farmhouse.

His hands were dirty and he walked down to the river to wash them and clean his knife. Besides, it would be safer to let the meat cool before loading it on the horse. The animal was steady, but Maeniel didn't want to have to talk to it for any length of time.

Horses tend to be thickheaded and somewhat impervious to rational persuasion. While working in the stables, he'd come to speak a little of their language, not a lot, but more than any human ever would. Like humans and wolves, they tended to differ in intelligence and personality, but they seemed to cross the line into irrational rage or panic more quickly than either the human tribe or the gray. Probably an advantage, considering their survival depended on unmonitored automatic reactions to threats posed by either nature or predators. But this strong tendency in their nature was a nuisance to the humans who enslaved them and expected a modicum of restraint and intelligence even from their slaves, human or otherwise.

Near the river he found a small pond dug out in a low area. It seemed it might once have had sluice gates so that it could be flooded from the river when it was high and to keep it filled when the water was low.

He tried to approach its edge and found the area around it was mushy. As he neared the water, he came close to sinking to his ankles.

He was annoyed at first, then the wolf woke. It shocked the man because he'd begun to believe his alter ego forever gone. It glared at him, yellow-eyed, from some hazy place of exile.

Fool! The words formed themselves in his brain out of his nightmare brother's disgust. *Have you become so enmeshed by their easy blindness to the world around you that you cannot hear the warning both wind and water shout to your eyes and nose?*

Yes, the earth was churned up at the pond's edge by the feet of both horses and men. Maeniel stood silent, as the wolf will, his mind emptied of all else, trying to read the mass of information pouring in.

Men, yes, no, not just men, soldiers: leather, steel, sweat but no fear. A woman! A young one, traces of perfume, raw sexuality, anger. A dominant she, like the mother of the pack. Horses, military mounts. They'd stopped here, relieved themselves, yes, even the woman, in the willow, cherry, and poplar thickets near the water. Then they ate, cooked food, bread, meat, cheese, and waited for someone. The absence of anger smells said they were not attacking or on the hunt.

What? What were they doing? He began to circle slowly. Actus.

Actus, a layer of odors. Man, clothing, perspiration, drink. Actus had the characteristic smell of those humans who ingested large quantities of wine. Anger and illness, peculiar to the man himself. He and only he left that signature in the air, on the ground, on leaves, trees, twigs, and bushes when he passed. Recognizable as a well-known face is to a human being.

Maeniel knew and understood them far better now, but this puzzled him. Yet he was not alarmed. They were all gone, no threat as far as he could tell to himself or anyone else.

He found a spot where he could wash his hands and clean his knife in a freshet that broke through the ice on the shingle riverbank. He rubbed the knife with deer suet to oil the blade before he sheathed it.

The sky was growing darker, but the light at the edge of the clouds was bright, and a pale, weak, setting sun shone through them, dusting the brown and gray winter landscape with swift golden light.

He thought of beauty as perceived by men. Yes, wolves knew that, too. A sense of rightness, the dialogue between the spirit of life and the souls of those who come and pass in the tides of time. No matter what happened to him, he would do well in the world, as either wolf or man, and he would be faithful to himself as either one.

The golden light faded and he turned to climb the hill, load the dressed deer on the horse, and return to the oppidum.

Mir was waiting at the gate when he returned, leading the heavily laden horse. The old man took the animal to the stable and told Maeniel to go help the cook.

The great hall was being readied for the feast. Fresh torches burned on the walls. A dozen joints of meat already hung over the fire pit in the center and, in a few moments, the two deer joined them. The four-pointer brought a gasp of awe from the gathering crowd. There was talk and laughter among the men and women readying the big room about who would claim the champion's portion from such a magnificent beast.

Maeniel left the hall and went to visit Mir. Dryas, Mir, Blaze, and Maeniel were quartered together. They'd taken a semiruined building at the farthest edge of the encampment. When they had arrived, the room was empty, the roof sagged, and snow had blown in and covered a floor already warped by rain. They cleaned it, covered the windows with oiled parchment, propped the roof, and moved in. Dryas and Mir slept in beds fitted into alcoves in the wall. Blaze had a cot and Maeniel stretched out on a table.

Maeniel had made a friend, Evars. It was she who swept the hearth and floor, then washed the clothes and bedding, placing it out in the snow to clear out lice or bedbugs. Dryas was clean and neat, rather in the way a soldier is, but not domestic. Evars could cook, and usually did, even when there was no need for it, like tonight. Soup bubbled on the hearth away from the fire, just at a simmer. Mir was reading, Blaze writing, and Dryas using a whetstone to sharpen the three javelins he'd used today.

Maeniel dipped himself a cup of the warm broth and sat down at the table. "I want the champion's portion tonight," he said.

Blaze continued writing and said, "Don't be a fool."

Mir continued reading and said, "Eh, what?"

Dryas rasped the whetstone at the tip of the spear and said, "It's yours if you want it, but you will probably have to kill one or possibly two men to get it."

Blaze and Mir both looked up, rather the way two birds at a fountain turn their heads at one time toward the same noise.

"He's not good enough," Blaze said flatly.

"He's not good enough. Is he?" Mir asked.

"Yes, he is," she said to the two men, then turned to Maeniel and repeated, "Yes, you are. You are the best I've ever seen and, for certain, the best I've ever trained. If you feel ready to accept the challenges of the other bulls, stand your ground. I can't guarantee you will win. No one can give you that sort of assurance, but I think it quite likely that you will."

"He is not noble. His blood—"

"Oh, be quiet," Dryas said to Blaze. "What is noble? He is the son of the giver of madness, she who inspires prophecy in women and battle madness in men. His house is the house of the wolf. He was their leader and will be a leader here among men."

She could feel the necklace and only just kept her hand from touching it. It crawled, actually crawled like a serpent, beneath her linen blouse. Maeniel raised his head and looked into her eyes. "I am not for you," she said. "If I were to return, I would have to bring a king to my people, and I may no longer do so. I am not fit to rule."

Mir shook his head. "Wolf, a child stretches out his hand to the fire. The child says, 'Pretty. I want that,' not truly understanding the nature and the dangers of what he so admires. You are yet as a child among men. I beg you, search your heart before you snatch at a prize because it seems attractive to your untaught eye."

"My name is not Wolf, it is Maeniel. You didn't tell them," he said to Dryas.

"No, your name is your own, seeing your patroness bestowed it on you—a name and much else. Mir's advice is good. Weigh it, then decide at the feast how you will proceed. If you snatch at a flower, you never know when there might be a wasp among the petals. Or even an adder coiled in a crown. But, being a certain type of male creature, you will probably need to find out. So, good luck. I think you will probably need it." Then, as she began oiling the spearheads, Evars entered to call them to the feast.

XVIII

LUCIUS ORGANIZED HIS HOUSEKEEPING ARRANGE-
ments. The old doorkeeper, Octus, looked to be an excellent
manservant, at least as far as Lucius was concerned. He was, as
Aristo said, quiet. He didn't fuss over Lucius, who loathed being
fussed over. He kept Lucius' clothes clean, made his bed, straightened
his things, and then left him alone to pursue such activities as he cared
to, without comment or complaint.

Lucius let one day go by. Philo was recovering well and was already up, walking around and eating everything Alia brought him.

Cut Ear brought his things from the Gallic senator's house and
moved in. His things were mostly more edged weapons and woolen
clothing. Cut Ear was sophisticated enough to have a banker in the
Forum and Lucius suspected his gold went there, except for the coin
Alia got.

Lucius told Octus he was going to visit Caesar and needed to
dress well. He bathed and Octus came in with a magnificent ivory
linen and silk tunic. Lucius climbed out of the tub in the tepiderium
and studied the garment. "It's not mine."

"I think it is. Your father bought you a number of nice things
after you left to do your military service. Somehow quite a few of
them found their way into Firminius' rooms. Aristo retrieved them."

It was very plain, but beautifully cut and woven. Then Octus
draped his senatorial toga over it.

It was near noon and Lucius wasn't looking forward to this interview at all. No, he didn't think he would wind up being beheaded, but confessing to Caesar that he'd been wrong about Philo having no information wasn't pleasant to contemplate.

When he arrived at the dictator's house, a soldier admitted him as before and he was shown into the same peristyle garden he'd seen the night before last.

He found the residence surprisingly modest for a man who commanded the wealth and power Caesar had now. But then, as he strolled around the pool in the center of the garden, he began to understand how a tired campaigner, worn out from the wars, might be grateful to come back to a quiet spot like this. In the sheltered garden the winter herbs—elecampane with its large yellow flowers, sage bearing tall blue spikes—bloomed everywhere. There were roses still, the sweet rose of Pistem, its petals growing purplish as the flowers aged; big rosemary bushes growing against each column of the porch; and even the sunburst calendula clustered around a sundial shaded by a blue-flowered chaste tree, its violet flower spears erupting from the dense, aromatic foliage. Orris, iris, and Egyptian lotus flourished in the pond along with a spiky blue waterweed that seemed to have run wild all around the margins of the peristyle pools.

A statue divided the two pools. The figure was diminutive, done in some sort of greenish black marble. At first, Lucius thought it a bronze, but then as he drew closer, he saw the material was oddly colored stone.

She was old now. This must have been done when she was young, because she wore a toga praetexta, the dress of an unmarried girl not yet a mature woman. It confirmed to Lucius that she had once been extraordinarily beautiful. Calpurnia, Piso's daughter, Caesar's wife, born to live and die between the two men.

He remembered how Philo had described her this morning. "Yes," the Greek had said. "A great lady and a very sick woman."

"She's not just jealous of Caesar, as they say?"

"No, they are wrong. She understands the duties and burdens of being married to one of the great political dragons of your city and she accepts them. She was brought up to be fully aware of her obligations to husband, family, city, and even class. Her family is shadowed by a problem of a mysterious and terrifying nature. I studied in Alexandria with a specialist in trephination. Do you know what that is?"

"Knocking holes in the skull."

Philo nodded. "Just so. She fears these headaches greatly because . . . she believes they sometimes bring with them a knowledge of the future. Who knows? She may be right. She foresaw her sister's death and her father's, but the big problem is the headaches have been increasing in the last few years. They've gone from two or three times a year to one every week to two weeks.

"They are terribly painful, but brief, only about a half hour by the clock. And I can make them shorter by administering a mixture of opium, feverfew, and valerian. But she needs the surgery and won't have it. I think it's now her only hope, but she fears it may leave her deranged, a very real possibility, or do no good at all, again a very real possibility. Sometimes it simply doesn't work.

"A male relative of her mother's had a trephination and lay as one dead for a week. Then to the chagrin and disgust of all his relatives, who were already dividing up his property, he made a complete recovery and survived to a more than ripe old age. However, his sister was left bereft of the power of speech and hearing, lost the use of the right side of her body, and died, as did one of Calpurnia's younger sisters. She was, after an apparently uneventful night's sleep, found dead still in a position of repose by her attendants when they went to awaken her in the morning."

"Mysterious," Lucius said.

"Yes, very, but at least in me she has someone who takes her pain and fear seriously and doesn't attribute it to her possession of a uterus rather than a prick and balls. I'm certain from my experiences in Alexandria that her disease is both real and quite dangerous."

"How so?"

"The increasing symptoms. When this disorder is benign, and it can be, the frequency and duration remain stable. But when it is not, and a rapid increase in frequency or even severity takes place, the physician is confronted with the potential for incapacitation or even death."

"Very bad, and in a lady of her rank, not so good for the physician either."

"Yes," Philo said glumly, "and don't think I haven't given that some thought from time to time."

But looking at her now, her youth frozen in stone as an image of beauty, grace, and delight, he could see why Caesar had to have her, and remained as faithful as a man of his kind ever could be, for so many years.

Just then, a secretary came to call him and told him Caesar would see him now.

Lucius followed the secretary through two large reception rooms filled with some of the most important, influential, wealthy, and powerful men in Rome. He knew and recognized most of them from the Senate chamber. He tried to avoid their eyes because he knew what they were all thinking: "Why is this low-class, skinny nobody being led into the presence of the first man in Rome ahead of all of us?" And Lucius was wondering about that himself.

Caesar sat at a writing table between two secretaries. He dismissed them both when Lucius entered and pointed to a chair. Lucius sat. "You sent me a note saying you wanted to see me."

"Yes, I . . ." Lucius' voice emerged as a croak. He cleared his throat. "I wasn't totally truthful . . . no . . . no, truthful is not the word I want to use, accurate is better, much, much better." Lucius noted in passing that his palms, armpits, and forehead were damp. "I . . . Philo, no . . . I and Philo, I mean we both . . . had a talk after he was . . . tortured. No, I don't really mean that word . . . tortured. Naturally you wouldn't—"

"Oh, yes I would," Caesar said.

"Certainly you . . . aah . . . would."

"What does Philo know?" Caesar looked both suspicious and angry.

Lucius was sick of the whole business. "Not one damned thing, but he heard rumors and, since I gave you my word, I feel I must . . ."

"Trip over your tongue every other sentence," Caesar supplied.

"Yes . . . no . . . yes . . ."

"Stop!" Caesar raised one finger. "Take a deep breath and tell me this rumor, Regulus." Caesar now looked amused.

"Regulus? Philo called me that. He's probably right. He usually is. The story goes some fifty senators have . . . are considering killing you."

Caesar raised his eyebrows. "Fifty. A nice round number. Sounds more like a faction than a conspiracy?"

"Some say forty," Lucius replied unhappily. "Some say sixty. I split the difference—the workings of the mercantile mind, Caesar. It runs in the family."

"Any names?"

"A few, about four certain, two probable. Tillius Cimber, Casca, Brutus," Lucius hesitated, "and Cicero."

"Naturally," Caesar said. "He hates me."

"Cassius and the other is a nonentity and I can't remember which one."

Caesar raised his hand. "Don't bother, but thank you. I know it was difficult for you to come here today, but I've been hearing these stories since I returned to Rome."

Lucius heaved a deep sigh of relief. "So it's nothing new. Well, I'm now glad I came. I feel much better. So you don't give any credence to these tales."

Caesar shook his head. "No, I don't. They're always vague and the names are different each time. Some of those mentioned today are my intimates, waiting in the antechamber out there to see me. What am I to do? Have my soldiers take one or two of them into the garden and behead them on the pretext that they are plotting treason?"

"They wouldn't see it as treason, Caesar, but as a form of service to the state."

Caesar leaned back in his chair and began laughing.

"It's not funny. They're dangerous."

Caesar's laughter ended in an ironic smile. "I'm betting they wouldn't have the courage."

"Too rich for my blood. I wouldn't make or take such a wager. The stakes are too high."

"What should I do? Load the dice?"

"In the games you play, the dice are always loaded, but I'd just make sure I had the best pair. They're not only dangerous to you, Caesar. I'm here to say I don't want to be entangled in their plotting and dragged to my doom for nothing."

"A sensible attitude. Very well, you may go. But before you do, I have a warning to give you. I value your sister's friendship and would not take kindly to any interference in or curtailment of her business or personal activities. So leave patria potestas and paterfamilias to molder in the law books where they belong."

Lucius felt a wave of rage sweep over him, one so powerful he could feel it in the pounding of his heart and the numbness of his skin. True, part of it was generated by the fear of this man's overwhelming power, but the other part was sheer, heedless outrage at the direct affront to his manhood.

He leaned forward in his chair, knuckles whitening on the curved finials of the arms. "Caesar, Fulvia and I understand each other. She stays on her side of the house and I remain on mine. She handles most of the family money and I don't care as long as I get whatever I want, when I want it. But she doesn't get a free pass to attack my friends, blow my nose for me, or use my penis and balls to make an heir for the Basilian family. And as for that sewer rat Firminius, he's a poisonous little viper that tried to sink his fangs into the heel of a friend of mine. He's lucky the law was on my side because if it hadn't been, I'd have used something else and he'd still be trying to pick up his guts from the floor of his fancy perfumed bedroom. As for those devious backstabbers in the Senate, no, you're right. I don't plan to join them in any of their vicious cabals, but not because I'm afraid of failing, but because when I go down, I plan to deserve it. Truly, richly, and deeply deserve it."

Caesar drew back. "Regulus indeed. I feel as if I've tapped a sheep between the horns and roused a lion." Then he gave a nasty chuckle. "Perhaps your sister's right. I should appoint you a legate and let you work off some of your vile temper on the battlefield. You'll find it a more appropriate venue for venting your considerable spleen than in the direction of a man with the power of life and death over you and your dubious associates."

Lucius felt his skin grow cold, but he was not ready to give ground. He felt he'd suffered enough indignities from Antony and this man. Being sent to the Senate as a spy. Being told with such casual cruelty to vacate his position as head of the family. Top that with an attempt on Philo's life. *No! Enough,* he thought. "Caesar, someday you're going to make one too many enemies."

"Yes, I may have already, but you won't be one of them. Do you know your father recommended your sister to me, but not you?"

"Doesn't surprise me much, Caesar. I don't think he was happy with my mother or cared much for her son."

"I think you might be wrong there. He said of you that you were as free of artifice as a child and as transparent as a crystal goblet. He forgot to mention you were as headstrong as an infuriated bull when finally angered."

"Coming from him, those aren't compliments."

"No, probably not, but think. Everyone fails to value candor and honesty. Truth has its uses. It's just not popular right now in Rome. Have you any political ambitions?"

"No."

"Good, then I might offer you a command. Not a high command, but if you serve on my staff, you would rise quickly. But I cannot find it in my heart to worry about your enmity. A man you were at odds with would always see you coming."

"Am I supposed to be reassured by that? You have a short way with your enemies. You had Vercingetorix strangled at your triumph and another one, the name escapes me, flogged to death. I talked to a centurion who was present when the sentence was handed down and carried out."

"The Gauls were impressed."

"So was the centurion and so was I. Thank you, but no thank you. I have no hankering to be placed between you and the Parthians. Now or ever. And I feel the same about the Senate. I would be very careful of those worthies, especially the ones closest to you."

"You believe them to be dangerous?"

"Yes."

"Indeed." For a moment, the ruler of the world looked sad. "I don't believe so. The Rome that destroyed Carthage and faced Hannibal down is no more."

"Yes, I agree, but they don't know that. Their thinking hasn't caught up with the times. They believe the Senate would be what it was if the new men polluting it were driven out. And if you were dead."

The mask dropped. The curtain slipped and, for the first time, Lucius saw the man himself. Or, at least, this was how he thought about it later, when he was alone and considering Caesar's words.

And in and for a split second, he understood how some men might have considered being allowed to commit suicide, rather than face a punishment devised by this man, a favor.

Caesar's face was stone, so still that when a muscle jumped in one cheek, Lucius flinched like one struck. He knew he was in mortal danger, and he knew that if the dictator wanted him dead, he would be dead, and in no more than a few seconds.

The dictator's voice was savage and meant for him and him alone. "And you think you can stand aside? How did you put it—stay on your side of the house and your sister on hers? Well, you can't. Will or nill, you're a player in the game and must abide the outcome." Caesar leaned forward on his desk, looking into Lucius' eyes. "Do you know when you became one?"

"No."

"The day your father sent me the money to raise one legion and pay the men for a year. And again when I crossed the Rubicon and received the price of an additional legion and their pay for a year from your sister. They both profited seven-fold from these transactions. Seven-fold is a conservative estimate. Ten- or fifteen-fold is more likely. Gallic gold dropped the price of the aureus by a third. The flower of their youth went to the auction block in Rome or in gangs chained together to work in the fields on the Basilian estates. The Gauls died in your mines, tended your vineyards, and poured a golden flood of oil and wheat into your father's cash boxes. Horses and a royal purple river of wine went into his ships to sell at a discount to every barbarian between here and the back of the north wind on the White Isle. So know this: both my friendship and respect can be purchased, but they don't come cheap. And if you want both, and the freedom to live as you please, then cut yourself in on the game, pick up the dice box, lay down your bet, and play!

"I agree those were no compliments your father paid you, but I believe he may have been wrong. Sometimes those who will not deceive others are themselves very difficult to deceive and I think that may be true in your case."

"Your hand is out."

"Yes, and it's not extended in friendship. It's been out since I made my first speech on the Rostra, more years ago than I care to remember. Now go! I've much other business to transact today and I've spent enough time with you already. I will pay the compliment of believing the time has not been wasted. Return when you're ready to talk business."

Lucius rose, mouth open, head spinning, and left.

THEY DIDN'T SIT TOGETHER IN THE HALL. THERE were three tiers of round tables overlooking the fire pit and then one half moon–shaped high table. The chief, Cynewolf, sat there and, since there was no help for it, Mir, Dryas, and Blaze must sit there also, because they were of the highest rank. But Maeniel, who apparently had no rank, sat on the third row near the door, where it was cold. He didn't notice the temperature, but he was aware of the slight.

Below the high table, the next highest in rank sat with their retainers. The second held most of the artisans and craft workers who lived in the town and their families, with the exception of young children.

On the third small inner ring, Maeniel sat with the low-ranking warriors attached to the household, and their women. Evars sat next to him. She'd appropriated the seat the night after they'd had their first sexual encounter and he'd stated he was pleased by her performance. She was a servant and, most of the time, servants ate sitting on the floor in the storerooms adjoining the kitchen.

She'd been bought from a tribe much deeper in the wilderness beyond the Rhine and she spoke a Gallic that was heavily accented, far more gutteral than the language he was used to.

Cynewolf freed his slaves, not out of the goodness of his heart, after the Romans burned the town for the first time. Often they had to seek other work because he simply could not feed them all. Those who had places to go left. The rest like Evars, who couldn't even tell anyone where she'd come from and didn't remember the names of her parents, remained. The oppidum was their home, the only one they had ever known.

As far as she was concerned, Evars was Maeniel's woman. She threatened a brunette girl who had also noticed that he was drop-dead handsome, kind, an expert lover, and, though not rich, was generous with what he had. Evars used a long, single-edged knife—one she carried in a sheath made from a bull penis and kept hidden under her skirt—to convince the girl of her determination. The brunette took the hint and ignored him thereafter. It was plain that Evars felt she'd come up in the world through her association with him.

The hall was almost beautiful tonight. Weavings were draped from the roof high up over the tables. The banners above were woven and dyed the colors that marked the heritages of the powerful families who supported Cynewolf, each bearing their own particular pattern and

color combination. Greens, yellows, all shades from the palest sunlight
to orange, summer verdure, delicate fern green, wine, and bloodred
flamed and danced in the banners, marked with the symbols each family
honored. Serpents, dragons, fantastic birds, even the bear and the wolf,
all drifted against the dark oak planks forming the ceiling.

Torches glowed on the wall sections. There were thirteen walls
and each held a torch in a bracket canted out over the tables below,
but away from the wooden walls. Pale, tanned deer hides covered the
benches, and tablecloths draped the tables.

Already there was music and song in the hall. The singers strolled
up and down the aisle.

The more important people on the top called for songs in praise
of this or that person or family. A general joyous party atmosphere
filled the air.

Next to Maeniel, Evars seemed caught up in the celebratory mood.
She was smiling, laughing, and guzzling the mead most probably intended for the men.

Oddly, Maeniel was more and more bothered as the evening
progressed. Shuddering, he remembered the gathering of ghosts that
preceded Imona's death. In spite of the laughter and song, he sank more
and more into an atmosphere of foreboding. He ignored the mead
and drank only a little wine mixed with water.

One of the distinguished guests pointed to Actus, who sat with
the warriors at the second table. Then general laughter followed and
Maeniel realized they were speaking of him. Not that they knew it.
Someone was recounting how Actus had encountered a dog that had
turned into a man, and then punched him in the face.

Actus flushed as laughter swept the small high table. Cynewolf
didn't look amused. Neither did Dryas, Mir, or Blaze. As for Actus,
he just glared at the glittering company sitting around his chieftain.

Maeniel added more water to his wine. He found he no longer
wanted to challenge anyone for the champion's portion.

The cooks had begun removing the joints of meat from over the
flames. They rested them on a table close to the fire and began passing out platters to the assembled company.

The biggest chunks—whole haunches, saddles, and racks of ribs—
went over the heads of Maeniel's companions to Cynewolf and his
guests. He distributed them with a liberal hand.

The people at the table near Maeniel received scraps, small pieces, and gravy. They were very happy sopping the juices with bread or lifting fragments of meat to their lips with their fingers. He relaxed and joined them.

The chopped pork, marinated then cooked in pepper, cinnamon, and wine, was delicious. Soup followed with plenty more bread, bread baked with walnuts, hazelnuts, and pine nuts worked into the dough, to dunk into the broth.

Evars drank more mead. Between the fire's heat and the strong drink, her skin was developing a nice flush and her flaxen hair, escaping the snood wrapped around it, was hanging in attractive ringlets framing her face.

She kissed him, tasting of honey mead and pork gravy. He didn't object and thought about meeting her in the barn later. Even though their association was widely recognized, he had no private place to take her and was annoyed by the fact.

He was thinking that he'd need to do something about finding a nice piece of land for next year and getting in a crop when he saw the shadow near the fire pit.

He turned away from Evars for a moment and saw Leon in cape and hood standing between himself and the flames with the mother of the pack at his knee.

A vast silence seemed to fall around Maeniel. Leon was dead, as was the mother of the pack. Her bones lay under a half ton of earth and rock on the mountainside beneath the snow. Leon was a scattering of blackened, gnawed bones resting below a linden tree.

Maeniel looked into Leon's eyes and saw he was really there. Not a shadow of what once had been or a vagrant memory, but a conscious presence. As Maeniel watched, Leon smiled at him with saturnine amusement. Oh, yes, he was there and enjoying some secret joke.

He couldn't be as sure about the mother of the pack. She seemed a bit more misty and remote, as if she had come from even farther away than Leon. She glanced at him once, then up. He followed the direction of her gaze to the table where Actus had been sitting, but he was unaccountably absent.

When Maeniel looked back at the flames, Leon still stood there, but she was gone.

"Evars," he whispered to the woman at his side, "go! Leave now! Hurry!"

"What?" she asked a bit muzzily. Drink fogged her eyes.

He caught her by the arm and tightened his fingers. She gave a yelp and a start. He spoke in her ear. "Go! Now! Leave. Right now! Go!"

She didn't go. All she did was rub her arm where his fingers closed around it. "What's the matter? You hurt me."

He stood and pulled her to her feet.

There was general laughter from everyone at the table and jokes about the impatience of some men, but he had a firm grip on her wrist and her strength was no match for his. He had her through the door and outside in a moment.

From the steps of the hall, he could look down on the whole town. His night vision was better than any human's. From where he stood, he could see that the gates were open and the shadowy figures of armed men were making their way through the streets.

Unceremoniously, he snatched her up and threw her over the wall. She landed with a scream on the other side. He turned just in time to dodge a spear thrust that would have pinned him to the palisade. He ripped the spear out of its owner's hand and broke his opponent's arm in the process. The man screamed, reaching for his sword with his left hand.

Maeniel shoved the arm aside and pulled the weapon from its sheath. He aimed for the man's stomach, but the blade skidded on the soldier's cuirass and went up through his throat.

Maeniel managed to get a good look around and saw no one else was near him. He sprinted toward the hall and, at the same time, saw flashes of light against the sky as a dozen flaming arrows arched through the air and embedded themselves in the outer walls of the chieftain's dwelling.

Maeniel knew he was screaming, but he wasn't sure what he was screaming as he leaped the steps up into the entryway. He dove through the door and landed rolling, only just able to stop himself before he landed in the fire pit.

On his knees, clutching the dripping sword in one hand, he stared up at the faces surrounding him. For a weighty second that seemed to last a thousand years, they stared blankly, mouths open, down at him, and then the screaming began in earnest.

There was no escape. In a few seconds, the hall filled with smoke. Its panic-stricken inhabitants trampled and fought each other to get to the door, but once they did, every man or woman who went through was cut down without mercy by the attacking troops outside.

The roof was fully involved. The rafters were covered only by thatch. A dreadful orange light, far brighter than torchlight, pervaded everything. It came from the proud banners hanging from the rafters. They were burning, falling to fragments and dropping strips of flaming cloth on the writhing human mass below.

The damp outer layer of thatch resisted the rivulets of fire for a few seconds and then went up with a roar that was echoed by a dreadful wail of despair from those trapped in the building. The whole roof seemed a seething mass of bright embers.

The wolf saw the chieftain die. One of the banners fell across his shoulders. His clothing caught and he plunged, running down the tiered tables and ended as a blackened writhing shape in the central fire pit.

Dryas followed, trying to help him. She stopped next to Maeniel, then looked away from whatever remained of Cynewolf. Her sword was in her hand. She seemed to carry an air of icy calm with her.

The wolf looked up beyond the smoke hole in the roof and saw stars, their calm beauty a foil to the unspeakable chaos around him. He could hear her voice above the din. "We must break out. We have no choice."

He ripped a section of the table from its legs on the floor. He didn't see Dryas pull something from around her neck and throw it into the very center of the fire pit. He balanced the table, holding the curved shape in his hands, and charged the doorway.

Dryas followed. The table slammed into the doorposts and, for a ghastly second, he was afraid they might hold. Then he felt the weight of the mob at his back and, with a rending crash, the doorposts snapped like dry twigs and the whole side of the building fell away.

In the streets, their attackers tried to move forward to close with their victims, but they wrought better than they knew when they fired the hall. A whole side of the roof slid down, like the flaming haystack it was, and landed in the street between the two groups. For a few moments, it held back the attacking force, allowing the fugitives from the ruined hall to make their escape.

The flames leaped up between them, but Maeniel noted Dryas didn't run. So he stood with her. The survivors from the hall were so demoralized that none of them tried to make a fight of it, though they probably outnumbered the attacking force. Too many of them were women; others were old like Blaze and Mir. They fled over the palisade, into the night. But Dryas faced their enemies, trying to give the oldest and weakest among them time to escape.

Maeniel thought privately she should worry about herself, and he was right because a rider among the raiders shouted, "That's her! Don't let her get away. A thousand golden aurei to the man who catches her! Bring her down!"

The soldiers charged Dryas, bringing mantles up to protect their faces as they plunged through the wall of flame. She cut the throat of the first within her reach and drove her sword into the eye of the next.

And Maeniel was again the gray wolf. Rage and wild delight surged in his heart. He plunged forward and hamstrung the third to reach her, then broke another's lower leg. But he knew there were too many and the street was wide. Both of them could be flanked.

Dryas was backing when the wolf saw a shadow loom over them. He howled a warning too late.

The blazing skeleton of the hall, timbers outlined in fire against the sky, toppled, falling down on them.

He turned tail and ran, but Dryas was locked in swordplay with one of her adversaries and couldn't or didn't disengage. Not in time.

The timbers disintegrated as they fell. One of them cracked Dryas across the head, showering sparks and framing her face with embers. Her opponent raised his shield and caught or deflected the debris raining down around them. Then he snatched up the woman and her sword from the street, threw her over his shoulder, and fled.

L UCIUS WANDERED AWAY, NOT AT ALL SURE WHERE he was going. He simply walked. The streets were crowded. Business of all kinds was being transacted around him. On the pavements, street hawkers sold everything from sex to household repairs.

In one block, a girl offered herself for two copper asses. She promised to accommodate him behind a nearby temple or inside the cella if he was squeamish about being seen. He accepted, paid her, but once inside the cella found himself completely incapable.

It was dark, the only light streaming in through two openings in the roof over the altar. There was no statue or even name emblazoned on the terra-cotta brick walls, and the altar itself was a square marble block with a dado at the top and base.

When he proved incapable, the girl looked frightened, but he gave her another copper and told her he wanted to be here alone with his thoughts. So he stood in the back, leaning against the wall, listening to the distant street noises.

He didn't reach any conclusions, but his whirling mind quieted. He walked toward the altar slab. On the step near the altar stood a brass pitcher, a platter with a few pieces of fruit on it, a basin filled with water, and a cup. The cup looked like brass. It was a plain gold metal, fluted at the edges, a bell beaker narrower at the base than the rim.

Without understanding quite why he did it, he lifted the pitcher and poured its contents into the cup, then drank.

The temple vanished. He felt he was somewhere near the Appian Way. The tall cypresses grew there, overlooking and outlining a roadway. He walked along a path overgrown by creeping thyme and moss, bordered by lilies. He'd never seen such flowers before. They were trumpets of flame, scarlet and yellow with brown-spotted throats. Scattered among the most brightly colored ones were patches of ivory and even green blooms. He walked along in the cool, damp shade under the cypresses.

Ahead, a stone road cut through the path he traveled along, and he heard horns behind him. He hurried, dodging to the side of the path, and stood among the lilies.

The quarry reached him first. A gigantic boar came into view, and Lucius was glad the hunt was right behind him. He would not have wanted that animal to pause near him. The beast's mouth was open, foam dripping around the jaws, and the tusks were almost as long as his forearm. The nasty little pig eyes swept over him, glowing with rage, and the beast turned toward him. Lucius knew an instant of terror. As far as a monster like this was concerned, he was helpless.

But the hounds were snapping at its heels. They were the largest hounds Lucius had ever seen, but they were clearly coursing hounds, slender, graceful, with lean bodies and short, tight coats, all marked in strawberry and blue, with sweet, clear voices.

Then the hunt appeared. Lucius gasped. All the steeds were white. Their coats glowed with a mother-of-pearl sheen and the wild, curling manes and tails reminded him of clouds receding into mist at the edges. They rode at him full tilt. He tried to back up and inadvertently pulled at his scar.

A jolt of electricity went through his back. He dropped to one knee. He looked up, trying to get his feet under him. At the same time, he was sure he was doomed and the fellow riding directly toward him would trample him. But he reckoned without *her*. She swept up from behind the leader. Her mount was black, a rich, shimmering darkness like the star-filled night sky. The weight of the gigantic animal pushed the glowing white one aside, nudging it away from Lucius. She passed within inches of him. Her right foot brushed his shoulder.

Then he watched open-mouthed as the magnificent creatures reached the road, a straight pathway made of smooth, hexagonal, blue-gray blocks. As they did, they soared into the air, floating almost like birds over the causeway.

He turned, jumping out from among the flowers at the edge of the path, trying to get a better view, but stumbled and found himself on his hands and knees on the temple floor.

The place he had been vanished. Both cup and pitcher were gone from the altar, but the bowl still rested near where they'd been. He found to his astonishment that he was looking down into the water, but her face looked back at him. The face was the woman who had prevented his being ridden down.

But then, on considering the matter for a few seconds, he decided it couldn't be *her* face. The woman on the midnight steed had a face like a goddess without mark or blemish. This dark haired, still-faced woman had wisps of hair escaping from a coif he really couldn't see and, while her features were as perfect as if they'd been chiseled and then polished from dense marble, she had a bruise on her right cheek and a small mouse under her left eye. She closed her eyes. He wondered if she were dead and found himself sad. Then he was surprised by his sadness. After all, why should he care if a woman, completely unknown to him, left the world or not? He tried to reach for her, touched the water, and found the basin was gone.

He knelt alone on the dusty floor. There was no altar, no pitcher, cup, or platter and the only light came from the door, seemingly far away, that opened into the street.

When he reached it, he was conscious that he'd run from the back of the temple. To his horror, he found the door barred by an iron gate. He found himself frightened by his own terror as much as anything else. He pushed at the door and found, to his great relief, that it opened at a touch. Then he was out, down the steps, and walking in the street. He didn't look back until he reached the Forum. It wasn't far away.

He couldn't see the temple from where he was. It wasn't until he reached into the draped folds of his toga to check his purse and find out if he'd come out with any money that he realized he held a plum in his hand. He looked down at it, astounded, then remembered the platter of fruit in the temple. The fruit was beautiful and he was hungry. The skin was smooth with the silken feel a ripe specimen of the fruit demonstrates and, for a second, he was tempted to eat it.

Then his hackles rose as he remembered where he got it. It was too beautiful, not like anything of this world. Blue, shading into violet, the color and fragrance were exquisite, carrying an essence of plumness. He placed it in the folds of his toga, then examined his purse.

Yes, he had money—a great deal of money, in fact. He became aware that the streets were emptying around him and the sun was high overhead. It was time for the siesta. There were a few people about and some shops were open. A lot of people didn't bother to take a long rest in winter.

He looked over at the Senate House and the public gardens overlooked by Pompey's Theater and the Temple of Venus.

He walked along the row of shops and saw someone he knew standing in a doorway—Lucrese. She turned toward him, a look of recognition in her eyes, then stepped back into the shadows of her cookshop.

He shrugged and walked on, but in a moment, a small, dark girl tapped him on the arm. "Sir! Handsome sir! My lady would speak with you."

He followed her into the cookshop where he had seen Lucrese. It was a small place and very clean. There were no patrons in it at present, but there were benches and tables that showed signs of frequent use.

The girl, and she wasn't more than a child, led him through the room and into a small herb garden with a grape arbor, a fountain, and a sundial. A table stood under the arbor and she seated him in a wicker chair beside it, then scurried away. She returned with a tray that held olives, cheese, and wine.

Differing spices and marinades flavored the olives. There were all sorts on this tray, each in its separate dish. Several varieties of cheese rested among the olives. The wine was one of those grown in the mountains near the coast: white, sweet, fragrant as an autumn mist, laden with the mixed scents of smoke, apples, hazel, and fennel.

The afternoon sun was warm on his face and neck. The sky was a hazy blue.

He relaxed and took the edge off his appetite with the olives and cheese. After a while, the child returned with a chicken and vegetable stew and a platter of bread cut into pie-shaped sections and flavored with hard cheese.

He used his fingers to eat the chicken and vegetables and the bread to sop up what remained of the gravy. All in all, he thought, it was one of the finest and most peaceful meals he'd ever eaten in his life.

When the child carried away the dishes, Lucrese brought him a platter of honey cakes. "How is Philo?" she asked.

"Sit down," Lucius said.

"I don't . . ."

"And I don't care. Sit down."

She sat on a small bench across from him.

"Not well," he told her. "He was tortured and had a very bad time of it."

"Oh, no!" she whispered, covering her face with her hands.

"Don't be upset. You probably saved his life."

She let her hands drop to her lap and looked away over the garden where neat rows of sage, thyme, fennel, cabbage, and mint grew in abundance.

"I just came from Caesar," he said. "Is anyone else here?"

"No." She looked suspicious for a moment. "Why?"

"The child?"

"No. She goes home to her mother. I pay her a few coppers a week to help me clean. I don't own this. Myrtus, Felex's aunt, does. She leases the shop to me and I pay her a weekly fee. Philo set it up for me. If all goes well, in ten years I'll own it." She crossed her fingers. "I hope. Why?" she asked again, still looking suspicious.

"I was just going to tell you what Caesar said."

She leaned forward, resting her chin on her knuckles. "Please do."

He recounted his conversation with the dictator.

"So," she said quietly when he finished. "That's how it works. Res publica, government of the people. You choose up sides, put your money in the hands of those you want to win, then winner take all."

He nodded, ate a honey cake, and drank a little of the wine. "What do you think? Should I pay?"

They both watched the sun travel and the shadow on the sundial showed more than an hour had passed since he arrived.

"Do you know how I got here?" Lucrese asked.

He shook his head. "No."

"The landlord wanted my father off his farm. My father defied him. You know what happened?"

Lucius nodded. "The landlord had him beaten or was it killed?"

"Beaten," she said, "but he died. Caesar's men came. My brother, who was tall and strong, marched off with the legions. He said he would return with rent money to pay the landlord, but he didn't. My mother died that winter. The landlord sold me to pay his rents." She stared directly into his eyes. "Lucius, I believe even the gods are bought and paid for.

"The sacrifices, bulls, rams, cows, and pigeons or doves purchased by the rich and powerful choke them with blood and meat, and blind them with smoke and incense until they have forgotten what virtue justice is, if indeed they ever knew."

"Yes," Lucius said, "and my sister is chaste."

"I know. I can't say the same. The first place I was sold into was a brothel. There I was sold again and again, sometimes as many as forty times a night, until I turned my face to the wall and refused food or water. The owner sold me in the hope of recouping his investment before I died. Yes, Lucius, pay Caesar. Pay him and count yourself lucky that you can protect those you love. I'm only sorry I couldn't care for my own. Protect them from your 'chaste' sister and her little rat, Firminius. And protect yourself. You're a good man and, on that account alone, I fear for you."

As he left, he realized the siesta hours were over, the street was filling up again. He paused at the door and pressed a coin into her hands.

"For the meal," he said.

"No, no," she said, trying to give it back to him.

He shook his head. "Myrtus is a very practical Greek woman. She wouldn't approve of your giving out free food." Then he hurried away.

She slipped it into her dress pocket. It wasn't until late that evening when she'd locked up and was standing alone next to her bed, braiding her hair by candlelight and preparing herself for sleep, that she remembered the coin, took it out of her pocket, and found a golden aureus.

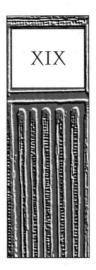

XIX

D RYAS AWOKE IN THE DARK. HER HEAD ACHED with a slow, miserable, dull throbbing. Her hands and feet were tied. She was in a cart. Not just a cart, but one hitting every bump and hole in the road they traveled along. She tried to open her eyes and her lashes brushed against something tied over them. She was blindfolded. Her stomach was queasy.

She remembered throwing the necklace into the fire. She was glad, even in this ugly situation, to be rid of the burden of imprisoning a creature she had come more to admire than not. She'd seen Cynewolf die and she was sickened to the bottom of her soul with what must have been her part in his destruction. The whole miserable business had been a fiasco from the beginning. Her life was over. She would not endure slavery.

Outside, she could hear voices and the jingle of horse trappings. Two people were talking; one had a voice like sliding gravel.

"She paid me," Gravel Voice said. "Good thing. This one isn't going to last. I'll be surprised if we get her to the ship."

"She'd be a novelty in Rome."

"I don't think she'd let them do that to her. They'd never get her to the arena. I don't believe that's what the Basilian bitch has in mind. What does she care about the mob? No, this one is intended for private use."

"Hers?" A question to Gravel Voice.

"Yes! No! Who knows? Someone with a taste for the extraordinary. She cost us enough. Miletus, Florus, Scipio."

"They wanted to go home rich like you."

"Tillius won't walk again. Achillas will be pissing lying down for a month."

"That was the dog."

"Dog! Dog, my ass," Gravel Voice exclaimed. "It didn't come until she crossed swords with us. No, she's a witch, too. Some of Caesar's legionnaires ran into them in Alba and said they were worse than men. Much worse. You bed down in what you think is a safe place to sleep and wake up with your throat cut. The whores put knives up their twats. You go to stick it in and next thing you're split like a cooked sausage. The Basilian cunt is welcome to her. When we reach Messene, I get off. I'll take my money and buy a farm on Campagna." Gravel Voice sounded relieved. "I won't even take ship with you. She can probably call a storm and have it sink the vessel before it reaches Ostia. I wouldn't put it past one of them. One of their witches."

Rome. Fulvia wants to take me to Rome. Caesar is in Rome, Dryas thought.

The horses the men rode picked up the pace and moved ahead of the wagon. She could no longer hear what they said. However, she could hear Fulvia speaking to Gravel Voice. His answer sounded insolent, but Fulvia continued to insist and apparently he agreed because the wagon stopped a few minutes later. Dryas felt two people climb in, one lighter than the other. *Fulvia and Gravel Voice,* she thought.

A second later, Dryas felt hands exploring her body. Big hands.

"I'll untie her feet," Fulvia offered sweetly.

"Don't untie anything!" Gravel Voice said forcefully. His hands moved over her breasts and stomach. "Nothing," he said.

Dryas tried to remain limp. He rolled her to one side. "Back. Aaah, right here," he said, and pulled out a knife she wore on a cord attached to her collar.

"Now the interesting parts," Fulvia sniggered as Dryas was turned on her back.

"Nothing about this sow is interesting to me," Gravel Voice said. "I watched her kill three of my men and if you're smart, my lady, you'll let me cut her throat right now and bury her under a crossroads with a stake through her heart and a big heavy rock holding her down so she won't get up and run with her friends the wolves."

As he spoke, he felt Dryas' belly and buttocks, then probed between her legs and thighs. "Yes, here's another strapped to her thigh. She comes with all the equipment she needs to . . ."

He stopped speaking because he'd lifted Dryas' tunic and had pushed his hand down her pants to get the knife she had concealed there. He was preoccupied with getting to the hilt so he could pull it free. He did and carelessly let the razor edge scratch Dryas' stomach. "Sorry," he said.

"Sorry!" Fulvia screeched. "Don't mark her up! Besides, who are you apologizing to? She's unconscious."

"No, she's not," Gravel Voice said. "She's lying doggo, hoping we'll think just that, but a couple of times I felt her flinch. She knows what's going on, but there isn't anything she can do about it." His hands moved down Dryas' legs while he spoke. "And yet another at the ankle." He removed the blade. "Now, I'll leave these with you, my lady."

"Sure you wouldn't like a little something for all your time and trouble?" Fulvia asked. "It's just the three of us here and you could pull down those trousers she's wearing and . . ."

"Force her," Gravel Voice said.

"Why not?" Fulvia's voice was husky with . . . Dryas wasn't sure what . . . but whatever Fulvia was feeling, she was doing her best to disguise it.

"No, my lady," Gravel Voice said. "Rape is an acquired taste, and as long as I've been a soldier, I never acquired it. Besides, you pay me to fight for you, not entertain you."

Dryas heard Fulvia's breathing quicken, but she said nothing more. Boards creaked as Fulvia climbed down from the wagon, then her feet hit the ground, but Dryas knew Gravel Voice must still be in the wagon, so she steeled herself.

Being taken in war was a risk shared by men and women alike. In that world, sexual abuse was commonly inflicted on both men and women. Perhaps it was a little more common with women, but men, especially young men, faced it also. The use of their bodies against their will. Dryas trained her students to expect that the worst might happen and to be ready to react with dignity and courage. She hoped she would be able in that grisly situation to be strong, but frankly found herself more outraged and annoyed than angry. She was sore and hurt in a dozen places. Now Fulvia and this loathsome piece of shit wanted to add to her misery. She wished an unpleasant fate on both of them if Gravel Voice acted on Fulvia's suggestion.

"No, brugia witch, I won't couple with you," Gravel Voice said. "I have what I want." Dryas heard the jingle of a sack of coins. "I wish she'd listened to me about cutting your throat. You might be better off and so might she." Then he was gone and she lay alone.

The wagon didn't move again and the sounds Dryas heard indicated they were getting ready to bed down for the night. She wondered how much time had passed since she'd been captured. Probably only a day, but there was no way for her to tell. She tried to roll over on her side and succeeded pretty well. She was lying on something soft, like cloth on top of straw. She was not too uncomfortable.

After a time, she smelled food cooking but no one offered her any. She wasn't surprised and eventually fell asleep.

When she next woke, she could hear night sounds, wind and a nearby owl calling. It was cold in the wagon, but someone, she was willing to wager not Fulvia, had covered her up with a coarse and none-too-clean blanket. It stank of horse manure and equine perspiration.

She was clearheaded and the headache was gone. *I should be grateful for small mercies. At least the blanket is warm.* She began a process of stretching herself, trying to keep her limbs from cramping too badly, exercising first her feet and ankles, then her legs, torso, upper body, and arms. She contemplated trying to turn over and was puzzled about how to do it without pushing off the blanket when she became conscious that she was no longer alone in the wagon.

Claws clicked on the wooden floor. Well, she had thrown the necklace into the fire. He seemed to have brought the cold night air in with him. She could smell cold fur and something else. Cold touched her cheek and pushed the blindfold up.

She found herself looking into his eyes. There was a sprinkling of snow on his muzzle. Here and there, ice crystals glittered on his coat.

He made a soft, very soft whine in his throat. She understood it to be an inquiry. Her own hounds often greeted her with such sounds when she rose in the morning. They would look into her eyes and join her when she went to empty her bladder down near the stream.

She wondered who lived in her rath now. Who fed the dogs and journeyed out at dawn with them to hunt? She was reasonably sure she would never see her beloved highlands again, and the home she loved would know her no more.

"I am well," she whispered to him, but two tears gathered at the corners of her eyes and coursed down her face. Since she was lying on her side, one slid across the bridge of her nose and another went under her eye and into the straw where her head rested.

He made a snorting sound and touched her cheek with his nose.

"I am well," she insisted. "They are taking me to Rome. It remains to be seen what, if anything, I can do . . . about . . . Just as well not to speak of that here. Go! Be free, fly far away. I would not see you chained to the chariot of our mad kind. Nor will I any longer try to make you a means to my ends. I wronged you in the first place by trying.

"Be free always, because of all things, freedom is best, though it is not easily won and must be chosen by those who will enjoy it. As an eagle on a crag chooses the freedom of the wind and a wolf on the hunt wears no one's collar. So, go with courage. There's not much chance for me to . . . score. But however little it is, I must take it and never count the cost." Then she closed her eyes.

He felt a cascade of brightness and cold fire and he was kneeling in the wagon beside her. "They have chained your wrists to the planks on this thing. Otherwise I'd have you out by now. I can follow them, pick them off one at a time before we ever leave the mountains. Help me."

She didn't open her eyes, but said, "No."

He heard footsteps outside and was wolf before he willed it.

The sentry peered into the wagon and met his eyes.

A FEW HOURS LATER HE WAS RUNNING ALONG THE slope of a mountain among the trunks of trees so ancient and tall they seemed clouds outlined against a brilliant star-flecked night sky. None had any branches closer than a hundred feet up. It had snowed, but only in some places had it reached the ground. It looked like splashes of silver against the black carpet of pine needles. The giant tree trunks lifted themselves as if they were the columns of some half-ruined temple submerged beneath the sea.

He ran among them, a shadow wolf against silver white snow and black damp drifts of needles returning the sun's bounty to the earth.

He became a man and stood looking up at the trees and the cold stars. He cursed first Dryas and then Imona, women both, and on errands incomprehensible to a wolf and even perhaps to most men. But he understood Imona better now because he knew Dryas. She, too, was willing to give her life in the service of her people. Imona had not listened to him and neither would Dryas.

He was a nurturing creature. She told him to go and be free, but he knew now there was no longer any freedom for him. He was not simply a wolf any longer, but had found a journey he wanted. That journey, or possibly *passion* was a better word, would haunt his heart for however long he would live.

We, the gray people and the brown, knew long ago our affairs were settled for us by . . . whatever makes life. Brings it into being, gave us our laws. They are imprinted on the engrams of our very thought processes. We follow the patterns our ancient ancestor, the dire wolf, knew. His law was mine and my mind can present me with memories of the hunt for monsters when glaciers rimmed the world. But in men, the world sees something new. They are not constrained by any law. Not back when they hunted across the ice, when all the world was winter, and not now. Their existence tantalizes as the woman did my first ancestor, when they allied themselves so long ago to hold back the night.

What they might become, he couldn't imagine, but this prey followed madly across all time was worth the pursuit, whatever the outcome might be. They were created to fall lower and also reach higher than his kind could ever imagine. He would join them in their journey because whichever way they went, they would bring him with them. They were blood of his blood and bone of his bone. What gave them life danced the everlasting measure from a world with dark seas and poisoned air into the stars scattered by the prodigal hand of the unknown—and, perhaps, unknowable—across an eternal sky.

Then he became aware that his feet were freezing, his nose was running, and it wasn't long till dawn. He had a duty to Blaze and Mir to tell them about Dryas. He didn't care to inquire how he'd come to acquire that particular obligation, but he felt the pull of it and followed as he'd once followed his pack mates.

Let's see what happens next, he thought, became a wolf again, and found himself much more comfortable as he trotted uphill with the wolf's effortless bicycling gait toward all that remained of the oppidum. He reached it near dawn and leaped the wall.

He found Mir, Blaze, and Evars at the house where they'd been living. Dryas' blood bay horse was in the barn. He greeted the horse. It returned the greeting perfunctorily and then buried its head in the manger. He had a mantle, tunic, and shoes in an empty stall. He dressed and went into the house.

Mir looked up from the table. "Did you find her?"

"Yes," he said, sitting down. Evars filled a bowl with oat porridge and placed it in front of him. He hadn't stopped to kill and was hungry.

"Well?" the old man prompted.

"She won't let me help her escape." He was putting away the porridge with a will. Not his favorite thing, oats, but he was hungry and chilled by his long night's run, and the porridge was warm.

"Why not?" Mir asked irritably.

"She thinks she can kill this Caesar if she finds a way to get close to him. I'm going to follow her to Rome."

Evars burst into tears. "And get yourself killed." She moaned.

"I take a lot of killing. You, Evars, need to go back with Mir. This is a worse place than where Mir was living. It's more dangerous here. Speaking of living, how many are left?"

"Not many," Blaze said, "and most are gone by now. They fled to friends' or relatives' places where they are welcome. A lot of the guests at the feast didn't live here, but in holds deeper into the forest. Cynewolf should have left, abandoned what used to be his lands on the Roman side of the river, and cut his losses. Now he's dead and most of the remaining lesser chiefs will find other lords to attach themselves to. I have an invitation to visit a people in Fresia. I had hopes of rebuilding something here, some resistance to these Romans, but Cynewolf was simply too weak a reed. The heart went out of him when . . ." He didn't finish.

"When they took his eldest son," Evars said. "He's in the bog with the child, the Veneti noblewoman—"

"Evars, be quiet!" Blaze ordered.

She glanced around the table, astonished. "Did I say something?"

"So," Maeniel said, looking at the two old men. "She was, what did you call her? A Veneti and a noblewoman."

"Yes, both," Mir said.

"It doesn't seem to have done much good," Maeniel said.

"No." The hand Mir used to spoon porridge into his mouth

trembled. "But she was all . . . the only one we had left and I had to try."

"Oh, yes, and now Dryas will try," Maeniel said. "She's not going alone. I'll join her and we can do our best against these Romans."

"What about me?" Evars asked.

"What about you?" Maeniel said. "If you like, you can come with me. If not . . ."

"I don't want to go to Rome," Evars wailed.

"I'll go talk to Dryas' horse," Maeniel said. "She feels a certain loyalty to her. I'll ask her if she's willing to carry me to Messene. Besides . . ." He glared darkly at Evars. "She makes more sense than anyone at this table."

"You will need money," Mir said.

"I know," Maeniel replied. "Dryas had a lot. I'll go get some. Dryas showed me where she hid it." Then he strode out.

"He will go speak to the horse," Mir said, placing his spoon in the empty bowl. "I must see this." Then he followed Maeniel out of the room.

"I don't want to go to Rome," Evars repeated stubbornly, her lower lip protruding.

Blaze sighed deeply and continued on with the porridge.

"I don't want to go to Rome," she repeated.

Blaze was deeply annoyed. "If I were you, I would be quiet. He's an unusual man."

"He's not a man at all," Evars snapped. "I saw him turn skin last night. And he can't just put me down like a sack of turnips and . . ." Then she looked disconsolate. "Yes, I suppose he can." She began to cry.

Blaze had spent his life settling disputes between people more hotheaded and stubborn than these two. He had a solution for both of them.

In the barn, Maeniel walked up to the stall. There was no door. The horse was tied to a ring on the wall.

She rolled her eye at him.

He snorted.

She blew between her lips.

Maeniel grunted a horse grunt.

She lifted her right forehoof and put it down with a thump.

He leaned against a beam and let go with what to Mir sounded like a few more grunts.

She pawed the dirt with a forehoof.

He said, "Messene."

The horse turned and presented him with her broad behind, looked back, and rolled an eye at him.

"Well?" Mir asked.

"She has to think about it, but she probably will. Then I'll turn her loose. She was borrowed from some people near the coast and is pretty sure she can find her way home."

"She told you all these things?" Mir asked with some skepticism.

"No," Maeniel said. "She told me about where she lives night before last. We were passing the time of day and I was practicing my horse. We aren't particularly friendly. Usually we eat them."

"I can see how that might make for an uneasy relationship."

"Yes, most of them won't speak to us, but when we do strike up a conversation with some, we tend to avoid antagonistic behavior in the future."

"Oh," Mir said.

"Yes, friendship has its advantages and benefits for both parties. I believe you have an aphorism that describes such situations. They can sometimes obtain advantages for us that we cannot obtain for ourselves and vice versa. As you say, you scratch my back and I'll scratch yours."

"Ah," Mir said. "Yes, that is certainly so."

"I NEVER HEARD ANYONE LET OUT SUCH AN AWFUL scream ever before in my life," Fulvia said.

Gravel Voice and Fulvia stood in the wagon looking at Dryas. She was sitting up, leaning against the side of the wagon, red-eyed with fatigue and discomfort.

"He said it was the biggest wolf he'd ever seen," Gravel Voice said, "but being that he probably hasn't seen a great many wolves, I don't think we need believe the beast was unusually large. What bothers me is, why was it here? What was it doing in this wagon?" He studied Dryas narrowly. "Do you understand us?" he asked her.

"Yes," she answered.

"She spoke very good Latin when we first met," Fulvia interjected. "I should think she does understand us."

"I did then, I still do," Dryas said.

"Why was the wolf here?" Gravel Voice asked.

"He's a friend," Dryas answered.

"What!" Fulvia screeched. "You are insolent, and a slave who is insolent . . ."

"Fulvia! You will not make me a slave!" Dryas said. "If you want something from me, this is the wrong way to get it."

Fulvia went white with fury. "You," she whispered hoarsely. "I'll have you flogged until you beg for death . . . until the skin hangs in red strips from—"

"My lady!" Gravel Voice said loudly, then he jerked a thumb at the clearing where the soldiers were preparing breakfast. He jumped down from the wagon and Fulvia followed.

He walked to the edge of the camp, then turned and spoke quietly. "My lady, I have no ax to grind. In a few days I'll leave you and I will probably never see you and your prisoner again. But I know these Keltoi and my people don't chisel all of those statues of them killing themselves because they're a gentle and malleable sort of people, especially not the noble and priestly classes. I think this woman is both, and if you do want to bring her to Rome alive, and if in Rome you want her to perform in the arena, I would show her some respect and give her reason to cooperate with you. Besides, I don't know what Lydius saw in that wagon last night, but if it's even half as big as he said it was, I wouldn't care to trifle with any person who has such . . . peculiar . . . and possibly unpleasant friends."

Fulvia didn't answer. Instead she looked away from him into the misty track leading to the coast. "You're right," she said at length, "and, curse it, I do want this woman to show herself as a fighter. An important friend of mine is, shall we say, enthralled by the thought of a genuine Amazon, about seeing one of them perform in the flesh. How do I handle her?" Fulvia could look appealing and sweet when she wanted to.

"Leave me alone with her for a while," he said. "Possibly, just possibly, I can persuade her to become more cooperative."

He returned to the wagon and looked in at Dryas. Her eyes were closed. "You have to be uncomfortable by now. If you like, I'll take you to a stream nearby and, if you promise not to run away, I can unchain you and get you something to eat."

Dryas opened her eyes and nodded.

"Your word," he insisted.

"Yes."

He had to help her down from the wagon since she was so cramped from being tied up, but he led her to the stream and looked away when she went behind a tree.

"A friend," he said.

"Yes."

"You wouldn't care to give me a more detailed explanation."

"No."

"I thought not."

She came from behind the tree, went down to the stream, and began to wash her hands and face.

He glanced uphill to where the soldiers were working around the camp. Fulvia was nowhere to be seen and the men were out of earshot. "You're important. She paid me a thousand in gold to bring you back. I'm not a fool. I know your kind and you wouldn't be alive now if you didn't want to be, so you must have something in mind. These Romans are bastards. So . . . let her bribe you and maybe push you a little. I told her I'd get you into a more cooperative frame of mind. Play along and I'll help you get to the coast alive. After that, you're on your own. Pretend you want money. Gold. That's the best tack to take with them. They're right about me, I do. But you, no. What's your name, dark woman?"

"Dryas."

He nodded. "Aquila."

"Thank you, Aquila."

"Good luck, Dryas."

WHEN LUCIUS ARRIVED HOME, HE WENT TO SEE Aristo. "How much money do I have?" he asked.

"A lot," Aristo answered.

"Good! Enough to raise a legion?"

"Yes, easily about three times that much."

"Send him, Caesar, enough for a legion and sufficient to pay the men for a year."

"This is what is desired?"

"Yes."

"And you will get what you want?"

"Yes. I also want a wooden bowl, but I can get that in the kitchen."

"To be sure," Aristo said. "I thought you might be contemplating some such transaction and have prepared the paperwork."

Aristo handed Lucius several sheets of paper. Lucius duly read them and then signed each.

"Yes," Aristo said. "Blood will tell. I believe you will probably be as successful as your grandfather was."

"My grandfather?"

"Yes, he really founded the fortunes of the Basilian family. I was only a young boy when we met. He bought me from a family that couldn't feed their children any longer. Those were the very bad times of Marius and Sulla. Many were impoverished during their proscriptions, my parents among them."

"How terrible!" Lucius whispered.

"No," Aristo said. "As it turned out, their misfortunes were my good fortune and, in the long term, theirs also. Because of your grandfather's wisdom, they recouped all they had lost and much more, as did I and my brothers and sisters. Your family is among the richest knightly families in Rome."

Lucius swallowed. "But you became a slave."

"My boy! My boy!" Aristo sighed. "Men have accepted slavery to acquire the position I got and that my father held before me, dispensator to a family on the rise, as yours was then. I believe my father felt your grandfather might be there to take advantage of our disaster— supporting Marius—but when we heard his offer . . . He tendered a princely sum, one that allowed my mother to live well and my sisters to make excellent marriages. Of course, Mother had to divorce Father. Too bad. She was hard hit by that. She loved my father. They were together at the end, though."

"Things don't always turn out so well though, do they?" Lucius asked. "Consider Octus."

Aristo frowned. "I wasn't aware you knew."

"It took a while to jog my memory. I didn't connect my mother's steward with the elderly porter in chains at the door. But when I saw him better dressed and walking about the house at liberty, I remembered. He deserved a lot better of this family. A lot better of my mother's son."

Aristo looked uneasy. "Possibly, but then your father may have had his reasons. I can't say. He didn't communicate them to me . . . or anyone. I can only speak for myself. And we, my family, prospered. My father received his freedom when your grandfather died. I got mine when your father passed on." The old man leaned back in his chair, lifted a small knife from the table, and sharpened the nib of his pen. "I didn't say this to elicit your sympathy, but only to make the point that in this life, sometimes we have no choice."

Lucius nodded. "I was maneuvered."

"Very probably. I can't prove it, of course, and even if I could, what would you be able to do about it?"

"Nothing." Lucius looked down at his fingers. "Who was the instigator?"

"Probably Antony. I tell you this because I believe you to be your grandfather's true descendant and cool enough to be able to use this information for your own benefit and those you are determined to protect. And by the by, your sister's idea about planting vines in Gaul is probably a good one, so stay out of her way."

He felt a sense of dismissal. Aristo bent over the papers on his desk again and his pen began scratching.

"They say there are sixty of them," Lucius said.

Aristo's pen halted and his head came up. He looked Lucius full in the eye. " 'They' say a lot of things. What do you think?"

"Folly! The worst kind of folly! I don't like politics. Gambling with money is bad enough. I don't care to risk my life."

"You may not have a choice." Aristo spoke quietly.

"Do you know, Caesar said the very same thing."

"Caesar is probably right. So were I you, I would prepare myself. By the way, you did a very nice job of bringing Firminius to heel. I don't think you'll have any further problems with him and neither will I. However, your sister is quite another matter."

"Speaking of my sister . . ." Lucius paused in the doorway. "There is a cookshop near the Curia. The proprietress . . . did me a . . . service."

"Say no more," Aristo interrupted. "Please!" His eyes were hooded.

Yes, Lucius thought, *not a safe topic. Not in this household. If Fulvia found out . . .*

"You don't look closely at papers you sign, do you?" Aristo asked. He proffered one to Lucius. Lucrese's debt to Myrtus was paid in full.

Lucius nodded, smiled, and handed the document back to Aristo while pondering the paradox that, in a world where few could read, a written communication was safer than speech. If he uttered one word about the matter, it might be repeated in every household in Rome before nightfall, but buried in a pile of dusty household accounts, no one would ever know. He smiled again and was gone.

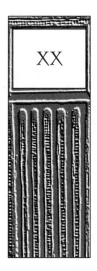

XX

I T WASN'T YET DAWN. DRYAS LOOKED THROUGH
the portcullis at the arena. Only a few torches burned outside
and, though she'd never seen one before, the arena matched
Mir's description. This wasn't very big, though. Yes, there were the
seats rising in tiers, one above the other, but there were no more than
eight or nine rows.

It had a box overlooking the sand-covered surface. The raised
box was ringed by a rail of iron spikes curved down so as to give a
good view of anyone sitting behind them, but placed to prevent any
of the participants in the entertainment, provided by humans or animals in the ring, from reaching these important spectators.

"Yes," she said quietly. She was alone. She had been brought to
Rome in the late afternoon. She had reached the ludus after dark and
heard part of a loud argument between the man who ran the gladiatorial school, the so-called lanista, and Fulvia. Or possibly it wasn't an
argument, only Fulvia laying down the law. She was fond of doing
so, as Dryas learned on the way to Rome.

Aquila was still present. Fulvia had bribed him to remain.

They had brought Dryas to a cell in the building. It had no provision for air or light, being a windowless box closed by an iron grating
and, during inclement weather, as it was now, by a door of three heavy
oak panels. Terra-cotta brick on one side of the tiny room formed a
raised platform. On it, she saw a roll of bedding.

She had been left with a small clay lamp, but it held only a dab of
oil. The flame was already guttering. Dryas used the few minutes of

light to unroll the bedding and then was almost sorry for the light because she saw that the straw tick was bloodstained in more than a few places.

A small earthenware pot with only a rag for a lid was pushed into the back corner of the cell. Dryas turned the bedding and saw even larger stains on the other side. The blanket included with the tick was as bad.

Outside, even with the door closed, she could hear the sound of rain and wind and the occasional thudding as the wind pushed the door back and forth. There must have been some provision for ventilation because, from time to time, Dryas felt the storm outside create a suction, and air flowed through the tiny room.

It was so small that when she stood in the center, her hand touching the back wall, she was within a few feet of the door. Standing in the center with her arms outstretched, her fingertips brushed the walls on either side.

The very animals the beastiarii fought were stabled better, but then that probably wasn't surprising. They were more expensive.

The lamp went out then, leaving Dryas alone in the dark. For a moment she felt fear, succeeded by sorrow and then despair. The damp brick walls were impregnated with the feelings of those criminals and war prisoners condemned to the arena.

And what had these unfortunates done? Dryas thought. Some, a few, probably deserved death, but with most, she as a judge would probably have let them off with a fine and restitution.

Most had probably committed petty crimes. Theft was the most usual one and Dryas knew the richer the rich got, the more they feared and hated anyone who tried to deprive them of even a small modicum of their wealth.

As for the war prisoners, she remembered what Aquila had said, "These Roman bastards believe the gods have given them dominion over the whole world. And anyone who says to them, 'You don't have a right to rule me or exert your sway over my little corner of land and people' is a criminal who deserves death.

"The saved is the slave, if they let you live. They have the right to do what they want with you. And trust me, that's all they mean by the rule of law: their laws and their rules."

He had sounded bitter. She knew they must have left a trail of anger and bitterness behind them everywhere they went. By their standards, she also was a criminal. Her people had ridden down from their highlands and helped the coastal peoples against Caesar, and no doubt would do so again. So by the Roman standard, a standard they hoped to impose on the whole world, she was worthy to be an objectification of their power. A demonstration of absolute rule. Because there is no more absolute power than the power to make men fight to the death and kill on your command.

It's one thing to consider this usurpation of godlike direction in the cold light of day; another to lie in the dark and feel agony, defeat, and pain-drenched loss seep out of the very walls around you. And listen to the rain.

She slept and dreamed somehow she'd broken free and was returning, climbing the thick grassy slopes to her home, and this evil fate was simply a nightmare to be forgotten as she ran with her hounds through the heather in the dreamlike purple, violet, blue, and pale rose of early dawn. Her soul was privy to a love of her own world so powerful it was an unending delight to her heart.

She woke to darkness and a despair so bottomless she knew it couldn't be her own. The lost soul wailed like an abandoned child and she quieted it with memories she searched out, finding them in her mind like the torn fragments of a parchment or a collection of drifting autumn leaves: red, yellow, orange, and gold floating on the surface of a still pool. The spirit yielded up its grief and slept. So did she.

Aquila woke her before first light. It was still dark outside. He handed her a cup of posca, the sour low-alcohol wine fed to soldiers and slaves. Dryas would have preferred one of her own teas, but this wasn't too bad. Someone, a woman possibly, had infused it with a fragrant herb, hyssop probably. In small doses it was a stimulant.

"Marcia, that is, the lanista's wife, she says you can use her latrine. It's off the kitchen and she'll find you something to eat," Aquila said.

Dryas nodded as she finished the sour wine.

Aquila led her down the stair. She'd been put on the third floor. From the walkway she could look down on an arena big enough to hold a few hundred spectators. There were more cells along the walkway.

"How big is this place?" Dryas asked.

"Holds about three hundred, more or less. Mostly less. Lately there haven't been any munera, and no games are planned until spring, so I doubt if there are more than a hundred men here."

"Munera?"

"Offerings of gladiators."

"Offerings? Is that what they are called?"

"They're offered as a memorial to someone dead."

"And this pleases his spirit?"

"I don't know," Aquila said. "I am a good Greek and we never figured out how we feel about the afterlife. If you want my opinion, and you probably don't at this hour of the morning, the Romans don't care in the slightest how many of their slaves they kill. And they enjoy the drama.

"As for Caesar, all he cared about at his munera was impressing everyone in Rome with how successful a conqueror he was and getting rid of any prisoners who were too brave, rebellious, or possibly even intelligent enough to defy him. The ones who bowed their necks to the yoke got off. The rest, well, if you murder most of the young men among any people, they won't be giving the Roman tax collectors any trouble for a long time."

They paused at the foot of the steps and Aquila rapped on the door of what looked like a small Roman house. A woman opened it.

"Here she is," Aquila said, giving Dryas a slight shove toward the woman.

The woman reached out and pulled Dryas into what was clearly a kitchen. Porridge was cooking in the corner of a charcoal grate. The smoke exited through an opening near the ceiling.

The woman was pretty, if faded, a Latin with dark, curly hair, olive skin, and an ample figure.

"Oh, no," she said to Aquila as he entered the kitchen behind Dryas. "What is the Lady Fulvia thinking? I expected some trollop, a circus performer, but she's a lady."

"Watch out, Marcia. Her Latin is very good, better than most pedagogues, and she can read and write it, too."

"Juno Matrona, she can't stay in those holes upstairs where they keep criminals and I don't know what." Marcia sounded scandalized. "Come, my dear." She took Dryas by the wrist and drew her through a curtain and past a wooden screen. The latrine had a wooden seat. There was a bronze bucket full of water next to it and a sponge on a stick hung from the wall. A table across from the latrine held a basin of warm water. Steam rose from the surface. Another sponge and a tunic and sandals hung across the back of a chair.

Marcia looked embarrassed for a moment and pointed to the sponge on the wall. "That one is . . ."

"I understand," Dryas said. "Vinegar?"

"Oh, yes," Marcia answered. "I didn't think of that, but it works well. Leave your clothing here. I'll wash it. Is that your sword? Aquila said it was, but I didn't really believe a woman would—"

"They do among my people, and I do. I'm supposed to. I received it from my teacher when I came of age."

Marcia's hands fluttered. "I see, I see. No, I don't see. You're a lady. Aquila said you were of high rank . . ."

Dryas shrugged and smiled. "I don't suppose that matters now."

Marcia left to let Dryas complete her ablutions.

As Dryas used the latrine, bathed, and dressed, she could hear them talking.

"What is she thinking?" Marcia repeated.

"I don't know. That's why I'm still here," Aquila said. "I swore I was going to leave them at Messene, but she's not what I thought. Marcia, she killed about six men and Lydius swears he saw a wolf visit her by night."

"How did she explain that?" Marcia asked.

"She said it was a friend."

Marcia didn't answer.

Dryas finished dressing and returned to the kitchen. Marcia gave her a bowl of wheat cooked with milk, and some flat bread. Aquila took his leave.

Dryas ate quickly. As she did, Marcia continued cooking, but watched her from the corner of her eye. She was just finishing when Aquila came back to the kitchen.

"Time to go," he said. "She wants you there by dawn. She wouldn't let me go with you. There's a litter outside . . ."

Marcia left and returned with a dark mantle, a palla. "Here, you'll catch your death." She wrapped it around Dryas.

The litter rested on the ground before the gates. It was still dark. Dryas parted the curtains and sat on the cushions. Aquila chained her ankle to one of the posts holding the curtains. He looked shamefaced. "I have to" was all he said, then pulled the curtain closed.

A powerful-looking man rode beside the litter. When Dryas tried to open the curtain, he snarled, "This is forbidden." But Dryas did manage to leave it open a little. Not that she saw anything that she felt would help her. Only dark, shuttered buildings, narrow streets, and the torches of outriders flaring against blank walls or locked and barred windows and doors.

There was a faint light in the east when they reached the arena outside the Basilian villa. The shackle on her ankle was unlocked and she was hurried through a tunnel into the cell where she stood looking out at the slow progress of the breaking day. The door was bolted.

With the growing light Dryas saw an earthenware jug and a cup on a bench built against the wall of the chamber. She sat down and poured some of the liquid from the jug. Posca, again. She shivered in spite of the mantle. It was cold so she drank some of the warm liquid.

She felt oddly relaxed. Her mind was quiet. She was sure she would die soon. Might a way open for her to take this Caesar with her? The wolf hadn't said he would follow her, but she thought just possibly he might. If he did, he might be a useful ally. She rested her back against the wall and waited in complete tranquility for what was to come.

OCTUS WOKE PHILO ABOUT THE SAME TIME DRYAS arrived. Philo got up and began to dress.

"She will want you," Octus said. He looked haggard.

"What happened?"

Octus leaned back against the whitewashed wall of Philo's cubiculum. "It's been a bad night. No sooner did she arrive than she began throwing things. All her maids are in tears, or at least all the ones not in hysterics are in tears. Firminius locked himself in his bedroom. Even Antye can't do anything with her."

"Antye?" Philo asked.

"Yes, her tirewoman. She and Firminius are usually the only ones she'll listen to when she's having a tantrum."

"Did you try waking Aristo?"

"I'm not completely mad. Do you think I want to wind up chained in that cell by the door again?"

"I don't think you would. *He* likes you."

Octus smiled, a bit tremulously. "Does he? He says so little one way or the other. I really wasn't sure."

"He does, very much." Philo put his hand on the older man's shoulder. "I don't think you have anything to fear at present."

"Well, in any case, my patron needs his sleep. I didn't think it would be wise. She broke a glass vase over Firminius' head and threw a hand mirror at Antye. Antye bore up well. She ducked, but Firminius ran screaming. He was barefoot and he cut his foot on the glass. I don't think he was very badly hurt, but he left bloody footprints all over her bedroom, the atrium, and the hall to his rooms. I don't think she hurt anyone else, though. But she was vowing to sell the whole lot of them in the morning."

"She doesn't mean it."

"No, probably not or she would have awakened Aristo herself. At any rate, you are to prepare some new gladiator for a private showing in her personal arena this morning."

"Very well," Philo said. "What was she so angry about?"

Octus' eyebrows rose. "I don't know. She came in, saw Macer and Afer playing doorkeeper, and sent for Firminius. Antye and the rest of the girls were undressing her. He came, she sent the girls out. Antye was her nurse and she trusts her, so she stayed. The next thing any of us knew, Firminius was screaming and running, so was Antye, and she was throwing things."

"You should have awakened me. I could have given her a sedative," Philo said.

"You should pay me protection," Octus said. "One of the people she was cursing besides *him* was you. Watch out for the new gladiator. She bought him in Gaul and I think she hopes you'll be his first kill. In any case, she wants to give Caesar a taste of her new star, so she has a wild boar waiting."

"Gladiator or beastiarius? Which one is he?" Philo asked. "There is a distinction, you know. One fights men, the other animals."

"If there's a distinction, it's lost on me, Philo. Every one I've ever seen is big, murderous, frightening, and unpleasantly agile. And that description fits not only the men, but the animals they fight also. At times it's difficult to tell the difference. Should I wake *him*?"

"Yes," Philo said. "If Caesar is coming, he might feel the head of the household should be present, for propriety's sake if nothing else. Our little mistress has to be oh so careful of her reputation."

Octus noted his face was stiff with disgust. "I'll get him now."

"Don't worry if he . . ."

Octus shook his head. "No, he's never gotten angry with me, never shown even the slightest impatience with me over anything."

Philo nodded. He knew why—Lucius felt abominably guilty about Octus. The loyalty he'd shown to Silvia should have been better rewarded, but Lucius had been doing his military service in Gaul when his mother died and he hadn't given much thought to the fate of her servants.

While Octus went to wake Lucius, Philo went to the armory and picked up a bundle of clothing, mail, and spears. The slave in the armory handed them to him without comment.

The sky was bright now, the sun only just rising. Philo balanced the spears against the wall and the bundle on his arm while he pulled his mantle more tightly around himself. It was cold. From nearby he heard squealing and roaring. He knew they must be torturing the boar to drive him into a frenzy so the creature would make an interesting fight of it. He shivered a little, remembering some of the things Antony's men had inflicted on him.

Wild boars were the most savage of killers, so he saved his sympathy for the man. One misstep around such a creature might find him struggling in agony on the sand.

Philo knew both the gladiators and the beastiarii well, and he wasn't afraid of any of them. In fact, he found them the most grateful of his patients. They were the most wretched individuals he'd ever known, war prisoners or criminals both. The war prisoners were those who weren't considered worth selling as slaves, and the criminals were drawn from the most impoverished classes of Roman society. Most, not all to be sure, were extravagantly grateful for the smallest kindness. The few who hated everyone who came near them didn't survive long.

Certainly not this one. He appeared rather small, sitting in silence, looking through the grating into the arena. The slender figure was in deep shadow. There was a big guard posted at the barred door. He opened it for Philo. At the clash of iron, the person on the bench turned toward him, and Philo realized he was looking at a woman.

LUCIUS WAS AWAKENED BY OCTUS, WHO TOLD HIM his sister had returned last night.

"I'm sorry I missed her," Lucius said.

"Yes," Octus answered, and prepared to shave him.

"Oh, no," Lucius moaned, moving back toward the warm bed.

"Caesar is coming," Octus said.

Lucius stumbled into the courtyard. He sat down in a chair out past the columned porch. The light was good. Octus shaved him. Alia brought his toga and woolen tunic.

"What am I doing that I need to dress in wool?" Lucius asked.

"Attending a munera with Caesar, Cleopatra, Antony, and your sister. She brought him a new gladiator from Gaul."

Lucius whispered something obscene under his breath, then in a still lower voice coupled Caesar and Antony with it, suggesting they do it to each other, take turns.

Octus drew back, razor in hand. "Sir . . ." he began.

"I know, I know," Lucius said. "I won't talk and I'll keep my face still."

Octus began again. Lucius noticed with some alarm that his servant's hand was trembling, but true to form, tremor or not, he had Lucius planed off within a few moments, hair combed, pomaded, and dressed in a few more, with purple-striped toga on and properly draped. Lucius noted that when the ill-fated Castor and Pollux had put the toga—a hellishly difficult garment to wear—on him, it slipped and slid, but Octus had the knack of vesting him in such a way as to keep the thing in position even in a high wind.

Thus sartorially correct, he was shepherded by Octus to the atrium. He was accompanied by Cut Ear, laconic as usual. The Gaul said, "Must see fight."

Caesar and Antony arrived, Antony cursing under his breath. When he saw Lucius he asked, "That Greek doctor of yours holding a grudge? Because if he is, I know a sure cure for grudges among slaves."

"Philo's not a slave," Lucius said.

"No," Caesar said. "Philo is a Roman citizen, as entitled to wear the toga as you are, Marcus Antonious, and he can vote in the assemblies."

Antony looked sour and then annoyed. "I didn't know you'd done that already."

"I have." Caesar smiled at Antony.

"Well," Antony rumbled, "I suppose I'll have to pay him then, but wherever he is, bring him on. I have the worst hangover since Zeus popped Athena out of his head. My tongue feels like it's been lying in a tanning vat for twenty years. My eyeballs are on stalks like a crayfish. I swear on my father's grave they're sticking out two or three inches. If not Philo, someone, someone have pity on me. Bring me a drink."

Octus bowed to Lucius and spoke to him in a low voice. "Philo is with the new gladiator, but if you wish, I know where the physician keeps most of his drugs. I can bring the gentleman a bit of what he—"

"Yes, yes," Antony said. "Even if you make a mistake, bring me something that will kill me outright. Better death than a lingering demise; I'm seared by the daylight. Seared, I tell you."

Cleopatra arrived, looking dewy-eyed and fresh. When she saw Antony, she snickered.

Fulvia arrived, on her best behavior. She ostentatiously kissed Lucius on the cheek and embraced Caesar. "My dear friend, you must see what I have for you." Then she exchanged kisses with Cleopatra.

Octus returned with a cup. He handed it to Lucius, bowed, and left. Lucius glanced at the contents. Yes, it had the same look and odor as Philo's hangover cure. He handed it to Antony.

"Come," Fulvia said. "See my new practice arena."

PHILO'S EYES WERE RIVETED ON THE WOMAN. She walked toward him and he handed her the three spears. She studied them critically. They were all of different shapes. She put one aside at once. Even Philo could see the head was loose. She brought the other two into the light. One she found satisfactory, the other she pronounced "Blunt," but she undertook to raise an edge using the stone bench. The metal, high carbon steel, sharpened quickly. When she was finished, she tested the edge cautiously with her thumb. "You wouldn't want to shave with it, but good enough. What is it, human or animal?" she asked Philo.

"A wild boar, I think."

"Fine, a wild boar. She doesn't want much, does she? Three spears, one with a loose blade, completely untrustworthy. The other two with no cross guards."

"Cross guards?" he repeated, even he thought a bit densely.

"Yes," she said. "A wild boar will walk up a spear and take the man holding it, or woman as the case may be." Her lips twitched in what might have been a small smile. Then she added, "Close your mouth or something might fly into it. What else have you there, any armor?"

He handed her the subligaculum and the mail.

She held up the mail and studied it against the light. It was rather beautiful, silver made with small rings. The neck and the hem that came to just below the breasts were decorated with large, glittering stones.

"Beautiful," she pronounced it, "and wouldn't stop a hangnail. If it is a boar and he gets me down, that pig's tusks will be in me before I can hiccup. And what is this?"

The subligaculum was scarlet silk. It was slightly more complicated than a loincloth. It had a belt of chain—big, flat links in gold. The silk came down across the buttocks, pretty well covering them, and then was drawn up between the legs, covered the stomach, and had fastenings to hold it to the thick chain belt and an end to pull down in front.

"Looks like she spent some money here," Dryas commented cynically.

"I'll go see if I can find you a better spear," Philo said. He hurried to the door and found it locked, the guard gone. He turned to Dryas, a look of utter dismay on his face. "We're locked in."

"Yes." She smiled. "Try not to look so much like you'd rather be locked in with a lioness."

He stammered . . . something. He didn't remember what it was afterward.

She laughed, then examined the portcullis. "Raised from the outside?"

Philo nodded.

"The spectators?" she asked, pointing to the box across the arena.

"Yes," Philo said. He recognized Fulvia, Antony, Lucius, Cleopatra, Caesar, and Cut Ear.

There was plenty of light. There was an awning over the box, but it was rolled back. The sun was up and the right-hand seats and the sand glowed with a quarter circle of yellow light.

"Turn your back," she commanded.

Philo began backing away slowly, keeping his eye on her. "The door is locked," he said. "I can't leave. I would if I could."

She said "Boo!"

He jumped two paces.

She said slowly, clearly, and distinctly, "Turn-your-back-I-want-to-dress."

"Oh, oh, ooh." The last was a sigh of relief. He turned and faced the side wall. He heard rustling noises behind him.

Across the arena, he heard snuffling, snorting noises, a loud thud, then the sound of hooves on the clay under the sand, then a loud crash against the portcullis behind him. He spun around.

The boar slammed snout and tusks against the iron grating for a second time. Immortal gods, the thing was big and it stank of blood, because the attendants had been baiting it, and pig piss. Its caretakers were afraid of it and kept it for long periods without cleaning the cage.

As Philo watched, the creature opened a big muzzle and he saw the teeth, worse than the ivory tusks on either side of the snout, long, yellow, and vicious. It gave vent to a grunting roar and slammed its tusks into the portcullis gate again. Its skin was black with bristles alongside the snout; they rose and formed a ridge along the back.

Dryas, watching it calmly, prodded one of its flanks with a spear. It lunged again, squealing and roaring; and, for a second, Philo thought the iron grate would give way.

Then he and Dryas heard shouts from above and small missiles rained down around the animal to drive it away from the portcullis.

Philo was horrified. "That thing, that thing will kill you." Belatedly he noticed that Dryas was dressed.

She smiled at him, a beautiful, curving, gentle smile.

Now out of the clumsy tunic, she was beautiful, and a picture of her smile and her body's grace in the abbreviated chain mail and loincloth impressed itself on his mind forever. Long, slim legs—they made most women's look stubby—muscular at the calf, narrowing at the knee, rising to powerful thighs. Slender hips, virginal almost, flat stomach ridged with muscle under a velvet surface. High, cone-shaped breasts, generous enough to hold the silver mail away from her abdomen. Arms, beautifully formed, like the legs well proportioned to her body, but strong, not bulky—rather the way the cables on a pulley give the impression of indomitable strength though they don't knot, but glide.

The boar was making a circuit of the arena and he arrived at the gate again. The portcullis began to rise. Shouts from above drove the animal back toward the center of the circle.

Dryas held a spear in either hand. The portcullis was going up, faster and faster.

"No!" Philo said. "No!"

"I'd better," she said softly, "or he'll get in here and kill both of us." Then, like lightning, she ducked under the gate and confronted the boar.

It charged. Dryas was alone now and a silence surrounded her. She ran right so the animal was charging directly at her. For a second, she lost it in the sun dazzle as the daystar rose over the eastern wall of the arena. When she saw it, the creature was almost upon her. She felt a tusk scratch her ankle and she drove the spear in her right hand into the boar's flank. It grunted, but wasn't even slowed. It turned; she clung to the spear, taking momentum from the creature's turning body, then abruptly let go, leaving the spear dragging from the boar's bloody side.

Now the sun was in its eyes. Dryas tossed the spear from her left hand to her right.

In the box, Lucius was still absorbing the fact that he was watching a woman. When the woman and boar were hidden for a second by a cloud of sand as it lowered its head and tried to drive its tusks in, he rose to his feet, an outcry forming in his throat.

Next to him, he heard Caesar say, "So soon. Too bad. I'd hoped for more of a fight."

Then he saw the spear enter the boar's body as she confidently skipped aside.

She was almost directly below the box.

Antony yelled, "By Bacchus, a woman! A hundred in gold on the boar."

"I'll take that!" Lucius yelled.

"So will I," Caesar shouted.

This time the boar lost Dryas in the sun dazzle, but her spear skidded across his ribs and fell into the sand, leaving her unarmed.

The boar paused for a moment, flanks heaving. Blood spurted from the wound in front of the hip. The spear still trailed behind him and Dryas noted that the foam-flecked jaws were red. Her second thrust, though seemingly ineffectual, must have nicked a lung.

But this killer was far from finished. It charged. Again, Dryas jinked left, he followed, then right. The creature seemed to anticipate her movements.

Dryas leaped like a tumbler, coming down on her hands just behind the beast's tail, somersaulted in the air, and landed on her feet in the center of the arena.

The boar turned with almost unbelievable agility, much more like a stoat or weasel than a pig, and came for her again.

In the box, Lucius heard Antony give an awed gasp. Caesar laughed. But the boar was a murderous adversary and Lucius found himself frightened for her. He leaned over the spiked railing, fists clenched on the iron pickets.

Dryas snatched up the spear and, to Lucius' horror, went to one knee before the charging animal. He knew what she was doing. He'd handled the sow in this way, so long ago when his own sword was driven into his back.

"No," he whispered, "no, don't. You've gotten him in the lung. In a few moments, he won't be able to breathe, then it's over." He knew this as well as she.

Dryas drove the spear between the charging animal's ribs, but it came up the spear, mouth open, yellow tusks ready to tear into her shoulder and neck. She leaped back, but she'd forgotten where she was and her body slammed into the stone side of the arena.

The gaping mouth closed on her ankle, but she was in motion, hands on the boar's back, in full vault over its back, feet in the air. One was bleeding and she landed on one side, catching herself on her left arm.

The boar turned, mouth agape, tusks low.

He has me, Dryas thought. *This is death.* Her hand skidded on the sand and she went down on her side, looking into the creature's eyes.

One step it came. Two steps. She'd driven the spear through its body. It wheezed, gurgled, and then it lay, legs folded under it, while Dryas got to her feet.

She found she was shaking all over, but it wasn't visible to the men in the box.

The boar wheezed again as Dryas backed away from it, then again as bright blood splashed from the gaping mouth down onto the sand. Then and only then did it die.

Dryas looked at her left hand. She'd skinned the side and the raw patches oozed blood. There were some shallow gashes near her ankle made by the animal's teeth. None of the injuries was serious.

Behind her, she heard the portcullis rising. The chains pulling it clanked.

Antony sat back. "What a fight." He pointed at Dryas. "But you can't tell me that's a woman. It just can't be. No, I don't believe it, not even if every vestal in Rome swore to it."

Dryas stared up at the men, her head tilted back slightly. Lucius found he didn't care much for the look she gave him—she hadn't directed so quelling a stare at the boar. Then she turned and walked toward the opening below the portcullis. In the bright morning light, it yawned like a cave.

Just before she reached it, she turned, pulled off the mail shirt and threw it to the sand. Then she tore away the scarlet loincloth, throwing it aside, and stood naked before them.

Lucius felt his mouth go dry and again he was glad he wore a toga, then realized he wasn't wearing it. He'd shrugged it off sometime during the fight. Then he noticed the other men weren't paying one bit of attention to the state of his soul.

Antony made a sound reminiscent of the boar.

And Caesar said, "I don't think there's any doubt we're looking at a woman. No! No doubt at all."

XXI

H E HADN'T KNOWN THERE WERE SO MANY OF them. He'd never seen this many before. How did they feed themselves? Keep from going insane? The crowding was appalling and he understood why their senses were so blunted. The city was so aroma laden that he found himself verging on losing his ability to think coherently. He simply—not even with a human brain—he simply couldn't process this much information at once.

He was riding in a litter and the grunting men, twelve of them bearing his weight, gave off an overpowering stench of fear and of the secretions of physical exertion that drenched their skins at both armpit and groin.

Fear because they were human beasts of burden and a driver followed them with a long whip coiled in his hand. The litter belonged to Amborux. When any of the slaves flagged or dropped below a certain pace, the whip cracked. Maeniel had noticed the men were marked by red welts on different parts of their bodies. Now he knew why.

The litter had been awaiting him in Ostia when he got off the ship. How Blaze had gotten the message to Amborux, he had no idea, but several of the Gaul's guards and the litter were at the dock. Maeniel loaded four sacks of gold and climbed in after them, wondering about the motive power of his transport. Now he knew. The men trotting along beneath him were very uncomfortable and, because they were, so was he.

The noise was overpowering. The shouts of hawkers mixed with those of patrons quarreling with the shopkeepers whose establishments verged on the street. The bustle and noise, the constant babble of human speech, footsteps, creaking handcarts, the thud of hammers and the scraping of plasterers when they passed a construction site. The omnipresent odors rising from cookshops, wine bars, butchers, sausage sellers, vintners, and bakeshops and underlain by stagnant sewage, urine, feces, damp timber, organic garbage, dry and damp rot, and decay, almost overpowered his senses.

Crack. Crack. Crack. The men under him began to jog as they entered the Forum. He hadn't believed they could move faster, but given encouragement of the driver's whip, he found they could. The guards pushed the crowd aside as they passed the Rostra.

The litter turned into a courtyard surrounded by stalls. Men sat in them, guarded by huge gladiators and chained mastiffs. Wolfhounds, he noted with some alarm.

The bearers set the litter down. "Gently!" the driver roared, and the whip cracked again. When the short legs on the bottom touched the cobbles, the wolf didn't feel a bump.

He stepped out of the litter before the largest stall. The shutters, reinforced with iron, stood open, and the proprietor sat next to a brazier. He was an acetic-looking bald Greek named Dophanes. Blaze and Amborux had recommended him.

Maeniel picked up the four sacks of gold. He placed them on the table in front of the banker. Two assistants scurried out and began to count the gold in the sacks. When they saw there were many other kinds of coins present besides the Roman aureus, they began separating them and brought out scales to weigh the unfamiliar ones.

Maeniel fished around in his purse and handed the driver two silver coins to buy refreshment for himself and his men. He asked that he include the bearers who, despite the chill air, looked thirsty and exhausted. This was a magnificent sum to men who were used, at best, to seeing only copper money.

Two of the guards, sent out to buy, soon returned with an armload of bread with sausage, onion, and pine nuts; four whole jugs of wine; fowl, including chicken, woodcock, and squab; sizzling sausages wrapped in some discarded book paper; and a clay pan of pork stewed with grape must, onions, turnips, and carrots.

Everyone sat down right where they were and fell to, while Maeniel, who had been warned by Blaze and Mir, kept an eye on the gold, making sure the count was an honest one.

Maeniel stood there in tunic and toga. No, he wasn't entitled to wear one since he was not a Roman citizen, but, after all, of what people are werewolves? He'd as well be Roman as not.

The slaves, who had been silently cursing him since Ostia, began not exactly blessing him, but were willing to believe he was a kinder man than experience suggested.

When the weighing and counting was finished, Maeniel found himself a wealthy man, even by Roman standards. However, instead of conducting him to Amborux's villa, he was taken to lodge with Manilius and Felex. He refused to get back into the litter and walked the rest of the way to the villa. He embarrassed, exasperated, and infuriated his guards by turns, because he wished to investigate everything.

He stopped at a sausage seller's stall and tried one of every kind, then ambled into a tavern where the tavernkeeper and a woman were putting one of the tabletops to an unusual use. The man's tunic was tucked up above his waist, as was the woman's clothing, but the outraged guards noted she wore the stola of a respectable married woman.

The guards were getting ready to hustle Maeniel out, when the man jumped off the screaming woman, snatched up a pot of soup from the stove, and threw it at all of them.

Maeniel only just avoided turning wolf by a hair. He caught the change and turned it back while he was ducking under a table. The guards fled in all directions, as did the woman. Some of the soup landed perilously close to her. The soup contained an unpleasantly large amount of fat, making for bad burns where it splattered on human skin.

The woman turned around at the door, screaming curses at her lover. The guards crept out of whatever refuge they had taken: most, like Maeniel, from under tables; one had been clinging to a ceiling beam; two others came from out in the street.

Then Maeniel found himself defending the unfortunate tavernkeeper from the guards who wanted to drown, or at least dip, him in a pot of boiling water. The woman added her vote to theirs: she was unhappy about the near miss with the soup. She went after her lover with teeth and fingernails since she was otherwise unarmed.

The neighbors gathered and were vastly entertained.

Maeniel noted a large man bearing down on them. Her husband? The crowd scattered. He was evidently known and feared in the vicinity.

The large man somehow became convinced Maeniel was insulting his wife, and the tavernkeeper was defending her honor. The large man had a sword.

Both Maeniel and the guards opted for the better part of valor and ran, followed by the litter bearers.

When they reassembled several streets away, Maeniel tapped the guards for explanations. They supplied them, along with a considerable catalog of obscenities, some of which didn't translate out of Latin well and in which Maeniel was deeply interested. He was aware of the private nature of the act of love, including the fact that humans were unhappy when interrupted, but he was in the dark so far as the outrage created by the woman's respectable dress in a less-than-respectable situation. He was duly enlightened. He was also persuaded to promise to be more circumspect in his explorations.

He kept his promise, detouring only long enough to buy bread with a delicious honey crust, enough for the whole party. They marched along, munching and drinking.

He paused to buy an unusual hat. Made to keep off the sun, it was in the form of a large cabbage with the leaves tied up with string at the center. The wearer untied as many leaves as were necessary to keep the rays from reaching face, ears, neck, etc.

His guards found it ridiculous enough to arouse them to laughter and even the litter bearers, the most repressed individuals in the group, managed a few grins and titters.

They were immediately sobered when Maeniel started a near riot in the Forum by throwing silver to some children who were dancing to the music of a double flute.

Thereafter he was hustled along more quickly until the whole party reached the house of Manilius and Felex on the Palantine.

The group was ushered through the door by a beautiful young man dressed as a woman. He had auburn hair and was wearing green silk, makeup, and perfume.

"Nice dress," Maeniel said to the doorkeeper.

"Yes, green, just my color." He purred and patted a rather elaborate coiffure done up with ringlets and a diadem.

He guided Maeniel into a peristyle crowded with people, about eight women and ten or so men, in various states of dishabille, all walking among very fresh-looking flowers and plants.

Early roses; irises; ferns; lilies; white, pink, and mauve sage;

magnificently blue flowering acanthus just lifting its complex spikes from its floret of decorative leaves. Violets were everywhere, blooming in low clay pans: purple, white, yellow-purple, ordinary yellow, and the odorous, shy, simple blue.

The human beings were, if possible, even more colorful. Everywhere the eye roved it fell on jewels: red, blue, orange amethyst, black onyx, hematite, and a rainbow of pearls—pink, white, blue, brown, and shimmering black. The dresses were of rainbow hue and material: silk, silk linen, wool linen, and block-printed cotton. Scarlet, green, orange, flame, bluebell, rose, yellow, brown, or even black: any and every known combination. And it went without saying all the faces were made up, and the air was heavy with perfume.

From his minders, Maeniel heard the sounds of stifled mirth, guffaws, hoots, giggles, coughs, and even strangulation as some tried too hard to control their amusement.

The ladies and gentlemen in the garden didn't trouble to hide their feelings. Several pointed at the cabbage hat and went into credible hysterics.

Manilius and Felex rolled their eyes heavenward.

"Oh, my dear," Felex moaned. "What has Amborux foisted off on us now?"

For a moment, Maeniel had the experience of standing between two groups of people both laughing at each other and, by the by, at him. He wasn't sure he was enjoying the situation, but he was a patient creature. So he swept off the cabbage hat, bowed to Felex and Manilius, and smiled.

Manilius pressed his palms together as if praying. "Oh . . ."

Felex looked bowled over. "My . . ."

The women rose from their chairs and migrated toward him in a group.

"My," said one wearing a flame-colored chiton, "isn't he . . ."

"Just adorable . . ." This lady wore a stola with about six layers of green silk gauze.

Maeniel began to kiss hands, a custom he really enjoyed.

L UCIUS WALKED AWAY FROM THE ARENA WITHOUT being aware of where he was.

Cut Ear murmured, "Caledoni."

"Wha-what?" Lucius asked.

"Caledoni. Her tribe." Cut Ear's face was stiff with disapproval. "Should be dead."

"I agree. She shouldn't have been able to kill that boar with two light spears, but she did," Lucius replied, still awed.

"No!" Cut Ear's voice was loud. "She be dead before allow . . . such use. Sacred war woman. No, is no Latin. War priestess, war queen, call Valkyrie, rider of storm on wind. Finger points." Cut Ear lifted his hand and pointed. "Finger falls on you, you dead. Put you first into fight naked, hand you over to battle power for victory. Caledoni." Then he would say no more, not in Latin anyway, and wandered off, muttering to himself.

Lucius sympathized with him. He felt more or less the same way himself, but for, no doubt, completely different reasons.

His imagination kept playing back a picture of her standing before the portcullis. His mind kept increasing the details of what he'd seen. No, she couldn't possibly have looked *that* good. *I have been without a woman too long. I should have done something about it weeks ago. I just need a little of the relaxation sex provides.*

By now, it was midmorning and the day was shaping up to be a warm one. He kept avoiding any spot where he might meet others. He wanted to be rid of the vision haunting him, and yet he didn't, finding his thoughts sought the picture of her standing proud and yet vulnerable, alone before the darkness, in the shadow of the ivory walls ringing the arena, on the white sand.

He was so deep in thought that he wasn't sure where he was until he stumbled on a flagstone pushed up by a tree root in a disused courtyard. He looked around, conscious for the first time where his straying feet had carried him.

This was the oldest part of the villa, but not remodeled like the peristyle near the atrium with its ancient cistern. He'd lived with his mother and father here during his youth until his sixteenth year, when the changes in Roman society had forced his parents to spend money modernizing their home, making it a fit residence for the rich, important Basilian family.

Near the entrance were the reception rooms where his father and Aristo met and greeted his business associates, dependants, and supporters—clients, in Roman parlance—creditors, freedmen, and slaves, all of whom were engaged in his various and manifold business ventures.

His mother had a suite of rooms near here where she assiduously cultivated her aristocratic connections with the Julian family, Caesar's relatives, as a means to her husband's ends. In the afternoon, she went off quietly to drink. As a child, he had never understood what the thick odor of alcoholic perspiration that always surrounded her by suppertime meant, but he sensed there was some unhappiness between her and his father. Still, they were both kind to him and, all in all, even with Fulvia's constant mischief, he'd been happy.

Now the garden was overgrown, the old flowerbeds infested with winter-brown weeds. However, the box hedges were still green, as were the tall cypresses. The pool was filled with cress and white-flowered water mint, and the carp he remembered as a child still lived there.

He thought *she* must still be here.

Yes, she stood among the cypress, box, and dead rose canes at the apex of the pool near his boyhood room: Venus stepping into the bath. The legs were greenish with damp, one forever poised over the water. She was no masterpiece, but a mass-produced product of one of the more commercial Hellenistic city-states founded by the successors of Alexander. A cheap knockoff of the classical statuary Greece was famous for.

Her face was ugly with a large, underslung jaw, but the sculptor had the body right. As an imaginative thirteen-year-old, her face hadn't been the part of her that interested him most.

He had been lonely then. As he made his way through the overgrown bushes and cypress to her side he thought, *And I'm lonely now.*

She wasn't very big, a little less than life-size. He remembered looking up at her face in his youth, but now he was larger than she was. He looked down at the top of her head. He put one arm around her slender waist and rested his cheek on the cold, marble hair. He recalled the woman in the arena and remembered where he'd seen her face before—in the deserted temple where he'd found the plum, a reflection in the basin of water.

A big old carp rose, took a fly on the surface, and vanished into the coiling waterweed. Dragonflies danced among papyrus clumps gone wild along the edges of the pool. A green frog, a very small one,

jumped on the statue's foot, the one over the water. Wonder of wonders, a green snake, marked with long black lines along its back,
paused and studied him with catlike amber eyes, pupils slit in the
bright sunlight, then eased into the water and vanished into the
murky depths.

He saw her face looking up at him from the water, eyes closed,
her body slender, white, rose-tipped breasts, dark pubic triangle softly
furred. Yes, that was what the dense, curly mound looked like, the
fur of a kitten.

The hand around the waist of the statue sought and seemed to feel
the texture of a moist, ripe peach. He didn't care to put what his hand
was feeling, a patch of moss perhaps, to the test. The sun shining over
his shoulder mirrored by the water suddenly shattered as the frog
leaped from the statue's foot into the gold-leaf disc. Pleasure leaped in
his body, tightened his loins almost painfully, then shot away like an
arrow loosed from a bow into the light, the air, and the silence,
leaving him drenched with perspiration and feeling weak. His lone
goddess of desire supported him upright and kept him from falling to
his knees in prayer, supplication, or despair.

F ULVIA WAS DELIGHTED. SHE OOHED AND AAHED
over Dryas, offered her money, jewels, slave attendants of her
own, a villa in Baiae, whatever she could possibly imagine.

Dryas was disgusted and depressed. She believed none of Fulvia's
promises and felt her situation hopeless. She'd heard enough to know
that Caesar was in the audience that had watched her this morning.
She hadn't even known which one he was. How could she kill him if
she couldn't even recognize him? She wasn't at all sure how to find
out what she needed to know to complete her mission.

All Dryas asked for was a bath and some food. She hoped Fulvia,
with her flood of chatter and exultation, would go away. She did.

Dryas accepted the sauna steam bath; her people enjoyed it, also.
The tepiderium surprised her. What luxury. Why did a people with
access to such comfort and beauty want to bother with thrill-seeking
behavior such as she'd been involved in this morning? Or go running
around trying to bully others as they had the people of Gaul? What a
waste of time for them.

Fulvia's maids applied perfumed oil to Dryas' body. The perfume stung the cuts on her ankle; they opened and began to bleed, as did the ones on her hand. The sight of her blood brought on immoderate— or what she considered immoderate—behavior among the women.

They flew around, crying out in an undignified manner. Their screeching annoyed Dryas, but she was well mannered. She was, after all, a guest, albeit an unwilling one. Among tribes whose tradition of hospitality went back time out of mind, the guest had an obligation of courtesy to the host, an obligation to accede to any reasonable request. She did not vent her annoyance on the guiltless maids, but promised to cooperate with the physician when he came.

The women draped her in a loose muslin gown and sent for Philo.

Philo met Lucius in the atrium. To Philo, he looked dour and unhappy.

"Where did they take her?" Lucius asked.

"Nowhere, she's in the baths. Antye sent for me. Seems the boar got her on the ankle. Fulvia told them to treat her like fine crystal. They are in mortal terror of their mistress's wrath. Antye called me to check on what are probably a few scratches. I saw the woman when she came back from the fight. By this evening, she'll have every tongue in Rome wagging. Caesar and Cleopatra had to borrow a bedroom before he could leave for the Senate. That jade's trick she pulled just before she dove for cover ruined every man in sight." He chuckled. "Antony even forgot he had a hangover."

Lucius made a gurgling sound. "No! No! Don't take another step. Don't move. Don't do anything till I get back." He danced around wildly. "I need . . . I need . . . I don't know what I need . . . a disguise of some kind. Can I be your assistant? Can I be a bath attendant? What can I be?"

"Oh, no, not you, too!"

"Yes, yes, yes!" Lucius danced up and down.

"Octus!" Philo called.

Octus appeared.

"A tunic: old, worn, holes and patches. Is there something like that in the vicinity?" Philo asked.

Octus nodded and, in a few moments, returned with a garment.

"It's not very attractive, but it will do nicely. Thank you," Philo said, and offered it to Lucius.

"Now I'll get over her." He said this confidently as he donned the tunic in a tiring room off the baths.

Philo nodded. "Yes, sometimes when we get a close look at something we have admired from afar, we find it doesn't live up to our expectations. Flaws hidden by distance appear more glaring and we see a coarseness. The very thing that made such an impact from a remote perspective repels us as too extreme when we approach and try to embrace it."

"Ah, yes," Lucius said. "Let's get going. I want to see what she really looks like."

"I thought that's what I said," Philo answered.

"No, no, you didn't. Or maybe you did when I untangle it, but right now—"

"Be quiet," Philo said. "You're a servant." He opened the door.

The filtered daylight from a skylight was not such as to flatter any woman. But Dryas was impervious to it. In fact, she looked to Lucius' eyes rather like some captive earth spirit.

The maids had washed, pomaded, and braided the ebony hair around a strange, spiked, copper crown. At close range, he could see how fair her skin was, rather like the finest, grainless marble. Not cold as marble would be, but brushed with rose, about the same pink color as the rose of Pistum with its gift of the double spring. He remembered the long canes twined at the Basilian country villa. Now, in the cool air and bright sunlight, they would just be beginning to bloom. The long, cruel vines would be alight with buds and flowers and the air would be drenched with their fragrance.

She was seated in a chair, one of those rather spare things the Greeks favored with a curved back and slender legs. The chair and the damp muslin gown hid none of the secrets of her body, but rather lent a slight softness to its outline. They created a seductive sense that one, stretching out a hand to bare her nakedness, would find something of the joy the eye finds in a landscape beautiful already in the morning mist, but becoming even more lovely in the new sunlight.

She was simply woman, without artifice, without embellishment, without pretense, without desire, even. Woman as she is, as God created her, born as much to quench lust as to create it. As ready to cradle a child to her breast, or a man searching for that burning delight touched with the mystery of creation between her thighs, and to share her delight in union with him, even as he brought his fire to rouse hers.

As Philo closed the door behind him, she looked at them.

Yes, he'd thought so this morning, her eyes were blue. Blue like the plum he picked up in the temple, blue as lapis polished as a gem, blue as the Aegean Sea in summer, blue and framed by dark lashes.

And, what was worse, she saw him. She had no filter between herself and others. He had his; he had not seen Lucrese as a human being, only as one of the household slaves, until her lover died.

But this woman had none, and he saw her eyes follow him as he and Philo approached the chair. The scar along his back pulled. He was barefoot. He'd discarded his sandals when he donned the worn tunic, and his scar troubled him more when he had not even the light support of a winter legionary boot.

She saw the limp, the worn clothing, the bowed head. He was a little afraid she might recognize him from this morning's fight, though he'd sat to the left of Antony and Caesar. He hoped she hadn't gotten a good look at his face.

He knew all of the evidence said "servant" to her, and not a particularly important one at that, but still she saw him and looked past the worn clothing, the limp, and the subservient air.

They reached her chair. He went down on one knee beside it and lifted her leg by the heel and calf, holding it up so Philo could see the shallow lacerations left by the boar's teeth.

She reached out and rested one hand on his shoulder. He looked up and met her eyes. Shock went through him like a bolt of lightning and, for a moment, they were alone together.

Yes, she saw him, and he saw himself through her eyes. She saw a servant, a young man with a limp, dressed as one who labors for his keep, one young but without much hope of ever attaining any better life. Yet struggling along as well as he could with the few small gifts he had been given: youth, straightly imprisoned in a house where it would never be allowed to grow and, at last, blossom into confident, generous, talented manhood; a human spirit, born to take wing to love, to hope, to achieve, lost to all the good it might do for itself and others, born only to be driven down into darkness and be utterly destroyed.

He felt her sadness and, oddly, her thirst for justice and he knew with an all-pervading certainty that she was his and had been in the past, his, and he had loved her for all time and would do so again. In life or death, he would yield her to no one. No, not to Caesar or Rome or even the very immortal gods themselves.

Then Philo was smearing an ointment on the ankle and reassuring Antye and the other women that the few scratches were nothing to worry about. Lucius replaced her foot on the floor and she lifted the hand on his shoulder and looked away.

He knew he got to his feet and left the room, but he didn't remember doing so. Nor could he ever recall the path he took to return to the deserted garden where his image of womanhood resided. He walked among the deep green of the overgrown cypress and the weed-choked yet somehow fecund pond blessed by the mother of all life who presided over it. He knew she had transmuted his desire from stone to flesh and sent him to look on her and she to gaze into his eyes.

THE WOLF ALSO BATHED, A RITE HE RECOGNIZED as important among these Romans. He also allowed Felex's "maids" to dress him. They were as adept at male haberdashery as female, and he entered the atrium at dusk every inch a proper Roman. He then asked Felex why he was to be lodged here and not as Amborux's guest.

"Oh, my dear, that would never do. A connection between the Arch Druid of Gaul and Amborux, a highly regarded Roman senator and citizen, might be useful at home, but it would never do here in Rome. So we are his stand-ins, you might say. He couldn't ignore a request from that direction, most unwise even with Gaul ostensibly under the Roman heel. They still have much too much prestige among the people, these Druid fellows, and while I'm sure they're perfectly nice people, the Romans don't approve of them at all."

"Mmm," Maeniel said. "I see." He did. He saw more than Felex wanted him to see.

"I don't want to be offensive, but we're having a little dinner tonight for some other senators of our acquaintance. You are used to Roman etiquette?"

"Recline, support myself on left arm, use first three fingers of right hand to pick up food. Don't slobber, fart, belch, snivel, spit, or scratch. Don't get drunk or start fights, discuss religion or politics, or tell off-color jokes when women are present—or grope the waitresses or waiters for that matter. Compliment the food, even if it isn't good, and don't hog the best dish . . . share. And," he took a deep breath, "wash before and after."

Felex blinked at him. "Yes, oh my, yes. I do believe that covers everything."

"Fine," Maeniel said.

"Don't mention Amborux in the same sentence with Druids. Actually, you probably better not mention either one of them at all."

"That goes without saying," Maeniel promised.

In a few moments, a model of Roman rectitude marched in, Marcus Junius Brutus, followed by an unhappy Antony.

"Caesar's sons," Felex said, driving an elbow into Maeniel's ribs.

"Aren't they a little old?" Maeniel commented.

"Well, you know, my dear, they aren't his real sons, but Brutus is his heir and Antony is heir apparent," Manilius told him.

"Mmm," Maeniel said. He was happier when they went in to dinner.

Antony and Brutus reclined at opposite tables. They eyed each other like a pair of wolves ready to undertake a disagreement over status. Maeniel had often been either a participant or bystander at such events and was surprised to note Manilius and Felex chose to pretend nothing was happening. He'd noted in the past that humans were not uniformly truthful with themselves or others, but this represented an astonishing degree of self-delusion.

The house was, as Lucius had noted, resolutely Greek and the dinner table no less.

Dinner began with a magnificent salad of octopus mixed with bitter greens in oil, dressed with a bit of lemon and more than a bit of oil. The sweet curlicues of tender meat were lightly peppered and salted and, as was more usual in Greece, bread was supplied to sop up the remaining oil and lemon.

Antony and Brutus eyed each other over the salad and, when both their fingers fell at the same moment on the same tentacle, they almost snarled at each other.

Had they been wolves, Maeniel thought, then thought again, No! They were no different from wolves. They even smelled like a pair who wanted, but didn't quite dare, to begin a confrontation, yet. Only when one or the other was sure he might win would this individual force the issue, and neither of them had reached that point yet. No, the only difference between this pair and wolves was that, among wolves, all would accept the change and go on much as before. While among humans, the consequences for the loser would likely be far more drastic.

When every scrap of the salad disappeared and the platter was carried out, fat dormice stuffed with pork, pepper, pine nuts, and sorrel appeared, a generous platter of them.

"Have you seen Caesar's new toy?" Antony asked Brutus, then added, "Sorry, I forgot you weren't invited."

Maeniel had to repress himself. He almost laughed. The wolf would have given the sharp bark wolves emit during play. It wasn't a laugh, but it was close.

Brutus lifted both eyebrows. "I heard about her, but the man is aware of my philosophical leanings and knows I don't approve of such . . . such lascivious entertainments. It is a profanation of the virtue shown by true gladiators. A woman, of all things. How can she possibly be primarius bellator, an outstanding fighter, and excel in hand-to-hand combat, as even prisoners and slaves do? They, at least, are men."

Dryas, the wolf thought. *They are speaking of Dryas.* "Where was this?" he asked.

Antony ignored the question entirely, and Brutus replied with disdainful hauteur, "A private matter. A disreputable exhibition of the charm that novelty has for weaker minds."

"Caesar seemed to be enjoying himself," Antony said, putting away his third dormouse.

"That's a measure of the degeneration of . . . the times," Brutus finished lamely.

Maeniel was enjoying himself. He understood Brutus had almost stumbled badly. Antony's eyes were glittering. He'd almost gotten Brutus to accuse the dictator of degeneracy.

"A woman, a woman gladiator," Manilius gushed. "How . . ."

Brutus and Antony both skewered him with their eyes.

"How . . . how different," he finished.

"Hardly a gladiator. Beastiarius is a better term," Brutus stated pedantically. "After all, she faced an animal, a boar. She is, I understand, said to be a Gaul. How apropos. A sacred animal to those barbarians, I believe."

"I don't know if it's sacred or not, but I know this one was big and vicious. She had at least one close call with it, maybe two. Killing an animal that size with a light spear is quite a feat. Ful—her owner, I mean, tells me she has a lion on tap for tomorrow," Antony said.

Maeniel considered wringing one or both men's necks. They

knew where Dryas was and wouldn't tell him, but Manilius and Felex exchanged a speaking glance.

"Oh, the naughty boy," Felex said. "And to think he was over here just last week for Aunt Myrtus' turbot in olive oil with capers, and didn't breathe a word about Fulvia's new acquisition."

"I see no one can keep secrets from the two of you." Antony laughed.

Maeniel saw satisfaction on the two handsome faces. Antony had just confirmed what both had already guessed.

"I can't see why anyone would try. The whole of Rome is talking," Manilius said. "She's said to be very beautiful, but, of course, you're both Caesar's intimates and only a few have been favored with a look at the woman. Why, she was brought to the house in a curtained litter and returned to . . . but then you know, don't you?" Manilius purred. "You must know where she's hidden."

Brutus smiled, Antony avoided his eyes, and Manilius and Felex looked disappointed.

Maeniel ate a dormouse. He'd eaten dormice before. These were spicy. He was trying to decide if the warm furry fresh ones were better than the oven-roasted variety and came to the conclusion that he enjoyed both. These were fatter than the wild variety and had been flavored with figs.

None of them knew where she was, that was obvious, but every one of them was hell-bent on finding out.

The dormice were gone. A beautiful blond girl arrived and carried off the empty tray. At least the person who carried off the tray was blond, beautiful, and looked like a girl, but the wolf informed him "she" was not female. Both Antony and Brutus appeared to think she was. Or, as a second alternative, it was possible they simply didn't care. *After all,* Maeniel thought darkly, *this is Rome.*

More wine made the rounds, the very famous Falernian. Maeniel found the legendary wine almost as good as its reputation promised.

"I am finding all this simply unbearable," Felex sighed. "Now, Antony, you are the only one here who has seen her. Is she as attractive as gossip paints her?"

"You're a friend of Lucius, I take it," Antony said.

Felex looked puzzled. "Yes, he shares our dinner every few weeks. A charming young man, though we haven't been able to interest him in . . ."

"Taking wives among your friends," Antony finished the sentence for him.

"Tut, tut," Manilius said. "Now, the ladies are respectably married, all of them, and only in search of a bit of adventure. Not every husband in Rome is able to keep his darling in a manner truly befitting her rank, and if they make a bit extra on the side . . ."

"Yes, but you know him better than anyone here. He must talk about his family to the two of you."

"Oh," Manilius said, taking a deep breath. "I see. I see where you're going." He tapped Felex on the wrist. "Dearest, think back. Our esteemed friend described a little exhibition bout that had a rather unpleasant, um, outcome, shall we say. But who was the exauctoratus, the man who was in charge of the ludus where the ladies trained?"

Felex frowned. "Give me a minute, just a minute. It's on the tip of my tongue." He snapped his fingers. "Of course, he's famous: Gordus, the great Gordus himself. That's where she's hidden. On the Campus Martius, in Gordus' place."

"Amazing," Brutus said. "Now, why would you want to know where she is?" The question was directed to Antony.

Antony grinned at Brutus, but didn't answer.

Both Manilius and Felex looked uneasy.

Just then the main course arrived. Pork, done over an open fire, with a hazelnut crust, stuffed with bread crumbs, honey, and the large mushrooms of the countryside.

Before he ate, Maeniel, with excuses to his hosts, had to go seek some relief in the latrine. He'd been drinking wine with the rest since the beginning of supper, and he wasn't used to large amounts of any intoxicant, not to mention the sheer volume of liquid.

When he was sure he was alone, he became a wolf and found he could hear the diners in the triclinium speaking to one another.

"You are to be warned," Brutus was saying to Antony. "Interfering with Caesar or anything the man wants is—"

"Don't be a fool," Antony interrupted. "Do you think I'd let an itch in my loins get between me and my loyalty to my own best interests, you—"

"Then why did you want to know where she's being kept?" Brutus interrupted in turn.

"Because no one would tell me." Antony sounded angry—really angry, not posturing.

"If you were not a man whose appetites lead him like a bullock with a ring through his nose," Brutus snarled, "then I think the dictator would find you more trustworthy."

"Trust! You Greek-loving sycophant. Who are you to talk about trust? If he'd been of Sulla's mind or even had any good common sense, he'd have ordered the lot of you Optimates to open your veins after the battle of Pharsalus and all that would be left of the lot of you would be ashes, wax, death masks, and unpleasant memories. The best thing Cato ever did was stick a sword into his stomach. But the rest of you . . . One by one, you came crawling to him, begging for mercy. And you got it . . . worse luck."

"Gentlemen, gentlemen." Manilius tried vainly to quiet the pair.

"I won't stay here to be insulted by a greedy, lecherous sot like you. A man whose only god is his belly, only brain is in his prick, and one who keeps faith only with a wine jar. Caesar's is the disgrace in that he trusts you, a fungus on the tree of the Republic, and that he's willing to turn to such a filthy object as yourself . . ."

Antony's bass rumble could be heard above Brutus' higher pitched orator's delivery.

"I told him, I told him when he pardoned the lot of you and welcomed your participation in setting up a new government, I told him he was cutting his own throat by doing it. Do you think he's a fool? Do you really believe I am? Do you think I'm deaf, dumb, and blind? When I get proof of what you and your senatorial friends are about, what you're planning, I'll have the lot of you smeared with pitch and hung on crosses to light the way the legions take when we ride to Parthia. You, your wives, and your children . . ."

There was another crash from the triclinium and an alarmed cry from Felex as Brutus stormed out of the house, calling for his litter to carry him home.

The wolf sat on the floor of the latrine. He could hear Antony laughing and Felex and Manilius fluttering around, making excuses for Brutus to Antony. Then he stood up a man and slipped his tunic back on. Without help, he could do nothing with the toga. It was unfamiliar to him and far too complex a garment for him to manage alone. Then he flushed the latrine with a bucket of water.

When he came out, the slaves were all standing in the kitchen, most with their ears against the triclinium wall. Several of them helped him with the toga and two produced a basin and a pitcher of warm water and helped him wash his hands.

"By the way." Antony sounded completely relaxed and calm. "Why did you invite me here tonight? Certainly not to quarrel with that constipated fool."

"No," Manilius replied. "Oh, what an evening. I'm completely undone. Everything is flown out of my head. My mind is a complete blank. Felex, my beloved, please . . ."

"Our guest, our guest!" Felex cried. "His banker is our banker and he did us the courtesy of informing us on how much this Maeniel, I believe his name is, has on deposit with him. We were amazed at the amount. Our friends told us he was a rich man, but we had no idea how rich."

"Well? Well," Antony said impatiently, "don't dance around so delicately. How much?"

"Six, no less than six golden talents."

"He's rich, all right. I'll talk to Caesar, see if we can't find a home for some of it. Trust me, he can't do any better than invest in our little foray into the east. The Gauls were only barbarians, but when Caesar began squeezing their balls, wagonload after wagonload of gold came back to Rome, and slaves by the thousands and tens of thousands. These Parthians are said to be even richer—" He broke off because Maeniel reentered the room.

Manilius and Felex explained that Brutus had been called away. Maeniel settled himself on the couch and accepted a portion of the roast, just now being carved.

Antony turned to Maeniel and smiled.

XXII

RYAS WAS RETURNED TO THE LUDUS IN THE litter that afternoon. She was brought back to the cell she'd been kept in the night before. Marcia must have been in, because the cell was swept and the bed, such as it was, made. She had contributed clean sheets and a blanket. Dryas still had the mantle, so she covered herself and went to sleep.

In the dark, she could feel the pain. He lingered with the dead here. She knew why he felt it. In the arena, he'd killed among his kin. He'd wanted to live. Three of the men he killed had been part of his life since he was a child and one was his brother. In the fragment of a dream, he knelt before her and asked her forgiveness. She couldn't give him that forgiveness.

She sat with him on a stone. It was dusk and the entertainment for the Roman crowd was over and it had been a magnificent event. A veritable river of blood had been shed. He was alive and everyone he had loved was dead. He took his sword to himself.

Dryas woke shivering.

Aquila was standing at the door of the cell. He held a lamp. "You screamed," he said. "You screamed and it was one of the worst screams I ever heard. What happened?"

"I don't remember screaming," Dryas said. "Nothing happened, but it's cold. Cold, and I must have been dreaming."

He unlocked the door, came in, and set the lamp down. The mantle had fallen from the bed and lay like a pool of ink on the floor. He picked it up and wrapped it around Dryas. He was clucking.

He's motherly, Dryas thought. *I was a mother, but never motherly. He could not possibly be a mother, but is.*

"Come," he said. "Marcia is roasting some chickens and we have dried dates and rosemary to stuff them with, and carrots on the side with bread and fresh cheese. I believe there are a few boiled eggs left over from lunch."

Dryas came quietly. It was late afternoon. Daylight glowed around them as they walked along the porch. As they passed the cell next to hers, she heard a loud thud and the door shook.

"Funny," Aquila said. "Gordus told me this tier was empty."

"No," Dryas replied quietly. "These cells aren't empty." As they passed the third, the door rattled even more loudly. They both saw it quiver and shake.

"That makes my skin crawl," Aquila said. "If it wasn't you who screamed, what did?"

Dryas didn't answer. They reached the stair leading down into the practice yard. There were no further disturbances.

They entered Marcia's kitchen and found Gordus seated at the head of the table. No reclining here. Marcia's chair was beside his and places were set for Dryas and Aquila. They sat.

Marcia was fixing a plate for someone who didn't come down to eat. Sliced chicken breast, gravy, a delicious-looking onion bread, date and rosemary stuffing, four or five slices of bread hot from the oven, a pot of fresh cheese with pepper, and a side of carrots with honey, oil, and cumin. She disappeared upstairs.

Gordus glared at Dryas and scowled, then cast the same look in Aquila's direction. Marcia returned and began serving her guests and ignoring her husband. His displeasure deepened, but only when Dryas and Aquila each had a plate with bread, chicken, stuffing, and carrots did she turn her attention to Gordus.

He muttered something under his breath.

She turned from a pot of beef barley soup she was dishing up for him and fixed him with a stare a Gorgon might envy. "Yes? I didn't quite catch that."

"How is he?" Gordus asked, sounding rather lame.

"Fine. Philo came today and pronounced the wound healing well. No thanks to you."

"He'd best thank his lucky stars I did no worse. The next time he has the temerity to face me, I'll cripple him permanently."

"Oh, you men," Marcia cried. "The boy loves you—"

"If he loved me, he wouldn't want to undertake a career in the arena. Tell me, woman, would you want him risking his life among those barbarian warriors, criminal reprobates, outcasts, murderers, and slaves? Men dead to all decency and faith, men who don't shrink from the worst possible—"

She smacked the bowl of soup down in front of him and whacked him over the head with the wooden ladle. "I married you, didn't I? And what were you when we first . . . met?" she finished a bit lamely.

"You knew what I was, but I . . . I—" he pointed to his chest. "—I raised myself from servitude, poverty, debt, and disgrace. Now I'm the owner of my own establishment. Eight, nine, ten times a year I fought, long after I had enough money to secure my discharge, so that you and the boy could be secure. Even now . . ." He favored Aquila and Dryas with another scowl. "If it weren't for the money, I'd tell my distinguished patroness to go straight to . . . for trying to turn my ludus into a brothel."

"Gordus!" Marcia shouted.

Dryas leaped to her feet.

Aquila did the same, hand on his sword hilt. "Sir, neither I nor the lady are here of our own will. She was, as many who have come here, captured in an honorable battle, and though as unfortunate as I believe you yourself once were, she has borne herself with discretion and courage since—"

"What are you?" Gordus snapped. "A soldier or an orator?"

"He's a Greek," Marcia said, as if it explained everything.

Dryas spoke. "I'm a guest here in your kitchen even if I am a prisoner in your cells. Politeness is incumbent on a guest even when the host is offensive. Please return me to my former accommodations if you think so little of me. I would not—"

"Please!" Gordus said, raising his hands to heaven in supplication. "I am sufficiently called to order." He rose and bowed to Dryas. "I apologize."

Dryas returned the bow and sat down.

He did the same in the direction of Aquila, who sat down, saying, "Actually I'd hate to miss your wife's roast chicken. And besides, those cells on the top floor are haunted."

Dryas seconded him. "Yes, they are."

Marcia, who was filling a plate for herself, turned her head toward her husband. "I told you so."

"I think it's Priscus," Gordus said.

"Yes." Dryas was consuming stuffing with a spoon. "He died in the cell I'm currently staying in."

"Gordus!" Marcia sounded outraged.

"How did you know?" Gordus sounded guilty.

"I am one who deals with the dead," Dryas said.

"What else do you do?" Marcia asked.

"I train young men for battle and I try to see the future when it is necessary."

Gordus looked somber when she said this.

"And yes," Dryas continued. "I know I am to fight tomorrow. I heard the women gossiping about it. What is it? A panther, a lion? I didn't understand the words they were using."

"It's not either one," Gordus said. "It—this thing—came from far away on the Silk Road. It's a cat or looks like one, though I never saw a cat like this before. It's big. Usually they use it to execute criminals, so it's a man-eater. And I don't think . . . I wish you were not at my table, young lady. I was hoping I wouldn't have to look at your face."

Dryas smiled, broke off a piece of bread, and dipped it in the chicken gravy.

"See," Aquila said. "Look at her. She's been like this since the beginning. That's why I'm here."

"Yes," Gordus said. "I see."

"Let me lay Priscus to rest," Dryas said. "He calls me to do my duty. He did wrong. He knows and cannot sleep. His kin went to the arena with him."

"Yes," Marcia said, "but what will they say when they see him?"

Dryas smiled again. "I am not a judge."

"Very well," Gordus said. "Then you will read my son's future."

"I will try," Dryas said. "I am not always successful, but I will try."

WITH ANTONY, MAENIEL WAS IN UNFAMILIAR TER-ritory. The leader of one wolf pack doesn't put his arm over the shoulder of another pack leader, breathe wine in his face, and suggest they visit a whorehouse.

"We'll find you something nice, eh?" Antony said. "This is the best place in Rome and that's saying something. Rome is the queen of cities, although Alexandria isn't bad. Reptens has everything, and he knows better than to try to fob off second-rate goods on my friends."

Maeniel bet he did. Antony had the charm of your average crocodile combined with the menace possessed by a cranky bear. It was more than obvious. Both Manilius' and Felex's knees rattled in his presence and they were probably not the only ones. Maeniel noticed that Antony's slaves were wary of him, extremely wary. But he did know where Dryas was, so when Antony sent home his litter bearers, they set out together into the night.

By then, it was growing late. The city was dark. The gateway to the two friends' house looked down on the Tiber. Mist was rising from the water. The air was cold and damp at the same time.

Maeniel took a deep breath. These crippled humans lived in a limited universe. From somewhere in the distance drifted the strangest variety of odors the wolf had ever encountered. But then the man knew—because Blaze had told him—they brought animals and humans from far away to entertain themselves by basically, yes, basically murdering them. This was probably what they planned for Dryas, Blaze had told him.

The gardens around and among the dwellings nearby had their own odor: pine, cypress, box, grass, and water, sleeping flowers and birds. Yes, both sleep. A rose at midnight has a different odor than a rose in the sun. As do humans. They in turn have a set of different smells when they sleep than either plants or animals do.

Yes, in his valley he would probably have killed by now and be at rest. He could gauge Antony's degree of drunkenness by his odor. The man shouldn't even have been walking around, much less stringing coherent sentences together, but Antony set off, singing a little ditty that interested the wolf because it contained a lot of the new words Amborux's guards had taught him to say. Antony was teaching him some new uses for perfectly respectable Latin words from everyday speech, comparing anatomical events to weapons, wells, caves, etc.

With the cool air and the night breeze, Antony's head began to clear and other impulses besides drunkenness moved him. He began to recount amorous adventures to Maeniel.

The wolf listened, wondering if the women would describe Antony in the same glowing terms as he did himself.

They reached a bridge over the Tiber. The guards recognized Antony. He greeted one.

"My lord," the man said, "it's very late, about the eighth hour. Out of the circle of light cast by the guardpost, all manner of unpleasant things happen in the Transtiber."

Antony laughed. "We're armed, aren't we?" He showed the guard the Spanish sword in his belt. "Now, my friend, my rich friend, what have you got?"

Maeniel pushed the toga aside. He wore the sword belt Mir had given him. The old man had given the sword to him before they left for the oppidum on the Rhine. Dryas pronounced it a magnificent gift.

I was going to put it into the well to rust to nothingness with the rest, but, properly speaking, it belongs to him, Maeniel remembered Mir's words.

The weapon and scabbard were very plain, but when drawn, the steel shimmered like a rainbow and seemed almost to glow with a light from within.

The legionnaire stepped forward, spear in hand. He was an impressive man, young, dark, with long hair streaming from under his helmet. He wore a muscle cuirass and a kilt of golden plates, bronze arm guards, and greaves.

"Draw that just a few inches," he ordered Maeniel.

Maeniel did.

"Gallic, and old!" he said. "Where did you get it?"

"It was a present from a friend."

"I wish I had friends like that," the legionnaire said. "You Gaul?"

"No," Maeniel said.

"Try not to stick it in anyone tonight."

"Not unless they deserve it," Maeniel replied.

"Yes. If they do, throw the remains into the river. Caesar doesn't like foreigners killing citizens, or wearing togas either. The garment is reserved for citizens and gentlemen of rank like Lord Antony here."

Maeniel smiled or rather bared his teeth. "I'll keep that in mind," he said quietly, and followed the still-singing Antony across the bridge.

Immediately, they entered a much poorer quarter. The houses were closer together and overlooked the streets menacingly. The smells were sharper and worse. Sewage, spilled wine, dirty bodies, fear, rotting food. Sex was a ripe reek in the air, almost a constant, as was blood, decay, and death. Away from the river, the street began to rise. Music flowed from behind closed and barred doors of taverns. Pipes wailed and moaned, drums pounded at various rhythms, and a waterfall of strings being plucked by expert fingers danced in the air.

Antony paused in the narrow street. Now he stank of more than wine. "Want to spill some blood?" he asked.

"I thought we were going to visit this Reptens? Remember? Girls?"

Antony gave a nasty chuckle. "My house is full of women. I crook my finger, tell one to share my couch, she drops her dress right then. No, I don't come here for women."

He turned and walked over to a door and pounded. "Let me in. I want wine. I'm thirsty. Let-me-in."

"Lord," the heavily accented voice behind the door whispered, "we don't cater to Romans."

Antony kicked the door open and felled the rather slight man behind it with one blow of his fist.

Another rushed out of the shadows holding a curved single-edged sword. Antony had his Spanish blade in his hand. He parried the first blow, then drove the heel of his hand into the base of his opponent's nose. There was a popping sound. The man's nose seemed to vanish into his face and a gush of blood poured from his mouth and nose, splashing on his tunic and then Antony's and then the floor.

Even in the dark, Maeniel saw something in the shape of a spider falling on him. He guessed where the neck was likely to be. Just as well because a knife sliced through the breast of his tunic, searching for his heart, even as he wrung whatever was in his hand. It was the neck or the spine somewhere. He felt the bones snap and one jumped through the skin and cut his fingers.

Antony laughed. "I hadn't hoped for entertainment this good."

Maeniel was amazed at his recklessness. He could only just see, and he was sure Antony must be blind. They were in a corridor. It jogged and ended in a courtyard hidden by the offset in the corridor.

"Are there any more of them?" Antony asked.

"No, not here," Maeniel answered. "But at the end of this hall . . . a lot."

"How many?"

"I can't tell."

"Well, if you know they're there, you should know how many." Antony sounded annoyed.

"I can smell them. A lot more than two hands."

"Over ten?" Antony whispered.

"Yes. Let's get out of here."

"Oh, no." Antony positively chortled. "This is the most fun I've had in weeks. I wouldn't leave here for anything in the world." He advanced down the hall.

Maeniel followed.

GORDUS BROUGHT DRYAS TO A PASSAGE UNDER the arena. It was dark. He preceded her, carrying a torch. Dryas followed along with Marcia. Aquila, with another torch, came last. The passage stank of cat urine and other barnyard smells of animals living in confined spaces. The passage ended in a larger stone-floored room that extended under the seats above. There were cages here. Most were empty. They were small and had wooden bars, but Gordus led them to the back, where a much larger cage with iron bars stood before them. It was also wheeled, so that it could be rolled along or drawn by mules. The length and breadth of the mass stretched out on the floor of the cage in the shadowy torchlight was astonishing.

Gordus shook one of the bars and shouted, "Wake up, Terror. Wake up and greet the lady."

The thing rose sluggishly, padded into the circle of light cast by the torches, lifted its immense head, bared its fangs, and roared.

Dryas stepped back a pace, drew in a deep breath, and let it out slowly. She glanced to one side and saw Aquila's face. His eyes were wide with horror. Marcia covered her mouth to stifle a shriek. Gordus seemed impassive.

Oddly enough, Marcia's and Aquila's reactions steadied Dryas. Her first impression was one of beauty. The bright orange hide with the black stripes was magnificent, as was the rippling grace of the muscles moving easily under the short coat. Yes, it was cat. The great head with its white ruff bent down as if to touch noses with her and two golden eyes, pupils contracted in the torchlight, studied her rather incuriously. Then it raised a paw to the bars and she saw the ends of the dreadful scimitar-shaped retractile claws. They extended themselves lazily from their furred sheaths and then slowly slid back in.

It turned, giving something on the cage floor a desultory nudge with its nose, and returned to the pile of straw bedding in the corner from whence it came.

Dryas looked closely at the thing the cat nudged, then drew back her lip, curled in disgust. It was the bloodless, mostly fleshless remains of a human arm, hand still attached, resting on the floor of the cage.

"It belongs to Antony," Gordus said. "They call the thing 'Terror' and it is. As I said, they use it for executions, and most of what it eats is human flesh because Antony throws it the remains of the men it kills. He says we pay even slaves something and Terror deserves his fee."

"I take it they won't throw me to it unarmed?" Dryas asked.

"No," Gordus said, "but then, how much good do you think a sword will do you? Even the men it executes are usually given something." He gestured toward the cage with the torch. "You can see even a sword and shield didn't do that one much good. I think that's what Antony enjoys. At least a few of them are game enough to make a fight of it, but they lose. Oh boy, how they lose."

"Thank you, Gordus," Aquila said. "I appreciate your solicitude. I really do."

Marcia wept quietly.

"I told you not to get involved," Gordus said angrily to his wife. "I told you you'd only get hurt. I told you to leave her alone."

"Hush!" Dryas embraced Marcia. "It's not the worst thing I've ever faced and trust me, death isn't the worst thing either." She kissed the older woman on the forehead. "Thank you for all your kindness. Now, let's go lay Priscus to rest. I promised him last night I would if I could."

They continued along the corridor under the arena until she sensed they were outside. Above, cut through the limestone rock, were light wells. By night, they showed only stars.

Then they came to the mortuary chapel.

"We don't invite outsiders here," Gordus said, placing his torch in a metal bracket on one side of the door. Taking his cue from Gordus, Aquila placed his on the other side.

The chamber they illuminated reminded Dryas of a banquet hall, and that was as it should be. There were four large stone couches grouped around a stone table in the center of the room. Along the walls there were benches, also stone, that could easily be covered by cushions to accommodate more people if necessary. The walls were whitewashed and painted. The dominant color was red, a brilliant flame-colored scarlet—the same color worn by the bride at a Roman wedding in a veil that draped her entire body.

At Dryas' feet was an opening into the floor where libations could be poured. It was surrounded by a shallow cone.

Dryas stepped around it and walked toward the table. Above it was a square light well leading up to the open and yes, there were the stars.

"Yes," she said. "This is entirely fitting." She could see it in her mind's eye by day. The light well illuminating the entire chamber with a soft glow, lighting the benches, stone couches, and even the table covered by cushions and cloths, filled with men reclining on the couches and seated or reclining on the benches around the walls. The head of the officiant would be covered, out of respect for the dead man, and he would make the offering into the libation hole. Bread, oil, meat, and wine given to the earth for their late comrade in arms that he might have food and drink as he undertook the long and sometimes difficult journey into eternity.

Then the rest would feast together, sharing among themselves the provisions brought in baskets to the tomb in thanksgiving that they each would have a little longer to take joy in the light, but knowing also that one day they must go, as this voyager had, on his last journey alone.

We love. Dryas remembered other loves. *We love and it is not eternal, but nonetheless, we love.*

"Even the damned need consolation in their damnation, so we built this," Gordus said. His voice echoed in the stone room. "Even the damned are due something from those who pronounce sentence, and they respect this. Woman, we will hold your rites here, if we must."

"Thank you," Dryas said. "I will endeavor to deserve it." Then she entered a small antechamber, the cubiculum of the gladiators where their ashes rested in niches in the walls. She found Priscus' amphora almost at once and carried it into the main room. It was perhaps a foot long, a smaller version of those used to hold wine. Marcia had a stand to hold the pointed amphora upright, and Gordus had oil and wine.

Aquila handed her his dagger without thinking twice about it. She used the metal hilt to break the seal on the amphora and the handle of one of Marcia's wooden spoons to grind the remaining bones to powder. Then she mixed oil and wine in the amphora with them and placed it in the stand on the table under the stars gleaming through the light well.

When she turned to set the piece of wood in her hand on fire, she saw that Gordus, Marcia, and Aquila had covered their heads with their mantles, so she covered hers, then pushed the wooden spoon handle into the torch flames. The oil caught and she returned to the table and dropped it into the ash-filled vessel.

For a moment, she was afraid it wouldn't catch, a bad omen, but then the oil flared and flames leaped from the top of the amphora. Up rose the smoke, carrying the oil, wine, and the perfumes used on Priscus' funeral pyre up, up toward the stars and the night sky beyond.

And she went with it. She saw Caesar, the author of so much misery. He sat alone, writing by the illumination of a five-branched bronze lamp cast in the form of six gladiators killing each other.

He looked up when the presence entered, as if he felt both minds bent on him.

He is old, she thought, *and this should have happened long ago.* She saw the hawk's profile, the hollow cheeks, the skin sagging at his throat, the everlastingly unquiet eyes probing the gloom in the corners of the room as if he willed himself to see them. See them and somehow prevent Priscus' escape from the greedy, controlling force that had destroyed so much and so many.

But they were moving, circling him, and even had he been able to see beyond time to where they were on the cusp of eternity, he would have had no more than a fleeting glimpse before they were in the night and gone.

Then Dryas found herself looking down at the stars. They were spread like an ocean before her. Burning in myriads before her, their thousand roads traced the pathless seas and the green continents, their movements certain and predictable from the beginning of time to its end and yet a vast mystery that she and her kind might never fully comprehend.

Then the presence that had been Priscus spread wider, the way smoke from a dying fire does when caught by the wind, vanishing, scattered into the air. He was gone, part of the ocean of stars.

Dryas awoke, back in the chamber, where she watched the amphora crack and fall. The dust, spun into a whirlwind by the air warmed by the fire, and pulling cold air from the dark chambers around her, rushed up the light well into the night beyond.

B EHIND THEM IN THE PASSAGE, SOMETHING moaned. Maeniel went cold, knowing it must be the first one. He was relatively sure the other two must be dead.

Antony didn't seem to hear. On they went. Once beyond the bend in the corridor the wolf could see and, being a wolf, see well. The courtyard was full of men. They were seated on low cushions around equally low tables. They watched a pair, girl and boy, dance. They were both naked. Maeniel and Antony stopped, brought up short by perhaps the most erotic thing they had ever seen.

At first, Maeniel thought they were children, but then on closer inspection, he saw they weren't that young. No, both were adults, though small. They were very brown with dark hair. The girl was standing center stage and the boy moved around, circling her, trying to draw close. Though standing still, her body undulated with an exquisite play of light and shadow as she slowly turned to remain face-to-face with her male partner. And though Maeniel had, at first, thought her naked, she was wearing something: snakes.

One serpent circled her waist like a belt and Maeniel saw as she and the boy slowly turned on the stage that it moved and was alive. She had two others, one on each arm, and each time the male drew near, she raised an arm and the serpent lifted its head, hissed, and the mouth opened as if to strike, and the boy drew back. He resumed his endless circling 'round and 'round the tantalizing she-creature and each time he tried to close with her, she threatened him again with the serpents, all to the whistling and skirling of the pipes and the heartbeat of the drum.

Braziers burned everywhere in the courtyard, keeping off the night chill. At Maeniel's side, Antony stood swaying, more than half-drunk, but Maeniel's head was clear. Still, something in the fumes from the braziers began clouding his mind, making it difficult to think and impossible to tear his eyes away from the couple in the center of the courtyard.

As he watched, slowly the dance changed. The girl began to bend her body back, legs apart until her shoulders were almost parallel to the ground. Then she rested the fingers of her right hand on the ground and the snake flowed down the arm to the earth, was caught by a handler, and placed in a basket. She did the same with the other until she was leaning back, supported on fingers and feet, her long hair brushing the ground, the snake at her waist the only one remaining.

Her partner, his body undulating as hers did, had a full erection and moved closer and closer to the wet red structures between her parted labia. Only the reptile encircling her waist held him off. It lifted its head and the mouth opened only a few inches from the male's phallic organ. Maeniel, feeling his blood heat, understood the point of the dance and he, like everyone else in the garden, was rigid, hypnotized by the young man's rhythmically swaying body. And the snake, seemingly equally caught up in the rhythms of the man's intensity, slowly lowered its head and, using her leg as a ramp, abandoned its post on her waist. The male dancer entered his kingdom, being welcomed through the gates in an intimate kiss by the woman's other lips.

Maeniel spun around, knowing they were there and knowing that they'd hesitated out of fear for the dancing couple's safety. He was right. There were at least a dozen men. He snatched the drunken Antony by the belt and dashed past the joined bodies of the dancers. It took every trick Dryas ever taught him to stay alive and moving until he reached a wooden gate in the wall. He used Antony's head as a battering ram to open it. Pushing the semiconscious man in front of him, he fled.

L UCIUS WAS AWAKENED BY A NIGHTMARE. AS IN ALL his worst dreams, it concerned some personal failure of his, but he wasn't sure what. Unlike most Romans, he had no servants sleeping in his room. At bedtime, he had dismissed Octus, propped himself with cushions, read till he became sleepy, then blown out the lamp.

Now, trying to remember his nightmare, he saw a light pass on the porch in front of his door and opened it, surprising Octus walking toward Philo's room, a few doors down. The servant turned and faced him.

"What's wrong?" Lucius asked.

"Nothing," Octus said, shielding the flickering lamp flame from the night wind. "I was going to call Cut Ear to accompany Philo. Calpurnia sent for him, a rather urgent summons. She's been taken badly with her usual problem. I hope our stirring around didn't awaken you."

"No, I had a nightmare. I saw your light." He lifted his mantle from a hook on the back of the door and wrapped it around himself. The dream was fading, but he still wanted company, though he couldn't put his finger on the source of his disquiet. The dream had shaken him badly and the fear lingered on into waking consciousness.

Yes, he understood what was gnawing at him: his fears for the woman who had fought the boar. Fulvia would tell him little. He assumed she was still smarting because of his treatment of Firminius and, though she didn't say or admit she knew, his visit to Caesar and what was certainly a payoff. She refused to communicate Dryas' whereabouts to him. Fulvia, shocked that her brother had shown any backbone at all, was probably looking for anything she could possibly use against him, something to push him back into what she considered his place among the relatives she either patronized or ignored.

As usual, he hadn't wanted to quarrel with her openly and couldn't think of any way to circumvent her at present, so he allowed himself to be fobbed off with promises of fuller explanations tomorrow.

She went to dine with Cleopatra and he fell asleep before she returned. Now, as he followed Octus to Philo's room, he was kicking himself for a fool. He should have forced the issue even if it meant airing their dirty linen in front of every single solitary person in the household, slave or free.

Fulvia didn't frighten him. Caesar did, and he remembered the Roman dictator's warning about interfering in her affairs.

Philo was up and dressed when Octus entered his room.

"What's wrong?" Lucius asked.

"This time? I don't know but—"

"When she snaps her fingers, you'd best run," Lucius finished the sentence for him.

Philo fixed his eyes on a point beyond Lucius' left shoulder and Octus turned toward the wall and studied its blank surface.

Lucius sighed and, seeing a folding camp chair open next to Philo's neatly made bed, sat down and rested his arms on the chair's arms. "Don't treat me like this," he said. "When have I ever . . ."

Philo raised his hand. "Please, our conclusions. The young lady you're worried about is probably at Gordus' ludus. Fulvia is his patron and the woman is more than likely there, locked in one of the cells. We were trying to think of some way to help her, but hadn't hit on anything yet.

"Now, the Lady Calpurnia is very ill. She is an extremely sick woman, though no one at present believes it, not even her husband. Many people with her problem, and other disorders similar to it, resort to the surgery I described, to relieve their symptoms—the headaches, visions, and odd optical phenomena that follow them all their lives."

"Wait a minute. Visions?" Lucius asked.

"She doesn't have just headaches," Octus said. "She becomes very ill. She was a friend of your mother's. Often, I accompanied your mother on visits to her house. At first, she will have a brief episode of . . ." He glanced in an uncertain way at Philo.

Philo nodded. "You might as well tell him."

"A brief episode of prescience, then for a few moments she's blind. She vomits and a terrible headache begins. The headaches are brief, but horribly painful. They seldom last more than a few hours, but those few hours are purest agony. In many ways, the prescience bothers her most. You see, she foresaw your poor mother's death. Months, no years before Silvia died, Calpurnia begged her to stop drinking. But the last time they met, I'm sure, from the Lady Calpurnia's manner, she knew it was already too late, as did I," he said sadly. "Now things are getting worse. She sees all manner of friends and acquaintances, about half the members of the noble families in Rome, covered in blood, dead on battlefields, on their funeral pyres. She is extremely frightened, and we believe she is right."

Lucius could see Octus was trembling. He gestured toward a low bench along the opposite wall from the bed. "Sit down. Please."

Octus didn't refuse. He sat.

Lucius turned to Philo. "What about you? If I ever saw a hard-headed, practical, skeptical Greek, it's you. How much credence do you attach to these visions? And, for heaven's sake, don't stand there towering over me. You sit down, too."

Philo sat on the bed. "At first, none. I've seen these type of disorders before and I reassured Octus, telling him I believed most of the sufferers were led astray by the disorder of their intellect during an attack, but I have begun, however reluctantly, to concur with Calpurnia's interpretation of her visions. They are in accord with what I know of Roman politics, Caesar himself, his unpleasant friend Antony, and the march of events.

"Tonight, for instance, at the house of your friends, Manilius and Felex, Antony picked a nasty quarrel with Brutus. We believe he did so at Caesar's orders. We think he, Caesar, feels it would be folly to leave Rome with such strong representation of the Optimate party holding seats in the Senate. We also feel that there is little we can do about it except to warn you to keep your head low. Antony is emerging as Caesar's sometime successor, but there is simply no way to know how long Caesar will last. And those betting against him have so often been wrong . . ."

"Yes," Lucius said. "You're sure the conspiracy among the Optimates, the best people, is real."

"Yes," Octus replied. "I wouldn't care for you to know my sources, but yes, it's real enough, though if they ever nerve themselves up to do more than talk . . ."

"I think," Philo said, "on balance the quarrel with Brutus was intended to force their hands. Make them bring their intentions to fruition, as it were."

"Yes, well put," Octus said.

"Nothing we can do?" Lucius asked.

"If you can think of anything, anything at all, please," Philo said.

Lucius shook his head. "Be careful, you two. I have been warned and won't take it lightly."

Philo rose. "Well, I must go. It doesn't do to make Cut Ear too impatient."

"No," Lucius said. "And you, Octus, go back to bed. Get some sleep. Wake me when you return, Philo, and we will go check on the ludus."

Octus conducted him back to his room and left.

Lucius stood looking at the plum. He still had it in a net bag hanging on the wall in his room. *It should be a prune by now,* he thought. Yet each time he examined it, the fruit remained plump and moist as ever. It grew no more ripe, it didn't rot, and it didn't dry. He reached out one finger and stroked it through the wide meshes of the bag.

Suddenly the room seemed to fill with cool air and the mixed fragrances of a garden of roses, lilies, lavender, and violets. He thought, *I want to go home,* but then wondered at his mind's drift. He was at home, wasn't he? Here, now. Wasn't he? *This is home. Here, isn't it?* But he had no answer to the question. He blew out the lamp and the fragrance of the garden remained, filling the darkness.

XXIII

THERE WAS NO PURSUIT. APPARENTLY THE PRO-
prietors of the establishment they'd just raided were satisfied
to let them go.

Maeniel found a quiet tavern still open for business and ushered
the staggering Antony into it. He seated his companion at a bench
along the wall and bought wine for them both.

He tasted his cup and found it good, only lightly watered. "Umm,"
he said, surprised.

The tavernkeeper, a muscular giant with one eye and multiple
scars, said, "You paid for good, I gave you good." Maeniel had indeed given him silver. "But you keep those swords in your belts and
don't start trouble in my place."

He took note of Maeniel's bloodstained clothing, his cut fingers
and skinned knuckles. Antony's head hadn't been the only thing to
come in contact with the courtyard door. He also took note of the
fact that the clothing under the dark mantles was expensive. "Gentry
like you and your friend think you can come down here and piss on
somebody else's doorstep and crap on the floors. You think we don't
notice you're a bunch of shithouse rats under the fancy clothes, but
we do. So watch yourself. You give me any trouble, I'll repay it with
interest. You got a guarantee."

Maeniel nodded and brought Antony his drink.

"You used my head to open the garden gate." Antony coupled the
word gate with an obscenity so vile that a man on the bench moved

363

down two seats simply on hearing it. Antony drank. "Not bad," he said, looking down into the cup.

"Yes," Maeniel said.

"You're pretty good. I never saw anyone move as fast as you did when it was time to get out."

"We killed two people in there. I was afraid," Maeniel told him quietly.

Antony managed to look indignant. "Of course I killed them. They blocked my way into the building. I'm a consul. A word from me and every filthy degenerate on this side of the river will be put to death, and I'll make sure the execution is lengthy and unpleasant for every one of them. Whatever suits my fancy—burning, crucifixion, sending them to the beasts or, as entertainment, forcing them to fight to the death in the arena."

"Well, I wouldn't throw my weight around in here. Being a consul won't do you any good if we're both found floating facedown in the Tiber. So drink up and let's get out of here. The proprietor isn't a friendly sort."

Antony made a suggestion about what the proprietor could do, but Maeniel noticed he did it in a low voice and no one was close by.

The wine seemed to sober him rather than otherwise. "I had my fun for the night," he said. "Now I have to visit Caesar. Want to come? Want to meet the most powerful man in the world?"

Maeniel nodded. He didn't trust himself to speak.

Antony laughed, rose, hitched up his belt, and gave the bar man the finger.

Maeniel, behind Antony, gave the proprietor a slight negative shake of his head as if to say, "Don't, it's not worth it," and mouthed, "He's drunk."

The bar man, not in the least intimidated, watched them both through the door and down the street.

Caesar's house was some distance from the Transtiber. Again the men of the Praetorian Cohort saluted Antony. If the condition of his clothing disturbed them, they didn't show it.

It was after midnight, about the ninth hour in Roman terms, when they reached Caesar's house. Behind the walls surrounding the villa there were lights and the sound of voices. Antony banged on the door and a soldier opened it.

"What's going on?" Antony asked him. "I know Caesar spends half the night at his desk, but usually everyone else goes to bed."

"The Lady Calpurnia was taken badly," the soldier said as he ushered them into the atrium. "Frightened the lights and liver out of me," he added in a low voice. "I don't know what she saw, but the expression on her face, and the scream she gave . . ."

He touched an amulet at his neck. "Isis protectoress. She came out of her room and spoke to the duty man. He said she asked him to fetch her physician. He came and sent for that Philo, but before she could get back to her room . . . I know. I was standing with him. She stared. Her face turned the color of bleached cloth and then she fell to the floor screaming and went into the worst fit I've ever seen in my . . . She looked just like a dog that's been fed poison. She has three physicians with her now."

"Women," Antony grunted. "You marry them, they fall apart."

"Want to use the baths?" the soldier asked him. "The two of you look like a smashup in a Circus chariot race."

"Bet your ass," Antony replied. "Caesar still with his wife?"

"Oh, for another half hour, likely, or an hour. She was taken bad."

Caesar's baths were surprisingly austere; the tepiderium in white and green, but very neat and comfortable. When they were finished bathing, Antony was conducted away to see Caesar and Maeniel was left to cool his heels in a dark garden.

The lights were going out in the house. From his spot in the peristyle, Maeniel saw the physicians leave, or people he assumed were the physicians. A soldier walking inside under the portico cut off access to the private rooms on that side of the house where Antony had gone.

Usually preternaturally alert, he wasn't aware of another presence until she settled herself beside him on the bench. "So," she whispered, "do you like my moon garden?"

He turned toward her. His reaction was similar to that of Lucius. Even in the half darkness, he was astounded by her beauty. Beauty is, and was always, an illusion. She wore a Greek chiton similar to the one she'd worn the night Lucius saw her. The very simple garment, only two rectangles of cloth sewn together at the sides and fastened with pins at the top, leaving room for the neck and head, suited her. She had a lush, graceful body and the draping showed it off to perfection. Her long hair was bound back with the vitta of a matron, white woolen fillets indicating she was a lady of rank.

As Maeniel watched, she crossed one leg over the other and let her hands drift up to clasp themselves at her knee. She was clothed in beauty, glowing from within.

"Moon garden," he repeated almost foolishly.

"Yes." She smiled and he felt honored. "I planted it to be seen by moonlight. These herbs take the color of the moon. She is nothing, the moon, or so the philosophers tell me. She shines only by the reflected light of the sun. But so beautiful, her silver mist. See." She touched one leaf, a lacy, deeply cut silver frond. "Artemesia, wormwood. There are three or four different kinds here. The priests use it to perfume the oil at sacrifice. I use it to perfume the oil in my bath. Behind it, rue."

This reminded Maeniel of the spatter marks made by water on trees and rocks in a light rain. Hundreds of tiny round leaves, they glowed almost blue in the fitful illumination allowed by the cloudy sky.

"Horehound," she said pointing to another. "It is eaten for the throat, and sage for the kitchen and for perfume." She broke a leaf and handed it to Maeniel.

Yes, to one of his kind such a fragrance was almost an intoxication. The wolf would never completely understand, but the man Dryas had led him to be was boundlessly appreciative.

"Those are some of the things here, and there are many others. See, there?" She pointed to some tall stalks rising from a rosette of silver leaves and bearing sprays of white flowers. "Valerian, an old friend, and the white poppy." Yes, he could see the delicate, papery flowers behind the valerian. "A new friend," she said.

"Your garden is very beautiful, but shouldn't you be in bed?" he asked.

She shook her head. "No, you don't know how hard it is to evade my maids. They watch me all the time now. Philo wants to send for a man in Alexandria whom he knows, a physician who will tap a hole in my skull. He says there's a chance my headaches and visions will go away, but I told him no. I won't let him. If Caesar goes to Parthia, I might take the risk then. I am vain and treasure my looks. I don't want to be bald and ugly. Besides, there's a great deal of risk. My sister had a similar thing done and she grew very ill and died. My mother did the same and she recovered from the surgery and, for a long time, the headaches and visions went away. But when she was old, they came back, but not so bad. She was a good age when she died and it was from lung congestion in winter, not the headaches."

"You love him so much?" Maeniel asked.

She laughed. It was a velvety sound, almost a caress, but then she quickly put her finger to her lips. "Oh, my, I must be quiet. Someone will hear. Oh, no, I don't love Caesar, but I'm afraid if I allow Philo's friend to come to Rome, Caesar might put off leaving for Parthia. If I do decide to let them make a hole in my head, I want to be alone to deal with the pain and the ugliness. I don't want him hanging over my bed. You see, he might explain things to me again. Since she came, the slithery Egyptian queen, he hasn't talked to me about affairs of state. I think he must tell her. I went to the Temple of Venus Gene-trex when he found her and made a thank offering of doves to the ruler of gods and men.

"I was so glad he found her. You see, the only thing I hate about it is that she gave him a child. I wouldn't, you see. He wanted children, even girls. He loved his daughter, Julia. Even his daughter. Many men don't care about daughters at all, but he welcomed her. Many husbands have daughters taken out and placed on the temple steps. The slave dealers come and pick the best and carry them off to be brought up for the brothel trade."

"What happens to the rest?" Maeniel asked, horrified. No one had told him of the common custom of abandoning unwanted children, so-called infant exposure.

"I suppose the dogs get them." She shivered. "A newborn is such a fragile thing. In the summer heat or winter cold, I don't imagine they live long. They are often left near the Temple of Vesta. One of the priestesses of the goddess told me many are abandoned at night and, by sunrise, most are dead. And unless picked up, the few that remain don't last till noon. In the summer the sun is too hot, in the winter the night too cold.

"But I never got pregnant and after a time . . . I was glad. Because . . . because he began to explain things to me and I'm afraid when he starts killing his enemies in the Senate, he'll explain to me why he had to do it. He's going to, you know—kill them. I've already seen it in my visions. I don't mind . . . he's explained to me why he had to do it. The philosophers I used to have read his dispatches from Gaul. They explained to me why he had to do those things—you know, sell so many into slavery. Torture their leaders when they wouldn't cooperate, when they wouldn't give him money.

"Yes, the philosophers explained it all and when he came back, he explained how Pompey got killed, how he had no part in it. I watched him and that bothered me when one of his legions revolted. They decimated it, you know, killed every tenth man, but there were so many. It didn't take long to behead them. Most cooperated.

"I couldn't understand why, but he and Antony explained it to me. They wanted to die quickly and die they must if the lot fell on them. That's how they're . . . chosen. By lot. If they fight back or try to run away, then they're hacked at until they die from blood loss or are eviscerated. They die of thirst or they smear pitch on them and burn them alive, so it's better if they kneel down and let the centurions cut off their heads. Sometimes the ones waiting even sharpen the swords the officers are using . . . So Antony says. They accept it as necessary to preserve discipline in the ranks.

"But when I was there, the corpses . . . got stacked so high . . . They stank so badly. You see, they couldn't burn them quickly enough and the ones who didn't behave, didn't accept death the way my husband says a proper soldier should, they screamed so . . . so . . .

"And, you know, soldiers don't have wives. It's against the law for them to have wives. I know Caesar and Antony explained that to me, too. But they have women like wives, not real wives . . . but women. And they had children . . . like real wives do. They begged and pleaded with the officers for their men's lives, but, of course, they were just making a nuisance of themselves and no one listened to them . . . I'm sorry. You are a guest. No doubt you understand these things—being a man—far better than I."

Maeniel shook his head as if trying to clear it. "No," he said. "I've never been a soldier and, after your description of a soldier's life, I'm not sure if I ever want to be one."

"Are you waiting to see my husband?" she asked politely, the way a child trying to accommodate a grownup does.

"No."

"Are you afraid of my husband?"

"No. I'm probably foolish not to be, but no, I'm not."

"How pleasant to be in the company of a man who isn't afraid of my husband and doesn't want anything from him. Why did you come to Rome, then? I can see you don't know much about us."

"I'm looking for a woman."

"Any woman or a particular one?"

"A particular one. Her name is Dryas."

"Oh, that one," she said flatly. "My maids told me about her. She fought a boar this morning and won, but tomorrow afternoon she will die. Antony wants to put her in the ring with Terror."

"Why? What is Terror?"

"Antony hates her. He lost money on her. He bet on the boar. He feels she made a fool of him."

"Why? By saving her own life?"

She shrugged. "There's no accounting for some of the things they do, but he bet Caesar she couldn't overcome Terror. Caesar bet Antony she could."

"What is Terror?"

"Terror is a big cat from India. They call it a tiger. It's like a lion. You've seen a lion?"

He had and said, "Yes."

"Terror's bigger. The hide is orange with black stripes. Antony uses it to execute criminals. Caesar says he wins either way. If she does kill Terror, he gets lots of gold from Antony. Even if she falls, the sight of her fighting heats his blood. You see, he wants to get Cleopatra pregnant again."

"He didn't explain that to you?" Maeniel asked.

She laughed. "No, no I overheard the maids talking about it when they thought the poppy drink Philo gave me had me knocked out. The poppy doesn't always put you to sleep, even though the person who's taken it looks like they are sleeping. Philo warned me about that and I've noticed that, like most of the things Philo says, it's true."

"Does he explain things to you, too?" Maeniel asked.

"No," she whispered, then looked back furtively over her shoulder. "Come," she said, rising. "I know a place where we can talk and not be disturbed. I was going there when I saw you and stopped to ask about the garden."

"From all I've heard, Caesar is a jealous husband. He said something about his wife being above suspicion."

She started to laugh again and then whispered, "Calpurnia, hush!

He's not jealous, not of me anymore. And that was just an excuse to divorce his wife and marry me. You see, he'd seen me at dinner in my father's house. He needed something to cement his relations with my father at that time and, having seen me, he decided he had to have me. But the only way he could get me to his bed was through marriage and he always gets what he wants. Both his friends and his enemies found that out about him long ago. Shh! Follow me."

He couldn't imagine where she could be going. This garden was a closed courtyard, a columned porch bordered on two sides. The rooms under the porch were the only entrances and exits. Two high stone walls edged at the top with caltrops bounded the back.

The moon shone brightly for a moment and, when it did, he saw a spot where the walls met and one shadowed the other. It seemed a very dark area, but two large rose trees in pots were set to each side where the fabric of the two walls met. They were beginning to bloom and a few white flowers could be picked out even in the darkness.

"Do you know," she said, pointing to the rose trees, "that you can make flowers from different plants? A gardener made these for me from the dog rose and the four seasons rose. They are very pale, almost white. The place I want to go is between them. Let me see if it's open." She strolled forward to the corner of the two walls and . . . vanished.

He reared back and then thought, *I have been among men too long. I know what this leads to.* He walked forward and the inky shadow swallowed him, too.

"Oh, good," he heard her say. "I've never shown this place to anyone before. I wondered if you could get in, too."

"Yes" was his low-voiced reply. "I have been here before." And he had, the time he chased the chamois from the cliff and fell. He had been near death. But he remembered the giant trees and, from above, the waterfall; the bracken and other ferns near the basin of the falls; then the mosses, growing on the inner rim. But, above all, he remembered the water seeming to glow in the dark.

It hadn't been quite night then, when he visited before, but it was now and when he looked up, the giant pines were open enough in their branching so that he could see the sky was clear and the half moon floated alone in solitary splendor. Yes, the water did glow. Its cold, blue-tinged fire appeared just after it began in the cliffs high above. The eye could follow the hazy moving light as it descended and then foamed in the basin at the foot where it yielded a glow so bright it was possible for him and Calpurnia to see each other. At this distance, over fifty feet away, the light was diminished, but still present as a background to the trees and rocks around them.

She shivered, rubbed her arms, and said, "I should have brought a wrap."

He pulled off his military mantle, removed the clean toga, and handed it to her. "Here," he said. "It's probably one of your husband's. Antony and I used his baths and the attendants gave us clean clothing."

"The baths! What happened that you had to bathe? Are you a friend of Antony's?" The second question was posed with some alarm.

He hastened to quiet her fears. "No, and after tonight I don't think I want to be one."

There were some rocks grouped near the brook that marked the overflow from the pool at the base of the falls. Despite the falling water's light when it became a stream winding off among the pines, all that remained of its fierce radiance were clusters of flashing pinpricks as it struck the pebbles and cobbles scattered along the stream bed, rather as if a thousand fireflies danced over the rippling water, driving off the shadows under the giant trees.

She chose a rock shaped like a chair and sat down. He picked out a formation of layered stone with a flat top.

He recounted all that had happened after they crossed the Tiber including the dance between the two young people in the garden.

"Mmm, I wish I'd seen that part," she said.

"I don't know about the morality of a pure wife . . ."

"Please," she said, pushing one hand out in a stop signal. "Whenever men begin to talk about morality, I know they mean sex. The things *they* do to each other—or, for that matter, to women—aren't important. *They* are never immoral, only other men or women.

"Look at Antony. He probably thinks what the two of you did when breaking in there was just fine, while the two young people are filthy degenerates. If he could find out who they were, he would punish them regardless of their motives. Possibly they were slaves forced to act out this play, but most likely they were only poor and needed the money they brought home for doing their little dance."

Maeniel didn't answer. Her statement seemed perfectly logical to him. "They seemed to be enjoying themselves," he said, "showing off their skills of serpent handling, balance, and dance. And, if it culminated in pleasure for them both, well, so much the better. But," he began to rise, "I'd best be going. It must be growing close to dawn and your servants will be looking for you."

"Oh, there is no time here." She sounded completely unconcerned. "I've come here when I couldn't bear the explanations, the headaches, the . . . I suppose despair is the word for it . . . any longer. I've remained several days, but whenever I've returned, no one has missed me. Neither sundial nor clepsydra—the water clock in the atrium—had changed. So, you see, no one will miss me."

"What drove you back?" he asked.

"Hunger, thirst. You see, I'm afraid to eat or drink here, especially that water." She pointed to the falls. "I drank some once; the poppy sometimes leaves me with a raging thirst. For a few hours, no one could see me, but I became visible in the baths and frightened my maids—they were in the tepiderium having a drinking party—almost to death. Living among slaves is a problem. Even my freedwomen don't trust me.

"Caesar has simply become too powerful. I am only a moon to his sun, but they will believe I have more power than I do when he begins to kill them. They will not come to my house, but their wives will, as the wives of those soldiers came to Caesar's officers, beseeching them to spare those they loved. So they will come to me and never believe I cannot help them. Never believe how little attention he pays to anything I say. They will never understand that my tears and pleas are as vain as theirs. He is inexorable. He will destroy them soon. I know, I have seen it in my visions and they never lie.

"So, you see, this place here is my only refuge. I won't let Philo's friend poke a hole in my skull. If the headaches and visions stop, I might lose this place. The pain is so terrible that, when Philo gives me the poppy drink, it opens the door. That's why, as soon as the drink tames the pain, I rise from my bed to seek this place. It is the pain that makes it possible for me to come here. Someday soon, when he starts killing them, I will come and drink deep at the pool and return no more." Then she sat silent and pensive in the cool darkness.

"You are very beautiful," he said quietly.

"Yes, and it's a misfortune. It drew his eye. But here in this place where no one can touch us, would you like to make love to me?"

"Yes. I was afraid to ask."

"So was I," she said, rising. She dropped the toga, then undid the shoulder pins on the chiton and the soft garment fell with a whisper to the ground among the ferns.

He spread the dark mantle on the ground. She looked up, her arms covering her breasts modestly. "While no time passes there," she said, "it passes here. The moon is low and I think it will soon be dawn."

He embraced her and, even in the darkness, his lips found hers. Then he knew that whatever women he had known or would know, none would ever bring him such grace and gentleness. Later, lying together, they watched the sunrise over a forest of pines that stretched away toward the horizon.

She said, "Go now," and kissed him good-bye near the pool. Before he reached the portal, he turned and tried to get one last look, but she was lost in the fiery light of the rising sun.

Then he found himself in the garden and, without looking back, strode through the atrium toward the entrance of the house. He retrieved his sword from the guard, who sent two soldiers to escort him to the house of Manilius and Felex.

A short time later Clea, Calpurnia's freedwoman, checked and found Calpurnia's couch empty and the maids asleep. She didn't awaken them. Their mistress seldom went far. Clea found her sitting in the garden on the bench, her head thrown back, sleeping in the last pale light of the setting moon.

She returned Calpurnia to her room, removed her dress, and combed out her long hair. While slipping the carmisa nightgown over her head, she noticed something she'd missed, a tuft of pine needles in her hair. She gently removed it and eased her lady down on the bed and covered her.

While shaking out the silk chiton, a dried fern frond fell to the floor. Clea carried the frond and the pine needles to a brazier glowing in the corner and dropped them on the coals, then touched an amulet she wore at her neck. She was a devotee of an Eastern goddess, a valued initiate into her mysteries.

She had been a slave welcomed by the other initiates because such worshipers were a valuable investment. Those who began as slaves often rose to great importance and affluence since they were trusted by their powerful owners. This was true of Clea. Calpurnia trusted her and she would never betray that trust.

For a second, the fragrance of pine filled the cubiculum as the brown needles glowed red and fell to dust. It wasn't the first time. Clea had found similar things caught in her lady's dresses and hair. It had happened before and she knew there were neither pines nor ferns anywhere in the garden.

PHILO WENT TO SEE LUCIUS WHEN HE RETURNED from Caesar's house. It was chilly and very near dawn. He looked in on Octus first and found the older man sleeping. Alia welcomed Cut Ear back. He was grumbling, but she put him to bed anyway.

Philo found Lucius pacing the floor, nervous, but by no means would he admit it.

"Do you think I should bathe?" Lucius asked.

"Yes."

"Why?"

"With women, bathing is better."

"This doesn't have anything to do with her," Lucius stated loftily.

"Oh?"

"No!"

"Bathe!" Philo insisted.

"No perfume. No pomade!"

"Yes, fine. Bathe."

"Shave?"

"With women, shaving is better."

"I hate to wake Octus. I'll shave myself."

"No, better you should wake Octus than cut your throat. Besides, he might feel it deeply should you not call on him when in need of his specialized services. He would be hurt. Deeply hurt."

"His hands shake sometimes."

"That's because he's afraid of your sister. He's not in the least nervous about you."

"I'm not sure that is a compliment. In fact, looked at in certain ways, it's not. Caesar said—"

"Do not quote Caesar to me." It was Philo's turn to be lofty. "Should you begin to do so on any regular basis, I would be forced to return to Greece. Almost anything can be observed from a variety of viewpoints. Some of which will make the most virtuous and laudatory actions look, at best, stupid and, at worst, meretricious and deceptive.

"He does not fear you because you, as he and almost everyone in the household has observed, can be irritable, depressed, or angry, but you are almost never spiteful and never, by any means, cruel. Your sister is vengeful, spiteful, and extremely cruel.

"Now, bathe, shave, and dress. The woman is at Gordus' establishment. She was seen there a short time ago and it is widely known some sort of entertainment using her . . . talents is planned for this afternoon in the arena at the gladiatorial school. A private showing for Caesar, Antony, and several hundred of his senatorial and knightly friends."

"Oh, no!"

"Yes. I'll go call Octus."

"Cut Ear?"

"No, let him sleep or whatever he and Alia do. You may need him later in the day."

A half hour later, Lucius and Philo left for the ludus.

D RYAS WAS AWAKENED ABOUT AN HOUR LATER BY Aquila. He handed her a cup of warm beverage through the open barred door of the cell.

"Posca?" she asked.

"No, Marcia put this together. I don't know what's in it. You can get sick on posca. I did when I was in the legions. But you can't get drunk. I know, I tried."

"That's probably how you got sick," Dryas said.

"Yes, it's vile."

Dryas tried Marcia's mixture, white wine with a few herbs steeped in it. She tasted mint and wintergreen, gently warmed. "Nice," she said.

"Almost anything's better than posca, but I don't know if you should be in a good mood when you go down to greet this . . . Lucius."

"Who is he?"

Aquila looked as if he didn't know what to say. He shifted his feet and bit his lip. "Probably . . . probably he's your real owner."

Dryas looked up at him. "And?"

"He is the brother of Fulvia, the woman who paid me to capture you."

"What does he want?"

"I don't know, but just in case he wants what I think he does . . ." Aquila extended one of the daggers he'd taken away from Dryas when he searched her.

She pushed it away. "No, the time for such things is past. I can't take that way out."

"Why not?"

"Your safety, Gordus and Marcia's safety; and they have a son and married daughter with children of her own. I have my honor and honor will not allow me to let others pay the price of my irresponsibility. So, please, close the door and let me dress."

Aquila shook his head and withdrew.

Dryas did dress. The cell was a lot more comfortable. Marcia had changed the bedding, burning the tick and sheets where Priscus died, and she'd found clothes for Dryas. A clean tunic—carefully sewn from used linen, it is true, but then dyed a warm brown ocher or rust. A palla made of finer wool—yes, often washed and somewhat worn, but mended and also redyed a dark blue and decorated with braid at the edges—and a pair of sandals, laced at the center with finely cut leather uppers, and worn with woolen socks.

Dryas braided her hair around the spiked copper crown as Fulvia's maids did yesterday. She wrapped the palla more tightly around herself and then told Aquila through the door, "I'm ready."

He kicked the door open. His face was stern and his color was high. He jerked the palla away from Dryas and manacled her hands behind her back, then replaced the palla over her shoulders and shoved her forward.

She walked ahead of him down the stairs. On the second flight, she stumbled briefly. He snatched at her arm, realizing she was in danger; with her hands chained she wouldn't be able to catch herself if she fell. But he didn't take off the chains. Instead, he kept hold of her arm until they reached the bottom where Marcia waited.

"Aquila, you stop that right now! If you're going to play the fool, go to your farm in Campagna."

"She won't even defend herself!" He undid the manacles.

Marcia embraced Dryas and helped her rewrap the palla. Marcia looked sad. "No, she won't. I didn't either. Sometimes it isn't safe for a woman to think about herself. I had my mother and a younger sister to consider. She has us."

"Of all the evil in this ugly thing, this is the worst meanness of all." Aquila's fists were clenched. "He wants to get to her before she faces . . . that . . . that . . . thing."

"Well," Dryas said, "I can't think I'll be much use to him after."

Marcia began to laugh. She hugged Dryas again and then started to wipe away tears. "After it was over, my mother helped me clean myself. There was some blood. I was only fourteen. I shrugged, looked at her dry-eyed, and said he wasn't much. That's true enough, he wasn't, but it hurt all the same. So I lied, but it was a good lie and I'm glad I said it. And when it's over, I have some porridge, bacon, and fresh-baked bread and you, Dryas, can sleep on the cot off the kitchen. Both Gordus and my boy are gone. I'll welcome the company until this afternoon."

"Well, I'm not fourteen and he's not going to think I enjoyed it," Dryas replied darkly. "I may not resist, but there are other ways to show how you feel and I won't spare him those. So warm the porridge; I'll return shortly."

This time, Aquila led the way.

WHEN MARCIA TURNED TO ENTER HER KITCHEN, she saw the dog. He was one of the biggest she'd ever seen. "More wolf than dog," she said under her breath. She was a bold woman. Some of the men confined in the ludus—not all, mind you, she would have said, but some—were more dangerous than any wolf.

So she had a smaller version of the old legionnaire's sword in a sheath near the door. A dreadful weapon, it could easily be used to decapitate a human or animal with one blow. The sure weight of the heavy, crooked, single-edged blade made it formidable even in the hands of a woman. She drew it from its sheath and poised herself in front of the dog.

But he seemed to have heard her comment. He sidled toward her, creeping, tail between his legs, tongue lolling, with an ingratiating whine.

She sighed and shook her head. "Another hungry one. All right, stay there." She threw odds and ends of discarded food in a pail near the grill. Some were stale, but the dog would probably be grateful.

She picked up the pail, turned, and found herself facing a large man not wearing much in the way of clothing.

With one hand, he shielded a strategic area with a somewhat less than adequate dishtowel. The other was extended in a gesture of supplication. He addressed her in formal Latin. "My apologies for disturbing you at such an early hour. If you could spare a piece of cloth a little larger than this, I also would like to see Dryas, and if you could see your way clear to some porridge and a little of that bacon, I would be most appreciative. You see, I've been on foot all night and—"

He had to break off and finish his speech a little later, because just about then, Marcia fainted.

"I'M NOT ABOUT TO MAKE IT EASY FOR HIM," Aquila snarled. He led Dryas to a chamber with one door opening into the arena. It was covered by a metal grating. The other end of the room was closed by a similar grating. He locked her in. The ceiling was curved. The gratings on either end suggested animals and the room smelled of cat piss and dung though the floor was clean, freshly swept. No doubt ready for the tiger.

Dryas composed herself and waited. Aquila and two men appeared in the corridor in the passage under the seats. She recognized both of them at once. One was the physician who treated her bruised ankle, the other the bath attendant who'd been with him. Only the bath attendant was dressed a whole lot better today.

Dryas walked toward them, then paused at the bars. A torch burned in the corridor. She gave both Lucius and Philo a look of deep disapproval. "Why the charade?" Her eyes looked directly into Lucius', as they had the day before. "Why didn't you simply identify yourself at once?"

Lucius found his mouth dry and he had no answer. He looked at Philo and Aquila. They were no help at all. Aquila's face was savage. Philo's expression more or less said, "You're on your own."

"Because . . . because," Lucius stammered, "anything, anything, even pity, would have been better than seeing hatred in your eyes."

Dryas smiled. "Why should it matter to you what I think of you?"

"Because I don't . . . What do I say? Normally a man doesn't have to do this for himself . . . not without help."

Dryas extended her hand through the grating and took his. He lifted it to his lips.

"Now, tell me what it is you want," she said quietly.

"What did you think I wanted?"

"To lie with me, with or without my permission," she answered.

"No." He shook his head and clasped her hand in both of his. "I came here to ask you to marry me."

Aquila looked as if he thought his ears had gone back on him. Even Philo seemed shocked.

But Dryas' eyes widened in horror. She let go of the mantle and it fell unregarded to the floor. She stretched out her left hand through the grating to touch his cheek. "Either this is the worst of deceptions," she whispered to him, "or you don't know!"

His direct gaze belied the very idea of deception. They stood only inches apart. He placed his right hand over her hand on his cheek. "What don't I know?" His face suddenly paled with anger and fear and then, in a voice not even Philo knew he possessed, he roared out the question, "What don't I know?"

XXIV

To GORDUS, THE DAY SEEMED BEAUTIFUL. HE and Martinus were walking along near the Forum. The sky was a fair warm blue with a haze of very high, white clouds that did nothing to dim the bright, warm sunlight.

"Do you think we will get to see Caesar?" Martinus asked.

"I don't know," Gordus said. "He has so many petitioners now that I can't think we'll be successful and, even if we do get in to see him, he might not grant our request."

"Surely he has some sense of fairness," Martinus said.

"My son, I wouldn't put my request to him in that particular way. In fact, I wouldn't put any request to a man as powerful as he is in that way."

"No," Martinus said. "I'll let you do the talking. I'm not good at explaining things and I'd probably just get tongue-tied and make a fool of myself."

"What did she tell you?" Gordus asked. "How did she read your fortune?"

Martinus looked pensive. "I don't know how to explain it. It just didn't seem like much, at least not to me, not at first."

"So?" Gordus asked.

"Very well."

They dodged a seller of stuffed bread—the man had his stove on his head—and then had to make their way around an aged soldier selling flowers, of all things. He sat on the steps to the Temple of Vesta with baskets of roses, lilies, violets, and narcissus scattered around him, along with pots of herbs for windows, balconies, and courtyards: sage, basil, one kind of sweet marjoram, and even long stalks of dill.

"She asked for her sword. Aquila went and got it for her and she drew it and placed my hand on the blade. Then, after a few seconds, she lifted it off. There were dark marks where my fingers touched it. She said I had to know, but you were right. I am not for the sword. I was sad because I honor you and I wanted to be as much . . ."

They paused because they were near the Temple of Venus and the dovecote in her shrine covered the paving with birds.

An old woman tried to sell them a small bag of grain. "Feed her doves," she said, "and you honor her. She has made you fair of face, young man, and must love you. Now ask her to make you lucky in love."

Martinus smiled and Gordus thought, *He is handsome. Light brown hair, so very fine and soft the wind ruffles it like dust, large, hazel eyes fringed by long, brown lashes, a beautiful smile coupled with a tall, strong body endowed with the grace of youth. If I saw him in the arena with a sword in his hand, I would die. My spirit cut from its fleshy root would lie down in darkness and never rise again. Thank you, Dryas. Thank you.*

Martinus paid the old woman a copper and took the bag of grain from her hands. Then he and his father sat on the temple steps and fed the doves. They were across the street from the awnings striped in red and yellow that marked the house of Caesar.

"As I said," Martinus continued, "I wanted to be as much like you as I could, but she said, 'No, the steel rejects you. Look at the marks you left on the sword.' Then she put her hand on my chest and closed her eyes. She frowned at first and then smiled and, for a long time, she was still. Then she gestured at the doorway. A girl walked through it. She was beautiful, the most beautiful woman I've ever seen. She smiled at me and then vanished. And, after that, I heard the laughter of children. Then Dryas asked me if I wanted the music."

"What music?" Gordus asked.

"The music I hear all the time," Martinus answered. "I never remember not being able to hear it. I sang in my crib and while I crawled around the kitchen floor behind Mother. Sometimes, when I hear a good bit, I memorize it and teach it to my friends. I can't imagine it ever going away, but I never told you or Mother about it because I was afraid you'd laugh at me."

"No," Gordus said. "No." His gray eyes were luminous with love.

"No, I would never laugh at you. Not about anything important. So, what about the music?"

"She said that if I went on with my training as a gladiator, when I fought my first match, the music would leave me forever. I said I'd rather be dead than live without it. She answered yes, she knew, but that's why she kept her hand on my chest so long. It was so beautiful and she was listening, too. She told me the girl at the door would be my wife and we would live a long, happy life. I would have many children and I would love them all and they would love me in return. The music would follow me all the days of my life and through the lifetimes of my descendants until the end of time. But not if I took the path of the sword.

"I wouldn't ever want to do anything to make the music end. I couldn't live without it."

Or I without you, Gordus thought. "We will think of something," he promised.

Burdened slaves trotting past, carrying a very expensive litter with ivory-and-gold poles and purple curtains, sent the doves into flight with soft piping cries and a whir of wings. The cloth bag was empty.

Gordus rose. "We will go to see Caesar."

To his surprise, they were admitted only about an hour after they arrived.

Caesar greeted them politely. "Yes," he said, "and I believe I saw the young man at the exhibition bout you gave." Martinus' arm was still bandaged. "He's not the swordsman his father is, but then that's hardly to be expected. Will you follow his profession?"

Martinus blushed and stammered. "No, I don't think so."

"Probably just as well," Caesar said.

"Yes," Gordus said. "My lord, it's about the woman at my ludus that I came."

Caesar had turned away from his desk to greet them. He looked back and cast an impatient eye at the parchments and papyrus piled there. "Yes, what about the woman? I've invited some people this evening to see her fight. Are she and what is it, a lion or whatever kind of cat, ready?"

"It's called a tiger, Caesar, and I came because I feel placing her in the arena with such a savage creature is nothing short of murder."

Caesar's eyebrows rose. He waved away the two secretaries still in attendance and rested his hands on his knees. "Strong words," he commented.

"I don't think so," Gordus said. "The young lady is no criminal. As far as I can tell, she has never been convicted by any Roman court of a crime whose penalty is damnatio ad bestias, that is, execution by being thrown to wild animals."

"I know what it is," Caesar said. "Don't presume to instruct me in law."

"No," Gordus said. "I would never presume to take any such line, but I would like her status clarified for me. The soldier, Aquila, tells me she was captured in an attack on a town ruled by an ally of ours called Cynewolf and carried off against her will to Rome."

"You have a sensitive conscience, Gordus, for a lanista and an ex-gladiator." Caesar rose and walked to the side of his office looking into the garden. There was a stiff breeze and the long linen curtains flapped and the rings rattled.

"Gordus," Caesar said, turning toward him, "I know what the young lady, as you describe her, is and I can tell you more about her." He reached up self-consciously and smoothed his balding head. "I can tell you more about her than she cares to tell you about herself.

"She is a Caledoni. They are the British tribe at the farthest remove from us. They live in the highest mountains, farthest away from the rest and, even among the fierce and wild tribes of Britain, the White Isle, they are considered the fiercest, the most savage, and the most lawless. They have no gods and worship only the dead who have gone before them. They feel all men are created equal and women, also, because they train their women in the arts of war and slaughter. And their daughters as they do their sons, teaching them to ride, hunt, and wield sword and shield as well as men.

"They account one man as good as another and will accept no curb on their passions, are moved as easily to laughter as to tears, to wrath as to terror. They are without consistency or control and are as wild and untamable as the wolves of their valleys or the eagles floating among the crags where they make their homes. The arena memorializes our victories. When I'm done with Parthia, I will return to the White Isle again.

"I would like to see this woman of the Caledonians fight. We cornered one of their she-wolves in Britain but we never knew she was a woman until she was dead. When I do return, I will capture as many more of her people as I can and bring them here, men and women, to fight and die for our entertainment. As this woman does for me now. Do you understand, Gordus?"

"Yes," Gordus said. "I believe I do, but will you at least let me allow her to have her own weapons to fight this Terror so she stands some chance? That's what they call the beast, Terror. The mail the Lady Fulvia wants to dress her in is weaker than most cloth. Let me give her some effective armor."

"Gordus, you weary me and that's not good for you or the lady. Next you will want me to send a cohort of soldiers into the ring with your fighter, to protect her against any harm that might befall her."

"You don't want her killed in the first few seconds, do you?"

"No," Caesar said slowly. "I would like her to survive, if at all possible."

"I am an experienced man in these matters," Gordus said. "Let me arm her."

"The exhibition of her body is part of the spectacle," Caesar objected.

Gordus swallowed. "She will look wonderful, I promise."

When they were out in the street again, to Gordus the sun didn't seem so bright or the day so beautiful as it had been.

"You failed," Martinus said.

"No, boy, no. Half a loaf is better than none, especially if you're dealing with men like Caesar. I didn't hope to get that much, but he did overrule that Basilian bitch who would have gotten our little priestess killed in under a minute. I'll do the best I can for her. She's formidable. He's right about that."

"Are any of those other things he said true? What does that stuff mean about memorializing our victories?"

"The other things, probably not. Does this Dryas seem to you to lack self-control or courage?"

"No," Martinus said. "Aquila told me she was some sort of judge among her people, which means they have laws, at least."

Gordus nodded. "As for memorializing our victories, he made me feel like spitting in his face. My father farmed his land in Campagna until he was chased out by soldiers when our land was expropriated by the Senate to settle some of Pompey's veterans. I'm as much a Latin as any member of the Senate. My grandfather supported the Gracchi when they tried to make land reforms. My father was a tenant farmer at Capua when the Campagnian law was passed, by Caesar no less, leaving our family completely destitute.

"So we went to Rome and tried to live on the grain dole. Bread and circuses, they say, have been the ruination of the Roman people, but I think my father and grandfather would rather have had their farms than any amount of panum and circuses. I went before the lanista at Capua, yes, the same ludus Spartacus came from later, and swore to be beaten by whips, burned by hot irons, or killed by steel if I disobeyed my master. I did it for money, money to try to keep my mother and younger brothers from poverty, but I never wanted such a life for you."

"Mother?" Martinus asked.

"Be quiet. What happens to a man may be spoken of openly, but women . . . that's different. I will say this: we played together as children and she lived only two streets away in the same village, and her blood is as Latin as is my own. But in the arena, I fought as a Gaul sometimes and, at others, as Samnite and once or twice as Thracian— all peoples defeated by the legions.

"Still, I can't see what Caesar thinks he's memorializing unless it's reducing our own people to slavery in a headlong quest for power. He's managed to do that all right. Still want to be a swordsman and shed your blood and that of your companions as 'entertainment' for men like him?"

"I'd rather have the music," Martinus said.

THE RESULTING FIGHT WAS PROBABLY BETTER than the one with the tiger, but not so public. Philo, who got a chance to watch, considered it one of the best rafter-lifting, window-rattling, knockdown, drag-out family fights he'd ever seen.

Lucius and Dryas were made for each other. On very slight acquaintance they stood, iron grating between them, and slugged it out, toe to toe, at the top of their lungs.

Lucius was all for taking possession at once and wanted Dryas to run away with him. *Now!* They would take ship from Ostia. *Now!*

And leave his friends and family to face the not-inconsiderable wrath of Caesar and Fulvia, not to mention Antony? Was he out of his *mind?* She had her *honor* and honor demanded certain types of behavior. Didn't he understand *that?*

What kind of honor could a woman and barbarian have?

It was just as well the iron grating was there, Philo thought. Not for Dryas' sake, but for Lucius'.

Dryas looked as if she might just kill him if she could get her hands on her suitor. In fact, if Aquila would bring her sword, she might do just that!

How dare she get him into such a condition that he was about to be driven mad for love of *her*!

His mental aberrations were hardly *her fault*! Had he not come from a nation of men so vain, arrogant, selfish, and heedlessly greedy that they could not be trusted to leave even their friends alone, she would not be . . .

At this point, Maeniel, Marcia, Gordus, and Martinus arrived. Lucius found himself seriously outvoted. He didn't take it quietly. He went down fighting, but he didn't get much help. Even Philo felt he had certainly taken serious, reckless, and, possibly, semipermanent leave of his senses.

Marriage! He was proposing marriage to a wild barbarian warrior woman. There were any number of proposals, not to mention propositions, the very practical Greeks of Philo's acquaintance might have made to this magnificent Amazon, but marriage was not one of them.

And the same went for Aquila, Gordus, and even Martinus. Aquila's mind inclined in that direction, but he could not, with any true conviction, see Dryas feeding chickens and pigs on a farm in Campagna. Or, for that matter, dwelling in the house of a rich Roman aristocrat like Lucius. She would cause a sensation, even if he retired to a villa in the country with her. The majority of Romans, patricians or even knightly, would find a desire even to cohabit with Dryas not only eccentric, but absolutely insane.

But Lucius was serious and it was obvious that he was because Maeniel and Gordus were tying his hands behind his back. Gordus looped a rope around his neck and prodded him at spear point up to the house.

With shaking hands, Dryas picked up her mantle from the floor of the cage, brushed the dust off, and joined, then passed, the procession heading upstairs to breakfast.

The kitchen was as warm as the area under the arena had been cold. Dryas walked over to the charcoal grate and began to warm her hands in the heat waves rising from the fire.

Three covered dishes rested on the table. Yes, Marcia had promised porridge, bacon, and bread.

Gordus marched Lucius into the kitchen, closely followed by Maeniel, Marcia, Aquila, Martinus, and Philo.

The table was in a corner. There were benches against the wall and on two sides. They sat him down on one of the benches against the wall, Gordus on one side, Maeniel on the other.

Marcia served up her version of posca, a much nicer one than Dryas had tasted at Fulvia's villa. In a few minutes they all had a cup, except Lucius, whose hands were tied.

For a few moments, everyone simply drank. Then Dryas, still at her position near the grate, turned to Lucius. "You say you want to marry me?"

"Yes," he answered defiantly. "I do."

"Dear lady—" Philo started to interject.

"Don't call me 'dear.' I'm not a domina. That implies slaves to order around and I don't own any and don't interrupt me when I'm speaking."

"Is she always like this?" Aquila asked Maeniel.

"Most of the time," he answered philosophically.

Dryas gave them a dark look to shut them up and looked again at Lucius. "Very well. Do you realize what marriage implies among my people?"

Lucius had to admit no.

"The man I marry stands a chance of becoming a king of the Caledoni. In order to make a match with me, you would have to face the ordeals involved in standing for kingship, and even if you fail, you would still become one of the ruler's companions."

"Caesar said you had no kings," Martinus said.

"Caesar is wrong," Dryas answered. "The king is a leader in war and a judge in peace. In a way, we, like the Romans, are suspicious of rulers and we, like you, prefer to order our own lives. Women like me live to give kings to the people, either by birth or marriage. Our bodies are not our own to dispose of. This is why I am asking these questions. If you truly want to make a match with me, I am bound to accept."

There was general consternation in the kitchen.

Philo threw his mantle over his head in a gesture of grief.

Marcia said, "What!" and hit the wooden table with the ladle she was dishing up porridge with. Aquila sat openmouthed and Maeniel, who felt most of the members of his shared species were already mad, took the news with complacency.

Martinus, alone, asked the salient question. "Why?"

"Because he can bring them Roman language, military arts, habits, knowledge, methods of fighting, and, last but not least, technical skills. There are many things done in Rome that they would be wise to learn," Dryas finished.

"Yes," Martinus said. "Caesar said that when he's conquered Parthia, he will send his men to the White Isle and they would bring back some of your people to fight in the arena."

"I couldn't pass up such an offer, were it made—" She frowned at Lucius. "—in all seriousness. But I believe you to be young, frivolous, and driven by the heat of desire, not by any sort of real ambition to be part of my life. When I went to meet you, I was determined to allow you to quench your desires, rather than take the chance you would harm my friends.

"You were then simply an inconvenience and if that is all you are, then go. Rome is full of whores, some expensive, some cheap, but all for sale. I am not. I assure you, I can only be your victim, not a willing partner in pleasure. I do have my duty and must fight this afternoon. So if you must, I will go into the latrine with you because such a place is where the kind of desire you express belongs.

"If not, and you are willing to accord me the respect you would give even a street girl—that is, not to trouble her when she has other than business matters to attend to—then go." Dryas pointed to the door. "And you will earn my thanks and respect for however long I live. So untie his hands, Maeniel, and allow him to do as he wishes. Unfortunately, he has powers that, at present, don't lie with us and, one way or another, I would have him be gone." Then she turned back to the grate and began to warm her hands. She found them still cold.

Gordus cut the ropes on his wrists. Lucius pulled his hands out from behind his back and looked down at them as if he wasn't sure to whom the appendages at the end of his wrists belonged. He studied Dryas, feeling somewhat as if he'd been hit hard between the eyes with a two-by-four.

The rust-colored tunic and blue mantle were attractive. Marcia handed her a bowl of porridge and a spoon. She began to eat where she was standing. She looked so ordinary. Yes, there was that wonderful body under the soft linen tunic, the hair drawn up and braided around the strange, spiked brass crown. The warmth of the stove brought a bloom to her skin he hadn't seen before and even the cut-lace sandals and woolen stockings couldn't disguise the grace of her legs, ankles, and high-arched feet. He could no more imagine forcing her out of raging lust than he could imagine himself doing any other unthinkable thing like killing a child, laying information against a friend or even an enemy before a tribunal, stealing, or harming another person for no good reason.

Finally he said, "You are completely safe from me. I would no more touch you against your will than I would jump from the roof of this building and try to fly. I do find your conditions for marriage staggering. I'm not sure I can meet them and I am very afraid for you. So afraid it nigh drives me out of my senses. I am the last man on earth you need fear. Yes, I will go if you wish it, but I would rather stay and offer you what comfort and assistance I can."

So saying, he rose, pushed past Maeniel, and went over to where Dryas stood. Again she saw the limp and it tore at her heart. She didn't know why.

"I can't think," he said humbly, "that I would make a good candidate for kingship among your people. I am scarred and my health will probably always be affected by my injuries and long illness."

He was just taller than she was and she tilted her head back slightly to look into his eyes. She didn't feel Marcia take the bowl and spoon from her hands and she didn't resist when he put his arms around her and rested her head against his chest. He stood, holding her, his lips resting on her hair, while she wept in sorrow that this moment had come to her, when she was sure she was going to die.

LUCIUS AND PHILO HURRIED THROUGH THE STREETS of Rome. What had started as a fine and beautiful day was quickly turning sour. An overcast moved in slowly, blotting out the warm sunlight and the fair skies, and the north wind began to rise, funneled by the narrow streets of the already ancient city. It whipped at the loose garments the Romans habitually wore, nipping noses and fingers and driving the damp winter chill to the bone.

The gray skies matched Lucius' mood. He was filled with grim anger and hate. He was walking so fast, Philo had to almost trot to keep up.

"I wish you wouldn't do this," Philo pleaded. "It's not wise to burn all your bridges at one time. Even if you leave, someday you may want to return . . ."

Lucius paused and waited a second for Philo to catch up to him. He didn't answer, only stared coldly into his friend's face. "No," he finally said. "I won't ever want to return. Not here, and not to being Lucius Cornelius Basilian. I'm done. If you don't want to come with me, I'll give you money, any amount you ask for. You can go wherever you like. The whole world is open before you, Philo. I'll make you a rich man, if that's what you want."

"Do you actually plan to marry this woman and run off to the ends of the earth with her?"

"Yes."

Philo began laughing. "I wouldn't miss this for the world." He wiped his eyes. "Do you know, my mother's favored novels were those Hellenistic romances about adventure and love. One of them was about Alexander and I wondered what it would have been like to follow the troops across half a world, to see Persia and India, to fight with men riding elephants. They climbed mountains, crossed deserts, saw the Hanging Gardens of Babylon when it was the largest city anyone had ever built. Even in that horrible slave dealer's shed at Cos, I felt a wild excitement in my heart. You never know where you will be sold or why. I was flabbergasted to end up in Gaul, of all places, looking at a very sick man . . ."

"Was I?" Lucius asked.

"Yes, you were yellow and your sister was threatening me."

"What would you have done if I hadn't recovered?"

"I don't know. I never got a chance to lay any plans. You began improving as soon as I persuaded you to stop drinking yourself into a stupor every night and take some nourishment. Most gratifying, an easy win."

"Yes?" Lucius asked ironically.

"No, actually it was touch and go there for a while."

"I thought as much. Well, this may not be a great adventure. We might come to an unpleasant end in an out-of-the-way corner of a foreign land."

"I'll risk it," Philo said.

"Well, then," Lucius said, and began walking again. He'd carried Dryas upstairs with Marcia in close attendance. He put her down on a cot in one of the sleep rooms upstairs. Then he removed her shoes, leaving the socks on. Marcia took off her belt.

Philo had mixed something. "Valerian," he told Marcia. "She needs her rest, but not any medication that would leave her groggy or with a hangover."

Aquila lifted her head and persuaded her to drink it.

Then they had adjourned downstairs to take counsel with one another.

"I can do nothing," Lucius told the rest. "If I asked for anything from my sister, she would take pleasure in doing the opposite just to spite me. She has Caesar on her side."

"Yes, I went to see him this morning," Gordus said.

"I take it you had no success," Philo said.

"On the contrary, I may have accomplished something practical." Gordus nodded. "I got him to overrule your sister's plans to dress her as a dancing girl and dump her in the ring with a killer cat. I'll put together some scale mail and I'll be able to give her a shield and her own sword. He still wants, as he put it, for her to exhibit her body, but . . ." He turned to Maeniel. "How good is she with a javelin?"

"Good," Maeniel said. "She's good with any weapon."

"Fine," Gordus said. "I may be able—"

He was interrupted when the door banged open and a man, unknown to him, stood in the doorway, pointed to Maeniel, and screamed, "That's him! Him! Get him before . . ."

But it was too late. A big wolf, one of the biggest Lucius had ever seen, was rolling clear of the worn tunic Maeniel had been wearing.

There was no other escape. The wolf charged the man in the doorway, shooting between his legs. He went down. The wolf dashed straight into Antony and five or six members of the Praetorian Cohort.

Maeniel had the advantage of surprise. They had the advantage of being armed to the teeth. One aimed a spear at him. It skidded along his ribs and struck a paving stone, showering sparks.

War at last! the wolf thought, and he hamstrung the spearman.

Antony tried to take his head off with a gladius and missed by only an inch or two, but he wasn't armored as the soldiers were. The wolf made a turn that would have done credit to a striking snake and sank his fangs into one big, well-fed Roman buttock.

Blood spurted; Antony screamed—or vice versa. At that point, nobody was keeping track, but Antony fell, driving his sword into the upper thigh of one of the other soldiers, grabbed another by the cuirass and brought him down also.

The wolf saw daylight and bolted.

Lucius, who had been watching the whole thing with complete astonishment, turned to Aquila.

"She says he's a friend of hers," Aquila said, and shrugged.

"My," Philo said, "your intended has some very peculiar relatives."

Lucius left Antony bleeding, blustering, and roaring in a fine patrician fury at Gordus, Marcia, Aquila, and even poor Martinus. He caught enough to know that Antony had been sent by Caesar to look after the tiger and he was not happy about it. He was accompanied by a man named Decius who evidently was an agent of Fulvia's and babbled endlessly about a man who turned into a wolf and back.

"I don't know about turning into a wolf, but turning back, that's impossible," Philo had said as he and Lucius made their way to the egress. Lucius did notice with some satisfaction that Philo made no move nor did he offer to help Antony.

Now he was on his way home, ready to raid the strongbox. In this respect, he was a true Basilian. Love mattered, but the next thing he thought of was money. If he was leaving with her for the ends of the earth, fine, but he wanted to travel in comfort and there are few situations in which money is not useful.

"Don't look now," Philo said, "but we're being followed by a large . . . dog?"

"Oh . . ." He paused for a second, foot in the air, put it down slowly, then abruptly turned down a street leading toward the river.

As in most modern cities, the central forum was surrounded by more-or-less seedy areas, and this street was one. Cramped, narrow shops, a few bars and small restaurants, even a mill being turned by a discouraged-looking mule with a baker next door. A wine importer's warehouse. A half dozen insulas, which were apartment houses with rooms overlooking the street. The windows were so close together, Lucius could hear women chattering back and forth over his head and there were only a few feet of clearance to admit light and air to the stepped passage below. Then Lucius saw what he'd been looking for: a bath. The entrance was in an alley. They turned and went in.

Once inside he was reassured. It looked respectable, a place patronized by poor laborers and the like. No luxuries, but you wouldn't get your throat cut for the contents of your purse. No marble, but the walls were whitewashed and the floor was the ubiquitous ruddy terra-cotta brick.

At this hour of the morning it was deserted. As they entered, the owner appeared out of the shadows at Lucius' elbow.

Lucius handed him a coin. "The steam room."

The man looked him up and down, then inspected Philo. "Want food, wine, a woman?"

"No," Lucius answered. "I have a hangover. Late party last night."

"Don't get many purple stripes 'round here." He eyed the senatorial stripe on Lucius' toga.

"Inquisitive, aren't you?" Philo said. He was now being a citizen, also togate.

"I can go blind," the man said.

"Do so," Lucius said, handing him another coin.

"Right. In there." He pointed to a wooden door. "Sheets in the dressing room. Watch your clothes." Then he vanished as quickly as he'd appeared.

The steam room wasn't bad, the sheets clean, benches along the walls. The steam was generated the old-fashioned way: rocks heated by a bed of coals. The room was warm and damp.

"No hypocaust," Lucius said.

"Is that good?" Philo asked.

"Yes. Sound carries through those things. Now we wait and see if our friend contacts us."

"I'm not sure whether to be sorry or relieved if he doesn't," Philo said.

"Yes."

But a few minutes later they heard sounds in the other room and then Maeniel entered, also wrapped in a sheet. He took a seat on the bench.

One of the bath attendants wandered in with a bucket, threw

water on the rocks to generate more steam, looked surprised to see Maeniel, and exited.

"You may have to pay extra," Maeniel said.

"A detail," Lucius said.

Sure enough, the owner arrived, hand out. Lucius placed another coin in it and he exited.

"Who was that hysteric at the ludus?" Lucius asked.

"His name's Decius. We met in Gaul. Some . . . relatives . . . of mine wanted to make a meal of him. I prevented them."

"Too bad," Lucius said.

"As it happens, yes. He was waiting for me last night at the house of Manilius and Felex. As soon as I walked in, he began screaming. I had to depart precipitously. Fortunately, I'm good at it. They didn't catch me."

"Obviously." Lucius nodded.

"Yes, but I spent all night wandering around Rome, trying to find the ludus. When I did, I discovered I had more trouble on my hands than I knew what to do with."

"You know her?" Lucius asked.

"Yes, very well."

"Care about what happens to her?"

"Yes."

"Why is she here?" Lucius asked, and saw evidence of an internal debate going on on Maeniel's face.

Finally the wolf answered, "Caesar," and made a throat cutting gesture.

"Pity," Lucius answered. "She never got close enough, but she's not the only one who finds the idea attractive. There are a number of others, myself among them, but I can't think of a way."

Maeniel nodded. "States the problem in a nutshell."

"Do you know what I would do?" Philo spoke for the first time.

"No," they chorused.

"Pay a call on Brutus."

"Brutus," Maeniel said. "Is he the one Antony quarreled with at dinner the other night at—"

"Yes," they chorused again.

"Word gets around. Calpurnia says Caesar's making a list, but I'm not sure what that means."

"Proscriptions." Lucius made a wringing motion with his hands.

"Does that mean what I think it means?" Maeniel asked.

"Yes, and you do get around. How well do you know that particular lady?" Lucius asked delicately.

"No," Maeniel said. "She has too much to lose."

"I think I'll go call on Brutus," Lucius said.

"I need clothes and money," Maeniel said.

"A detail," Lucius told him.

T HE FIGHT SHOWED EVERY SIGN OF BEING AN event. Marcia guarded Dryas' sleep and she did sleep well. The room above the kitchen was warm.

The arena was not a very big one. The seating was shallow, only about five tiers, but it was set in the middle of the five-story ludus. Two colonnaded porches overlooked the ring on three sides. They were comfortable and sheltered from the wind by the back of a theater across the street. Nothing else nearby was tall enough to block the light.

A beautiful arrangement, really, Gordus thought. He'd presented private munera for Caesar before. The men in the audience usually gravitated down into the seats. Food and wine were spread out for the spectators on the porches, where there was more comfortable seating for the women. They had a good view, and if bloody spectacles weren't to their taste, they could spend their time nibbling and gossiping while their menfolk were involved with the violence of the arena.

Now he must think of a way to keep the little priestess alive. That was how he'd thought about her since the night in the mortuary chapel.

Gordus was a hard man. He trained gladiators for Caesar and others. He'd sent many men out to die. In almost every munera, he lost a few. That's why he'd built the columbarium, the tomb. Even these outcasts needed to know they would receive a proper burial and be feasted, at least, by their fellows when they died. It was part of the discipline of the ludus. The oath of acceptance, stating they would face punishment by whips and hot irons or even death by steel if they failed in obedience to their owners and trainers, was not a hollow one. He himself had felt the whip and even the iron occasionally and he inflicted them with a free hand when he had men in training. There was no place for kindness or even, most of the time, for mercy in his profession.

But, oddly enough, few of those he taught hated him and a lot actually seemed to like him. After a taste of just how hard he could be, they accepted the discipline of the ludus and he was unrelentingly thorough in imparting the skills they needed to survive the arena. Many were grateful and came back to work for him when they earned their discharge from owners who made money.

Like many hard men, he was sentimental about women. Wives and daughters were ritually pure. Yes, things had happened at the hands of soldiers when Marcia's father and his fell trying to protect what little they had. He knew some of the men in his village accepted being put on the roads, driven into poverty rather than allow their wives and children to suffer as his mother and Marcia's had. He understood this. He hated and resented it to the very bottom of his soul, but he understood.

Once, men like his father and grandfather had been important. They were the backbone of the legions. They stood and protected Rome when Hannibal crossed the Alps into Italy and threatened the city itself. Men of his family soldiered with Scipio and Fabius, fought the Samnites and, in Tuscany, helped lay the foundations of awesome Roman power. They had felt they and their sons would be rewarded one day with prosperity, security, and peace.

But they were wrong. Even his grandfather had been sure the Gracchi would deal justly with the small landowners near Rome. At that point, faith ran out. Gordus was sure his father had fallen in despair. He himself saw clearly how the game was going.

The only two classes that mattered now were the publicani—the knights who looted the provinces for their own profit—and the patrician generals who were paid by these successful thieves to go out and conquer more people, so they in turn could be looted, exploited, and enslaved until the wealthy classes were so bloated with their gains that they fell to cutting one another's throats in a mad brawl over the spoils.

He made his own separate peace, as many men and women have over the long ages, turned his eyes inward, and resolved to protect his own. By whatever means necessary.

He knew ugly things had happened to Marcia before he could buy her freedom and her mother's, but they were not her fault. She had done what she must, but, even now, he noticed she wore the vitta, the woolen fillets of a chaste wife and, over them, an old-fashioned linen veil lest any think she might be careless about her virtue because of the past.

Dryas did not belong here. No woman did. The ludus was a certain special sort of hell, for men only. Only men could deserve it.

He felt an absolute contempt for Caesar because he colluded with Fulvia in placing Dryas here. He admired discipline and courage. They were the only virtues that mattered to him in one of his fighters and were, as far as he was concerned, central to all others.

Despite being a woman, Dryas upheld those standards. He would do his best for her, so he began to assemble a wardrobe.

The boots were tricky. He used sandals reinforced in the legs with leather wrappings, then gilded the results. They were handsome.

Then he cut her a cuirass of chain mail on the inside with scale mail on the outside. The beast fighters liked scale mail because talons, claws, and teeth couldn't get a purchase on it, but chain mail was stronger. So she had the best of both worlds—he hoped. He did have to tack the finished product up so it would leave her midriff bare, but the sleeves extended almost to the elbow and would give some protection to her arms.

Aquila gave him her sword and two daggers. He drew the sword. Even in the dull light of the overcast sky, rainbows shimmered in the metal. "Razor sharp," he commented.

Aquila nodded.

"How did they ever lose?"

"Sometimes they didn't," Aquila said.

He brought the things to Marcia, who stood at the foot of the stairs.

"She's still asleep," Marcia said.

"Good. The caterers are just setting up for the food," he told her. "Let her sleep as long as she can."

Two men, both experienced gladiators, sat at the table, having some wine. Both were exauctorati; they had been discharged. He could trust them. He joined them. Marcia went upstairs.

"You open for her," he told the men. "The two boys I picked are tyros, just trainees. Nice-looking kids. Don't cut their faces. I told them don't press you and don't try any tricks. You aren't supposed to cripple or kill them. Don't make a liar out of me. Exhibition only. Caesar will be there. He knows."

"Girl and the tiger. Is it a real thing or just a tumbler?" one of them asked.

"It's real, all right," Gordus answered.

The other man seemed taken aback. "A woman. It doesn't seem right."

"It isn't," Gordus said, "but then what do you do?"

Both men nodded and helped themselves to more wine.

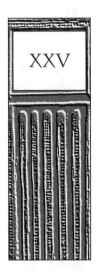

XXV

COOKS PREPARED ROASTED MEAT WITH HONEY and herbs, suckling pigs, roast chickens, geese, pigeons, guinea hens, and even swan. A whole pig turned over an open fire, being basted with its own drippings.

Another table held cold food: olives of all kinds, fresh cheese, pickles of cucumber, small squash, onions and leeks, ham and citron. There were breads with cheese, dates, nuts, and pungent breads with olives and onions.

Amphoras of white wine chilled in the snow and there was an ample supply of the justly famous Falernian, the most admired of all reds.

Litters arrived at the gates and disgorged beautifully dressed men and women. They climbed the stairs to the colonnaded porches over-looking the arena where slaves, supplied by Caesar and Antony, of-fered them wine in gold and silver cups sprinkled with rose petals. A gustatio of spiced eggs, small sausages, smoked cheese, and small as-paragus with a savory of coriander, lovage onion, and wine sauce made the rounds.

Caesar arrived with an enormous entourage including Brutus, Cicero, Fulvia, Cleopatra, Cassius, and Lucius. Lucius knew Dryas' best chance was for no one to see he gave a rap for what happened to her.

Antony—who was pleased to see Lucius coming around, as he thought, to a more sensible point of view—arrived, as did a horde of other senators, military officials, publicani, knights, and assorted leeches, sycophants, and gate-crashers, including Maeniel.

They wandered around the porches seeing, being seen, and exhibiting jewels, gold, silver, amber, garnets, sapphires, amethysts, rubies, and a plethora of pearls. Fine clothes: velvet, silk, linen silk, wool. The men distinguished in white. The women as gaudy as multicolored butterflies. Exchanging witticisms, inanities, banalities, stupidities, injuries, cruelties, and whatever else entered their minds.

No one listened to anyone else and no one seemed to see anyone else, or so it appeared to Lucius, who was sure Dryas was going to be killed for the amusement of these worthless parasites, murderers, extortionists, and thieves. He indicated as much to Maeniel when he met him investigating the spiced olives on the lowest porch over the seats to the arena.

"Not if I can help it," Maeniel said, ingesting some black olives steeped in wine, oil, and bay leaves.

"It is an incongruity that you would like olives," Lucius said. "Wouldn't you prefer some nice fresh, bloody meat?"

"No," Maeniel said. "I get a lot of that as it is. I wouldn't underestimate her. I did once and paid dearly for it."

"You didn't see that tiger."

"Oh, yes, I did," Maeniel said. "But we're early and I thought I'd try the food. Problems are best faced on a full stomach. If you don't eat, you often regret it later. So don't be self-indulgent. She isn't, not in the least, I assure you."

MARCIA HELPED DRYAS DRESS. THE GILDED FOOT-wear was a rather basic thong sandal with uppers that reached to just below the knee. These lent support to the ankle and some protection to the lower leg.

Of course, the standard loincloth, red silk, but Gordus had reinforced the belt and had given back the two knives she carried. The spiked crown was again braided into her hair.

Marcia wrapped the strophium—breast binder—showing Dryas how to wear it in such a way that it supported her breasts and protected them from the mail shirt.

"Tumblers do it this way," Marcia explained, "so they won't jiggle."

Dryas laughed, then admitted, "Yes, they can be a terrible nuisance. Yet I've always been sorry I didn't have bigger ones."

"Oh, the small ones work just as well as bigger ones, on men and babies both."

"Yes, I know. I expected to have trouble nursing my son, but I didn't."

"Your son?"

"He's dead." Dryas looked away.

"I saw stretch marks on your stomach," Marcia said. "I have a lot of them myself. I had four; only two lived, Martinus and Tullia. Tullia's married. She married well, considering . . ." She didn't finish. Marcia had once been a slave and she meant "for the child of a freedwoman."

Dryas nodded and hoped Marcia wouldn't ask her any more questions. She didn't.

Then Marcia produced a pair of wrist guards. They were leather, and they strapped into place. "Gordus had to look high and low for a pair small enough," she said.

"I've always considered them an affectation," Dryas said as she examined them.

"Gordus does, too, on some of these men who have fists the size of sledgehammers, but your wrists are slender. On small, slightly built men, he's found them a help. They support the wrist at its narrowest, weakest point."

Dryas strapped them on, finding they did give a bit of extra support. The thongs ran up between her fingers and a soft leather pad rested on her palm. "Yes, good," she said, and elected to carry her sword rather than wear the belt and scabbard. "Only in the way," she said regretfully.

"Well, we are done," Marcia said.

The abbreviated costume was chilly, so Dryas wrapped herself in the woolen palla.

Marcia handed her a cup of warm liquid. "Philo," she said. "He mixed this, some of his herbs. He's good. Gordus was happy to get him. All the men say unless you're dead when they drag you out, Philo will put you back together and have you laughing at his jokes while he's doing it."

Then they walked to the window and began watching the beautiful people of Rome arrive. Marcia chuckled when one particularly overdressed woman climbed out of a litter. "Now, she should know better than that. She's fifty if she's a day." Marcia knew most of them.

"Not that they know me, you understand, but some of them show up every time Caesar sticks his head out.

"Servila." She pointed to an older woman who was very dark and conservatively dressed. "Greediest woman in Rome. Hard to know what she has the most letch for: Old Baldy or his money. During the last proscriptions, he must have had eight or nine of the condemneds' biggest estates knocked down to coppers for her. She's not only the greediest woman in Rome, she's one of the richest."

"I hate the thought of being paraded in front of those people in this," Dryas said, opening the palla and looking down at the abbreviated costume. "Half naked."

"You won't be," Marcia said. "There's a tunnel to the arena entrance. You don't have to go near them. Just as well; you're probably the best looking thing in here. All of the men will be salivating when they see you. Take these women . . . No don't take them, soft as hot butter, muscles sagging, tits sagging, white lead not only on their faces but on their breasts and asses, rouge on their cheeks, tits, and where they squat to piss, kohl on their eyelids and under the eyebrows, tight binders so their flat little titties will have cleavage, corsets that are more harness than a horse wears, just so they look like they still have figures.

"They lie on their couches all day, pop sweetmeats, cakes, cookies, have abortions when they get knocked up, never do any work except to scream at their slave women. Piss and moan when they have to walk as far as the latrine. No wonder Lucius went head over heels for you. Yikes, a woman with some brains and guts who doesn't look like a fat dairy cow when she's naked and isn't afraid to tell a grab-ass aristocrat where to head in. Doesn't surprise me in the least."

Someone knocked at the door.

"Is it time?" Marcia asked.

"Yes," Gordus answered.

A few minutes later, Dryas was waiting in one of the entrances to the arena behind an iron grate.

Gordus handed her a shield. "I can't give you one the cat couldn't destroy. This one is good for only about one swipe."

"No," Dryas agreed. "I couldn't carry one strong enough to resist the claws of an animal that size. The sheer weight would be too much for me."

In the arena outside, the second warm-up match was ending. The tyro, a very handsome blond boy, had an ugly scalp wound. The older man drew away, having done all Gordus paid him to do.

The lanista, one of Gordus' assistants acting as referee, separated the two men.

"Not bad," Dryas said. "They look impressive, scalp wounds."

Gordus nodded. "The way they bleed. He's not bad, though, the German kid. I usually don't like blonds. Bad eyes and they cut and ooze like chopped meat. But this kid's fast. He may live awhile if he doesn't try to jump the bones of every teenager in Rome."

"Popular?" Dryas asked.

"Have to chase away a few every time he goes out to practice. You wouldn't believe the things they try to give him. Clothes, jewelry, perfume." He paused.

Dryas supplied, "Used underwear."

Almost against his will, Gordus began laughing.

The arena was clear now, empty. The sun was westering. Above, the overcast came and went. The sun lightened and darkened. Now the white sand and light limestone bleachers were a monochrome blue-gray, setting off patches of white where the bleached tunics and togas of the senatorial classes formed the bulk of the crowd, and then suddenly the sand and limestone oval would sparkle, aflame with transient golden light.

"How do you want your funeral?" Gordus asked. "That's how we wish each other good luck here."

Dryas nodded. "Makes sense."

The tiger padded into the arena and yawned lazily, showing a massive array of lethal-looking ivory choppers. The crowd drew in an awed breath. Just then the sun returned, shining through a gap in the fleecy tiles above.

"How beautiful," Dryas said. And it was. The black markings were set off like a velvet appliqué against the sleek orange coat. Under the fur, the big muscles elongated and contracted with a supple grace that seemed almost impossible in a creature so large. Then the tiger's head turned and the big killer's yellow eyes, looked, it seemed, with a vast indifference into Dryas' own, as if to say, "I am waiting."

Dryas nodded. "We wouldn't want that. Open the gate."

She moved out into the open. The shield she carried was a nice match to the red silk loincloth she wore. It, too, was red, bound in brass with an upper and lower rim of the yellow metal.

The sun reappeared and glistened on the copper crown, the scale mail she wore as a shirt, and the high, laced, gilded sandals.

She held the shield negligently to one side. *Best give them a good look. It's the least I can do for my friends.*

The tiger turned smoothly and took three steps toward her, then glided into a run with almost unbelievable speed and leaped.

At the last second the shadow of the rising animal covered her. She pivoted on her right foot and slashed, catching the cat across the tender pad of its left forefoot with the edge of her sword.

The right paw simply tore the shield from her arm. Her whole left arm went numb as the handle and strap were ripped loose from her hand and forearm, but she got the tiger across the face with the edge of her blade.

She should have died then, and was certain she was going to, but the animal broke off the attack.

Dryas, remembering the mouse-hunting cats she'd seen, moved away very slowly. *That's what I am. A mouse,* she thought. Her entire consciousness fixed on her adversary.

The tiger shook the paw she'd injured, then shook it again, showering the sand with red drops. Then it began its stalk.

Dryas managed to spare a glance for her numb left arm. Blood dripped from a laceration on her forearm, but her fingers were red only where the shield had pulled free of her hand. She flexed them gently and felt the life returning. She kept moving away. The tiger followed. Yes, she was a mouse and . . . *In a second, yes,* she thought, *here it comes.*

It was a blur of motion. She leaped toward it as it came, a warrior's choice. She had the sword two-handed. She slammed into it. She felt the sword sink through muscle, against gristle, and grate on the bone. It stank and she was blind, wondering if its jaws were closing on her head.

Then she was struck a simply unbelievable blow in the ribs. Her hands were torn free of the sword hilt—she hadn't known she was still clutching it—and she was flung into the air.

Automatically, as her teachers had taught her so many years ago, she turned herself into a ball. She rolled. When she stopped, she saw the tiger coming like a striking hawk. It was only inches away. The impulse was reflex and she never knew where it came from. She had a handful of sand; it exploded in the tiger's eyes.

She felt something like icicles move across her bare thigh and, a second later, she stood in the center of the arena, watching the animal try to clear its vision.

Somewhere in the far distance, she heard the crowd, but they were screaming and shouting in some hazy otherworld. Only a vast silence enveloped her.

Her eyes raked the beast. She'd hurt it. The sword was buried to the hilt in the animal's chest. Every time it took a breath, air bubbled out around the wound. Between the sand and the blood on its face from the sword cut, one eye was hazed, but its vision didn't seem more than slightly inconvenienced. When the big animal moved, it limped.

She'd been clawed. Blood was sheeting down her left leg from the long, shallow thigh wounds. She'd been bitten on the right shoulder, but the mail had done its work. The whole arm and shoulder was painful when she moved it. She was sure the fangs had tightened, but not penetrated. She had lighter claw marks on her left arm, merely scratches.

Kill it, she thought. *Kill it.* A litany in her brain. *Kill it. How?* They circled each other. *Kill it.*

The shield lay where the tiger had torn it from her arm. She still had her knives. Again, it was a warrior's choice. She was not as badly hurt as it was. She could outlast it.

The ridges made by the claws on her upper thigh were the worst and they were scabbing over. She could feel them tightening as the blood clotted, but the cat's eyes were clearing. The injured one was tearing and the yellow orb was bright again and following her movements.

There was more light. She was vaguely aware torches were being placed at measured intervals around the arena. She and the cat padding along, moving from one puddle of flickering yellow light to another. Always it was closer and closer.

The shield lay where it had fallen, near the spot where she had entered the arena. She remembered the frog from Mir's lake. *I am the mouse,* she thought.

The tiger drew closer and closer. Now or never. In a moment it would be too close.

She dove for the shield. Her fingers closed on the rim. She hurled it, spinning, flashing in the torchlight.

The tiger had a choice: the woman in deep shadow or the shield glimmering, glittering in the light. It went for the shield, batting it out of the air.

Dryas ran for the tiger. No, she didn't seem to run, but to fly, and she leaped, landing on the animal's back.

The tiger reared like a maddened horse, biting at the muscular legs holding the woman on its back.

Dryas grabbed at the loose neck skin and got a fold in her left hand. It tightened like a claw. With her right hand, she drew the knife, her longest one. The orange neck with its midnight stripes was twisted toward her left arm digging in, holding like death.

She slashed down as hard and deep as she could. She heard the roar, not the voice of the cat, but the air rushing out through the ringed cartilage as it parted.

Then she was flying, head over heels, trying to turn her body into a ball again. She failed, landed on her neck, and found herself paralyzed for an instant. It couldn't have been more than an instant because she was on her feet so quickly some of the spectators didn't realize she'd been down.

The tiger was down. It gave two or three roaring breaths and tried to rise, then died.

Dryas felt dizzy. She looked up and saw stars beginning to pick themselves out in the blue gloaming above.

She walked toward the tiger and looked down at it, then raised her arms and looked up at the spectators in the seats.

The crowd went wild.

The plaudits of the multitude, she thought.

Then she looked down at the tiger again, crouched, lifted the ritual handful of dust given to the fallen who cannot be buried properly, stood, and let it trickle in a stream from her fingers down on the orange-and-black striped shoulder.

The cheering crowd was abruptly silent as Dryas walked toward the doorway. Not everyone understood the gesture she'd made, but enough did to realize she'd just treated them with supreme contempt.

Inside the entrance to the arena, Lucius and Maeniel stood with Gordus. Maeniel held a spear.

She staggered in. The crowd buzzed loudly.

Gordus was laughing. "The first families in Rome might riot over that and kill all of us."

Lucius grabbed her and wrapped the mantle around her.

Maeniel pointed at the spear. "We were here. You didn't need it."

"No," Dryas said.

"I told you she was good," Maeniel said.

There were shouts, squeals, and screams from above. "The party's getting started," Gordus said. "The dancing girls are here. The wives and mothers are going home. Some of them will party all night at one another's houses. The Senate doesn't meet again until day after tomorrow."

Maeniel and Lucius gazed at each other in the half darkness. "I'm going to kill him," Lucius said.

"For this?" Maeniel asked.

"If for nothing else," Lucius said.

"I don't want to be present during this conversation," Gordus said.

Dryas said nothing, but sagged against Lucius' body in a way he found extraordinarily gratifying, even though he would never, by any means, admit it.

MAENIEL EASED ALONG THE DARK PASSAGE UNTIL he found a half-empty room that held spare weapons, a few stage props, and assorted broken and discarded entities—things that collect around all human dwellings: nonfunctional objects, useless but too good to throw away, the "maybe it can be fixed and sometime I might need it" stuff.

The room was pitch-black except to the wolf and it smelled of mold and damp. He hung up his tunic and toga and trotted out on all fours.

He was thinking of Calpurnia. The rain that had been threatening all day came sweeping in in sheets and curtains. The crowd hurrying to their litters dissolved into a pack of fleeing individuals.

The wolf stood in the shadow of one of the arena entrances and watched them. *Just as well,* he thought. The dog tribe accepted the taboo about killing within the pack and he considered humans pack. He had seldom seen so much ineptitude in any group of creatures. Were wolves in any closer association with them now, they would constitute a standing temptation. Ah, well.

The rain slowed. The slaves carrying the litters might get wet, but no one worried about them, and the area around the gates cleared.

The wolf trotted away from the arena. A soldier stationed near the gate to protect the late-leaving and somewhat drunken spectators gave a quick gasp when he saw the wolf ease through and past him in the shadows. The gleam of big yellow eyes flashed and then was gone.

White silk gown was how he thought of her. *Woman grace.* He moved through the Forum. It was still misting rain and even the shops that normally stayed open late were closed. The few lights that were still lit glowed on the cobbles.

When he reached Caesar's villa he circled it, baffled. He had the same problem he'd had when he tried to rescue Imona. Locked out.

A uniformed guard complete with helmet, pilum, and sword stood in front of Caesar's door.

The wolf paused in front of him and sat down.

"Go away." The legionnaire swung the butt of the spear at him.

The wolf lifted his muzzle to the sky and howled. This set off every dog in the neighborhood for miles around—yelping, howling, barking, whining—creating an unearthly uproar.

The sentry picked up a clod of earth and hurled it at the wolf.

He dodged easily and gave the sentry a big tongue-lolling, toothbaring smile.

The sentry whispered something obscene under his breath.

The wolf howled again. This wail was louder and longer, drawing on the full resources of the wolf yodeling power. All the canines in the vicinity sounded as if they were going insane.

The captain of the guard opened the gate. "What in the name of . . ." This was as far as he got. The wolf dove past him and vanished into the darkness of the atrium.

"It was the dog!" the young soldier said. "He ran into the house."

His captain looked at him as if he'd grown another arm in an unbelievable spot, say in the middle of his forehead.

"I'll have the watch look for him. Maybe he belongs to someone inside."

"I don't know. I never saw him before."

"Yes, well, if he doesn't belong to the house, why would he want to get in?"

"I don't know," the sentry said, "but maybe we should ask—"

"Ask who? The Lady Calpurnia is asleep. Caesar's in the arms of you-know-who at her villa. You just go ask him if it's his dog and let me come along. I want to watch. I want to watch what happens to you when you do. Now, be quiet and stop upsetting those damned dogs!" Then the door slammed shut, provoking another outburst of barking.

This night was moonless as yet and the house was a maze. Maeniel moved quickly from shadow to shadow. He had no idea where she was. He crouched down, letting his senses inform him.

Male soldier on a pillared walkway. Yes, he had all the indications: metal, perspiration, male, heat, young. Yes, soldier.

More males, not soldiers, in a room, a tablinium office nearby, colder, musty garments, drink, food. He could hear them laughing and talking together. Caesar's secretaries? Probably.

Lovers, two of the house slaves? Together in an empty triclinium nearby. The smell of sex heated him.

Avoiding the sentry, he drifted along in the shadows of a porch to another courtyard. Roses, yes, those roses. The white ones in jars against the wall. The gates of her own private garden. Their fragrance saturated the damp, still air, almost as if they beckoned, saying, "Come, come." Yes.

She awakened. She'd had a headache today. It began while Dryas fought the tiger, and this time she'd seen *him*. She knew the ordeal that had been her life would soon come to an end—the ordeal that began when he saw her at the age of eighteen and asked her father for her hand, and continued, day after day, until now.

It had taken him more than twenty years to realize how much she hated him and, even so, it wouldn't have mattered in the least to him, had she been able to give him a son.

It took a further five years for him to understand that she had destroyed each of her pregnancies in turn and twice came near death in quite successful attempts to prevent others.

Now she was past all of that. Cleopatra had given him a son and tonight, hoping for another, he lay in her arms.

The room was dark and her maids were huddled shapes on couches surrounding her bed. She closed her eyes and smelled the roses. When she opened them, she saw the eyes. They glowed, gathering light and mirroring it back. An animal. A cat? No, too high. A dog? But there was no dog in the house.

She seldom slept in the cubiculum, her bedroom to one side of the porch. She preferred this room. It was round and her husband sometimes called it the Temple of Vesta, not wholly in jest. Pillars of green and white marble alone separated it from her garden.

The floor was decorated with a winged horse picked out in mosaic. Only fragile curtains separated her room from the garden. They drifted to and fro in the night breeze. No, she'd had one cat and one dog. She'd never have another. The dog annoyed him and one day she found it had been buried alive. The small animal must have struggled for a long time before it died.

She hadn't known how angry he was over the cat, kitten really, until she found it wandering and crying in the garden with the pins sticking out of its eyes.

It was then that she resolved never, never, never to give him any children, and she hadn't. But in the last few days he'd begun to explain things to her again, and a vast weariness weighed down her spirit like a cenotaph.

The eyes moved toward her. She wasn't afraid. He had so terrorized her and for so long that simple fear no longer had any meaning.

The animal vanished and a man she recognized stood beside her. "It's you," she whispered.

He stretched out a hand, helped her rise.

"How convenient you're able to be something else, then turn human." Her voice was so low he could barely hear her. "What sort of animal are you?"

"A wolf," he said, helping her down from the bed. They slipped out of the room hand in hand.

"I imagine it gets you out of all sorts of inconvenient situations," she said.

"Yes." He pulled on a tunic he found. "Yes," he repeated, "but it creates all sorts of unpleasant ones when I turn at the wrong time."

"I can't say I'm surprised. In fact, last night I was sure there was something strange about you. After all, you came into my garden so easily."

The roses were in front of them. They walked between them, hand in hand.

It was a little after daybreak. The light—rose, fuchsia, violet, and drenched with amethyst—was unutterably beautiful. He could just see her. See her and the world they'd entered.

"This is a different place," he said.

"I know." She drew very close to him. The gown, as last night's, was silk, but this one was so thin as to be almost transparent. "I've been here before. I must meet someone here."

"Now?"

"No, not until the sun is high in the sky. Make love to me."

"Yes," he said, and drank at her lips. They were cool and refreshing as the water of an icy spring. Her flesh was soft as a rose petal and as fragrant. They stood near a stone balustrade. A few paces away, three marble steps led up to a stone porch covered by low ground cover with silver leaves and blue flowers. Beyond the porch, there was no house, only a grove of young pines.

They were infant trees with trunks no more than a few inches in diameter. In the early light, the thickly woven branches bearing long needles were green-black. It was dark under the clustering low limbs. They lay together on a thick carpet of brown needles. The rich scent of pine resin wafted around them.

"Does anyone live near this garden?" he asked.

"If they do, I have never seen them." He'd pulled the tunic off and she ran one hand slowly down from his shoulder, across his chest, then stomach, creating a delightful anticipation. When it reached its goal, they both smiled and lost themselves in kisses, caresses, and the search of one body in another's for divine delight, as the morning re-created the first day of the world around them.

Afterward, they slept for a time and, when they woke, the sun was driving long shafts of light down among the young pines. The heavily needled branches wove patterns of gold on their skins and the forest floor.

They looked out on parkland of small groves and open meadows sown with a rainbow of flowers. Before them, the world fell away in shallow steps toward a misty horizon and, far away, his wolf's ear detected the sound of the sea. A summer sea, ebbing and flowing, long, warm, shallow combers landing as lightly as a child's footstep on a sandy shore.

They walked across a meadow. The flowers burned gold against dark, browning summer grass, then blue in the green growing shadow of long-stemmed hanging Babylonica willow. The trailing branches rested on a gigantic broken urn buried in the turf. Beyond the urn, a cascade of vines bearing scarlet flowers dropped to a blue pool caught in the shadow of the luxurious weeping trees.

Something drank at the pool. Something the wolf couldn't quite see, but it lifted its head and whickered when it saw his companion, who hurried forward with a happy cry.

They joined each other, laughing and dancing together in the grass and flowers.

The wolf saw a soft, almost black nose and then an eye, shiny and dark, fringed with long lashes. A dark, dappled gray shoulder glowed with a metallic gleam. Then, for a moment, he saw a horn in the center of its forehead.

It reared, a patchwork of substance and shadow, and then wings unfurled. For a moment, they darkened the sun with a massive shadow. The wings of a steed this large must stretch out the span of a racecourse from end to end, almost a mile from tip to tip. It didn't wear them, but called them from wherever it lodged, as it called the horn, and hooves that could dance on air.

All he saw was a big, dark, dappled gray, its coat glowing like pure hammered silver, with a curling mane and tail, soft as a fair woman's hair, but abundant as a skein of fine wool.

It knelt for a second, inviting her to mount. She demurred, laughing, but kissed its nose and hugged the big neck.

Then the wings opened with a snap, the report as loud as a ship's mast breaking in a storm, and it vanished in a swirl of wind.

She stood, hand raised in farewell.

"Your friend?" he asked.

"Yes. He is becoming impatient. I must leave next time the visions present themselves."

He walked down to join her and they sat on a broken bench near the pond. It was thickly overgrown with lotus, and the big pink-violet flowers were opening in the sunlight.

From the pool, to one side, a stair led down. The shallow, half-overgrown steps sloped away across low terraces, each filled with green sward surrounded by different gardens, some filled with roses, lilies, flowering trees, and more ponds decorated with statuary, some of it broken, some intact, some pale, others darkened by lichen and moss. A riot of flowers bloomed in the borders around them: hollyhocks; pinks; daisies; calulena; foxglove; nightshade; poppies white, pale violet, and red; and in the shadows were henbane and monkshood. Each garden was a separate entity. Each invited exploration and contemplation.

"Your friend defeated the tiger," she said.

"Yes, but I don't know what to do now."

"Kill him," she said.

"You're sure?"

"Yes."

"I can't think that whoever replaces him will be any better," Maeniel said.

"Yes, they will, especially from your friend's point of view. As far as I'm concerned, it doesn't matter. As far as Rome is concerned, he's done all the damage he can. He cannot create. All he can do now is destroy. Once, I wouldn't have said that, but now, I must.

"He has perfected his skills. Another ten years and he will have laid waste with both hands. In ten years, nothing will rise from the ruins he leaves behind. There is no one like him. No one as strong."

"They say he has good qualities."

"What?" she asked.

"Mercy."

She began laughing. "He doesn't know what the word means. What looks like mercy is his ability to ambush. He pardons all and waits to see who will be of use to him, who may be crushed, their spirits broken and enslaved, and who must be killed because they will defy him to the last.

"Of those, he will select a few and allow them to live, for a time, that they may entertain him with their suffering. Remember the pirates? They captured him and demanded a ransom. He raised it, but promised he would return and crucify them. And so he did."

"I was told he had them strangled before he put them on the crosses," Maeniel said.

"Yes, after a time, some of them, but only when he became bored with his cruelty and their sufferings. He's good at cowing others through those they love. In fact, he deprived me of everyone I loved long ago. Think about your friends. All those hostages in Gaul. They bow the knee because they fear for their loved ones.

"Now I am free. I have become a hindrance to him. When he returns from Parthia and the White Isle, he will wish to marry the Egyptian. Of what use is a middle-aged wife to him? He was seen tampering with one of Philo's medicines, the concoction I take for my headache. A bit more opium and I will sleep not for a few hours, but forever."

Maeniel caressed her cheek and kissed her on the forehead.

He started to speak, but she pressed her finger to his lips. "No, he has chosen and so have I, because there is no damnatio here, only choice. His is a plane of stone where the dead rise at dawn, wounds livid in their pale flesh, eyes emptied of all but hatred. They contend again each day for victory and power, but the only victory they have is the few hours before sunset when the dead sleep in nonexistence. Wrapped in death's silence, they rest and rise at dusk to drink and boast, waiting for the dawn, going out again to relive the agony of their death wounds. They wait for him. He cannot escape them because he understands nothing else."

"And you?" he asked.

"Shh." She put her finger on his lips again. "I have never felt such love. I cannot walk in darkness because it lights me from within and I may, on my steed born of wind and rain, ride forth to all the worlds beyond.

"Now, share this final beauty one more time before I am summoned and must go. We will love each other in the bloody dust of time before I must turn and enter the portals of eternity."

XXVI

THERE WERE BATHS AT THE LUDUS. SPARTAN, TO be sure, but equipped with all the latest appliances. The hypocaust had been fired. The room was very warm and Marcia waited for Dryas. The warm bath was a simple, tiled pool filled by a pipe protruding from the wall on the side. She opened a stopcock and warm water began to fill the plunge bath.

"Go away, you men," Marcia said.

"No," Lucius replied. "I have a right." He settled Dryas on a bench against the wall and began removing her sandals. They had quite an audience: Gordus, Aquila, Philo, and Martinus.

"Do you say he has a right?" Gordus asked Dryas.

Dryas, still staggered by the enormity of what she had done, said, "Yes."

The others left, all but Marcia, who unbraided her hair and then began helping her undress.

Dryas sank gratefully into the pool, basking in the warm water. As she relaxed, she watched him, standing by the side of the pool, talking to Marcia.

She closed her eyes and thought for a long time of her house with its bright wall hangings and the dogs clustered near the fire pit. The bedroom curtains partitioned it off from the rest of the house. She'd seen how these Romans lived.

What would he think of it on a wild night when the sea leaped at the rocks only a few miles away, the wind drove the rain ashore in gray curtains, and an icy mist hung over forest and heath?

She closed her eyes and it seemed she could smell salt air, a faint perfume of heather and wild fennel mixed with the odor of wood-smoke and roast meat. Here, in this hot, moist bathhouse a half a world away, her heart hungered for the chill, but oh so clean wind and the distant sound of the sea.

At the assembly, when she had communicated her decision to her people and among the women who were the queen's companions, she was surprised by their sorrow. Surprised they loved her, at least some of them.

Sachna came, her closest friend, riding as she did like the nomadic horsemen, without bridle or rein, so well did she and her mount understand each other. She begged Dryas to return if only for her sake. When Dryas refused and tried to tell Sachna good-bye, the little redhead turned her back, wouldn't listen, and rode away.

But from a distance she turned at last, and Dryas could hear the tears in her voice. "I won't believe you won't return. I won't. I know you. You will come back and I'll see to your horses and hounds until you do. The same wind that blows you away will bring you back. I know. I've never been wrong about you before, and I'm not now."

Then the ship's captain cast off and the rowers, sculling her lightly as a bird, turned the hull out into the open sea.

It had been, yes, over two years, almost three since she last heard her friend's voice. Now this Roman, this strange man offered mar-riage and she could not refuse him.

No, I cannot refuse him, but can I be a wife to him? I need to know. She looked down at her body in the pool. Her wounds colored the water with a pinkish haze. The worst were the claw marks on her thigh, but they'd stopped bleeding and were being cleaned by the water. The ones on her arm were only scratches. Her right shoulder was sore, swollen, and purpling.

The cat had got in a bite. The mail Gordus made for her had done its work well. Had she been wearing the silver gauze Fulvia had wanted to dress her in, she would now be dead or at least badly in-jured. As it was, she would recover in a day or so.

Her eyes closed and she rested, listening to the stream from the flow pipe pouring into the bath, letting it gently lave the injured shoulder.

She must have slept for a moment, or possibly more than a moment, because she awakened with a start and found Marcia was gone. He was on one knee near the stair down into the bath. His expression and posture reminded her that he had pretended to be a servant simply to get close to her. She smiled at him, almost pityingly.

"Don't!" he said. "You might tempt me to take advantage of you. That smile is so lovely."

"Take advantage of me," she said invitingly.

"No." His face darkened. "Come up and let me tend your wounds."

There was a chair near the bath with a thick linen sheet spread over it. He helped her get up the stair from the pool and, very gently, seated her, then wrapped the sheet around her, leaving her leg bare. He dried it carefully, looking at the gashes in her thigh. The tears in the skin looked raw, the edges livid and ugly.

Philo had given him clean linen bandages and a vulnerary powder that stank of sulfur. The men at the ludus swore by it and so did he. The heat and swelling of the wound in his back had begun to subside from the first time Philo used it. Now he scattered it on the claw marks; then, because he'd learned a thing or two from Philo, he bandaged it expertly.

He began dressing her, beginning with the most intimate garment first, the loincloth, a new one made of white silk. He handled her body the way another woman would, without passion.

He could tell by the expression on her face that she was shocked. She had expected the usual force, perhaps with a tacit gesture of conciliation, an attempt to make use of her without causing her pain or even too much discomfort. Male rut, possibly with its more ugly and unpleasant aspects suppressed, but much the same as she'd encountered before.

He proved as expert with the strophium as he had with the loincloth. Then he dressed her in a shift of white silk and added a red silk stola. He placed sandals on her feet. They were soft suede with a thong between her toes and tied at the ankle.

Marcia returned just then. She carried a white woolen palla and vitta, the fillets that bound a married woman's hair. She finished dressing Dryas, braided her hair, and placed on her the vitta and a belt called a cingulum, tied in a ritual knot.

"Only he can untie this," Marcia instructed her. "And only when you give him your permission."

"I am not a virgin," Dryas said. "I have borne a child."

"Yes," Marcia said, "but it doesn't have anything to do with virginity. It signifies something much more important."

"What?"

"He must persuade you to accept him as a husband, to lay aside whatever fears you have, so the two of you can become one."

"I don't know if I can do that," Dryas said.

"Yes, I was afraid of this," Lucius said. "But whatever happens tonight, I won't accept less and I'll try to return you to your people. We can part as friends, even if we can't be lovers. I don't want the specter of violence between us, even implicit violence."

"So I see," Dryas answered. Then she wrapped herself in the soft woolen mantle and accompanied Marcia and Lucius to the gate.

Aquila was waiting at the gate. He kissed Dryas on the cheek. "Good-bye now, little fighter. Take good care of her," he told Lucius. "I'm going on to Campagna." He touched Dryas' cheek with callused fingers.

She found her eyes filling with tears and caught his outstretched hand with both of hers. "Thank you."

He nodded and echoed the first words he'd spoken to her as a person. "Good luck, Dryas. Take care of her," he told Lucius again.

"I'll try. It isn't always easy," Lucius said.

Then Aquila turned, went through the gate, mounted his horse, and was gone.

Lucius helped Dryas into a litter.

"Yours?" she asked.

"Hired," he said, and they started out for the Basilian villa.

A few seconds later, she saw a pair of eyes reflecting the torchlight. She told the bearers to stop. The eyes came in closer to the litter, but did not approach the men carrying it because it moved as some of them drew back. "If you would," Dryas asked, "see to it he gets home safely?"

The eyes vanished.

"Do you think he will do as you ask?" Lucius questioned her.

Dryas nodded. "I believe yes. He's very kind and I'm worried about Aquila."

Lucius signaled the litter forward. "Close the curtains." Dryas obeyed. Lucius nodded. Yes, she was too intelligent a woman to quarrel about minor matters.

When they reached the house, he sent the litter to the utility courtyard. He assisted her out and led her past his old rooms to the part of the villa where his parents had lived. He'd asked Philo to tell Aristo to move the things stored there elsewhere and refurbish the place, but he had no idea how far along they were. Now he found Octus, Philo, and Alia there to greet him.

The triclinium was swept and the table laid. Couches and chairs were present. The others took their leave.

"Would you care to recline?" he asked Dryas.

She smiled. "I have never eaten in such a way."

"Well, sit," he said.

The chairs were old and comfortable, well padded with cushions. Octus entered with a tray of gustatio and placed it in front of them. Olives, cheese, fruit, and some white wine.

Dryas looked up at him. "Thank you. What is your name?"

Octus drew back. He wasn't used to being seen or even noticed.

"This is Octus," Lucius said. "He's a body servant—takes care of my clothes, shaves me, that sort of thing. Who's cooking? Don't tell me my sister allowed that temperamental Greek chef of hers to—"

"No," Octus said. "Alia is in the kitchen. There's a separate one in this part of the house. I had to get the chimney unblocked from the old swallows' nests, but when I did, she said she could use it."

"Fine! Alia's a good cook."

Octus departed, closing the curtain separating them from the garden. The room was bright. There were four standing lamps near the table, each sporting six flames. The room was made brighter by the fact that the walls were done in white, decorated with green garlands. The floor tessare picked up the green, being a simple acanthus design, also in green and white.

"You don't have a lot of servants?" Dryas asked.

"There are a lot of servants in the house, but no. I don't have a great many, not for myself."

She frowned at the olives and cheese. "Is this all?" she asked.

"No, it's the first course. Something to nibble on while Alia cooks."

"Oh," Dryas said, then she dipped her fingers and enjoyed the olives.

"Try some of the cheese with the olives."

"I see," she said in a few moments. "The combinations are pleasing."

"Yes." He filled her cup.

She sipped. "Sweet."

"Water," he said.

"You water it?"

"Yes, most men, all women."

"I see. One loses status if one doesn't."

"Yes."

She nodded and added water to the wine.

"What do you drink on your isle?"

"Mead, barley beer, sometimes wine. The rich tribes near the coast drink wine. We aren't rich, but poor, at least by their standards and probably yours, also."

"What do you do for them? Gordus called you a priestess. Aquila, also, but Cut Ear said you were a queen."

"Yes, I am royal. Mainly, I do three things. I must give the people a king by either marriage or birth. Speak law. Perform rites for the dead. When you asked to marry me, I spoke law. I told you what my laws say about me."

The olives and cheese were gone. Octus pushed aside the curtain and took the tray.

Lucius looked and felt very uncomfortable, but he had to know. "How many men in your life?"

"Two," Dryas said.

"Is that all?"

"It's enough. One is the father of my son, the other the wolf."

Lucius found himself violently jealous. "The father of your son?"

Dryas was quiet for a second. "I'm not sure I can explain. It was political."

"Political?" Lucius asked. "How could it be—"

"Don't tell me you don't understand? Marcia said at least half the marriages among the Romans are political. He had to be accommodated. We aren't Romans. The only thing that holds us together is good faith. He and his lineage threatened to withdraw when their queen died in childbirth. I stood in for her, as did several others. They have heirs and remain our allies."

"The wolf . . . Why didn't you marry him and return him to your people?"

Octus entered then, interrupting her response. He had three covered dishes on a tray. "Alia's outdone herself. I hope you're hungry."

He set the tray down. "Roasted hare with an herb sauce," he said as he uncovered the first, "pork stew with leeks and quince, and a capon larded with bacon and stuffed with mushrooms. For wine, Falernian."

The capon was a hit, the pork stew only a little less appreciated, but Dryas, as ravenous as the tiger she'd killed, found room for some of the hare also. At length, she sighed, sipped from the wine cup, wiped her mouth with the napkin, and answered his question.

"The wolf's not human. He was a menace to the people near where he lived and had to be tamed."

"And you succeeded."

"Yes. I was lucky, and he is sweet-natured and brave. Otherwise, I would have failed."

"But you don't love him?"

"No. He is different. For a time, any people of his would love him, but, in the end, whatever was between them would fail and he would return from whence he came. I don't know what his destiny will be, but it does not lie with us or with me." She sipped again. Her long lids came down over her eyes and she looked almost asleep.

"Where is your son?" Lucius asked.

"He's dead."

"Cut Ear told me you or any woman of your rank would have taken her own life if you hadn't had a purpose in coming here. Besides, I've spoken to the wolf," he finished rather uncertainly. "I don't think we should talk about what he said. I trust the people around me, but . . ."

"Yes," Dryas said. "I will tell you how my son died."

Octus entered just then with passum, a sweet raisin wine, and dried figs preserved with bay leaves.

It must be the wine, Dryas thought. The wine seemed to produce a curious detachment in her or, just possibly, grief was dying away. She didn't know, but the nature, extent, and depth of grief, however boundless, didn't matter. The whole point was, should grief be a barrier not only to love, but also to duty?

He means the offer, she thought. *Whatever else he may be—foolish, deluded, reckless, to be drawn by a life and people he'd never seen or known— the man was honest. And I must meet him with honesty of my own. To do less would be the worst possible crime.*

"I don't know if I can love you," she said. "I don't know if I can give my life into your keeping." She paused. The pause seemed a long one, several breaths, a dozen heartbeats. "But I will try."

"Let us sacrifice to the household spirits." He rose and led her to the peristyle. He stood at one end of the pool. An amphora, a very old amphora, very much of the sort the poor placed on graves to receive offering for the dead, protruded from the soil and the flagged pavement.

He covered his head with the folds of his toga. Dryas followed his lead and covered hers. The servants, Octus, Philo, Alia, and even Cut Ear, stepped up beside him.

Lucius spoke. "I have come here to seek a blessing on my marriage and a farewell. To ask for blessings here is usual, to say farewell is not. But I am here to do so because we have forgotten where we came from.

"Generations ago my family came here. We took this land and, when we did, we promised to care for it, to love it, and to defend it. My ancestors were probably not always good people. Some were, no doubt, greedy, others cruel, and all bear the traces of autocracy as well as strength. But they were wise and tempered power with mercy and justice. Their faults were redeemed by courage and honor.

"Now, no more. Love for the land has become a desire to dispossess others of what is rightfully theirs, and defense is an excuse to lay waste and pillage all within reach of our arms, as indeed we have. So I must set out as they did once, if the tales be true, when they faced the ruin of their world.

"So, at their first altar, I commit my life to this woman and her people."

Alia handed oil and wine to Dryas, who passed it to Lucius. He poured both into the neck of the amphora.

A second later, everyone was startled and frightened when the statue at the other end of the pool fell, crashing into the water, and shattered into hundreds of pieces.

Lucius walked down to the end of the pool and stood quietly looking down at the fragments in the dark water.

"Is it a bad omen?" Philo asked. "What do you think?"

"No," Lucius said. "It means she's leaving this place to come with me."

Then the rest drifted away, leaving them alone in the dark garden.

"Ritual," Dryas said. "Ritual awakens things."

"Yes," he said, and led her to the marriage bed.

The cubiculum was a larger one than he was used to. The walls here, as in the dining room, were painted in the more restrained style of an earlier age. The floor was white and green, bordered with a garland of spring flowers. The walls were painted a very light green, just the color of new leaves in spring, and each panel sported a bouquet of the same flowers decorating the floors: iris, hyacinths, daisies, and the pink, sweet spring rose.

A brazier in the corner cut the night chill and a lamp with ten flames burned next to the bed. It was an old iron one, but padded with four down mattresses, silk sheets, and heavy pillows.

Dryas took the fillets from her hair and let it spill down her back, then turned to him and pointed to the knotted belt at her waist. "Untie it."

THE WOLF DID AS DRYAS HAD ASKED. HE PICKED UP Aquila's trail outside the ludus and followed it. Aquila had left Rome by the Via Appia. If he saw the wolf, who took an easier route moving along through belts of trees and over farms, keeping track of Aquila by scent and distant sight, Aquila gave no indication of it.

At length near Terracina, Aquila took a back road and turned toward the coast. The area was mixed farms and forest.

The wolf increased his speed and closed the gap between himself and Aquila. He trotted along in the shadows of trees bordering the road. *A nice constitutional by moonlight,* the wolf thought. Absolutely nothing happened.

The hour was late, the farmhouses shuttered and dark. Even the dogs must be in their kennels because not one had run at him, barking.

Aquila yawned and nodded on his horse. Insects chirped and thrummed in the grass and even the wolf was tempted to find a comfortable spot nearby and take a nap.

About a mile from the coast, Aquila turned off the two ruts in the mud, the farm road, and entered a still-narrower track. It led up into the rolling hills near the sea. It was so steep his horse had to scramble a bit to pass the rough spots.

The wolf smelled wild things for the first time—deer, rabbits, boar, and even, very faintly, cats. Not the domestic variety, but the small, rather fierce *felis silvestris*, not yet exterminated in Italy.

The wolf found this small corridor of wilderness comforting. But nothing whatsoever happened to Aquila. He reached his remote villa safely.

Disgusted, the wolf settled down under a bush and watched Aquila get ready for sleep. The house was set high up among its vineyards. Below, the coast road curved in and out near the water.

The wolf looked for cover. He certainly was not going to make the long trip back to Rome tonight, not without a rest. In high dudgeon, he stalked toward the house. It had a large porch in back sheltered from the sea breeze.

Inside, Aquila blew out his lamp. The porch held extra pruning hooks, amphoras, stakes, hoes, and a pile of warm sacking. Ah, just the thing.

The wolf stretched, turned 'round and 'round . . . then paused. Something had changed. What?

Inside, Aquila began to snore.

Down below on the shore road, noise. What noise?

Yes, very faint, the tramp of feet. Soldiers! Here, of all places.

The wolf ran around the house. Soldiers, yes, and marching toward the town whose lights the wolf could just see about a mile away. Oh well, no reason to get excited.

The wolf sat. He wondered what Dryas and Lucius were doing, then decided not to overexert his imagination. He had no difficulty guessing. He thought, with some envy and not a little spite, *I wonder if she thinks he's as good as I am.* He hoped not. *When the soldiers go by, I can get some sleep.*

But they didn't go by. Instead, they turned and marched up the road toward Aquila's house.

The wolf circled the house at top speed. It had a square, tiled roof and few small windows, all barred, and probably a courtyard in the center.

There was no time to be lost. The wolf ran as far into the vines as he could, then charged the house at top speed. His leap carried him over the ridgepole and down on the tiles covering the porch roof surrounding the courtyard.

A wolf really has no ability to scream and, for once, Maeniel regretted this greatly because, if he could have, he would have and at the top of his lungs.

He had been sure the inner roof would be as wide and flat as the outer, but it wasn't. It was both narrow and steep. His claws clicked helplessly on the pantiles as he struggled to get purchase on something, anything, but he failed.

Aquila, very much liking the night's coolness, slept in the courtyard.

LUCIUS LAUGHED UNTIL HE WEPT. "I WISH I'D SEEN his face. I just wish I'd seen his face when a hundred-and-seventy-pound wolf . . ." Then he broke down again.

Dryas had to turn away. She, also, was somewhat overcome.

Maeniel was scarlet with mortification and anger. "You're both in danger, terrible danger," he said furiously.

"I know," Dryas replied, and collapsed into Lucius' arms with a scream of laughter.

"What happened . . ." Lucius began.

"I asked him for a sword and something to wear," Maeniel said.

This set Lucius off. "A sword and something to wear," he repeated weakly.

"It was cold." Maeniel's anger hadn't cooled.

Lucius, holding his sides, said, "Stop! Stop! I'm going to die . . ."

Octus, who stood nearby with torch in hand, covered his mouth.

"Go on," Dryas said, wiping her eyes.

"He was recovering," Maniel continued. "I'd knocked the wind—"

"I believe that," Philo interjected.

"He asked me why," Maeniel plowed on. "He looked surprised."

Lucius staggered away. Dryas felt the need to sit down. She did, on a bench near the porch. "I can't imagine why," she said in a faint voice.

"I told him we were about to have company," Maeniel finished. "And it isn't funny. The soldiers were with the Egyptian queen and what she wanted to ask Aquila was if Dryas can really read the future."

Lucius abruptly stopped laughing. He walked over to Dryas and put his arms around her. "It's freezing out here. Octus, get her mantle." Philo took the torch from the servant's hand. "Sounds harmless enough," Lucius said. "If she presses you, fob her off with the usual— good spirits attend on you, Caesar will get you pregnant as many times as there are days to summer and, each and every time, the child will be a boy. I remember a rather dried-out-looking Syrian telling my mother that. Silvia smiled and gave her some copper coins."

Dryas' eyes seemed to darken, but she didn't speak.

"Yes," Octus said. "I remember the woman, also. Silvia died only six months later." Then abruptly he colored. "Please, excuse me."

"No," Lucius said, patting him on the back. He took the white mantle from his servant's hand and wrapped it around Dryas. "No need to excuse yourself. It's true. I think she was right about one thing. Good spirits did attend on her. Silvia was a loving woman."

"I never remember an unkind word," Octus said quietly, and withdrew into the shadows.

"Yes, well, *she* isn't a Syrian on a street corner," Maeniel said, pointing. "She is Dryas, lady of Caledoni."

"I not only fought a tiger, but once a dragon," Dryas said. "And yes, I do read the future when requested and I am never wrong."

"Dragons don't exist," Lucius said.

"So you say," Dryas told him. "So most say, but what didn't exist bit me." She turned and showed scars on her right calf, three ugly white depressions from deep puncture wounds.

Lucius pushed Dryas to arm's length. "There are no dragons."

"Yes," Maeniel said, "we know. Let us argue dragons at some more convenient time. The problem is not what the exalted lady asked Aquila, but what she said on the way back to Rome to one of her intimates, Iris."

"Yes, there are two of them, Iris and Charmain," Dryas said.

"How could you overhear that?" Lucius asked.

"Please," Maeniel said.

"I'll take it on faith," Philo said.

Lucius nodded.

Maeniel continued. "She was heard to say, 'I must keep Caesar from proscribing them for at least the next few days.'"

"Yes," Lucius said. "I thought it might be something like that." He took the torch from Philo's hand and, accompanied only by Maeniel and Dryas, walked toward the other end of the garden.

When they were out of earshot of the rest, he asked Maeniel, "Have you any proof? They won't move, none of them will, without proof."

"No," Maeniel said, "but I think I could get some. Don't ask how."

"Let's go," Dryas said. "Ostia is only an hour's ride away. Ships from there set sail for every corner of the world."

"No," Lucius said. "He has agents in every corner of the world. How far do you think we'd get? No, now it's either him or us. Once I'm not sure if I would have cared, but now I have too much to lose."

"Besides," Maeniel said to Dryas, "you were the one set on coming here."

"Yes," Dryas said, "but now . . . He's old and I'm not sure . . ."

"Age doesn't blunt a snake's fangs. If anything, they just get more lethal," Maeniel said. "And he's a viper if I ever saw one. Trust me. If he decided to kill the two of you, you'd be just as dead no matter what age he is."

"If I could only get that fool, Brutus, to act." Lucius drove his right fist into the palm of his left hand with a loud crack. "Do you really think there is some way to get proof positive that he's going to begin proscribing his enemies?"

"I think I can get it. I told you, don't ask me how."

"I'm not dumb enough to ask either of you how you do anything, but I want to come along. She talks about reading the future. I've seen what you can do. Then she has dragon bites. Sometime, I want to meet this dragon."

"All right, but don't be surprised at anything that happens," Maeniel said.

"I haven't been surprised by anything that's happened since I met the two of you. Let's go."

D RYAS WATCHED THEM OUT OF SIGHT IN THE street in front of the door. Cut Ear and Octus were with her. When she turned to enter the house, Fulvia stood there. She made as if to close the door, but Cut Ear placed his big hand on it and Dryas passed her without comment.

"How dare you!" Fulvia said. "How dare you . . . and dressed like a respectable woman."

"I am a respectable woman," Dryas said.

Then Fulvia pushed past her, followed by Firminius, her tiring woman, two maids, and Lucius' ex-servants, Macer and Afer, plus a half dozen chair bearers and two or three more ex-gladiator guards.

Aristo waited in the dimly lit atrium. He introduced himself to Dryas and began discussing finances with her.

Her *dress allowance*! Her *jewelry allowance*! Her *maids*!

"What maids? What clothes? What jewels?" was Dryas' contribution to the conversation.

Yes, she might need a few more dresses, possibly as many as two or three. Ordinary undyed linen or woolen cloth was fine. She would cut and sew them herself and, if possible, she'd like to see some horses today. She would probably need a good strong gelding or mare, saddle broken and gentle if possible. Otherwise, she was just fine. She would care for her own things. She always had and didn't want anyone fussing around her weapons or clothing, thank you. She was used to caring for them herself. Then she returned to the old part of the house where Lucius had lodged himself and his servants.

Dryas returned to the cubiculum where she and Lucius had spent the night. Only a wax light burned on a table beside the bed. Two light wells in the ceiling were beginning to let in the first pale gray morning light. Alia was up and stirring, so the bed was made.

Dryas took off the expensive wedding garments and dressed herself in the simple tunic and mantle given her by Marcia. She thought of the three—Gordus, Marcia, and Martinus—with affection.

A surprise. The trip had been filled with surprises. The kindness of the people she'd met was one of them. The love she'd found had been another. She had come here to kill, if possible, and, if necessary, to die. She had done neither. Instead, she found friendship, hope, and, at last, love. Because she was in love and had realized it during their night together.

He had none of the wolf's innocence or his compelling attraction or even his physical beauty. The slender, scarred Roman knew exactly what he was doing. He'd shown her his expertise, in fact, shown off his expertise, something the wolf would never have done at their first encounter.

He played her body like an exquisite instrument, getting each and every response he wished as often and as intensely as he wished.

Yet, all the while, he thought of her. She could tell he was delighted with the return of his own virility and happy he'd waited for such a beautifully responsive partner as herself to share these delicious moments with him.

Their second encounter was a virtuoso performance. She had never considered herself beautiful, but he did and told her so, praising charms usually hidden by her clothing. She had not known there were so many specific terms for the body parts he investigated or that the Latin language contained so many words with double meanings. In fact, he seemed to take delight in shocking her, so that he, as he put it, could see her blush all over.

"My delight," he whispered, "the flush covers your whole body. Here, there, everywhere. My heart, my soul, my own . . ." At some point, they'd both drifted off to sleep only to be awakened by Philo's knock when Maeniel arrived.

Philo startled her from this reverie by knocking again. "My lady, Alia has prepared breakfast. I must excuse myself. I have to apply restoratives to Aristo, a chilled towel and ardent spirits. A bride who refuses money and asks to see horses the day after her wedding was almost too much for him. My advice to you is to take the money. It comes in handy. Money always does."

"Yes," she replied through the door, "and make sure he purchases the horses—one each for you, Alia, Lucius, me, Maeniel, Cut Ear, and Octus. Don't forget Octus. Send him on right away, along with Alia, to Ostia to wait for us. Get both of them out of the city now." Then she came out on the porch to face him.

"You mean that?"

"I certainly do. The only people who should remain here are those who can hold up their end in a fight: me, you, Lucius, Cut Ear, and Maeniel. Nothing says you have to obey my orders."

Octus arrived just then. "Oh, yes, Lucius told us to do exactly what you said."

"Yes." Philo looked uneasy. "He did say—"

"Well then, move!" Dryas said. "And tell this man—Aristo, you called him—to get mounts for every one of us within the hour."

"Yes, my lady," Octus said, and hurried away.

Philo looked taken aback.

"You did say there was money?" she asked.

"Ye-yes," he stammered. "Lucius gave me quite a lot."

"Good," Dryas said. "Bring it to Gordus and tell him I want to see him as soon as possible."

"It was for you . . . just in case he . . ."

"Didn't come back," she supplied.

"Yes," Philo said.

"Gordus can probably lay it around more expertly than we could. Put every cent into his hands and tell him to get together every man he can find. He'll know enough not to call in fools or blabbermouths. Did you say something about breakfast?"

Philo pointed to a table under an arbor near the door.

She glanced at it. Bread, cheese, fruit, porridge, posca. Always posca. "Fine," she said.

Philo continued to stand staring at her.

"Well?" she asked. "Is there anything else you want to tell me?"

"N-no."

"Get moving!"

He did.

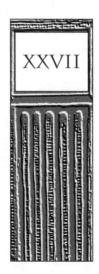

XXVII

MAENIEL AND LUCIUS WALKED ALONG TO-
gether until they were about a hundred yards from
Caesar's house, then Maeniel stepped into an alley.

"You don't mind taking risks, do you?" Lucius asked. "Suppose
two other cutthroats had gotten here first?"

"I've decided that if anyone tries to rob me, I'll eat them. It will
delay me, but I'll do it."

"Yes," Lucius said slowly. "Are humans tasty?"

"Can't say," Maeniel said. "I've never had one, but trust me, tasty
doesn't matter to a wolf. Humans gormandize. Wolves eat. As far as
they're concerned, any dinner is tasty. Take care of my clothes."

They dropped to the ground in front of Lucius and the wolf
stepped away. He strolled down the street to Caesar's door.

The same young legionnaire was on guard. The wolf sat down and
gave him a big, curly tongue grin. "Son of a bitch," the soldier said.

The wolf's grin grew wider.

"If I don't, you'll howl, won't you?" the legionnaire asked.

Maeniel panted a bit then closed his mouth. He lifted his muzzle
toward the stars.

"No, no, no, no, no," the legionnaire said. He turned and rapped
on the door.

It opened a crack.

"That dog's back." He sounded unhappy.

"You woke me up to tell me that?" The man inside sounded
even more unhappy.

431

"Yes. He's going to start howling."

"You can read his mind?"

"He's getting himself into position."

"Well, let him in."

"We still don't know if he belongs here," the legionnaire argued.

"Who cares? He's a dog. What's he going to do?"

The young legionnaire stepped aside. Maeniel drifted in, tail elevated, waving gently. He nodded to the sentry inside, lying on a cot near the door, then moved into the atrium, past the death masks, past Lares and Penates. He felt a brief, unhappy frisson of power. They mattered. He sensed something old, but still powerful. The hair on his back lifted in a ridge on his spine. Yes, something was going to happen soon. He went in search of Calpurnia.

She was awake, walking in the garden. When she saw him she said, "He's not here." She led him to the baths where clothing was stored on shelves.

In a few moments he returned, dressed in a tunic, mantle, and sandals. He sat down next to her. By the first light of day, he could see how haggard she was. "Another one last night?" he asked.

"Another ones. Every few hours now, they come. I simply take Philo's medicine. It's the only thing that helps and it doesn't help much now." She rested her head against his shoulder. "I want to die, but I waited."

"Why?" he asked, resting his hand against her cheek.

"Because there's something I need to do."

There was movement in the villa. As the light grew, he could hear the slaves in the kitchen lighting the fire and starting breakfast.

One of her maids came out of the round bedroom and looked shocked to see Caesar's wife in the arms of a man, a young man.

"What do you want her to do?" Maeniel asked.

"Go away!" Calpurnia said.

Maeniel looked up at the woman. "Go away." The girl went.

"Come with me," Calpurnia said. Her fingers tightened painfully on his hand.

He helped her to her feet, and she led him out of that garden and down a long colonnade into another garden.

"I'm almost blind in one eye," she said, "and I can barely walk. But your friends will die unless you have this. So I must give it to you before I depart."

She walked quickly in spite of her protestations about both pain and blindness. From time to time, she would lurch and stagger against his arm and, once or twice, she might have fallen had he not been there.

"I'm anxious to get it over with. You cannot imagine how tired I am of him, of Rome, the Senate, the whole mess. But for the roses, they might have ruled my life and I would have died much younger, worn out by sorrow."

As it was, the wolf thought, she was dying of sorrow.

By then, they reached Caesar's office. There was a lock, but he broke it easily with his fingers. The doors slid back. Caesar's office was empty, as were the public rooms all around it. The writing table where Caesar worked was bare except for a leather folder. A basket nearby held paper trash. She tipped it over and began to rummage through the contents.

"This is a trick I learned many years ago when I was anxious to learn his mind. He makes more than one draft of everything, usually two or three. Then he removes all extraneous material. This is why some of his toadies praise his style, and he has a good one, very lean, yet graceful. It almost makes you think he's telling the truth.

"Ah ha!" She rose to her feet with the list in her hand. She passed it to Maeniel. He could not read well, but he could, thanks to Mir's best efforts, read.

The list named individuals and their possible reasons such as "he's surely in on intrigue by now," "wife is tired of his jealousy—besides, he's one of the richest men in Rome, will split profits with wife sixty-forty," "would love to stick a knife in me," and "hates me, curses me every time my back is turned."

But the most striking name on the list was Marc Antony. *Him, too,* the wolf thought. But his name was crossed off, the notation "not yet" and "drunken, pussy-whipped fool." Next to another one's name, "I just want to see his face," and yes, there was Lucius, but the only notation by his name was "father?" The list included Brutus, "oh yes, my son."

The paper was badly crumpled, dirty and torn. "It's in his handwriting and they will recognize it," Calpurnia said.

Maeniel smoothed the paper, folded it, and helped her out of the room. In the short time they'd been in the office, the sky had darkened perceptibly. Though dawn, it was a gray one and the clouds rolled ominously; even as the day brightened, they turned thicker and blacker.

Outside, in the garden, Calpurnia looked up. "Yes," she said, "presently. Don't be impatient. Give me but a few moments more."

Distant thunder rumbled a warning.

"Yes," she said. "I know, I know."

Maeniel put his arm around her waist and she hurried, as well as she was able, to the roses. To his surprise, she didn't use the entrance, but plucked a rose, a single rose, and handed it to Maeniel.

"You don't want to go in?" he asked.

"It's not necessary now. Don't stand near the jars when I begin to die."

The light was green now. A sprinkling of big drops splashed on the pavement. The fragrance of roses was almost overpowering. The wolf could smell the components of rose, pepper spicing, a cloying sweetness mixed with the smell of rain on the wind, sadness, bitter regret. Do these things have an odor? To him, they did.

They kissed and he was surprised that though the air was thick with rose, she was perfumed by sea breezes and something less enduring like a flower. Not a heavy scent, but a light one touched with sharpness, exquisitely piercing, the most like the fruit of limes. One offering itself to the senses, but never caught in the net of the perfumer's art, only experienced when the fresh green fruit is bruised.

Yes, she was unique and could only be experienced, but never captured or possessed. But that, Caesar had never known, he could not conceive of anything he could not possess and anything barring him from possession, he would destroy.

The wolf greedily kissed her again, picked her up, and carried her toward the frightened maids.

He barely reached the circular room when the storm struck. He laid her on the bed and backed out of the room. Rain drenched the gardens behind him and, as he turned away, her women began to scream. Her body convulsed as her spirit struggled to break free of the confining, but beloved flesh.

Was that thunder? No, it was deafening. The hooves landed on the cobbles and Maeniel saw the steed clearly for the first time. He was the color of the storm clouds, like old hammered silver, dappled from dark to light, and big, bigger than the largest horse Maeniel had ever seen. This time, he wore a saddle with ivory and gold trappings.

Lightning flashed white, blinding, closely accompanied by a clap of thunder that shook the walls. The wolf heard a cry. The head was beautiful, eyes onyx, nostrils wide and red against the velvety soft muzzle.

He reared, striking the pavement with his forehooves as he dropped back. The long, curling mane and tail seemed somehow made up of, or part of, the storm clouds, sending down rain in gossamer curtains between heaven and earth.

Boom! He struck the earth with one forehoof and the stone where it fell boiled, sending up water in a cloud of steam.

Then she came. The form in the bed surrounded by her hysterical women was still now. Servants and soldiers ran in from everywhere in the house, alarmed by the women's cries.

She paused next to Maeniel and smiled. "Good-bye. I can't kiss you because I'm not really here, but live long and be well. Don't stand near those stone jars when he leaves. The gates are going to close."

Her steed knelt as he had before and, in a second, she settled herself in the saddle.

The wind roared, but even Maeniel could hear the creature's cry of joy and triumph above the rage of the elements. Rain slashed at his face.

It leaped, driven upward by its back hooves, high into the air, clear of the villa and its walls, into the roaring wind and wild storm above it. Then, with a snap louder than the thunder, the giant wings opened and it was gone.

He remembered her warning and dashed back to her chamber. A two-forked bolt of lightning struck the jars filled with roses. The plants themselves hissed, steamed, then burst into flame. The jars exploded, showering the courtyard with pottery fragments and dirt, and sending every human being within sight or sound of them diving for cover.

Maeniel covered his head, the paper, and the rose with his mantle and ran. On his way, he passed the two legionnaires who had been guarding the door. They were sheltered from both storm and confusion near the altar of the household gods.

"I told you," the young one said, "we shouldn't have let that dog in here."

"You really think he had something to do with this? Caused all this commotion?" the other one asked.

"I suppose it sounds silly . . ." his friend replied.

"You planning to make a career of the army?"

"I don't—"

"Yes, well, I do," said the older man. "You go telling your commanding officer stories like that, you wind up guarding goats in farther Hispania. There aren't anything but goats in farther Hispania."

"I see."

"I sincerely hope so because I don't plan on joining you there at any time in the near future. The first thing any soldier should learn is never volunteer. The second is—"

"Don't tell me," the youngster said. "When to shut up."

The older man didn't answer. He just nodded.

DRYAS GOT HER HORSES; ARISTO WAS EFFICIENT. She mounted Alia and Octus on the best ones and sent them on ahead, telling both of them, "Find inconspicuous lodging and don't tell anyone who you are or why you're there. If we don't follow you by tomorrow, don't try to contact us. If we aren't there by the following day, we won't come. Don't return and look for us. Keep on going." Since she spoke to Alia in her own language, Alia understood her well enough. "Find a Caledonian ship if you can," Dryas said, "and go beyond the reach of Roman arms or power." Then she gave both of them money and sent them on their way.

Then she asked, "Philo?"

"No," he said. "I'll stay."

"He will worry," she said.

"I know, but I'll stay anyhow."

"Stubborn," she said.

"We are known for it" was the reply.

"Cut Ear?"

Cut Ear laughed. "You should run first. Little, small, woman. What you do here?"

"Bring him back to my people or die in the attempt," Dryas flared back at him.

"Ya, die in the attempt, because Caesar is here now with his woman."

They heard the tramp of booted feet on the street. Dryas hurried back to the old part of the house where Lucius made his home and waited in the garden. Aristo showed Caesar into the garden. He was accompanied by Cleopatra, Fulvia, Firminius, and about a dozen soldiers.

"You see," Fulvia said, pointing to Dryas. She sounded shrill. "He's trying to marry her."

"Well, he can't," Caesar said calmly. "It's against the law."

Dryas tried to catch Cleopatra's eye, but the queen avoided her gaze.

"Fulvia," Caesar said, "a word to the wise. When she has served her purpose or, should I say, my lady's purposes—" He nodded to Cleopatra. "—let him have his fling. In a month or more, he will likely grow tired of her or, quite possibly, she will weary of him. After all, they can't have that much in common. Here she can't claim any rank much higher than a slave or, at best, a freedwoman belonging to your house."

"What about the . . . other matter?" Fulvia asked. Her lips were a tight white line and her eyes glittered with malice.

Caesar gave Fulvia a glance that still made strong men quail. "I had believed you to be a person of intelligence and well-ordered judgment. Don't make me change my opinion. Your father made his choice. Had he any doubts about your brother's paternity, he simply could have ordered the infant exposed. A father's rights in that respect are absolute. He didn't, and since he is now beyond all human questioning, his judgment is final. I will not have such a case brought at law. Every legitimate heir in Rome would be howling for my head. I would do a lot for my friends, but this I will not do."

Yes, Dryas thought, *keep on, Fulvia, and your name will find its way on to one of his lists. His or hers.*

Caesar gazed at Dryas. "My lady—" He indicated Cleopatra. "—believes you have the power to read the future and she wants you to look into ours."

"Why do you think I can do this?" Dryas asked.

Caesar's face hardened. "I don't plan to explain myself to you. Do as my lady asks."

The command was unmistakable. Dryas tried again to catch Cleopatra's eye. The beautiful queen wouldn't look at her; instead she rested her hand on Caesar's arm and gazed into his eyes. He returned her adoring look with one of his own.

He's besotted with her, Dryas thought. *I have no choice.* She felt an increasing sense of foreboding. *I want to destroy him, but why am I afraid?*

"She is the dragon's own," Cut Ear growled from behind her. "From the sea." He pointed to Dryas' leg. "He marks her. Look at leg."

Dryas lifted the long tunic as high as her calf, showing the marks of the puncture wounds.

"Women trouble," Cut Ear said. "All trouble." He pointed at Dryas. "This woman, worst kind of trouble. You smart man. So smart, nobody get 'round you. To you, chiefs, warriors, like children. Play fool, you spank. Play worse fool, you kill. They learn. The ones still alive learn. Lucius, Roman fool. She snare him. She take him. Let have him. Nothing to you. Have many more young fool. Ya. But cheap. Lots. Follow you for free. Pick of lot. Ya."

He pointed to Dryas again. "Old, old, old people. She is one. Live in mist, rain, darkness. Gods fight in sky. Look into other world. Mouthpiece of hag. Dragon queen. Star singer. Men steal first magic from woman, this kind woman. All trouble, worst kind. No good reason she come here. No good. I ever tell you wrong?"

"No, my friend," Caesar said. "You never lie. Is what he says true?" he asked Dryas.

"Yes," she answered. "I would urge you to take his advice."

Cut Ear grunted.

"This begins to intrigue me," Caesar said. "You can really tell a man his fate?"

"No," Dryas said. "Only about himself. I have never known anyone who wanted to know as much as I can tell him. Never."

"Just possibly I do," he said.

"Yes, well, you will face the woman. When?"

"I have never been afraid of women. Now. What do you need?"

"Nothing. A quiet place where we will be undisturbed."

"Day or night?"

"Now, as you demanded," she said.

"The Temple of Vesta. The ladies, the virgins, will be happy to favor me. She, Vesta, is, after all, a woman."

THE TEMPLE WAS AN ANCIENT ONE, PERHAPS THE oldest in Rome. It was, in the course of centuries, rebuilt many

times. It housed a fire and, really, that was all. Its stark simplicity perhaps replicated the huts built by the first settlers. Probably they were
from Greece, those who came and settled the stony, hot soil of the
seven hills beside the Tiber.

Its center was the hearth where they first gathered for protection
against the cold and dangers that lurked in darkness. In those days, the
last sight people had before they slept was the banked coals of the
night fire, and the first, the rising flames of a morning before sunrise
as the woman, keeper of the flames, built it higher to cook the day's
first meal.

She was Vesta, guardian of the family, the chastity of wives and
daughters, protector against misfortune, hunger, and disease, keeper
of the flame and, perhaps, the spirit of fire, itself forever dividing men
from beasts. Yielding to men the gift of heaven, placed in the trembling hands of our kind's first immortal dreamer; the first to lift her
eyes and hands from the mire, and stretch them out toward the star-
filled sky.

Yes, Dryas thought, *this is one of those places like Delphi, Tara in the
Irish valley, or the one on Salisbury plain. A seal is set here. Yes, she will
come. I am sure and Cut Ear is right. It is a foolish man who meddles with
women's magic. Who would have thought it? This Caesar, a fool. She will
destroy him and possibly me, too, in the process.*

The temple was a small, though imposing, structure. Round; the
fire burned alone on a circular marble altar in the center, tended day
and night by its guardian vestals. The walls were white limestone surrounded by marble Corinthian columns. Once inside, Dryas could
see that there were no paintings or statues, only plain white walls and
a rotunda over the altar with the fire.

Dryas felt a deep dread slowly creeping over her.

The day outside was warm, almost unseasonably warm. The sky
above the Forum was filled with high-topped cumulus clouds, white
at the tops, but darker at the base where they rode the thermal layer
above the city.

Dryas took a last look at the light and air beyond the heavy, cedar
double doors. Caesar spoke with the vestal on duty. She nodded and
departed.

Two of the soldiers closed the heavy doors and the room grew
dark. The fire on the altar didn't shed much light, but the roof had a
double dome, a smaller one atop the larger, and windows surrounding

the division between them let in clear, bluish-white light, as did the smoke hole in the roof that served as a chimney.

It was oddly familiar to Dryas, and then she remembered. The ancient building was very like Cynewolf's hall, almost as if a command once given echoed still in the human mind and soul, and would forever more. *I do not ask for worship, but honor me this way. I would be remembered for your sake and mine.*

Caesar saw Dryas' waxen paleness in the firelight. "What is it, sorceress? Have you made promises you cannot keep and are afraid?"

Dryas removed her belt and then unbraided the copper crown from her hair while answering. "I am afraid, Caesar, but not of you. She is a being of immeasurably greater power. The promises are not mine to keep, but hers. I am now certain she will keep them."

She handed her crown and belt to Cut Ear, who stood near her. Her long hair hung like a thick dark curtain, framing her face. Then she walked toward the altar and around it until she faced Caesar over the flames.

"Since you ask!" she said.

Cut Ear backed away very quickly because he knew the creature looking back at him over the flames was not Dryas.

"Why do you summon me to this place without light or air? I find it inconvenient," she said. With that, they found themselves somewhere else.

Dryas would have known the place, but Dryas was securely tucked away, somewhere where there was no time. They stood on the sloping side of the mountain where the spring became a waterfall and the giant conifers held the mountaintop.

These woods were more ordinary and friendly. Stone pines with their cloudlike tops mixed with holum oaks. Rowan with its blazing berries ringed a clearing at whose center a fire burned on a flat stone. The air was clear and an intermittent breeze blew, cooling the air and fanning the fire. Birdsong filled the trees and bushes around them.

"Have you a question?" Dryas and not Dryas asked. "Be quick because this mortal cannot bear my touch for too long and I won't be party to the destruction of this woman. Although she is utterly unimportant to you, Caesar, her people need her to accomplish a great purpose. Speak!"

"What is my destiny?" Caesar asked.

Dryas–not Dryas appeared impatient. "You yourself would know the answer to that question if you but bent your considerable intellect to an analysis of the facts. But then, humans like you don't really want to know. The answer is: It is time for you to die.

"All roads you take will bring you to death, not distant mortality, but death, soon, especially if you go to the Senate tomorrow. Stay away from the Senate during your remaining sojourn in Rome and you will leave for Parthia alive. Mourn your wife; give that excuse."

"My wife is not dead. Her maids tell me she is resting. A bad storm this morning frightened her."

"She is not resting, Caesar. The important part of her has already departed. True, she breathes yet, but, by morning, the discarded envelope of flesh she once wore will fail and it will begin its journey down the path to dust. That wasn't a storm, but of that I will say no more."

"The Ides of March," Caesar said. "Every soothsayer in Rome has been moping and whining about them for months. Seems however powerful you are, Dryas, you are still a charlatan like all the rest."

"Caesar, when a man goes with an ax to fell a tree, he can determine from where he makes the cut how to make the tree fall in the spot he wishes. Once the cuts are made, then the tree is destined to fall in that spot. So it is with a man. The forces that will kill him begin their work at birth and continue throughout his life. There are many kinds of forces. Some are purely physical, others are concerned with the soul, and there are yet others, moral in nature.

"Even mere mortals can read these patterns and see the end. Philo is an expert at certain kinds and foretold your wife's death some months ago."

Caesar sighed. "It seems that I am condemned to be talked down to by women. These are truisms you utter. I hear nothing new."

Dryas–not Dryas was unmoved. "Caesar, disabuse yourself of the idea that you are speaking to a woman or, for that matter, anything human at all. Tell me, do you discuss politics with your horse?"

Caesar's face colored. It was the first time he'd seemed ruffled by anything. "No! I do not."

"Well, no more than you could explain politics to a horse, could I explain the ordering of the universe to you. Trust me. It is both vaster and far more complex than you comprehend—could possibly comprehend. Believe me when I tell you all paths now carry you toward death, and soon.

"For instance, should you escape death here in Rome and leave for Parthia, there are some among those people who, spurred by a great fear of you, have studied your deeds and writings. They are searching for weakness and have, they think, detected several. I do not believe you will find them so easy to destroy.

"But that is not all. You are threatened from within. You are old, old before your time, worn by the struggles of a lifetime. But not only your body fails. Your chief terror is the decline in your mental facility. You are more forgetful than most men of your age. How often do you lose the thread of your discourse and have to be recalled by your lady, Cleopatra?"

"I won't listen—" Caesar shouted.

"Oh, yes, you will," Dryas–not Dryas said. "You will listen for as long as I choose and certainly until I am finished."

Everyone in the clearing—Philo, Cut Ear, Fulvia, and Cleopatra—knew he would, would listen for as long as whatever inhabited Dryas' flesh desired.

"Do not forget—" Her voice crackled with power. "—that you summoned me and I am not dismissed until I care to leave. So be silent."

Then she continued. "There are those carefully concealed seizures and the fact that you have awakened and, for a few minutes, have found yourself unable to move your right side or speak. Soon, even in your reckoning of time, this condition will become permanent and you will lie, a helpless, drooling wreck, cared for by your own slaves like a child until, at last, you will not be able to eat or drink enough to sustain life and, imprisoned in your rotting body, you will die."

Caesar's face was pale now and, even in the morning coolness of the forest, he was perspiring.

"This is cruel," Cleopatra cried.

"You, you charge me with cruelty to him?" Dryas–not Dryas raged. "What has he ever been but a monster of cruelty? He who was given everything: beauty, strength, intellect, wealth, health, and, yes, even love. His life could have been an arc of light against the empyrean.

"He could have been one who purified his people and brought them to greatness, but what did he do with his gifts? He used them in a shallow taste for minor cruelty, to gratify a deep thirst for power and what became an obsessive drive for primacy. First Man in Rome."

Philo didn't think he could ever convey the freight of absolute contempt in that statement.

"Nonsense," Caesar answered. "The Romans aren't fit for greatness. I gave them what they asked for: wealth, boundless wealth, and, at last, power. They will rule the world. I have seen to that. What greatness could I have given them? Answer me that."

Dryas—not Dryas looked weary. "You still don't understand, do you? No matter what I say, you *will not* understand. The greatness was yours to discover. Yours to bring into existence. I could not give it to you, but you might have invented it for yourself. In that sense, I was wrong to compare you to a horse. A divine fire burns in each one of you. It is yours to accept or deny and, in your narrow, selfish soul, you denied it and so failed yourself and your people."

"And so, for this crime of . . . omission, I must receive some . . . form of punishment?"

Caesar's question was ironic, but fearless.

"No!" she answered. "We do not punish, and I see, even at this very moment, you are struggling to find a way to get the better of me. Never, never understanding that true greatness is not a matter of victory or defeat. No, of all things, what I most deplore is pointless suffering. No! In the normal course of time, you die. All of your kind do. It is inherent in your nature. You could not live, if you did not also die. No, I merely warn you how close you are to that final moment. Come here, Cut Ear."

For once, the giant warrior looked afraid.

"Come, I said," she repeated.

He came, drawing close to her side.

"Wait!" It was Philo's voice that piped up. "I . . . I . . . want to ask a question . . . please? Just one?"

"What? I said we have not much time." The reply was a stern one.

"Who . . . what are we?" Philo stammered.

She, Dryas—not Drayas, almost smiled. "Ah, the Greeks. I cannot remember when I took such joy in a people . . . I will give you an absolutely truthful answer, but you will not understand it."

"I don't mind," Philo said. "Someday, somewhere, sometime, someone will."

"Yes," she answered. "You are stardust."

Then she turned and spoke in a low voice to Cut Ear. "I have an affection for this woman. Do not fail me. Catch her, for when I leave her, she will fall. I'm going. Now!"

Dryas' face and body went slack. Cut Ear caught her and then, unaccountably, they were in the temple again. The fire burned quietly in its brazier on the altar. The soldiers ranged around the temple walls didn't seem to have noticed they'd been gone.

Fulvia had a magnificent fit of hysterics. Cleopatra wept. Caesar looked pale. Philo found his legs wouldn't hold him up and sat down, right there on the temple floor.

Dryas slumbered peacefully in Cut Ear's big arms.

DRYAS WOKE ON A COT IN GORDUS' LUDUS WITH Lucius bending over her. She smiled at him in a completely beautiful way. He embraced her thankfully.

Outside, the seats were filling and torches were being placed to illuminate the sand.

Wide-eyed, Dryas looked around the room. They were all present: the wolf Maeniel, Gordus, Marcia, Martinus their son, Philo, and even Octus. "What happened?" she asked.

Lucius avoided her eye.

"Dryas," Philo said, "you were a bit too successful in telling Caesar's fortune."

"So she came," Dryas said.

"Oh, yes, oh my, yes, did she ever. She came close to frightening everyone to death, even that invincible lout Cut Ear. Fulvia is locked in her chamber, probably still having the vapors and terrorizing her maids. Cleopatra, I think, has dried her tears. She is a woman of infinite composure. But Caesar is in a fury. He believes, must believe, that somehow you engineered the whole thing. He is bent on revenge."

"What sort of revenge?" Dryas asked.

Gordus answered. "You and I are to fight to the death. The stakes . . . the lives of our loved ones."

Marcia burst into tears. "It's my fault," she cried. "I was the fool who told that Egyptian bitch—"

Dryas went to comfort her and Marcia wept in her arms.

Antony came to the cell door. "I see she's come out . . . her little nap is over."

"Antony," Philo asked deliberately, "don't you ever get tired of being Caesar's pimp?"

"Just for that, Philo, I'll make sure, if the lot falls on you, your death will be particularly unpleasant."

Gordus studied Antony as if he were a large piece of dung. "I cannot think he will let any of us live."

"Oh, yes, he always keeps his word. Never doubt it," Antony replied. "The winner will not only be allowed to live, but rewarded handsomely."

"So this is what killed Priscus," Dryas said, speaking of the soul she'd put to rest.

"Yes," Gordus answered. "He faced his kin and killed them in order to survive."

Dryas embraced Marcia and then she left to go to Lucius. They didn't embrace, but spoke together in low voices. Philo stood near them.

Gordus also spoke quietly to Marcia and Martinus.

Maeniel stared coldly at Antony. "Go away," he said, "or I'll find a way to tear you limb from limb." Then he snarled and there was nothing human in the sound.

Antony stepped back from the grilled door, for a moment very glad it was present, then left.

Lucius rested his hand on Dryas' cheek. "I'll understand if you . . . lose."

"Yes," she said. She took the hand in both of hers and kissed the palm.

"I'm sorry, Philo," Lucius continued. "You shouldn't have tweaked Antony's nose."

"I have a quantity of opium concealed on my person, enough, more than enough, for both of us," Philo answered in a low voice. "Neither of us need suffer, Dryas. Don't worry, at least not about that."

"Yes," she said, then kissed Lucius on the lips and Philo on the cheek. "I'd better go and get dressed."

Marcia stepped away from Gordus and took her hand.

Octus stood in the shadows near the door. He was, as usual, very quiet.

"I thought I told you . . ." Dryas began.

"Forgive me, domina, for my disobedience, but I had compelling reasons to return."

"Come, Dryas," Marcia said. "We have not much time. Half the luminaries in Rome are seated outside. At Caesar's invitation, I might add. Hottest ticket in town. Sorry I can't enjoy the excitement, but having my life or death riding on the main event is sort of . . . a distraction."

Dressing didn't take long. When Gordus and Dryas turned back, he wore only the gladiatorial loincloth, the subligaculum. Dryas had one on, also, and the chain mail she'd worn when she fought the boar. Lucius noticed she'd rendered the fragile garment more respectable by placing a strophium under it, and her hair was braided up around the copper-spiked crown.

Antony stood at the door again. He held two swords. He presented them at the grating, hilt first.

Dryas drew hers, then Gordus took his. Together, they walked toward the arena entrance.

It was dark now, but there were many torches and the arena was brightly lit. She heard a cheer and saw Caesar enter what would become the imperial box. Cleopatra was at his side.

The gate in front of them began to rise and they stepped out into the arena.

"Are we supposed to greet him?" Dryas asked.

"No," Gordus rumbled. "Only condemned criminals do the 'we who are about to die' speech. I may be condemned, but I refuse to consider myself a criminal. Or to behave like one."

"Yes." Dryas nodded. When they reached the center, they turned and faced each other. Both could see Caesar from the corners of the eyes.

"When he drops the handkerchief," Gordus said.

IN THE CELL, LUCIUS STOOD WATCHING THE TWO of them through the iron grating. He couldn't find it in his heart to say anything to the rest, not even Philo.

The soldiers had been waiting when he and Maeniel returned to the villa. Dryas was already gone and Cut Ear nowhere to be found. The big Gaul had somehow managed to melt into the Forum crowd and Caesar had not cared to pursue him. Octus came to the back gate when Caesar's soldiers were placing them under arrest. He simply joined them, as usual without saying much, and was taken away with the rest. Though why he should bother to put his life at risk for an owner almost certainly doomed to die soon was a mystery to Lucius.

He, like Gordus, was sure Caesar would not let any of them live, not in the long run. Caesar had a record of merciless destruction. His opponents might win temporary clemency from him, but—like the legion who revolted against him—he ultimately exterminated them.

As far as Lucius was concerned, whatever Dryas chose to do was all right with him.

ANTONY ENTERED THE ARENA.
"So, he's going to play lanista, is he?" Gordus' eyes narrowed. "Might be a way to make him pay for it."

"I wish," Dryas said.

"We both do."

But Antony stood well back from the combatants, sensing they were both faster and more deadly than he was.

Caesar dropped the handkerchief.

Dryas and Gordus crossed swords. Antony backed far away and even Lucius, whose life was riding on the event, moved away from his position at the door of the cell beneath the arena.

Gordus came in fast, trying to muscle her.

Dryas remembered the words from her earliest training: "My dear, they are stronger than we are and will try to use that first."

Yes, Dryas thought. Both swords, polished to a high gloss, flashed in the torchlight like flames of gold.

Dryas gave ground so rapidly at first that Lucius was sure Gordus, in his immense skill, would overtake and kill her. But he was wrong. Instead, she subtly made Gordus pay for the pressure he was putting on her, catching him across the knuckles with her sword tip, and then slashing his arm.

Gordus became aware he was enjoying himself. A man of his kind, to survive, had to learn to live in the moment. This was a particularly fine one. He'd never had such a practiced opponent. She countered each of his moves with an equally effective one of her own, constantly negating his greater strength with her quickness and skill.

The crowd was silent. Not many of them knew how brilliant an exhibition this was, but almost all realized they were seeing something they would never encounter again.

To Gordus, Dryas was a problem to solve. No, muscling would not do it. What? He pushed her arm high and then went low. Nearly got her, but paid the price in a quick slash to the inside of his forearm. The Gallic sword was razor sharp. Had she managed to cut a bit deeper, she might have crippled him. He began to push her toward the wall in earnest, hoping to trap and kill her.

Dryas saw it coming, allowed him to press her, then, when she picked up the arena sides in her peripheral vision, she changed the sword from her right hand to her left and ducked under his arm.

Gordus had heard of the maneuver, but had never seen it worked or even seen anyone try it. But as he recovered and pivoted, he saw Dryas backing away from him. There was nothing for it but a straight-out contest of skill.

She was breathing hard. This was where women failed against men. A man's body is adapted for strength. Men don't carry as much normal body fat as women and the apex of the body is in the shoulders, whereas a woman's is in the hips. Everything on men is bigger—heart, lungs, and muscles. Women, most women, simply don't have the endurance men do.

Gordus went in for the kill.

He's fast, Dryas thought. It was simply terrifying how fast he was. Their blades sang and danced in the firelight. Dryas knew it was taking everything she had to match him. He, with his size and weight, would have more than she did. If she fought his fight, she would die.

Antony tried to break them.

Gordus cursed him.

Dryas realized Gordus was putting everything into this last push.

Antony dropped back, or perhaps the two fighters simply left him in the dust.

Dryas sensed she was beginning to slow. Now or never! Last gamble!

On the next parry, she didn't push the blade down far enough. The tip entered her right thigh. *Take one to give one,* she thought as she hooked Gordus' hilt and tore the sword from his hand.

It went spinning, tearing a bigger gash in her thigh than Gordus had intended. She felt the hot blood sheet down her leg. The amphitheater was silent, but in the distance, she heard Marcia scream.

Gordus stood in front of her, arms akimbo, hands empty, unarmed.

Antony arrived, panting. "Ask for mercy, Gordus."

"No," Gordus answered. "I won't do that." He stared into Dryas' eyes.

Around them, the spectators were in ecstasy, screaming, shouting, pounding at the benches and seats.

"Kill him, Dryas," Antony ordered. "Caesar's thumb is down."

"Go away," Dryas said, "or I will kill you."

"Back up," Gordus rasped. "She means it. I don't care how many guarantees you give. None of us feels we have anything to lose."

Antony backed away.

Dryas raised the blade and kissed the steel, saluting Gordus, then she extended the hilt to him.

He took it.

Dryas threw off the chain mail, but remained modest since she wore the strophium under it. "I will not dishonor my sword or myself. Do a clean job, Gordus. Philo and Lucius have opium. Live until tomorrow. Caesar is dead. Brutus has the list of proscribed men. They will kill him in self-defense, if nothing else.

"Here," she said, pressing her fingers below the strophium on the left side. "Here is the shortest distance to the heart."

"No, Dryas, you won. I won't die like Priscus from a broken heart." Gordus threw the sword aside and began the long walk back to the gate.

Dryas walked toward the blade where it lay glinting, reflecting the yellow torchlight. As she stooped to pick it up, a shadow loomed over her. Antony!

He picked the sword from the ground and ran it through her body.

The outcry from the crowd alerted Gordus. He spun around, charged back, and saw what happened to Antony.

Some shock seemed to knock Antony backward about twenty feet. The sword hissed, flared, smoked, and then the hilt turned red-hot in his hand. He flung it away with a scream of agony.

Gordus snatched up Dryas. She was mortally wounded. The blade had entered the right side of her chest. Now she would drown in her own blood.

She gasped. Blood poured from her mouth.

The gate was dark. There should have been lights behind it. Gordus wondered if they had all been killed while he and Dryas fought. He would believe such an evil trick from the dictator—his kind brooked no opposition. Gordus knew. He'd seen the naked power of this kind of man shown openly and often. Caesar was hardly the first bloodthirsty tyrant to dominate politics in Rome, but only one, and not the last, of a long line.

Carrying Dryas, Gordus sprinted for the gate. He met Maeniel just inside. The rest, his wife and son, were gone.

Maeniel cradled Dryas and thrust something between Gordus' lips. There was a terrific flash of light and he sprawled on the moss near a natural spring high on a mountain.

Maeniel came next, but he was no longer a man, but a giant wolf.

Then Dryas fell bloody, but no longer bleeding, into Lucius' arms. She was pressing Calpurnia's rose to the wound in her side. As he watched, it healed, becoming a red line, a puckered scar and then clean, soft, unbroken skin.

Octus thrust a cup of cold water into Gordus' hands and he drank and drank and drank.

THE IDES OF MARCH CAME RAINING. A THICK, SOFT-gray overcast sent its burden of showers to Rome.

Caesar stood and watched at Calpurnia's bedside. He had begun to believe the little witch woman was right. Calpurnia was dying. She resisted all attempts to awaken her; instead her breathing was becoming more and more shallow, her pallor was increasing, and her hands and feet were cold. Sad, so sad. She had once been so lovely.

Outside, a small rainstorm came and passed, rain pattering down, increasing the weight of moisture in the trees, bending the limbs lower. The brief shower turned to a mist, but the sky brightened only slightly. The light in the room where she lay was a green gloom. A gust of wind shook the trees, sending a flurry of droplets to the stone pavement and rings dancing in the mirrored surface of the pool, as if, far away, something wept for the beauty that had been hers and the promise that had been his.

After the fight yesterday, when he had told the story of Dryas' prediction to Antony, he had strongly denied any feelings of disquiet or even that anything unnatural had happened in the temple.

Antony had been soaking his burned hand in cold water and swearing that the Caledonian woman was the most powerful sorceress anyone had ever encountered. And he hoped he, personally, had brought about her demise by stabbing her with her own weapon. But he hadn't seen her die and they hadn't found her body, so he would go tomorrow and offer a brace of oxen to Jove the Protector in the fervent hope—

This was as far as he got because Caesar found himself disgusted with his legate's pissing and moaning and told him to shut up.

"Faugh!" Caesar said. "First, the oracle. Well, Dryas was near the fire and probably threw something in it that disordered our senses. So she managed to convince the rest of them that she was some goddess.

"And, as to their escape, all that demonstrated was that Gordus knew more about his own ludus than anyone else did. Sooner or later they must surface. And then . . ." Well, he would make sure the barbarian scum paid the price of their folly.

Then he ordered Antony to take care of his hand because they had more important matters to address in the next few days. The army was ready to march, and this number of executions of the conspirators would take time to carry out, even if they took place—as planned—in the camp where the prisoners would be surrounded by his own loyal men.

No, he would never admit to Antony or any of the others that he believed every word she—whatever vixen had possessed the witch—spoke was the truth. And nothing but the truth.

No, whatever he was, he, Caesar, was not a fool. No human being could have done what Dryas did.

And no one could have escaped the way they had from the cell where he had imprisoned them.

Yes, it was over and he knew it with a finality that left him helpless for the first time in his life. Helpless and with nowhere to turn.

In the bed, Calpurnia sighed deeply and, for a short space, stopped breathing. Everyone, the women gathered around her and Caesar, waited until, at last, she began to breathe again.

Last night, the physicians who'd seen her had informed him this was a harbinger of approaching death. The pauses would grow longer and longer and, in time, she would . . . cease. Cease to be. Was that what happened? Should he have asked the "woman," as Dryas called her? But then, she had given him no comfort about anything else. Why should she send him hope of a life to come? No, best not to know.

He studied the three possibilities she'd offered him. Of the three, the best was to go to the Senate today.

The second option, to die in Parthia . . . well, the Parthians had gutted Crassius, leaving him on the field, dying in agony. His own slaves had to finish him off.

The third, to stay in Rome and avoid the Senate, to live and die in such a way, helpless, strangling when he tried to eat or drink, unable to speak or even perhaps think, soiling himself, lying in filth, at the mercy of his attendants. No.

A soldier, one of the legionnaires who guarded the house, came to tell him Antony and the rest were here.

Oh, well. Go now.

Then he remembered Philo the Greek's strange question and its even more peculiar answer.

Stardust! What madness, and how typically Greek not to ask any question whose answer would confer an advantage for him, but rather would fly off in the direction of metaphysics.

But then, that was why the Romans had found them so easy to conquer and why so many of their intelligent, cultivated, well-educated, and talented citizens found themselves in the Roman slave markets, undergoing the dehumanizing process of being treated as commodities and sold as slaves.

No. Wealth and power, or perhaps only power, were worth having, worth suffering or struggle to get.

He had achieved supreme power, as so many other conquerors had. And . . . and he found it a disappointment. Inexplicable . . . but he did.

Why? What more could there be?

He never answered the question because Antony waved to him from the reception room near the atrium. Without a backward look, Caesar went to join him.

———————

MAENIEL WAITED AT THE FOOT OF THE CURIA steps. He had his hand on the hilt of his sword, concealed under his toga.

The rain had ended, but the walks between the trees in the public gardens were still wet. The sky showed patches of blue.

They had emerged last night from the place of the spring and the mountain, returning to the hills near Aquila's farm. The wolf had led them because Calpurnia had shown him other portals leading away from Rome, and he had no doubt that were they willing to travel far enough, they might reach any spot on the earth. Aquila had given them shelter for the night, and there was no need to go farther.

They found, when they returned to the city, the conspirators had raised a substantial force of ex-gladiators, as had Gordus.

Beyond the public gardens loomed the high wall behind the proscenium stage of Pompey's theater. They were in the theater, the rest—Lucius, Dryas, Philo, Aquila, Cut Ear, Gordus, and about twenty of the toughest, most determined swordsmen Gordus could hire. His wife and son were in Ostia along with Octus and Alia.

"You see," Octus had explained after Philo went to Gordus, "I spoke to Aquila. No one was watching me and I got that, what shall I call it, plum from the wall of your room, my lord. I knew it was no natural thing. In the course of nature, it should have been a prune. So, after I spoke to Aquila, I went to join you. Your friend—" He pointed at Maeniel. "—told me what it was, but I couldn't think of a way to give it to you until Aquila overpowered the guards. The only thing I really feared was that Gordus or Dryas, one of them, would kill the other, but that didn't happen."

"And," Maeniel said, "I had Calpurnia's rose."

But now they were coming, a knot of men in white tunics, togas surrounding the most powerful man in the world.

Maeniel wondered if he was going to have to use the sword.

Antony was the only man who knew him, but before they reached the dozen or so marble steps up to the portico, someone threw an arm over Antony's shoulders and drew him aside.

Caesar hurried past and, for a moment, Maeniel met his eyes. He found himself sorry to be part of the human journey. He couldn't tell what he was reading there, bewilderment that it had passed so quickly, sorrow for the loss of the beloved kaleidoscope of existence itself, a final awareness of ultimate aloneness. No way to know. One thing he did know, those eyes and the expression in them would haunt him as long as he lived.

Maeniel's fingers tightened on the sword hilt, but then Caesar was past and gone.

The multibreasted figure of some eastern goddess looked down on Maeniel and away into the rainy public gardens. His hand slid away from the sword hilt. Above, even beyond the double bronze doors of the Curia, he could feel it, smell it, sense it in ways no human ever could.

He shivered as the pack closed in.

ABOUT THE AUTHOR

ALICE BORCHARDT shared a childhood of storytelling with her sister, Anne Rice, in New Orleans. A professional nurse, she has also nurtured a profound interest in little-known periods of history. She has published three previous novels: *Devoted* in 1995, *Beguiled* in 1997, and *The Silver Wolf* in 1998. She lives in Houston.